'I'm just not good at relationships. It feels like a risk,' Nicole told him.

'You took risks all the time at the bank. You're taking a risk now on the Electric Palace.'

'Those were all calculated risks,' she pointed out. 'This isn't something I can calculate.'

'Me, neither. But I like you, Nicole. I like you a lot. And I think if we're both brave we might just have the chance to have something really special.'

'I'm not sure how brave I am,' she admitted.

'It's harder to be brave on your own. But you're not on your own, Nicole. We're in this together.'

FALLING FOR THE SECRET MILLIONAIRE

BY
KATE HARDY

MILLS & BOON

First Published in Great Britain 2016
By Mills & Boon, an imprint of HarperCollins*Publishers*
1 London Bridge Street, London, SE1 9GF

© 2016 Pamela Brooks

ISBN: 978-0-263-92008-6

23-0816

Our policy is to use papers that are natural, renewable and recyclable products and made from wood grown in sustainable forests. The logging and manufacturing processes conform to the legal environmental regulations of the country of origin.

Printed and bound in Spain
by CPI, Barcelona

Kate Hardy always loved books and could read before she went to school. She discovered Mills & Boon books when she was twelve and decided this was what she wanted to do. When she isn't writing, Kate enjoys reading, cinema, ballroom dancing and the gym. You can contact her via her website: www.katehardy.com.

For my friend Sherry Lane, with love
(and thanks for not minding me sneaking
research stuff into our trips out with the girls!).
xxx

CHAPTER ONE

'ARE YOU ALL RIGHT, Miss Thomas?' the lawyer asked.

'Fine, thank you,' Nicole fibbed. She was still trying to get her head round the news. The grandfather she'd never met—the man who'd thrown her mother out on the street when he'd discovered that she was pregnant with Nicole and the father had no intention of marrying her—had died and left Nicole a cinema in his will.

A run-down cinema, from the sounds of it; the solicitor had told her that the place had been closed for the last five years. But, instead of leaving the place to benefit a charity or someone in the family he was still speaking to, Brian Thomas had left the cinema to her: to the grandchild he'd rejected before she'd even been born.

Why?

Guilt, because he knew he'd behaved badly and should've been much more supportive to his only daughter? But, if he'd wanted to make amends, surely he would've left the cinema to Nicole's mother? Or was this his way to try to drive a wedge between Susan and Nicole?

Nicole shook herself. Clearly she'd been working in banking for too long, to be this cynical about a stranger's motivations.

'It's actually not that far from where you live,' the solicitor continued. 'It's in Surrey Quays.'

Suddenly Nicole knew exactly what and where the cinema was. 'You mean the old Electric Palace on Mortimer Gardens?'

'You know it?' He looked surprised.

'I walk past it every day on my way to work,' she said. In the three years she'd been living in Surrey Quays, she'd always thought the old cinema a gorgeous building, and it was a shame that the place was neglected and boarded up. She hadn't had a clue that the cinema had any connection with her at all. Though there was a local history thread in the Surrey Quays forum—the local community website she'd joined when she'd first moved to her flat in Docklands—which included several posts about the Electric Palace's past. Someone had suggested setting up a volunteer group to get the cinema back up and running again, except nobody knew who owned it.

Nicole had the answer to that now. She was the new owner of the Electric Palace. And it was the last thing she'd ever expected.

'So you know what you're taking on, then,' the solicitor said brightly.

Taking on? She hadn't even decided whether to accept the bequest yet, let alone what she was going to do with it.

'Or,' the solicitor continued, 'if you don't want to take it on, there is another option. A local development company has been in touch with us, expressing interest in buying the site, should you wish to sell. It's a fair offer.'

'I need a little time to think this through before I make any decisions,' Nicole said.

'Of course, Miss Thomas. That's very sensible.'

Nicole smiled politely, though she itched to remind the solicitor that she was twenty-eight years old, not eight.

She wasn't a naive schoolgirl, either: she'd worked her way up from the bottom rung of the ladder to become a manager in an investment bank. Sensible was her default setting. Was it not obvious from her tailored business suit and low-heeled shoes, and in the way she wore her hair pinned back for work?

'Now, the keys.' He handed her a bunch of ancient-looking keys. 'We will of course need time to alter the deeds, should you decide to keep it. Otherwise we can handle the conveyancing of the property, should you decide to sell to the developer or to someone else. We'll wait for your instructions.'

'Thank you,' Nicole said, sliding the keys into her handbag. She still couldn't quite believe she owned the Electric Palace.

'Thank you for coming in to see us,' the solicitor continued. 'We'll be in touch with the paperwork.'

She nodded. 'Thank you. I'll call you if there's anything I'm unsure about when I get it.'

'Good, good.' He gave her another of those avuncular smiles.

As soon as Nicole had left the office, she grabbed her phone from her bag and called her mother—the one person she really needed to talk to about the bequest. But the call went straight through to Susan's voicemail. Then again, at this time of day her mother would be in a meeting or with one of her probationers. Nicole's best friend Jessie, an English teacher, was knee-deep in exam revision sessions with her students, so she wouldn't be free to talk to Nicole about the situation until the end of the day. And Nicole definitely didn't want to discuss this with anyone from work; she knew they'd all tell her to sell the place to the company who wanted to buy it, for the highest price she could get, and to keep the money.

Her head was spinning. Maybe she would sell the cinema—after all, what did she know about running a cinema, let alone one that hadn't been in operation for the last five years and looked as if it needed an awful lot of work doing to it before it could open its doors again? But, if she did sell the Electric Palace, she had no intention of keeping the money. As far as she was concerned, any money from Brian Thomas ought to go to his daughter, not skip a generation. Susan Thomas had spent years struggling as a single mother, working three jobs to pay the rent when Nicole was tiny. If the developer really was offering a fair price, it could give Susan the money to pay off her mortgage, go on a good holiday and buy a new car. Though Nicole knew she'd have to work hard to convince her mother that she deserved the money; plus Susan might be even more loath to accept anything from her father on the grounds that it was way too late.

Or Nicole could refuse the bequest on principle. Brian Thomas had never been part of her life or shown any interest in her. Why should she be interested in his money now?

She sighed. What she really needed right now was some decent caffeine and the space to talk this through with someone. There was only one person other than her mother and Jessie whose advice she trusted. Would he be around? She found the nearest coffee shop, ordered her usual double espresso, then settled down at a quiet table and flicked into the messaging program on her phone. Clarence was probably busy, but then again if she'd caught him on his lunch break he might have time to talk.

In the six months since they'd first met on the Surrey Quays forum, they'd become close and they talked online every day. They'd never actually met in person;

and, right from the first time he'd sent her a private message, they'd agreed that they wouldn't share personal details that identified them, so they'd stuck to their forum names of Georgygirl and Clarence. She had no idea what he even looked like—she could have passed him in the street at any time during the three years she'd been living at Surrey Quays. In some ways it was a kind of coded, secret relationship, but at the same time Nicole felt that Clarence knew the real her. Not the corporate ghost who spent way too many hours in the office, or the much-loved daughter and best friend who was always nagged about working too hard, but the *real* Nicole. He knew the one who wondered about the universe and dreamed of the stars. Late at night, she'd told him things she'd never told anyone else, even her mother or Jessie.

Maybe Clarence could help her work out the right thing to do.

She typed a message and mentally crossed her fingers as she sent it.

Hey, Clarence, you around?

Gabriel Hunter closed his father's office door behind him and walked down the corridor as if he didn't have a care in the world.

What he really wanted to do was to beat his fists against the walls in sheer frustration. When, when, *when* was he going to stop paying for his teenage mistake?

OK, so it had been an awful lot worse than the usual teenage mistakes—he'd crashed his car into a shop front one night on the way home from a party and done a lot of damage. But nobody had been physically hurt and he'd learned his lesson immediately. He'd stopped going round with the crowd who'd thought it would be fun to spike his drink when he was their designated driver. He'd knuckled down to his studies instead of spending most of his time partying, and at the end of his final exams he'd got one of the highest Firsts the university had ever awarded. Since then, he'd proved his worth over and over again in the family business. Time after time he'd bitten his tongue so he didn't get into a row with his father. He'd toed the party line. Done what was expected of him, constantly repented for his sins to atone in his father's eyes.

And his father still didn't trust him. All Gabriel ever saw in his father's eyes was 'I saved you from yourself'. Was Evan Hunter only capable of seeing his son as the stupid teenager who got in with a bad crowd? Would he ever see Gabriel for who he was now, all these years later? Would he ever respect his son?

Days like today, Gabriel felt as if he couldn't breathe. Maybe it was time to give up trying to change his family's view of him and to walk away. To take a different direction in his career—though, right at that moment, Gabriel didn't have a clue what that would be, either. He'd spent the last seven years since graduation working hard in the family business and making sure he knew every single detail of Hunter Hotels Ltd. He'd tried so hard to do the right thing. The reckless teenager he'd once been was well and truly squashed—which he knew was a good thing, but part of him wondered what would have happened if he hadn't had the crash. Would he have grown out of the recklessness but kept his freedom? Would he have felt as if he was really worth something, not having to pay over and over for past mistakes? Would he be settled down now, maybe with a family of his own?

All the women he'd dated over the last five years saw him as Gabriel-the-hotel-chain-heir, the rich guy who could show them a good time and splash his cash about, and he hated that superficiality. Yet the less superficial, nicer women were wary of him, because his reputation got in the way; everyone knew that Gabriel Hunter was a former wild child and was now a ruthless company man, so he'd never commit emotionally and there was no point in dating him because there wasn't a future in the relationship. And his family all saw him as Gabe-who-made-the-big-mistake.

How ironic that the only person who really saw him for himself was a stranger. Someone whose real name he didn't even know, let alone what she did or what she looked like, because they'd been careful not to exchange those kinds of details. But over the last six months he'd grown close to Georgygirl from the Surrey Quays forum.

Which made it even more ironic that he'd only joined the website because he was following his father's request to keep an eye out for local disgruntled residents who might oppose the new Hunter Hotel they were developing from a run-down former spice warehouse in Surrey Quays, and charm them into seeing things the Hunter way. Gabriel had discovered that he liked the anonymity of an online persona—he could actually meet people and get to know them, the way he couldn't in real life. The people on the forum didn't know he was Gabriel Hunter, so they had no preconceptions and they accepted him for who he was.

He'd found himself posting on a lot of the same topics as someone called Georgygirl. The more he'd read her posts, the more he'd realised that she was on his wavelength. They'd flirted a bit—because an internet forum was a pretty safe place to flirt—and he hadn't been able to resist contacting her in a private message. Then they'd started chatting to each other away from the forum. They'd agreed to stick to the forum rules of not sharing personal details that would identify themselves, so Gabriel had no idea of Georgygirl's real name or her personal situation; but in their late-night private chats he felt that he could talk to her about anything and everything. Be his real self. Just as he was pretty sure that she was her real self with him.

Right now, it was practically lunchtime. Maybe Georgygirl would be around? He hoped so, because talking to her would make him feel human again. Right now he really needed a dose of her teasing sarcasm to jolt him out of his dark mood.

He informed his PA that he was unavailable for the next hour, then headed out to Surrey Quays. He ordered a double espresso in his favourite café, then grabbed his phone and flicked into the direct messaging section of the Surrey Quays forum.

And then he saw the message waiting for him.

Hey, Clarence, you around?

It was timed fifteen minutes ago. Just about when he'd walked out of that meeting and wanted to punch a wall. Hopefully she hadn't given up waiting for him and was still there. He smiled.

Yeah. I'm here, he typed back.

He sipped his coffee while he waited for her to respond. Just as he thought it was too late and she'd already gone, a message from her popped up on his screen.

Hello, there. How's your day?

I've had better, he admitted. You?

Weird.

Why?

Then he remembered she'd told him that she'd had a letter out of the blue from a solicitor she'd never heard of, asking her to make an appointment because they needed to discuss something with her.

What happened at the solicitor's?

I've been left something in a will.

That's good, isn't it?

Unless it was a really odd bequest, or one with strings.

It's property.

Ah. It was beginning to sound as if there were strings attached. And Gabriel knew without Georgygirl having to tell him that she was upset about it.

Don't tell me—it's a desert island or a ruined castle, but you have to live there for a year all on your own with a massive nest of scary spiders before you can inherit?

Not quite. But thank you for making me laugh.

Meaning that right now she wanted to cry?

What's so bad about it? Is it a total wreck that needs gutting, or it has a roof that eats money?

There was a long pause.

It needs work, but that isn't the bad thing. The bequest is from my grandfather.

Now he understood. The problem wasn't with what she'd been left: it was who'd left it to her that was the sticking point.

How can I accept anything from someone who let my mother down so badly?

She'd confided the situation to him a couple of months ago, when they'd been talking online late at night and drinking wine together—about how her mother had accidentally fallen pregnant, and when her parents had found out that her boyfriend was married, even though her mother hadn't had a clue that he wasn't single when they'd started dating, they had thrown her out on the street instead of supporting her.

Gabriel chafed every day about his own situation, but he knew that his family had always been there for him and had his best interests at heart, even if his father was a control freak who couldn't move on from the past. Georgygirl's story had made him appreciate that for the first time in a long while.

Maybe, he typed back carefully, this is his way of apologising. Even if it is from the grave.

More like trying to buy his way into my good books? Apart from the fact that I can't be bought, he's left it way too late. He let my mum struggle when she was really vulnerable. This feels like thirty pieces of silver. Accepting the bequest means I accept what he—and my grandmother—did. And I *don't*. At all.

He could understand that.

Is your grandmother still alive? Maybe you could go and see her. Explain how you feel. And maybe she can apologise on his behalf as well as her own.

I don't know. But, even if she is alive, I can't see her apologising. What kind of mother chucks her pregnant daughter into the street, Clarence? OK, so they were angry and hurt and shocked at the time—I can understand that. But my mum didn't know that my dad was married or she would never have dated him, much less anything else. And they've had twenty-nine years to get over it. As far as I know, they've never so much as seen a photo of me, let alone cuddled me as a baby or sent me a single birthday card.

And that had to hurt, being rejected by your family when they didn't even know you.

It's their loss, he typed. But maybe they didn't know how to get in touch with your mother.

Surely all you have to do is look up someone in the electoral roll, or even use a private detective if you can't be bothered to do it yourself?

That's not what I meant, Georgy. It's not the finding her that would've been hard—it's breaking the ice and knowing what to say. Sometimes pride gets in the way.

Ironic, because he knew he was guilty of that, too. Not knowing how to challenge his father—because how could you challenge someone when you were always in the wrong?

Maybe. But why leave the property to *me* and not to my mum? It doesn't make sense.

Pride again? Gabriel suggested. And maybe he thought it would be easier to approach you.

From the grave?

Could be Y-chromosome logic?

That earned him a smiley face.

Georgy, you really need to talk to your mum about it.

I would. Except her phone is switched to voicemail.

Shame.

I know this is crazy, she added, but you were the one I really wanted to talk to about this. You see things so clearly.

It was the first genuine compliment he'd had in a long time—and it was one he really appreciated.

Thank you. Glad I can be here for you. That's what friends are for.

And they were friends. Even though they'd never met, he felt their relationship was more real and more honest than the ones in his real-life world—where ironically he couldn't be his real self.

I'm sorry for whining.

You're not whining. You've just been left something by the last person you expected to leave you anything. Of course you're going to wonder why. And if it is an apology, you're right that it's too little, too late. He should've patched up the row years ago and been proud of your mum for raising a bright daughter who's also a decent human being.

Careful, Clarence, she warned. I might not be able to get through the door of the coffee shop when I leave, my head's so swollen.

Coffee shop? Even though he knew it was ridiculous—this wasn't the only coffee shop in Surrey Quays, and he had no idea where she worked so she could be anywhere in London right now—Gabriel found himself pausing and glancing round the room, just in case she was there.

But everyone in the room was either sitting in a group, chatting animatedly, or looked like a businessman catching up with admin work.

There was always the chance that Georgygirl was a man, but he didn't think so. He didn't think she was a bored, middle-aged housewife posing as a younger woman, either. And she'd just let slip that her newly pregnant mother had been thrown out twenty-nine years ago, which would make her around twenty-eight. His own age.

I might not be able to get through the door of the coffee shop, my head's so swollen.

Ha. This was the teasing, quick-witted Georgygirl that had attracted him in the first place. He smiled.

We need deflationary measures, then. OK. You need a haircut and your roots are showing. And there's a massive spot on your nose. It's like the red spot on Mars. You can see it from outer space.

Jupiter's the one with the red spot, she corrected. But I get the point. Head now normal size. Thank you.

Good.

And he just bet she knew he'd deliberately mixed up his planets. He paused.

Seriously, though—maybe you could sell the property and split the money with your mum.

It still feels like thirty pieces of silver. I was thinking about giving her all of it. Except I'll have to persuade her because she'll say he left it to me.

Or maybe it isn't an apology—maybe it's a rescue.

Rescue? How do you work that out? she asked.

You hate your job.

She'd told him that a while back—and, being in a similar situation, he'd sympathised.

If you split the money from selling the property with your mum, would it be enough to tide you over for a six-month sabbatical? That might give you enough time and space to find out what you really want to do. OK, so your grandfather wasn't there when your mum needed him—but right now it looks to me as if he's given you something that you need at exactly the right time. A chance for independence, even if it's only for a little while.

I never thought of it like that. You could be right.

It is what it is. You could always look at it as a belated apology, which is better than none at all. He wasn't there when he should've been, but he's come good now.

Hmm. It isn't residential property he left me.

It's a business?

Yes. And it hasn't been in operation for a while.

A run-down business, then. Which would take money and time to get it back in working order—the building might need work, and the stock or the fixtures might be well out of date. So he'd been right in the first place and the bequest had come with strings.

Could you get the business back up and running?

Though it would help if he knew what kind of business it actually was. But asking would be breaking the terms of their friendship—because then she'd be sharing personal details.

In theory, I could. Though I don't have any experience in the service or entertainment industry.

He did. He'd grown up in it.
That's my area, he said.
He was taking a tiny risk, telling her something per-

sonal—but she had no reason to connect Clarence with Hunter Hotels.

My advice, for what it's worth—an MBA and working for a very successful hotel chain, though he could hardly tell her that without her working out exactly who he was—is that staff are the key. Look at what your competitors are doing and offer your clients something different. Keep a close eye on your costs and income, and get advice from a business start-up specialist. Apply for all the grants you can.

It was solid advice. And Nicole knew that Clarence would be the perfect person to brainstorm ideas with, if she decided to keep the Electric Palace. She was half tempted to tell him everything—but then they'd be sharing details of their real and professional lives, which was against their agreement. He'd already told her too much by letting it slip that he worked in the service or entertainment industry. And she'd as good as told him her age. This was getting risky; it wasn't part of their agreement. Time to back off and change the subject.

Thank you, she typed. But enough about me. You said you'd had a bad day. What happened?

A pointless row. It's just one of those days when I feel like walking out and sending off my CV to half a dozen recruitment agencies. Except it's the family business and I know it's my duty to stay.

Because he was still trying to make up for the big mistake he'd made when he was a teenager? He'd told her the bare details one night, how he was the disgraced son in the family, and that he was never sure he'd ever be able to change their perception of him.

Clarence, maybe you need to talk to your dad or whoever runs the show in your family business about the situation and say it's time for you all to move on. You're not the same person now as you were when you were younger. Everyone makes mistakes—and you can't spend the rest of your life making up for it. That's not reasonable.

Maybe.

Clarence must feel as trapped as she did, Nicole thought. Feeling that there was no way out. He'd helped her think outside the box and see her grandfather's bequest another way: that it could be her escape route. Maybe she could do the same for him.

Could you recruit someone to replace you?

There was a long silence, and Nicole thought maybe she'd gone too far.

Nice idea, Georgy, but it's not going to happen.

OK. What about changing your role in the business instead? Could you take it in a different direction, one you enjoy more?

It's certainly worth thinking about.

Which was a polite brush-off. Just as well she hadn't given in to the urge to suggest meeting for dinner to talk about it.

Because that would've been stupid.

Apart from the fact that she wasn't interested in dating anyone ever again, for all she knew Clarence could be in a serious relationship. Living with someone, engaged, even married.

Even if he wasn't, supposing they met and she discovered that the real Clarence was nothing like the online one? Supposing they really didn't like each other in real life? She valued his friendship too much to risk losing it. If that made her a coward, so be it.

Changing his role in the business. Taking it in a different direction. Gabriel could just imagine the expression on his father's face if he suggested it. Shock, swiftly followed by, 'I saved your skin, so you toe the line and do what I say.'

It wasn't going to happen.

But he appreciated the fact that Georgygirl was trying to think about how to make his life better.

For one mad moment, he almost suggested she should bring details of the business she'd just inherited and meet him for dinner and they could brainstorm it properly. But he stopped himself. Apart from the fact that it was none of his business, supposing they met and he discovered that the real Georgygirl was nothing like the online one? Supposing they loathed each other in real life? He valued his time talking to her and he didn't want to risk losing her friendship.

Thanks for making me feel human again, he typed.

Me? I didn't do anything. And you gave me some really good advice.

That's what friends are for. And you did a lot, believe me. He paused. I'd better let you go. I'm due back in the office. Talk to you later?

I'm due back at the office, too. Talk to you tonight.

Good luck. Let me know how it goes with your mum.

Will do. Let me know how it goes with your family.

Sure.

   Though he had no intention of doing that.

CHAPTER TWO

By THE TIME Nicole went to the restaurant to meet her mother that evening, she had a full dossier on the Electric Palace and its history, thanks to the Surrey Quays forum website. Brian Thomas had owned the cinema since the nineteen-fifties, and it had flourished in the next couple of decades; then it had floundered with the rise of multiplex cinemas and customers demanding something more sophisticated than an old, slightly shabby picture house. One article even described the place as a 'flea-pit'.

Then there were the photographs. It was odd, looking at pictures that people had posted from the nineteen-sixties and realising that the man behind the counter in the café was actually her grandfather, and at the time her mother would've been a toddler. Nicole could definitely see a resemblance to her mother in his face—and to herself. Which made the whole thing feel even more odd. This particular thread was about the history of some of the buildings in Surrey Quays, but it was turning out to be her personal history as well.

Susan hardly ever talked about her family, so Nicole didn't have a clue. Had the Thomas family always lived in Surrey Quays? Had her mother grown up around here? If so, why hadn't she said a word when Nicole had bought her flat, three years ago? Had Nicole spent all this time living only a couple of streets away from the grandparents who'd rejected her?

And how was Susan going to react to the news of the bequest? Would it upset her and bring back bad memories? The last thing Nicole wanted to do was to hurt her mother.

She'd just put the file back in her briefcase when Susan walked over to their table and greeted her with a kiss.

'Hello, darling. I got here as fast as I could. Though it must be serious for you not to be at work at *this* time of day.'

Half-past seven. When most normal people would've left the office hours ago. Nicole grimaced as her mother sat down opposite her. 'Mum. Please.' She really wasn't in the mood for another lecture about her working hours.

'I know, I know. Don't nag. But you do work too hard.' Susan frowned. 'What's happened, love?'

'You know I went to see that solicitor today?'

'Yes.'

'I've been left something in a will.' Nicole blew out a breath. 'I don't think I can accept it.'

'Why not?'

There was no way to say this tactfully. Even though she'd been trying out and discarding different phrases all day, she hadn't found the right words. So all she could do was to come straight out with it. 'Because it's the Electric Palace.'

Understanding dawned in Susan's expression. 'Ah. I did wonder if that would happen.'

Her mother already knew about it? Nicole stared at her in surprise. But how?

As if the questions were written all over her daughter's face, Susan said gently, 'He had to leave it to someone. You were the obvious choice.'

Nicole shook her head. 'How? Mum, I pass the Electric Palace every day on my way to work. I had no idea it was anything to do with us.'

'It isn't,' Susan said. 'It was Brian's. But I'm glad he's finally done the right thing and left it to you.'

'But you're his daughter, Mum. He should've left it to you, not to me.'

'I don't want it.' Susan lifted her chin. 'Brian made his choice years ago—he decided nearly thirty years ago that I wasn't his daughter and he is most definitely not my father. I don't need anything from him. What I own, I have nobody to thank for but myself. I worked for it. And that's the way I like it.'

Nicole reached over and squeezed her mother's hand. 'And you wonder where I get my stubborn streak?'

Susan gave her a wry smile. 'I guess.'

'I can't accept the bequest,' Nicole said again. 'I'm going to tell the solicitor to make the deeds over to you.'

'Darling, no. Brian left it to you, not to me.'

'But you're his daughter,' Nicole said again.

'And you're his granddaughter,' Susan countered.

Nicole shrugged. 'OK. Maybe I'll sell to the developer who wants it.'

'And you'll use the money to do something that makes you happy?'

It was the perfect answer. 'Yes,' Nicole said. 'Giving the money to you will make me very happy. You can pay off your mortgage and get a new car and go on holiday. It'd be enough for you to go and see the Northern Lights this winter, and I know that's top of your bucket list.'

'Absolutely not.' Susan folded her arms. 'You using that money to get out of that hell-hole you work in would make me much happier than if I spent a single penny on myself, believe me.'

Nicole sighed. 'It feels like blood money, Mum. How can I accept something from someone who behaved so badly to you?'

'Someone who knew he was in the wrong but was too stubborn to apologise. That's where we both get our stubborn streak,' Susan said. 'I think leaving the cinema to you is his way of saying sorry without actually having to use the five-letter word.'

'That's what Cl—' Realising what she was about to give away, Nicole stopped short.

'Cl—?' Susan tipped her head to one side. 'And who might this "Cl—" be?'

'A friend,' Nicole said grudgingly.

'A *male* friend?'

'Yes.' Given that they'd never met in real life, there was always the possibility that her internet friend was actually a woman trying on a male persona for size, but Nicole was pretty sure that Clarence was a man.

'That's good.' Susan looked approving. 'What's his name? Cliff? Clive?'

Uh-oh. Nicole could actually see the matchmaking gleam in her mother's eye. 'Mum, we're *just* friends.' She didn't want to admit that they'd never actually met and Clarence wasn't even his real name; she knew what conclusion her mother would draw. That Nicole was an utter coward. And there was a lot of truth in that: Nicole was definitely a coward when it came to relationships. She'd been burned badly enough last time to make her very wary indeed.

'You are allowed to date again, you know,' Susan said gently. 'Yes, you picked the wrong one last time—but don't let that put you off. Not all men are as spineless and as selfish as Jeff.'

It was easier to smile and say, 'Sure.' Though Nicole

had no intention of dating Clarence. Even if he was available, she didn't want to risk losing his friendship. Wanting to switch the subject away from the abject failure that was her love life, Nicole asked, 'So did you grow up in Surrey Quays, Mum?'

'Back when it was all warehouses and terraced houses, before they were turned into posh flats.' Susan nodded. 'We lived on Mortimer Gardens, a few doors down from the cinema. Those houses were knocked down years ago and the land was redeveloped.'

'Why didn't you say anything when I moved here?'

Susan shrugged. 'You were having a hard enough time. You seemed happy here and you didn't need my baggage weighing you down.'

'So all this time I was living just round the corner from my grandparents? I could've passed them every day in the street without knowing who they were.' The whole thing made her feel uncomfortable.

'Your grandmother died ten years ago,' Susan said. 'When they moved from Mortimer Gardens, they lived at the other end of Surrey Quays from you, so you probably wouldn't have seen Brian, either.'

Which made Nicole feel very slightly better. 'Did you ever work at the cinema?'

'When I was a teenager,' Susan said. 'I was an usherette at first, and then I worked in the ticket office and the café. I filled in and helped with whatever needed doing, really.'

'So you would probably have ended up running the place if you hadn't had me?' Guilt flooded through Nicole. How much her mother had lost in keeping her.

'Having you,' Susan said firmly, 'is the best thing that ever happened to me. The moment I first held you in my arms, I felt this massive rush of love for you and that's never changed. You've brought me more joy over the years than anyone or anything else. And I don't have a single regret about it. I never have and I never will.'

Nicole blinked back the sudden tears. 'I love you, Mum. And I don't mean to bring back bad memories.'

'I love you, too, and you're not bringing back bad memories,' Susan said. 'Now, let's order dinner. And then we'll talk strategy and how you're going to deal with this.'

A plate of pasta and a glass of red wine definitely made Nicole feel more human.

'There's a lot about the cinema on the Surrey Quays website. There's a whole thread with loads of pictures.' Nicole flicked into her phone and showed a few of them to her mother.

'Obviously I was born in the mid-sixties so I don't remember it ever being called The Kursaal,' Susan said, 'but I do remember the place from the seventies on. There was this terrible orange and purple wallpaper in the foyer. You can see it there—just be thankful the photo's black and white.' She smiled. 'I remember queuing with my mum and my friends to see Disney films, and everyone being excited about *Grease*—we were all in love with John Travolta and wanted to look like Sandy and be one of the Pink Ladies. And I remember trying to sneak my friends into *Saturday Night Fever* when we were all too young to get in, and Brian spotting us and marching us into his office, where he yelled at us and said we could lose him his cinema licence.'

'So there were some good times?' Nicole asked.

'There are always good times, if you look for them,' Susan said.

'I remember you taking me to the cinema when I was little,' Nicole said. 'Never to the Electric Palace, though.'

'No, never to the Electric Palace,' Susan said quietly.

'I nearly did—but if Brian and Patsy weren't going to be swayed by the photographs I sent of you on every birthday and Christmas, they probably weren't going to be nice to you if they met you, and I wasn't going to risk them making you cry.'

'Mum, that's so sad.'

'Hey. You have the best godparents ever. And we've got each other. We didn't need them. We're doing just fine, kiddo. And life is too short not to be happy.' Susan put her arm around her.

'I'm fine with my life as it is,' Nicole said.

Susan's expression said very firmly, Like hell you are. But she said, 'You know, it doesn't have to be a cinema.'

'What doesn't?'

'The Electric Palace. It says here on that website that it was a ballroom and an ice rink when it was first built— and you could redevelop it for the twenty-first century.'

'What, turn it back into a ballroom and an ice rink?'

'No. When you were younger, you always liked craft stuff. You could turn it into a craft centre. It would do well around here—people wanting to chill out after work.' Susan gave her a level look. 'People like you who spend too many hours behind a corporate desk and need to do something to help them relax. Look how popular those adult colouring books are—and craft things are even better when they're part of a group thing.'

'A craft centre.' How many years was it since Nicole had painted anything, or sewn anything? She missed how much she enjoyed being creative, but she never had the time.

'And a café. Or maybe you could try making the old cinema a going concern,' Susan suggested. 'You're used to putting in long hours, but at least this time it'd be for you instead of giving up your whole life to a job you hate.'

Nicole almost said, 'That's what Clarence suggested,' but stopped herself in time. She didn't want her mother knowing that she'd shared that much with him. It would give Susan completely the wrong idea. Nicole wasn't romantically involved with Clarence and didn't intend to be. She wasn't going to be romantically involved with anyone, ever again.

'Think about it,' Susan said. 'Isn't it time you found something that made you happy?'

'I'm perfectly happy in my job,' Nicole lied.

'No, you're not. You hate it, but it makes you financially secure so you'll put up with it—and I know that's my fault because we were so poor when you were little.'

Nicole reached over the table and hugged her. 'Mum, I never felt deprived when I was growing up. You were working three jobs to keep the rent paid and put food on the table, but you always had time for me. Time to give me a cuddle and tell me stories and do a colouring book with me.'

'But you're worried about being poor again. That's why you stick it out.'

'Not so much poor as vulnerable,' Nicole corrected softly. 'My job gives me freedom from that because I don't have to worry if I'm going to be able to pay my mortgage at the end of the month—and that's a good thing. Having a good salary means I have choices. I'm not backed into a corner because of financial constraints.'

'But the hours you put in don't leave you time for anything else. You don't do anything for *you*—and maybe that's what the Electric Palace can do for you.'

Nicole doubted that very much, but wanted to avoid a row. 'Maybe.'

'Did the solicitor give you the keys?'

Nicole nodded. 'Shall we go and look at it, then have coffee and pudding back at my place?'

'Great idea,' Susan said.

The place was boarded up; all they could see of the building was the semi-circle on the top of the façade at the front and the pillars on either side of the front door. Nicole wasn't that surprised when the lights didn't work—the electricity supply had probably been switched off—but she kept a mini torch on her key-ring, and the beam was bright enough to show them the inside of the building.

Susan sniffed. 'Musty. But no damp, hopefully.'

'What's that other smell?' Nicole asked, noting the unpleasant acridness.

'I think it might be mice.'

Susan's suspicions were confirmed when they went into the auditorium and saw how many of the plush seats looked nibbled. Those that had escaped the mice's teeth were worn threadbare in places.

'I can see why that article called it a flea-pit,' Nicole said with a shudder. 'This is awful, Mum.'

'You just need the pest control people in for the mice, then do a bit of scrubbing,' Susan said.

But when they came out of the auditorium and back into the foyer, Nicole flashed the torch around and saw the stained glass. 'Oh, Mum, that's gorgeous. And the wood on the bar—it's pitted in places, but I bet a carpenter could sort that out. I can just see this bar restored to its Edwardian Art Deco glory.'

'Back in its earliest days?' Susan asked.

'Maybe. And look at this staircase.' Nicole shone the torch on the sweeping wrought-iron staircase that led up to the first floor. 'I can imagine movie stars sashaying down this in high heels and gorgeous dresses. Or glamorous ballroom dancers.'

'We never really used the upper floor. There was always a rope across the stairs,' Susan said.

'So what's upstairs?'

Susan shrugged. 'Brian's office was there. As for the rest of it… Storage space, I think.'

But when they went to look, they discovered that the large upstairs room had gorgeous parquet flooring, and a ceiling covered in carved Art Deco stars that stunned them both.

'I had no idea this was here,' Susan said. 'How beautiful.'

'This must've been the ballroom bit,' Nicole said. 'And I can imagine people dancing here during the Blitz, refusing to let the war get them down. Mum, this place is incredible.'

She'd never expected to fall in love with a building, especially one which came from a source that made her feel awkward and uncomfortable. But Nicole could see the Electric Palace as it could be if it was renovated—the cinema on the ground floor, with the top floor as a ballroom or maybe a place for local bands to play. Or she could even turn this room into a café-restaurant. A café with an area for doing crafts, perhaps like her mum suggested. Or an ice cream parlour, stocked with local artisan ice cream.

If she just sold the Electric Palace to a developer and collected the money, would the building be razed to the ground? Could all this be lost?

But she really couldn't let that happen. She wanted to bring the Electric Palace back to life, to make it part of the community again.

'It's going to be a lot of work to restore it,' she said.

Not to mention money: it would eat up all her savings and she would probably need a bank loan as well to tide her over until the business was up and running properly.

'But you're not afraid of hard work—and this time you'd be working for you,' Susan pointed out.

'On the Surrey Quays forum, quite a few people have said how they'd love the place to be restored so we had our own cinema locally,' Nicole said thoughtfully.

'So you wouldn't be doing it on your own,' Susan said. 'You already have a potential audience and people who'd be willing to spread the word. Some of them might volunteer to help you with the restoration or running the place—and you can count me in as well. I could even try and get some of my probationers interested. I bet they'd enjoy slapping a bit of paint on the walls.'

'Supposing I can't make a go of it? There's only one screen, maybe the possibility of two if I use the upstairs room,' Nicole said. 'Is that enough to draw the customers in and make the place pay?'

'If anyone can do it, you can,' Susan said.

'I have savings,' Nicole said thoughtfully. 'If the renovations cost more than what I have, I could get a loan.'

'I have savings, too. I'd be happy to use them here,' Susan added.

Nicole shook her head. 'This should be your heritage, Mum, not mine. And I don't want you to risk your savings on a business venture that might not make it.'

'We've already had this argument. You didn't win it earlier and you're not going to win it now,' Susan said crisply. 'The Electric Palace is yours. And it's your choice whether you want to sell it or whether you want to do something with it.'

Nicole looked at the sad, neglected old building and

knew exactly what she was going to do. 'I'll work out some figures, to see if it's viable.' Though she knew that it wasn't just about the figures. And if the figures didn't work, she'd find alternatives until they *did* work.

'And if it's viable?' Susan asked.

'I'll talk to my boss. If he'll give me a six-month sabbatical, it'd be long enough for me to see if I can make a go of this place.' Nicole shook her head. 'I can't quite believe I just said that. I've spent ten years working for the bank and I've worked my way up from the bottom.'

'And you hate it there—it suppresses the real Nicole and it's turned you into a corporate ghost.'

'Don't pull your punches, Mum,' Nicole said wryly.

Susan hugged her. 'I can love you to bits at the same time as telling you that you're making a massive mistake with your life, you know.'

'Because mums are good at multi-tasking?'

'You got it, kiddo.' Susan hugged her again. 'And I'm with you on this. Anything you need, from scrubbing floors to working a shift in the ticket office to making popcorn, I'm there—and, as I said, I have savings and I'm happy to invest them in this place.'

'You worked hard for that money.'

'And interest rates are so pathetic that my savings are earning me nothing. I'd rather that money was put to good use. Making my daughter's life better—and that would make me very happy indeed. You can't put a price on that.'

Nicole hugged her. 'Thanks, Mum. I love you. And you are so getting the best pudding in the world.'

'You mean, we have to stop by the supermarket on the way back to your flat because there's nothing in your fridge,' Susan said dryly.

Nicole grinned. 'You know me so well.'

* * *

Later that evening, when Susan had gone home, Nicole checked her phone. As she'd half expected, there was a message from Clarence. Did you talk to your mum?

Yes. Did you talk to your dad?

To her pleasure, he replied almost instantly.

No. There wasn't time.

Nicole was pretty sure that meant Clarence hadn't been able to face a row.
What did your mum say? he asked.
Even though she had a feeling that he was asking her partly to distract her from quizzing him about his own situation, it was still nice that he was interested.

We went to see the building.

And?

It's gorgeous but it needs work.

Then I'd recommend getting a full surveyor's report, so you can make sure any renovation quotes you get from builders are fair, accurate and complete.

Thanks. I hadn't thought of that.

I can recommend some people, if you want.

That'd be great. I'll take you up on that, if the figures stack up and I decide to go ahead with getting the business back up and running.

Although Nicole had told herself she'd only do it if the figures worked out, she knew it was a fib. She'd fallen in love with the building and for the first time in years she was excited at the idea of starting work on something. Clarence obviously lived in Surrey Quays, or he wouldn't be part of the forum; so he'd see the boards come down from the front of the Electric Palace or hear about the renovations from some other eagle-eyed person on the Surrey Quays website. She really ought to tell him before it started happening. After all, he was her friend. And he'd said that he had experience in the entertainment and service industry, so he might have some great ideas for getting the cinema up and running again. He'd already made her think about having a survey done, which wouldn't have occurred to her—she'd just intended to find three builders with good reputations and would pick the middle quote of the three.

But, even as she started to type her news, something held her back.

And she knew what it was. Jeff's betrayal had broken her trust. Although she felt she knew Clarence well, and he was the only person she'd even consider talking to about this apart from her mum and best friend, she found herself halting instead of typing a flurry of excited words about her plans.

Maybe it was better to wait to tell him about it until she'd got all her ducks in a row and knew exactly what she was doing.

What's stopping you going ahead? he asked.

I need to work out the figures first. See if it's viable.

So your mum said the same as I did—that it'll get you out of the job you hate?

Yes, she admitted.

Good—and you're listening to both of us?

I'm listening, she said. But it's still early days, Clarence. I don't want to talk about it too much right now—

She couldn't tell him that she didn't trust him. That would mean explaining about Jeff, and she still cringed when she thought about it. How she'd been blithely unaware of the real reason Jeff had asked her to live with him, until she'd overheard that conversation in the toilets. One of the women touching up her make-up by the mirror had said how her boyfriend was actually living with someone else right then but didn't love her—he was only living with the other woman because his boss wasn't prepared to give the promotion to someone who wasn't settled down, and he was going to leave her as soon as he got the promotion.

Nicole had winced in sympathy with the poor, deluded woman who thought everything was fine, and also wanted to point out to the woman bragging about her fickle lover that, if he was prepared to cheat on his live-in girlfriend with her, there was a very strong chance he'd do exactly the same thing to her with someone else at some point in the future.

The woman had continued, 'She's a right cold fish, Jeff says. A boring banker. But Jeff says he really, really loves me. He's even bought me an engagement ring—look.'

There were encouraging coos from her friends; but Nicole had found herself going cold. Jeff wasn't exactly a common name. Even if it were how many men called Jeff were living with a girlfriend who was a banker? Surely it couldn't be…? But when the woman had gone on to describe cheating, lying Jeff, Nicole had realised with devastating clarity that the poor, deluded woman she'd felt sorry for was none other than herself.

She shook herself. That was all baggage that she needed to jettison. And right now Clarence was waiting for her reply.

She continued typing.

In case I jinx it. The building's going to need a lot of work doing to it. I don't mean to be offensive and shut you out.

It is what it is, he said. No offence taken. And when you do want to talk about it, Georgy, I'm here.

I know, Clarence. And I appreciate it.

She appreciated the fact he kept things light in the rest of their conversation, too.

Goodnight, Georgy. Sweet dreams.

You, too, Clarence.

CHAPTER THREE

'IT'S A PIPE DREAM, Gabriel. You can't create something out of nothing. We're not going to be able to offer our guests exclusive parking.' Evan Hunter stared at his son. 'We should've got the land on the other side of the hotel.'

'It was a sealed bid auction, Dad. And we agreed what would be reasonable. Paying over the odds for the land would've wrecked our budget and the hotel might not have been viable any more.'

'And in the meantime there's an apartment block planned for where our car park should be,' Evan grumbled.

'Unless the new owner of the Electric Palace sells to us.'

Evan sighed. 'Nicole Thomas has already turned down every offer. She says she's going to restore the place.'

'It might not be worth her while,' Gabriel pointed out. 'She's a banker. She'll understand about gearing—and if the restoration costs are too high, she'll see the sense in selling.' He paused. 'To us.'

'You won't succeed, Gabriel. It's a waste of time.'

Maybe, Gabriel thought, this was his chance to prove his worth to his father once and for all. 'I'll talk to her.'

'Charm her into it?' Evan scoffed.

'Give her a dose of healthy realism,' Gabriel corrected.

'The place has been boarded up for five years. The paint-work outside is in bad condition. There are articles in the Surrey Quays forum from years back calling it a flea-pit, so my guess is that it's even worse inside. Add damp, mould and vermin damage—it's not going to be cheap to fix that kind of damage.'

'The Surrey Quays forum.' Evan's eyes narrowed. 'If she gets them behind her and starts a pressure group...'

'Dad. I'll handle it,' Gabriel said. 'We haven't had any objections to the hotel, have we?'

'I suppose not.'

Gabriel didn't bother waiting for his father to say he'd done a good job with the PR side. It wasn't Evan's style. 'I'll handle it,' he said again. 'Nicole Thomas is a hard-headed businesswoman. She'll see the sensible course is to sell the site to us. She gets to cash in her inheritance, and we get the space. Everybody wins.'

'Hmm.' Evan didn't look convinced.

So maybe this would be the tipping point. The thing that finally earned Gabriel his father's respect.

And then maybe he'd get his freedom.

The figures worked. So did the admin. Nicole had checked online and there was a huge list of permissions and licences she needed to apply for, but it was all doable. She just needed to make a master list, do some critical path analysis, and tackle the tasks in the right order. Just as she would on a normal day at her desk.

Once she'd talked to her boss and he'd agreed to let her take a sabbatical, she sat at her desk, working out how to break the news to her team.

But then Neil, her second-in-command, came in to her office. 'Are the rumours true?'

It looked as if the office grapevine had scooped her. 'What rumours?' she asked, playing for time.

'That you're taking six months off?'

'Yes.'

He looked her up and down, frowning. 'You don't *look* pregnant.'

Oh, honestly. Was the guy still stuck in the Dark Ages? 'That's because I'm not.'

'Then what? Have you got yourself a mail-order bridegroom on the internet—a rich Russian mafia guy who wants to be respectable?' He cackled, clearly pleased with himself at the barb.

She rolled her eyes, not rising to the bait. Neil liked to think of himself as the office wise-guy and he invariably made comments for a cheap laugh at other people's expense. She'd warned him about it before in his annual review, but he hadn't taken a blind bit of notice. 'You can tell everyone I'm not pregnant. I'm also not running off to Russia, thinking that I've bagged myself a millionaire bridegroom only to discover that it was all a big scam and I'm about to be sold into slavery.' She steepled her fingers and looked him straight in the eye. 'Are there any other rumours I need to clarify, or are we done?'

'Wow—I've never heard you…' He looked at her with something akin to respect. 'Sorry.'

She shrugged. 'Apology accepted.'

'So why are you taking six months off?'

'It's a business opportunity,' she said. 'Keep your fingers crossed that it works, because if it doesn't I'll be claiming my desk back in six months' time.'

From him, she meant, and clearly he recognised it because his face went dull red. 'No offence meant.'

'Good,' she said, and clapped him on the shoulder. 'Little tip from me. For what's probably the six millionth time I've told you, Neil, try to lose the wisecracks. They make you look less professional and that'll stand in the way of you being promoted.'

'All right. Sorry.' He paused. 'Are you really going today?'

'Yes.'

'Without even having a leaving do?'

'I might be coming back if my plans don't work out,' she reminded him, 'so it would be a bit fake to have a leaving do. But I'll put some money behind the bar at the Mucky Duck—' the nearby pub that most of her team seemed to frequent after work '—if you're all that desperate to have a drink at my expense.'

'Hang on. You'll pay for your own sort-of leaving do and not turn up to it?'

That was the idea. She spread her hands. 'What's the problem?'

Neil shook his head. 'If it wasn't for the fact you're actually leaving, I'd think you'd be slaving behind your desk. You never join in with anything.'

'Because I don't fit in,' she said softly. 'So I'm not going to be the spectre at the feast. You can all enjoy a drink without worrying what to say in front of me.'

'None of us really knows you—all we know is that you work crazy hours,' Neil said.

Which was why nobody ever asked her about how her weekend was: they knew she would've spent a big chunk of Saturday at her desk.

'Do you even have a life outside the office?' Neil asked.

And this time there was no barb in his voice; Nicole squirmed inwardly when she realised that the odd note in his voice was pity. 'Ask me again in six months,' she said, 'because then I hope I might have.' And that was the nearest she'd get to admitting her work-life balance was all wrong.

'Well—good luck with your mysterious business opportunity,' he said.

'Thanks—and I'll make sure I leave my desk tidy for you.'

Neil took it as the dismissal she meant it to be; but, before she could clear her desk at the end of the day, her entire team filed into her office, headed by her boss.

'We thought you should have these,' he said, and presented her with a bottle of expensive champagne, a massive card which had been signed by everyone on their floor, and a huge bouquet of roses and lilies.

'We didn't really know what to get you,' Neil said, joining them at Nicole's desk, 'but the team had a whip-round.' He presented her with an envelope filled with money. 'Maybe this will help with your, um, business opportunity.'

Nicole was touched that they'd gone to this trouble. She hadn't expected anything—just that she'd slip away quietly while everyone else was at the bar across the road.

'Thanks. You'll be pleased to know it'll go to good use—I'll probably spend it on paint.'

Neil gaped at her. 'You're leaving us to be an artist?'

She laughed. 'No. I meant masonry paint. I've been left a cinema in a will. It's a bit run-down but I'm going to restore it and see if I can get it up and running properly.'

'A *cinema*? Then you,' Neil said, 'are coming across to the Mucky Duck with us right now, and you're going to tell us everything—and that's not a suggestion, Nicole, because we'll carry you over there if we have to.'

It was the first time Nicole had actually felt part of the team. How ironic that it had happened just as she was leaving them.

'OK,' she said, and let them sweep her across the road in the middle of a crowd.

The next day, Nicole was in the cinema with a clipboard and a pen, adding to her list of what she needed to do when her phone rang.

She glanced at the screen, half expecting that it would be her daily call from the lawyer at Hunter Hotels trying to persuade her to sell the Electric Palace, even though she'd told him every time that the cinema wasn't for sale. Not recognising the number on her screen, and assuming it was one of the calls she was waiting to be returned, she answered her phone. 'Yes?'

'Ms Thomas?'

'Yes.'

'It's Gabriel Hunter from Hunter Hotels.'

Clearly the lawyer had realised that she wasn't going to say yes to the monkey, so now it was the organ-grinder's turn to try and persuade her. She suppressed a sigh. 'Thank you for calling, Mr Hunter, but I believe I've made my position quite clear. The Electric Palace isn't for sale.'

'Indeed,' he said, 'but we have areas of mutual interest and I'd like to meet you to discuss them.'

In other words, he planned to charm her into selling? She put on her best bland voice. 'That's very nice of you to ask, but I'm afraid I'm really rather busy at the moment.'

'It won't take long. Are you at the cinema right now?'

'Yes.'

She regretted her answer the moment he asked, 'And you've been there since the crack of dawn?'

Had the Hunters got someone spying on her, or something? 'Not that it's any of your business, but yes.' There was a lot to do. And she thought at her best, first thing in the morning. It made sense to start early.

'I'd be the same,' he said, mollifying her only slightly. 'So I'd say you're about due for a coffee break. How about I meet you at the café on Challoner Road in half an hour?'

'Where you'll have a carnation in your buttonhole and be carrying a copy of the *Financial Times* so I can recognise you?' She couldn't help the snippy retort.

He laughed. 'No need. I'll be there first—and I'll recognise you.'

Hunter Hotels probably had a dossier on her, including a photograph and a list of everything from her route to work to her shoe size, she thought grimly. 'Thank you for the invitation, but there really isn't any point in us meeting. I'm not selling.'

'I'm not trying to pressure you to sell. As I said, I want to discuss mutual opportunities—and the coffee's on me.'

'I'm not dressed to go to a café. I'm covered in dust.'

'I'd be worried if you weren't, given the current condition of the cinema. And I'd be even more worried if you were walking around a run-down building wearing patent stilettos and a business suit.'

There was a note of humour in Gabriel Hunter's voice. Nicole hadn't expected that, and she quite liked it; at the same time, it left her feeling slightly off balance.

'But if you'd rather I brought the coffee to you, that's fine,' he said. 'Just let me know how you take your coffee.'

It was tempting, but at least if they met in a neutral place she could make an excuse to leave. If he turned up at the cinema, she might have to be rude in order to make him leave and let her get on with things. And, at the end of the day, Gabriel Hunter was working on the business next door to hers. They might have mutual customers.

So he probably had a point about mutual opportunities. Maybe they should talk.

'I'll see you at the café in half an hour,' she said.

She brushed herself down and then was cross with herself. It wasn't as if he was her client, and she wasn't still working at the bank. It didn't matter what she looked like or what he thought of her. And if he tried to push her into selling the Electric Palace, she'd give him very short shrift and come back to work on her lists.

So Nicole Thomas had agreed to meet him. That was a good start, Gabriel thought. He'd certainly got further with her than their company lawyer had.

He worked on his laptop with one eye on the door, waiting for her to turn up. Given that she'd worked in a bank and her photograph on their website made her look like a consummate professional, he'd bet that she'd walk through the door thirty seconds earlier than they'd agreed to meet. Efficiency was probably her middle name.

Almost on cue, the door opened. He recognised Nicole immediately; even though she was wearing old jeans and a T-shirt rather than a business suit, and no make-up whatsoever, her mid-brown hair was pulled back in exactly the same style as she'd worn it at the bank. Old habits clearly died hard.

She glanced around the café, obviously looking for him. For a moment, she looked vulnerable and Gabriel was shocked to feel a sudden surge of protectiveness. She worked for a bank and had worked her way up the management ladder, so she most definitely didn't need protecting; but there was something about her that drew him.

He was horrified to realise that he was attracted to her.

Talk about inappropriate. You didn't fall for your business rival. Ever. Besides, he didn't want to get involved with anyone. He was tired of dating women who had preconceived notions about him. All he wanted to do was talk to Nicole Thomas about mutual opportunities, point out all the many difficulties she was going to face in restoring the cinema, and then talk her into doing the sensible thing and selling the Electric Palace to him for a price fair to both of them.

Nicole looked round the café, trying to work out which of the men sitting on their own was Gabriel Hunter. Why on earth hadn't she looked him up on the internet first, so she would've known exactly who she was meeting here? Had she already slipped out of good business habits, just days after leaving the bank? At this rate, she'd make a complete mess of the cinema and she'd be forced to go back to her old job—and, worse still, have to admit that she'd failed in her bid for freedom.

Then the man in the corner lifted his hand and gave the tiniest wave.

He looked young—probably around her own age. There wasn't a hint of grey in his short dark hair, and his blue eyes were piercing.

If he was the head of Hunter Hotels when he was that young, then he was definitely the ruthless kind. She made a mental note to be polite but to stay on her guard.

His suit was expensively cut—the sort that had been hand-made by a good tailor, rather than bought off the peg—and she'd just bet if she looked under the table his shoes would be the same kind of quality. His shirt was well cut, too, and that understated tie was top of the range. He radiated money and style, looking more like a model advertising a super-expensive watch than a hotel magnate, and she felt totally scruffy and underdressed in her jeans and T-shirt. Right then she really missed the armour of her business suit.

He stood up as she reached his table and held out his hand. 'Thank you for coming, Ms Thomas.'

His handshake was firm and a little tingle ran down Nicole's spine at the touch of his skin against hers. How inappropriate was that? They were on opposite sides and she'd better remember that. Apart from the fact that she never wanted to get involved with anyone again, the fact Gabriel Hunter was her business rival meant he was totally out of the running as a potential date. Even if he was one of the nicest-looking men she'd ever met. Didn't they say that handsome is as handsome does?

'Mr Hunter,' she said coolly.

'Call me Gabriel.'

She had no intention of doing that—or of inviting him to call her by her own first name. They weren't friends; they were business rivals.

'How do you like your coffee?' he asked.

'Espresso, please.'

'Me, too.' He smiled at her, and her heart felt as if it had done a backflip.

'If you haven't been here before, I'd recommend the Guatemala blend.'

'Thank you. That would be lovely,' she said politely.

This was the kind of café that sold a dozen different types of coffee, from simple Americanos and cappuccinos through to pour-over-and-siphon coffee; and she noted from the chalk board above the counter that there were a dozen different blends to choose from, all with tasting notes, so this was the kind of place that was frequented by serious coffee drinkers. The kind of coffee bar she half had in mind for the Electric Palace, depending on whether she kept it as a cinema or turned it into a craft café.

But Gabriel Hunter unsettled her.

She wasn't used to reacting like that towards someone. She hadn't reacted to anyone like that since Jeff. Given her poor judgement when it came to relationships, she really didn't want to be attracted to Gabriel Hunter.

Focus, Nicole, she told herself sharply. Business. Work. Nothing else.

Gabriel came back to the table carrying two espressos, and set one cup and saucer in front of her before sitting down opposite her again.

She took a sip. 'You're right; this is excellent. Thank you.'

'Pleasure.' He inclined his head.

Enough pleasantries, she decided. This was business, so they might as well save some time and cut to the chase. 'So, what are these mutual interests you wanted to discuss?' she asked.

'Our businesses are next door to each other. And they're both works in progress,' he said, 'though obviously the hotel renovation is quite a bit further on than the cinema.'

'Are you thinking mutual customers?'

'And mutual parking.'

His eyes really were sharp, she thought. As if they saw everything.

'Are you really going to run the place as a cinema?' he asked.

She frowned. 'Why would I discuss my business strategy with a competitor?'

'True. But, if you are going to run it as a cinema, I'm not sure you'll manage to make it pay, and it's not going to be good for my business if the place next door to me is boarded up and looks derelict,' he said bluntly. 'Most people would choose to take the Tube into the West End and go to a multiplex to see the latest blockbuster. One screen doesn't give your customers a lot of choice, and you'll be competing directly with established businesses that can offer those customers an awful lot more.'

'That all depends on the programming.' She'd been researching that; and she needed to think about whether to show the blockbusters as they came out, or to develop the Electric Palace as an art-house cinema, or to have a diverse programme with certain kinds of movies showing on certain nights.

'With your background in banking—' well, of course he'd checked her out and would know that '—obviously you're more than capable of handling the figures and the finance,' he said. 'But the building needs a lot of work, and restoring something properly takes a lot of experience or at least knowing who to ask.'

'It's been boarded up for the last five years. How would you know the place needs a lot of work?' she asked.

'Because if you leave any building without any kind of maintenance for five years, there's going to be a problem,' he said matter-of-factly. 'Anything from damp caused by the tiniest leak in the roof that's built up unnoticed over the years, through to damage from mice or rats. None of it will be covered by insurance—assuming that there was any premises insurance in place at all while it was closed—because that kind of damage counts as a gradually operating cause.'

There was definitely insurance in place. That was the first thing she'd checked. But she also knew he had a point about uninsured damage. And she'd noticed that he was using legal terms as if he was very, very familiar with even the tiniest of small print. She'd need to be very careful how she dealt with him.

'And then there's the state of the wiring and the plumbing,' he continued. 'Even if the rats and mice have left it alone, the cabling's probably deteriorated with age, and do you even know when it was last rewired? For all you know, it could still be nineteen-fifties wiring and it'd need replacing completely to make it safe. Without safe wiring, you won't get public liability insurance or any of the business licences you need.'

Just when she thought he'd finished, he continued, 'And then there's lead piping. Unless your water pipes have been completely replaced since the nineteen-sixties, there's a good chance you'll have lead piping. You'll need to get that replaced—just as we're having to do, next door.'

She didn't have a clue when the wiring had last been done, or even how to check what its current state was like, or how to check the water pipes. 'That's precisely why I'm having a survey done,' she said, grateful that Clarence had suggested that to her. 'So then I'll know exactly what needs to be done and what to ask builders to quote for.'

'So where are your customers going to park?' he asked.

'The same place as they would at the multiplexes in town—there's no need to park, because they'll either walk here or take the Tube,' she countered. 'Where are yours going to park?'

Even though he was pretty impassive, there was the tiniest flicker in his eyes that gave him away. And then she realised. 'That's why you want to buy the Electric Palace,' she said. 'So you can raze it to the ground and turn the space into a car park.'

'It's one option.' He shrugged. 'But if the building is

in better condition than I think it is, it could also work as the hotel's restaurant or conference suite.'

She shook her head. 'It's not a restaurant. It's a purpose-built cinema.'

'But it's not a listed building. The use could be changed very easily.'

She stared at him. 'You've already checked that out?'

'As we do with any building we consider developing,' he said, not looking in the slightest bit abashed. 'If a building's listed, it means we'll have to meet strict criteria before we can make any alterations, and it also means extra site visits and inspections—all of which adds time to a project. And time is money.'

She blinked. 'Are you saying you rush things through?'

'No. Cutting corners means offering our clients a substandard experience, and we don't do that. Hunter Hotels is about high quality,' he said. 'What I mean is that if a building isn't listed, then we don't get the extra admin hassle when we renovate it and we don't have any enforced down-time while we wait for inspections.' He looked her straight in the eye. 'Then again, if the council were to decide your cinema ought to be listed...'

'Are you threatening me?'

'No, I'm pointing out that you need to get various licences. The council might look at your application and decide that a purpose-built Edwardian *kursaal* really ought to be on the Statutory List of Buildings of Special Architectural or Historical Interest. Especially as there aren't many of them left.'

His voice was bland, but she was pretty sure he was enjoying this. Gabriel Hunter was a corporate shark—and he'd just spotted a weakness and was playing on it. She narrowed her eyes at him. 'It feels as if you're threatening me.'

'Not at all. I'm just warning you to be prepared, because you clearly don't have any experience of dealing with premises—and, as your building's been boarded up for the last five years, there's a pretty good chance you have hidden damage that's going to take a lot of time and money to sort out. The longer it takes to get the building up and running, the longer it'll be before it starts to pay for itself, and the more likely it is that you'll run into other roadblocks.'

Gabriel Hunter was being perfectly polite and charming, but Nicole thought that he was definitely trying to worry her to the point where she'd think that the burden of restoring the cinema would be too heavy and it would be easier to sell the place. To him. 'The Electric Palace isn't for sale,' she repeated. 'So, unless you have some constructive suggestions—like offering my clients a special pre-movie dinner menu—then I really don't think we have anything more to talk about, Mr Hunter.'

'A special dinner menu is a possibility. And in return you could offer my clients a special deal on ticket prices.'

'You seriously think we could work together?' And yet she couldn't shake the suspicion that this was all a smokescreen. She knew that Hunter Hotels wanted her to sell. 'I've just refused to sell my cinema to you. Why would you want to work with me?'

'It is what it is,' he said.

She looked at him in surprise. 'Clarence says that all the time.' The words were out before she could stop them.

'Who's Clarence?' he asked.

She shook her head. 'Nobody you know.' Clarence had nothing in common with Gabriel Hunter, and it was extremely unlikely that they knew each other. Even if they did know each other, in real life, they were so different that they probably loathed each other.

* * *

Clarence.

It wasn't exactly a common name. Gabriel didn't know anyone else called Clarence, whether in real life or online.

Surely Nicole couldn't be…?

But, as he thought about it, the pieces fell rapidly into place. Georgygirl had just inherited a commercial building—a business she'd been mysterious about. He knew she hated her job, and was planning to take a sabbatical to see if she could turn the business around and make it work.

Nicole Thomas had just inherited the Electric Palace and, according to his sources, she was taking a sabbatical from the bank.

So was Nicole Thomas *Georgygirl*?

This was the first time he'd actually connected his online and real life, and as the penny dropped it left him reeling.

The girl he'd met online was warm and sweet and funny, whereas Nicole Thomas was cool and hard-headed. Georgygirl was his friend, whereas Nicole Thomas had made it very clear that not only were they not friends, they were on opposite sides.

The whole reason he'd resisted meeting Georgygirl was because he'd been afraid that they'd be different in real life, not meeting each other's expectations. And then he'd lose her friendship, a relationship he'd really come to value over the months.

It looked as if his fears had been right on the nail. Georgygirl was completely different in real life. They weren't compatible at all.

Nicole clearly hadn't worked out yet that he was Clarence. Even if she'd researched Hunter Hotels, she wouldn't have connected Clarence with Gabriel. He'd let it slip that he worked in the leisure industry, but that was such a broad category that it was unlikely she'd connect it with hotel development.

Given that they didn't like each other—he ignored that spark of attraction he'd felt, and that surge of protectiveness he'd felt towards her—maybe he could leverage the ruins of their friendship. He could keep pointing out the downsides of the building and the difficulties she was going to face; then he could offer her an easy option. One he hoped she'd take, and she'd sell the Electric Palace to him.

OK, so he'd lose Georgygirl's friendship completely. But he'd pretty much lost that anyway, hadn't he? Once she knew who he was, she'd turn away from him. He'd be naive to think it could be different and could ever lead to anything else.

'I guess you're right,' he said. 'We probably don't have mutual interests. I'll let you get on. Thank you for your time.'

'Thank you for the coffee,' she said.

He gave her the briefest of nods and walked out before his disappointment could betray him.

Later that evening, a message came in on Gabriel's screen.

Hey, Clarence. How was your day?

OK, I guess, he typed back, feeling slightly uneasy because he knew exactly who she was, while he was pretty sure she still didn't know the truth about him. How was yours?

Pretty grim. I met the guy who wants to buy my business.

Uh-oh. Clarence would be sympathetic; Gabriel wasn't so sure he wanted to hear what she had to say about him.

OK... he said, playing for time.

He's a corporate shark in a suit, she said.

Ouch. Well, it was his own fault. He should've told her face to face who he was when he'd had the chance. Now it was going to get messy. He'd limit the damage and tell her right now.

I had a meeting today too, he said. With someone I was expecting to be my enemy, but who turned out to be someone I've been friends with for a long time.

That's good, isn't it? she asked.

He wasn't so sure. But he was going to have to bite the bullet.

Nicole, I think we need to talk.

Nicole stared at her screen. She'd never, ever given Clarence her real name. So why was he using it now? How did he know who she was?

Then a seriously nasty thought hit her.

She dismissed it instantly. Of course Clarence couldn't be Gabriel Hunter. He just couldn't. Clarence was kind and sweet and funny.

But he knew her real name without her telling him. And there was no way he could have connected Georgy-girl with Nicole Thomas. They'd never shared real names or the kind of personal details that would link up. So the only logical explanation was that Clarence was Gabriel.

Are you trying to tell me *you're* the corporate shark? she typed, desperately wanting him to tell her that he wasn't.

But his reply was very clear.

I don't think of myself that way, but you clearly do. Yes. I'm Gabriel Hunter.

Clarence really was Gabriel Hunter?

She couldn't quite take it in.

And then she felt sick to her stomach. Yet again, she'd fallen for someone and he'd turned out to be using her. Jeff had only asked her to date him and then move in with him because he'd wanted promotion and his boss had a thing about only promoting young men if they were settled. And now Clarence had betrayed her in exactly the same way: he hadn't made friends with her because he liked her, but because he'd wanted to leverage their friendship and persuade her to sell the Electric Palace to Hunter Hotels.

What a stupid, naive fool she was.

How long have you known who I am? she demanded, wanting to know the worst so she could regroup.

I only realised today, he said. When you talked about Clarence. Then the pieces fitted together. You'd inherited a business and you were taking a sabbatical to see if you could make it work. So had Georgy.

But you didn't say a word to me at the café.

I might have got the wrong end of the stick. There might've been another Clarence.

Because it's *such* a common name? she asked waspishly.

OK. I wanted time to get my head round it, he said. Right then I didn't know what to say to you.

So how long have you known that the Electric Palace was mine?

We knew it belonged to Brian Thomas—we'd approached him several times over the last couple of years and he'd refused to sell. We didn't know who his heir was until his will was made public. Then we contacted you—and at that point I didn't know you were Georgy.

He really expected her to believe that?
But now it's out in the open, he continued.
And how.

There's something I'd like you to think about.

Against her better instincts, she asked, What?

You know that art café you talked to me about, a couple of months ago? If you sell the cinema, that'd give you the money to find the perfect place for it. To find a building you're not going to have to restore first. It'll save you so much time and hassle. It'd give you the space to follow your dreams straight away instead of having to wait while you rebuild someone else's.

Nicole stared at the screen in disbelief. He was picking up on the private dream she'd told him about in a completely different context and was using it to pressure her into selling?
You actually think you can use our former friendship to make me sell to you? she asked, not sure whether she was more hurt or disgusted. Oh, please. You're a corporate shark through and through. The Electric Palace

isn't for sale—not now and not in the foreseeable future. Goodbye, Clarence.

She flicked out of the messaging programme and shut down her laptop before he could reply.

It was hard to get her head round this. Her friend Clarence was actually her business rival, Gabriel Hunter. Which meant he wasn't really her friend—otherwise why would he have tried to use their relationship to put pressure on her to sell?

And to think she'd told him things she'd never told anyone else. Trusted him.

Now she knew who he really was, her worst fears had come true. He wasn't the same online as he was in real life. In real life, she disliked him and everything he stood for.

She'd lost her friend.

And she'd lost the tiny bit of her remaining trust along with that friendship.

CHAPTER FOUR

GABRIEL'S MOOD THE next day wasn't improved by another run-in with his father—especially because this time he couldn't talk to Georgygirl about it and there was nobody to tease him out of his irritation.

He also couldn't share the bad pun that a friend emailed him and that he knew Georgy would've enjoyed. He thought about sending her a message, but she'd made it pretty clear that she didn't want to have anything to do with him. That 'Goodbye, Clarence' had sounded very final.

She didn't message him that evening, either.

Not that he was surprised. Nicole Thomas wasn't the kind of woman who backed down. She was a cool, hard-headed businesswoman.

By the following morning, Gabriel realised why his dark mood refused to lift. He *missed* Georgygirl. She'd made his life so much brighter, these last six months. It had felt good, knowing that there was someone out there who actually understood who he really was, at heart. And he was miserable without her.

Did she miss Clarence, too? he wondered.

OK, so Nicole had called him a corporate shark. Which he wasn't. Not really. He wasn't a pushover, but he was scrupulously fair in his business dealings. His real identity had clearly come as a shock to her. Hers had been a shock to him, too, but at least he'd had time to get his head round it before he'd talked to her, whereas he hadn't given her a chance to get used to the idea. Then she'd accused him of using their former friendship to make her sell the cinema to him, and he knew she had a point. He *had* tried to leverage their former friendship, thinking that it was all that was left.

But if she missed him as much as he missed her, and she could put aside who he was and see past that to his real self—the self he'd shared with her online—then maybe they could salvage something from this.

In any case, their businesses were next door to each other. It would be the neighbourly thing to do, to take her a coffee and see how she was getting on. The fact that he was attracted to her had nothing to do with it, he told himself. This was strictly business, and maybe also a chance to fix a relationship that he valued and he missed.

He dropped in to his favourite coffee shop—the one where he'd met Nicole the other day—picked up two espressos to go and two dark chocolate brownies, then headed for Mortimer Gardens.

The front door to the cinema was closed, but when he tried the handle it was unlocked. He opened it and went into the lobby. 'Hello?' he called.

Nicole came into the lobby from what he assumed was the foyer, carrying a clipboard. 'What are you doing here?' she asked.

'I brought you coffee.' He offered her the paper cup and one of the two paper bags.

She frowned. 'Why?'

'Because we're neighbours. You've been working hard and I thought maybe you could do with this.'

'Thank you,' she said coolly and politely, 'but there's really no need.'

He sighed. 'Nicole, I don't want to fight with you—and I could drink both espressos myself and eat both brownies, but that much caffeine and sugar in my system at once would turn me into a total nightmare. Take pity on my staff and share it with me.'

'I...'

He could see the doubt in her face, so he added, 'For Clarence and Georgy.'

She shook her head. 'Forget Georgy. She doesn't exist. Any more than Clarence does.'

'We do exist—we're real. And can you please just take the coffee and cake instead of being stubborn and stroppy? They don't come with strings attached.'

She stared at him. Just when he was about to give up and walk away, she gave the tiniest nod. 'I guess. Thank you.' She took the coffee and the brownie. 'Though actually I do feel beholden to you now.'

'There's no need. It's just coffee. As I said, no strings. I'm being neighbourly.'

'I guess I should be neighbourly, too, and invite you to sit down—' she gestured to his suit '—but you're really not dressed for this place.'

'Maybe.' He noticed that she was wearing jeans and another old T-shirt, teamed with canvas shoes; her hair was pulled back tightly into a bun. Out of habit from her banking days, or just to try and stop herself getting so dusty? Who was the real Nicole—the banker, or the girl who dreamed of the stars?

'I was just working through here.'

Gabriel followed her through into the foyer, where she'd set up a makeshift desk at one of the tables. She'd taken down the boarding on one of the windows to let some light in.

'Lighting not working?' he asked.

'The electricity supply's due to be reconnected some time today,' she said. 'I'm using a torch and this window until then.'

'And you have some spare fuses in case some of the circuits blow when the electricity's back on?'

She folded her arms and gave him a narrow-eyed look. 'I might be female, Mr Hunter, but I'm neither stupid nor helpless.'

He sighed. 'That wasn't what I was implying. You know I know you're not stupid or helpless. What I'm saying is that I have a couple of electricians next door if you run into problems, OK?'

'Since when does a hard-headed businessman offer help to the business next door?'

When it was owned by a friend, one whom he happened to know was doing this single-handedly. Not that he thought she'd accept that. And part of him thought that he was crazy. Why *would* he help her, when he wanted her to sell the place to him? He ought to be making life hard for her, not bringing her coffee and offering help from his staff.

Yet part of him wondered—was there a compromise? Could he forge a deal that would both please his father *and* help his friend? 'Damage limitation,' he said. 'If your place goes up in smoke, it's going to affect mine.' It was true. The fact that he couldn't quite separate Nicole from Georgygirl was irrelevant.

'Right.' She grabbed a cloth and rubbed the worst of the dust from one of the chairs. 'Since you're here, have a seat.'

'Thank you.' He sat down.

'So why are you really here?' she asked.

Because he missed her. But he didn't think she was ready to hear that. He wasn't sure he was ready to hear that, either. 'Being neighbourly. Just as you'd do if you were a lot further on in the restoration here and I'd just started up next door.'

'With the exception that I wouldn't be trying to buy your hotel so I could raze it to the ground to make a car park for my cinema,' she pointed out.

'I did say that was one option. There are others,' he said mildly. He just hadn't thought them all through yet. He wanted the land for car parking. Restoring the cinema instead and using it as part of the hotel was unlikely to be cost effective. To give himself some breathing space, he asked, 'Why did you call yourself Georgygirl on the forum?'

It was the last question Nicole had expected. She frowned. 'What's that got to do with the cinema?'

'Nothing. I'm just curious. Before I knew who you were, I assumed maybe your name was Georgina, or your surname was George. And then afterwards I thought of the film.'

'A film that's half a century old and has never been remade—and you loathe romcoms anyway.' Or, at least, Clarence did. She didn't know what Gabriel Hunter liked. How much of Clarence had been real?

'OK. So I looked it up on the internet. But the synopsis I read—well, it doesn't fit you. And neither does the song. You're not dowdy and any male with red blood would give you a second glance.'

'I wasn't fishing for compliments,' she said crisply. 'For the record, I'm not interested in flattery, either.'

'I was merely stating facts. Though there is one thing,'

he said. 'You're Nicole on the outside and Georgy on the inside.'

Two parts of the same person. Was it the same for him? Was the nice side of Gabriel Hunter—Clarence—real? But he'd lied to her. How could she trust him? Especially as she'd made that mistake before: putting her trust in the wrong man. She'd promised herself she'd never repeat that mistake again.

'So—why Georgygirl?' he asked again.

'It's not from that film. If you must know, it's George, as in Banks, because I'm—well, was—a banker, and girl because I'm female.'

'George Banks from *Mary Poppins*,' he said. 'I don't think you'd believe that feeding the birds is a waste—so I'm guessing that you never find the time to fly kites.'

'Clever.' And a little too close to the truth for her comfort. 'So why did you call yourself Clarence?'

'Because my name's Gabriel.'

She frowned. 'I'm not following you.'

'As in the angel,' he said.

She scoffed. 'You're no angel.'

'I don't pretend to be. I just happen to have the name of an angel.'

The Archangel Gabriel; and an angel called Clarence. '*It's a Wonderful Life*.' Her favourite film: the one she watched with her mother every Christmas Eve and wept over every time the townsfolk of Bedford Falls all came with their savings to help George Bailey. She shook her head. 'No. You should've called yourself Potter.'

'Harry?'

'Henry,' she corrected.

He grimaced. 'I know you think I'm a corporate shark, but I'd never cheat or steal like Henry Potter.' He looked her straight in the eye. 'For the record, that wasn't my teenage mistake, or have you already checked that out?'

'Once I found out who you really were, I looked you up,' she admitted. 'I saw what the papers said about you.'

'It is what it is.' He shrugged. 'So now you know the worst of me.'

'Yes. It's a hell of a teenage mistake, crashing your car into someone's shop.'

'While drunk. Don't forget that. And my father had enough money to hire a top-class lawyer who could get me off on a technicality. Which makes me the lowest of the low.' He suddenly looked really vulnerable. 'And you think I don't know that?'

She winced. Clarence had told her he regretted his teenage mistake bitterly. That he was still paying for his mistake over and over again. There was a lot more to this than the papers had reported, she was sure.

And she'd just been really, really mean to him. To the man who'd made her life that bit brighter over the last six months. How horrible did that make her?

Then again, Gabriel had tried to leverage their friendship to make her sell the cinema to him. Which made him as much of a user as Jeff. And that was something she found hard to forgive.

'Mr Hunter, we really have nothing to say to each other.'

'Georgy—Nicole,' he corrected himself, 'we've talked every night for months and I think that's real.'

'But your company wants to buy my cinema.'

'Yes.'

'It's not for sale. Not now, and not ever.'

'Message received and understood,' he said. 'Have you spoken to a surveyor yet?'

'No,' she admitted.

'I can give you some names.'

'I bet you can.'

He frowned. 'What's that supposed to mean?'

'A surveyor who'll tell me that there's so much wrong, the best thing I can do is raze it to the ground and sell you the site as a car park for your new hotel?' she asked waspishly.

'No. I'm really not like Henry Potter,' he said again. 'I was trying to be nice. To help you, because I have experience in the area and you don't.'

'Why would you help me when we're business rivals?'

'Because we don't have to be rivals,' he said. 'Maybe we can work together.'

'How?'

'What do you intend to do with the place?'

'You've already asked me that, and my answer's the same.' She looked at him. 'Would you tell a business rival what your strategy was?'

He sighed. 'Nicole, I'm not asking for rivalry reasons. I'm asking, are you going to run it as a cinema or are you going to use the space for something else? You once said if you could do anything you wanted, you'd open a café and have a space where people could do some kind of art.'

'It's a possibility,' she allowed. 'I need to sort out my costings first and work out the best use of the space.' And she really had to make this work. She didn't want to lose all her savings and her security—to risk being as vulnerable as her mother had been when Nicole was growing up, having no choices in what she did.

'If you want to set up an art café,' he said, 'maybe I can help you find better premises for it.'

'And sell you the cinema? We've already discussed this, and you can ask me again and again until you're blue in the face, but it's not happening. Whatever I do, it'll be done right here.'

'OK. Well, as a Surrey Quays resident—'

'You mean you actually live here?' she broke in. 'You didn't just join the forum to listen out for people protesting against your development so you could charm them out of it?'

He winced. 'That was one of the reasons I joined the forum initially, I admit.'

So she'd been right and their whole relationship had been based on a lie. Just as it had with Jeff. Would she never learn?

'But I do live in Surrey Quays,' he said, and named one of the most prestigious developments on the edge of the river. 'I moved there eighteen months ago. And I'm curious about the cinema now I'm here. It's been boarded up ever since I've lived in the area.'

'You seriously expect me to give you a guided tour?'

'Would you give Clarence a tour?' he asked.

Yes. Without a shadow of a doubt. She blew out a breath. 'You're not Clarence.'

'But I am,' he said softly. 'I know things about you that you haven't told anyone else—just as you know things about me. We're friends.'

Was that true? Could she trust him?

Part of her wanted to believe that her friendship with Clarence wasn't a castle built on sand; part of her wanted to run as fast as she could in the opposite direction.

Hope had a brief tussle with common sense—and won. 'All right. I'll show you round. But it'll have to be by torchlight,' she warned.

'Cinemas are supposed to be dark,' he said with a smile.

She wished he hadn't smiled like that. It gave her

goose-bumps. Gabriel Hunter had a seriously beautiful mouth, and his eyes were the colour of cornflowers.

And why was she mooning over him? Ridiculous. She needed to get a grip. Right now. 'This is the foyer—well, obviously,' she said gruffly, and shone the torch round.

He gave an audible intake of breath. 'The glass, Nicole—it's beautiful. Art Deco. It deserves to be show-cased.'

The same thing she'd noticed. Warmth flared through her, and she had to damp it down. This was her business rival Gabriel Hunter, not her friend Clarence, she reminded herself.

'The cinema itself is through here.'

He sniffed as she ushered him through to the auditorium, then pulled a face. 'I'm afraid you've got a mouse problem. That's a pretty distinctive smell.'

'They've chomped the seats a lot, too.' She shone a torch onto one of the worst bits to show him.

'There are people who can restore that. I know some good upholst—' He stopped. 'Sorry. I'll shut up. You're perfectly capable of researching your own contractors.'

She brought him back out into the foyer. 'From what you said the other day, you know that this place was originally an Edwardian *kursaal* or leisure centre. The downstairs was originally a skating rink and the upstairs was the Electric Cinema.'

'Does that mean you have a projection room upstairs as well as down?' he asked.

'I'm still mapping the place out and working my way through all the junk, but I think so—because in the nineteen-thirties it was changed to a ballroom upstairs and a picture house downstairs.'

'So is upstairs still the ballroom?'

Upstairs was the bit that she hoped would make him

change his mind about ever asking her to sell again. Because surely, working for a company which renovated old buildings and redeveloped them into hotels, he must have some appreciation of architecture? Clarence would love it, she knew; but how much of Clarence had been designed simply to charm her and how much of Clarence was really Gabriel? That was what she hadn't worked out yet. And until she did she wasn't prepared to give him the benefit of the doubt.

'The stairs,' she said, gesturing towards them.

'That's beautiful, too. Look at that railing. I can imagine women sweeping down that staircase in floaty dresses after waltzing the night away.'

Just as she'd thought when she'd seen the staircase. And there was no way that Gabriel could've known she'd thought that, because she hadn't told him. So was his response pure Clarence, and that meant Clarence was the real part of him, after all?

'And this room at the top,' she said as they walked up the stairs, 'was used by Brian as a store-room, or so Mum says.'

'Is your mum OK?' he asked.

She frowned. 'OK about what?'

'This place. It must have memories for her. And, in the circumstances...' His voice faded.

'She's fine. But thank you for asking.'

'I wasn't being polite, and I wasn't asking for leverage purposes, either,' he said softly. 'I was asking as your friend, Nicole.'

Gabriel wasn't her friend, though.

Saying nothing, she opened the door to the upper room and handed him the torch. 'See what you think.'

He shone the torch on the flooring first. 'That looks like parquet flooring—cleaned up, that will be stunning.'

He bent down to take a closer look. 'Just look at the inlay—Nicole, this is gorgeous.'

But it wasn't the really stunning bit of the room. She still couldn't understand why her grandfather had wasted it by using the room as storage space.

'Look up,' she said.

Gabriel shone the torch upwards and she actually heard his intake of breath. 'Is that plasterwork or is it pressed tin?' he asked.

'I assume it's plasterwork. I didn't even know ceilings could be made of anything else. Well, except maybe wood?'

'Do you have a ladder?' he asked.

'It doesn't tend to be something that a banker would use in their everyday job, so no,' she said dryly.

'I'll bring one over from next door later this afternoon, so we can take a closer look,' he said.

We? she wondered. It was *her* cinema, not his. But at least he seemed to appreciate the ceiling.

'Do you still want to raze the place to the ground, then?' she asked.

'No,' he admitted. 'If that ceiling's tin, which I think it might be, that's quite rare in England and it'll probably get this building listed. Look at those Art Deco stars— they're absolutely amazing.'

He'd already told her that if a building was listed it meant extra work and delays. 'You mean, that ceiling will get the building listed if someone drops the council an anonymous letter telling them about it?' she asked sharply.

'If you mean me or anyone at Hunter's, no. That's not how I operate. But I've got experience in this sort of thing, Nicole. I can help you. We're not on opposite sides.'

'It feels like it.'

'We've been friends for a while. We probably know more about each other than most of our non-online friends know about us.'

'But do we really?' she asked. 'How do we know it wasn't all an act?'

'It wasn't on my part,' he said, 'and I'm pretty sure it wasn't on yours.' He held her gaze. 'Have dinner with me tonight.'

No. Common sense meant that she should say no.

But the expression in his eyes wasn't one of triumph or guile. She couldn't quite read it.

'Why do you want to have dinner with me?' she asked.

Gabriel couldn't blame her for being suspicious. He *had* been trying to buy her cinema, planning to turn it into a car park for his hotel. But now he'd seen the building and its potential he was looking at the whole thing in a different light. Maybe there was a way to compromise. OK, so he wouldn't get the parking, but he might get something even better. Something that would benefit them both.

'Because then we can talk. Properly.' He sighed. 'Look, you know my background's in the service and entertainment industry. I've worked with several renovations, bringing a building kicking and screaming back to life and then into the modern age. I've got a lot of knowledge that could help you, and a lot of contacts that would be useful for you.'

'And what's in it for you?'

She was so prickly with him now. And he wanted their old easy-going relationship back. 'Does something have to be in it for me?'

'You have a reputation as a very hard-headed businessman. I can accept that you'd maybe do charity work, because that would double up as good PR for Hunter Hotels, but I'm not a charity.' She looked at him again. 'So why would you help me for nothing?'

'Because,' he said softly, 'I live in Surrey Quays and this building is part of my community. Plus Georgy-girl's my friend and I'd like to help her make her dreams come true.'

'And there's really nothing in it for you? At all?'

Maybe this was the time for honesty. And she was right in that there was some self-interest. 'Do you remember suggesting to me that I ought to take the family business in a different direction—that I should do something that really interests me, something that gives me a challenge?'

'Yes.'

'Maybe this would be my challenge.'

'And that's it? To help someone you think is your friend and to give yourself an intellectual challenge?'

And to give him some freedom. But he wasn't quite ready to admit how stifled he felt. Not to Nicole. Georgy was a different matter; but right now Nicole wasn't Georgy and she didn't trust him. 'That's it,' he said. 'Have dinner with me tonight and we can discuss it properly.'

Nicole intended to say no, but the words that came out of her mouth were different. 'Only on condition we go halves on the bill tonight—and I owe you for the coffee and brownie.'

'You can buy me coffee later in the week,' he said. 'I'll be around next door.'

'You're trying to tell me you're the boy next door, now?'

He shrugged. 'My business is next to yours and I have a Y chromosome, so I guess that's the same thing.'

She shook her head. 'It's a million miles away, Mr Hunter, and you know it.'

He didn't argue with her; instead, he said, 'I'll book somewhere for dinner. I already know we both like Italian food. I'll pick you up at, what, seven?'

'I suppose you've already looked up my address,' she said, feeling slightly nettled.

'On the electoral roll, yes.' He paused. 'It would be useful to have each other's phone number in case one of us is delayed.'

'True.' And in the meantime she might be able to think up a good excuse not to meet him, and could text him said good excuse. She grabbed her phone from her pocket. 'Tell me your number, then I'll text you so you'll have mine.'

It only took a matter of seconds to sort that out.

'Thank you for showing me round,' he said. 'I'll see you later.'

'OK.'

But she couldn't stop thinking about him all afternoon. Was she doing the right thing, going to dinner with him? Could they work together? Or was she just setting herself up for yet another fall and it'd be better to call it off?

Halfway through the afternoon there was a knock on the front door, and she heard Gabriel call, 'Hello? Nicole, are you here?'

She was about to ask what he thought he was doing when she realised that he'd changed into jeans and an old T-shirt—making him look much more approachable than his shark-in-a-suit persona—and he was carrying a ladder.

'Why the ladder?' she asked.

'Remember I said I'd bring one over? I thought we could take a closer look at your ceiling,' he said.

'Don't you need to be somewhere?'

He smiled. 'I don't have to account for every minute of my time. Anyway, I promised you a ladder. Given that you've already said a ladder isn't part of your everyday equipment—whereas it *is* part of mine—I'll carry the ladder and you do the torch?'

'No need for a torch. The electricity's back on now.'

'The fuses are OK?'

'So far, yes, but obviously I'll need to get the wiring checked out properly.'

This time he didn't offer help from his team next door; part of her was relieved that he'd got the message, but part of her was disappointed that he'd given up on her so quickly. Which was ridiculous and contrary. She didn't want to be beholden to Gabriel Hunter for anything. But she missed her friend Clarence.

'Let's go take a look at that ceiling,' he said instead.

In the old ballroom, he rested the ladder against the wall.

'So you're going to hold the ladder steady for me?' she asked.

'Do you know what to look for?' he checked.

'No, but it's my ceiling.' And she wanted to be the first one to look at it.

He grinned, as if guessing exactly what was going through her mind. 'Yes, ma'am. OK. You go up first and take a look.' He took the camera from round his neck and handed it to her. 'And photographs, if you want.'

She recognised the make of the camera as seriously expensive. 'You're trusting me with this?'

'Yes. Why wouldn't I?'

He clearly wasn't as suspicious and mean-minded as she was, which made her feel a twinge of guilt. 'Thanks,' she said. She put the camera strap round her neck so it'd leave her hands free, then climbed up the ladder. Close up, she still didn't have a clue whether she was looking at plasterwork or tin. But she duly took photographs and went back down the ladder.

Gabriel reviewed her photographs on the rear screen of the camera.

'So can you tell whether it's tin or plasterwork from the photographs?' she asked.

He shook his head. 'Would you mind if I went up and had a look?'

'Go ahead. I'll hold the ladder steady.'

As he climbed the ladder, Nicole noticed how nice his backside looked encased in faded denim. And how inappropriate was that? She damped down the unexpected flickers of desire and concentrated on holding the ladder steady.

'It's definitely pressed tin,' Gabriel said when he came back down. 'It was very popular in early twentieth-century America because it was an affordable alternative to plasterwork, plus it was lightweight and fireproof. So I guess that's why it was used here, to keep the ceiling fireproof. The tin sheets were pressed with a die to make patterned panels, then painted white to make them look as if it was plasterwork. Though, if that's still the original paint up there, it's likely to be lead, so you need to be careful and get a specialist in to restore the panels.'

'It sounds as if you've come across this before.'

He nodded. 'There was a tin ceiling and tin wainscoting in a hotel we renovated three or four years ago. Basically you need to strip off the old paint to get rid of the lead—for health and safety reasons—then put on a protective base coat, patch up any damage and repaint it.' He paused. 'Usually the panels were painted white, but there seem to be some traces of gold on the stars.'

She looked up at the ceiling. 'I can imagine this painted dark blue, with gold stars.'

'Especially with that floor, this would really work as a ballroom—and ballroom dancing is definitely on trend. There are even fitness classes based on ballroom dance moves. You could take the *kursaal* back to its roots but bring it into this century at the same time.'

He was talking a lot of sense. Putting things into words that she'd already started to think about. 'It's a possibility.' She continued staring at the ceiling. 'There are all kinds of styles around the cinema, everything from Edwardian through to slightly shabby nineteen-seventies. It's a mess, and it'd be sensible to take it back to one point in time. And, with features like this, it'd make sense to restore the building back to how it was when it was a ballroom and cinema. It's a shame there won't be any colour pictures to give me any idea what the original decorative schemes looked like, though. There definitely isn't any paperwork giving any details.'

'Actually, there might be colour photos,' he said, and grabbed his phone. After a few seconds' browsing, he handed the phone to her so she could see for herself. 'Just as I thought. According to this website, colour photos exist from as far back as the middle of the eighteen hundreds.'

'But weren't they coloured by hand, back then—so they were colourised rather than actually being printed in colour?' Nicole pointed out.

'Look, you can see the three different print overlay colours at the edge of this one.' He pored over the screen with her. 'But it also says the process was time-consuming.'

'And expensive, so it'd be reserved for really big news stories—unless I guess someone was really wealthy and did it as a hobby. Though would they have taken a picture of the building?'

'There might be something in the local archive office,' he said. 'Photos or sketches that people haven't seen for a century.'

They looked at each other, and Nicole thought, he's as excited by this as I am. But was this Clarence standing next to her or Gabriel? She couldn't be sure. And, until she was sure, she didn't dare trust him. 'Maybe,' she said carefully.

He'd clearly picked up her wariness, because he said, 'It is as it is. I'd better let you get on. See you at seven.'

'OK.'

Though when Nicole got home it occurred to her that he hadn't told her where they were going, and she didn't have a clue whether she was supposed to dress up or dress down.

She thought about it in the shower while she was washing her hair. If she wore jeans, she'd feel uncomfortable in a posh restaurant—and would he take her somewhere posh to try to impress her? But if she dressed up, she'd feel totally out of place in a more casual bistro.

Little black dress, she decided. Something she would feel comfortable in no matter the situation. And high heels, so he'd know she wasn't intimidated by him.

Bring it on, she thought.

Bring it on.

CHAPTER FIVE

GABRIEL PARKED OUTSIDE Nicole's flat. Nerves fluttered in his stomach, which was absolutely ridiculous, and completely out of character. This wasn't a real date; it was discussing mutual business interests. There was no reason why he should be feeling like this.

Yet this was Nicole. Georgygirl.

And that made things that little bit more complicated.

He and Nicole were on opposite sides. Rivals. And yet Georgy was his friend. The girl he'd got to know over the last six months and really liked. The one person who saw him for who he really was.

How ironic that, now they'd met in real life, she didn't see him at all. She saw Gabriel Hunter, the ruthless businessman: not Clarence, her friend.

He shook himself. It was pointless brooding. Things were as they were. All he could do was make the best out of it and try to salvage a few things from this mess. Maybe he could reach a better understanding with her, in business if nothing else.

Nicole lived in a quieter part of Surrey Quays, in what he recognised as a former industrial complex that had been turned into four-storey apartment blocks. The brickwork was a mellow sand colour; one side had floor-to-ceiling windows and the three upper storeys had a wrought iron balcony. There were trees and raised planted beds in the square, and the whole thing was pretty and peaceful—exactly the kind of place where he'd expected Georgy to live.

He pressed the button to her intercom.

'I'm on my way,' she said.

Economical with words, as usual, he thought with a smile.

But he was blown away when she walked out of the doors to the apartment block. She was wearing a simple black shift dress, with high-heeled black court shoes and no jewellery. Her hair was still pulled back from her face, but this time it was in a sophisticated updo that reminded him of Audrey Hepburn.

'You look amazing,' he said, before he could stop himself.

She inclined her head. 'Thank you.'

And now he felt like he was on his first date all over again. Which was stupid, because as a teenager he'd been overconfident and reckless, never worrying about what people thought of him. He took a deep breath. 'It's only a short drive from here.'

'Short enough to make it more sensible to walk? I can change my shoes.'

'We'll drive,' he said.

He half expected her to make an acerbic comment about his car—a sleek convertible—but she climbed into the passenger seat and said nothing. It wasn't exactly an easy silence between them, but he had no idea what to say, so he concentrated on driving. And she did nothing to dispel the awkwardness between them, either.

Was this a mistake?

Or was she as confused by this whole thing as he was?

Once he'd parked and they were out of the car, he gestured to the narrowboat moored at the quay. 'The food at this place is excellent,' he said.

She read the sign out loud. 'La Chiatta.'

'Italian for "the barge",' he translated.

'Effective.' But then she looked at the narrowboat and the ramp which led from the quay to the deck. The tide was low, so the angle of the ramp was particularly steep. From the expression on her face, Nicole clearly realised she wouldn't be able to walk down that ramp in high heels. Although clothing was something they'd never really talked about in their late-night conversations, Gabriel had the strongest feeling that Nicole almost never wore high heels and had only worn them tonight to prove a point.

'We have two choices,' he said. 'We can go somewhere else that doesn't have a ramp.'

'But you've booked here, yes? It's not fair to the restaurant if we just don't turn up.'

He shrugged. 'I'll pay them a cancellation fee so they don't lose out.'

'What's the second choice?'

Something that would probably get him into trouble, but he couldn't stop himself. 'This,' he said, and picked her up.

'Gabriel!'

It was the first time she'd used his given name and he rather liked it.

But maybe picking her up had been a mistake. Not because she was too heavy, but because she was so close that he could feel the warmth of her skin and smell the soft floral scent of her perfume, and it made him want to kiss her.

That was so inappropriate, it was untrue.

'Hold on tight,' he said, and carried her down the ramp before setting her on her feet again.

'I don't believe you just did that,' she said, sounding shocked.

Clearly tonight she was seeing him as Gabriel the corporate shark, not Clarence. 'No, it was a solution to a problem. By the time we've finished dinner the tide will have changed and you'll be able to walk up the ramp relatively easily.'

She gestured towards the ramp, where a man and a woman were gingerly making their way down together. 'He's not carrying her.'

'Probably because she's wearing flat shoes. No way could you have walked down that ramp in *those* without falling over.' He gestured to her shoes.

'You could've warned me.'

'I didn't even think about it,' he admitted.

'Or I could have taken off my shoes just now.'

'And ended up standing on a sharp stone or something and hurting yourself? My way was simpler, and it's done now so there's no point in arguing about it.'

'If you say, "It is what it is",' she warned, 'I might just punch you.'

He laughed. 'Think about it. It's true. Come and have dinner, Nicole. Have you been here before?'

'No.'

'The pasta is amazing.'

She didn't looked particularly mollified, but she thanked him politely for opening the door for her and walked inside.

This was supposed to be a business discussion, Nicole thought, so why did it feel like a date?

And she still couldn't quite get over what Gabriel had

just done on the ramp. Even Jeff, back in the days when she was still in ignorant bliss of his affair and trusted him, wouldn't have done something like that.

What was worse was that she'd liked being close to Gabriel—close enough to feel the warmth of his skin and smell the citrusy scent of whatever shower gel he used.

And, just before he'd set her back down on her feet, she'd actually wondered what it would be like if he kissed her.

She needed to get this out of her head right now. They weren't friends and they weren't dating; this was strictly business.

Once the waitress had brought their menus and she'd ordered a glass of red wine—noting that Gabriel was sticking to soft drinks—she looked at him. 'Is there anything in particular you recommend?'

'The honeycomb cannelloni is pretty good, and their ciabatta bread is amazing.'

'Sounds good.' At least their tastes meshed when it came to food. He hadn't lied to her about that, then.

Once the waitress had taken their order, he leaned back in his chair. 'Thank you for agreeing to meet me tonight, Nicole.'

'As you say, it's business and neither of us has time to waste. We might as well eat while we discuss things, and save a bit of time.'

She really hoped that it didn't show in her voice how much she was having to fight that spark of attraction. She was absolutely *not* going to let herself wonder what it would be like to run her fingers through his hair, or how the muscles of his back would feel beneath her fingertips.

To distract herself, she asked, 'So what really happened?'

He looked puzzled. 'When?'

'Your teenage incident.'

* * *

Gabriel really hadn't expected her to bring that up. Where was she going with this? Was it to distract him and make him agree to a business deal that, in a saner moment, he would never even have considered? Or maybe he was just being cynical because he'd spent too long in a ruthless business world. Maybe she really did want to know. He shrugged. 'You said you'd read up about it, so you already know the details.'

'I know what was reported, which isn't necessarily the same thing.'

That surprised him, too. She was more perceptive than he'd expected. Then again, how could he tell her the truth? It felt like bleating. And at the end of the day he was the one who'd done something wrong. He shrugged again. 'I was nineteen years old, from a wealthy and privileged background and full of testosterone. My whole crowd was identikit. I guess we all thought we were invincible.'

'I don't buy it,' she said.

'Why not?'

'It was your car, right?'

'Yes,' he admitted.

'Even full of testosterone, I don't think you would've been stupid enough to get behind the steering wheel of a car if you'd been drinking.' She gestured to his glass of mineral water. 'And I notice you're not even having one glass of wine now—which I assume is because you're driving.'

It warmed him. Even if Nicole did see him as her business rival, someone she shouldn't even like, she was being fair to him. And she'd picked up on the thing that the newspapers hadn't. 'It is. I wouldn't put anyone at risk like that.'

'So what really happened?'

He shook his head. 'It doesn't matter now. I was the one behind the wheel with alcohol in my bloodstream, I was the one who crashed into the shop, and I was the one whose father's expensive lawyer got me off on a technicality. It was my fault.'

'You didn't actually know you'd been drinking, did you?'

He knew she was perceptive, but that really shocked him. 'What makes you say that?' he asked carefully.

'Because,' she said, 'even given that you might've had a lot of growing up to do back then, there's a massive difference between high spirits and stupidity, and you're not stupid. Not with the highest First your university had ever awarded and an MBA from the best business school in the country.'

'So you really did do some digging on me.' He wasn't sure if he was more impressed or discomfited.

'Just as you did on me,' she pointed out, 'so get off your high horse and answer the question.'

'You're right. I didn't know I'd been drinking,' he said. 'I assume there was vodka in my orange juice—something I wouldn't have tasted.'

'So the people who spiked your drink got away with it.'

'I got away with it, too,' he reminded her. 'On a technicality.'

'Maybe Gabriel did,' she said. 'But I know a different side to you.'

She was actually recognising who he was? Gabriel was stunned into silence.

'You've stuck out a job you don't enjoy, out of loyalty,' she continued, 'because your dad sorted out the mess you made, so you didn't have a criminal record and could finish your law degree. And I think Clarence would've done something more. At the very least, Clarence would've gone to see the shop owners and apologised.'

He squirmed. Now he really understood why she'd made it up the ranks so swiftly at the bank, despite not having a degree. She was the most clear-sighted person he'd ever met. 'Do we have to talk about this?' Because he could see where this was going, and it made him antsy.

'If we're really going to work together in any way, shape or form,' she said, 'I need to know who you are. Are you the heir to Hunter Hotels, who dates a different woman every week?'

'Strictly speaking, I haven't dated at all for the last six months.' Since he'd first started talking to her on-line. Which hadn't actually occurred to him until now. Was that why he hadn't dated? Because part of him was already involved with her?

'Or are you really my friend Clarence?' she asked.

'It's not that black and white,' he said. Part of him was Gabriel, the heir to Hunter Hotels, desperate to make up for his past mistakes and yet feeling stifled. And part of him was Clarence, a man who actually connected with people around him. If the crash hadn't happened, what would his life have been like? He wouldn't have had to spend so much time biting his tongue and reminding himself to be grateful. Maybe he could've been Clarence all the time. 'I could ask you the same. Are you Nicole Thomas, the workaholic banker, or are you Georgygirl, who dreams of the stars?' He paused. 'And you've got the stars, right on the ceiling of your cinema.'

'Maybe I'm a bit of both,' she said.

'And so,' he said, 'am I.'

'So what did you do?'

He sighed. 'You're not going to let this go, are you?

Nicole, it's not public knowledge and I want it to stay that way.'

'Who else knows?'

'Two others.'

'Not your father?'

'No,' he admitted. Evan Hunter had decreed that everything was done and dusted. The shopkeeper had been paid off, Gabriel didn't have a criminal record and, although Evan hadn't said it in so many words, Gabriel would be paying for that mistake for the rest of his life. He certainly had, to date. And he felt as if he'd never earn his father's respect.

'The shopkeeper, then,' Nicole said. 'And his wife.'

She was good, he thought. Incisive. Good at reading people and situations. 'I'm saying nothing until I know this stays with you,' he said.

'Do you trust me?'

'Do you trust me?' he countered.

She sighed. 'We're back to the online-or-real-life thing. Two different people.'

'Are we? Because I'd trust Georgygirl and I think you'd trust Clarence.'

She spread her hands. 'OK. It's your decision.'

If he told her, it would give her leverage.

If he didn't, it would tell her that he didn't trust her and she couldn't trust him.

He thought about it. Was it a risk worth taking? Strategically, it meant giving a little now to gain a lot in the future.

'Obviously my father paid for the damage to the shop,' he said. 'But you can't solve everything with money.'

'So what did you do?' Her voice was very soft. Gentle. Not judgemental. And that made it easier to tell her.

'I went to see the Khans,' he said. 'With a big bouquet

of flowers and a genuine apology. And I said that money alone wasn't enough to repay the damage I'd done, so until the end of my degree I'd work weekends in their shop, unpaid, doing whatever needed doing.'

'Stocking shelves?'

'Sometimes. And sorting out the newspapers for the delivery boys—which meant getting there at five in the morning. And don't forget sweeping the floor and cleaning out the fridges.'

She raised her eyebrows. 'It must've killed your partying, having to be at work for five in the morning at weekends.'

'The crash kind of did that anyway,' he said. 'It was my wake-up call.'

She looked straight at him. 'You weren't just a shopboy, were you?'

'I was at first,' he said. 'It was six months before the Khans started to believe that I wasn't just a posh boy slumming it, but eventually I became their friend.' He smiled. 'I used to eat with them on Sundays after my shift in the shop. Meera taught me how to make a seriously good biryani, and Vijay taught me as much as my father did about business management and having to understand your own business right from the bottom up. Though in return when I did my MBA I helped them streamline a few processes and negotiate better terms with their suppliers.'

'Do you still see them?'

'Not as often nowadays, but yes. Their kids are teenagers now; they were very small when the crash happened. Sanjay, their eldest, is off to university next year, and I've given him the lecture about partying and getting in with the wrong crowd.' As well as sponsoring the boy through the three years of his degree, but Nicole didn't need to know that.

When the food arrived, she tasted her cannelloni and looked thoughtful.

'Is it OK?' he asked.

'More than OK. You were right about the food, just as you were right about the coffee on Challoner Road.' She paused. 'What you did for the Khans…that's what I'd expect Clarence to do.'

'Clarence wouldn't have been stupid enough to go round with the over-privileged crowd in the first place,' he pointed out.

'You're human. We all make mistakes.'

Which revealed that she had a weakness, too. That she'd made a life-changing mistake. One that maybe held her back as much as his did him. 'What was yours?' he asked softly.

She shook her head. 'It's not important.'

'I told you mine. Fair's fair.'

She looked away. 'Let's just say I put my trust in the wrong person.'

'And you think I'm going to let you down, the same way?'

She spread her hands. 'Gabriel Hunter, known for being a ruthless businessman—is it any wonder I think his offer of help with the cinema comes with strings?'

'Or you could see it as Clarence,' he countered, 'who really needs a new challenge, and a way to take the family business in a different direction.'

'OK. Just supposing the Electric Palace was yours… what would you do?'

'Bring the building back to life, and then get it listed so nobody can ever try to raze it to the ground and turn it into a car park,' he said promptly. 'In that order.'

She smiled. 'Right. But seriously?'

'You've got two main rooms, both with projectors, yes?'

'Yes?'

'Do you know the capacity of the rooms?'

'There are three hundred and fifty seats in the lower room.'

'The upper room's smaller. We'd need to measure it properly, but I'd guess we could fit seventy-five to a hundred.' He looked thoughtful. 'I really like your idea of taking the Electric Palace back to how it was when it was first built. You've got the ceiling upstairs, the parquet flooring and the amazing glass in the foyer. We need to look in the archives and ask on the Surrey Quays forum to see if anyone's got any old newspapers or magazines, or anything that has pictures or sketches or a detailed description of how it was.'

'But originally it was a cinema and ice rink,' she reminded him.

'I don't think an ice rink would bring in enough footfall or spend,' he said. 'The next incarnation would work better—the cinema and the ballroom. But keep the Art Deco glass. That's too stunning to lose.'

'You really want to turn the upstairs room back into the ballroom?'

'No. I think it'd work better as a multi-purpose room,' he said. 'If you didn't have fixed seats, you could use it as a cinema; but you could also use it as a ballroom and a conference venue.'

'Conference venue?' she asked.

He knew he was probably speaking too soon, but it was the perfect solution. A way to work together, so he could help his friend *and* impress his father. 'Conference venue,' he confirmed. 'The chairs you use for the cinema—they could be placed around the edge of the dance floor on ballroom nights, and they could be moved easily into whatever configuration you need for a conference, whether it was horseshoe or theatre-style. And if you use tables that fit together, they'd also work as occasional tables for the cinema and ballroom nights.' He warmed to his theme. 'Or for any club that wants to hire the room—you could still do the craft stuff. Offer people crafternoon tea.'

'Crafternoon tea?' She looked mystified.

'A session of craft—whether it's sewing or painting or pottery—followed by afternoon tea. Hence crafternoon tea,' he explained.

'That's the most terrible pun I've ever heard,' she said. 'Maybe. But would anyone really hire that room for a conference? I can't see it.'

'You have a hotel next door,' he said. 'Which would hire the room as a main conference suite, and there could be breakout rooms for the conference next door.'

'What about refreshments and meals for the conference delegates?'

'Depends on your staff and facilities. That's when we'd work together,' he said. 'We'd have to sort out costings and come up with something that was fair to both of us. I'm thinking out loud, here, but maybe you'd do the coffee and a buffet lunch, and I'd do the evening sit-down meal, because my kitchen has a bigger capacity than yours.'

'Right,' she said.

'And then there's downstairs,' he said, ignoring the fact that she didn't seem enthusiastic—once he'd worked out the costings and she could see it would benefit both of them, she'd come round. 'We have the main cinema. We can restore the seats. As I said, I know specialist upholsterers who can do that.'

'The seats are old and uncomfortable. The multiplexes offer VIP seating. Maybe that's the sort of thing I should put in.'

He shook his head. 'We can't compete with the multiplexes, not with one full-time and one part-time screen. They have twenty or more screens and can offer staggered film times. We can't.'

'So maybe we need to offer something different.'

He wondered if she realised that she was using the word 'we'. Though he wasn't going to call her on it, and risk her backing away again. 'Such as?'

'When I was looking at what my competitors offer, I saw an idea I really liked—a place that had comfortable sofas instead of traditional cinema seating, and little tables where people could put their drinks or food,' she said.

'Like having the best night in, except you've gone out for it?' he asked. 'So you've got all the comfort and convenience of home, but professional quality sound and vision—actually, that would work really well.'

'And when the ushers take you to your seat, they also offer to take your order for food and drink. Which they bring to you and put on the little table.'

'I like that. A lot. But serving alcohol and hot food means getting a licence,' he said, 'and we'd have to think about what we offer on the menu.'

'We could have cinema-themed food,' she said. 'But it has to be easy to eat. Pizza, burgers, hot dogs and chicken.'

'Would that replace traditional cinema snacks?'

'No. Not everyone would want a meal. I think we need to include the traditional stuff, too—popcorn, nachos, bags of chocolates. And tubs of ice cream from a local supplier.'

Her eyes were shining. He'd just bet his were the same. Brainstorming ideas with her was the most enjoyment he'd had from anything work-related in a long, long time. And he had a feeling it was the same for her.

'You know what this is like?' he asked.

'What?'

'Talking to you online. But better, because it's face to face.'

Then he wished he hadn't said anything when she looked wary again.

'Excuse me,' she said. 'I need the Ladies'.'

'The toilets are that way.' He indicated in the direction behind her.

'Thanks.'

On her way to the toilets, Nicole stopped by the till and handed over her credit card. 'Mr Hunter's table,' she said. 'The bill's mine. Please make sure that you charge everything to me.'

'Of course, madam,' the waiter said.

She smiled. 'Thanks.' It would save any argument over the bill later. And, given that Gabriel had already bought her two coffees and a brownie, she felt in his debt. This would even things out a little.

You know what this is like? Talking to you online. But better. His words echoed in her head.

He was right.

And she really didn't know what to do about it, which was why she'd been a coward and escaped to the toilets.

Tonight, Gabriel wasn't the corporate shark-in-a-suit; he was wearing a casual shirt and chinos that made him far more approachable. He'd attracted admiring glances from every single female in the restaurant—and it wasn't surprising. Gabriel Hunter was absolutely gorgeous.

But.

They were still on opposite sides. They shouldn't be wanting to have anything to do with each other, let alone help each other. And could she trust him? Or would he let her down as badly as Jeff had?

She still didn't have an answer by the time she returned to their table. And she was quiet all through pudding.

And when he discovered that she'd already paid the bill, he looked seriously fed up. 'Dinner was my idea, Nicole. I was going to pay.'

'And I told you, the deal was that we went halves.'

'So why did you pay for the whole lot?'

'Because you bought me two coffees and a brownie, and I don't like being in anyone's debt. I pay my way.'

'Now I'm in your debt.'

She smiled. 'That suits me.'

'It doesn't suit me. And we haven't really finished our conversation.'

Excitement fluttered in her stomach. So what was he going to suggest now? Another business meeting over dinner? Coffee at his place?

'We kind of have,' she said. 'You've agreed that the Electric Palace should be restored, and you know it's not for sale.'

'But,' he said, 'we haven't agreed terms for conference hire, or whether you're going to use my kitchen facilities to save having to build your own.'

'That assumes I'm going to develop the cinema the way you see it. I have my own ideas.' At the end of the day, this was *her* business. She'd spent ten years marching to someone else's tune, and she wasn't about to let Gabriel take over—even if he did have more experience than she did.

'I think we need another meeting,' he said.

He looked all cool and calm and controlled. And Nicole really wanted to see him ruffled.

But maybe that was the red wine talking. Even though she'd stuck to her limit of no more than one glass. Cool, calm and controlled would be better for both of them.

'I don't have my diary on me,' she said.

His expression very clearly said he didn't believe a word of it, but he spread his hands. 'Text me some times and dates.'

So now the ball was in her court?

She could turn him down.

Or they could explore this. See where the business was going.

See where they were going.

She damped down the little flicker of hope. She couldn't trust him that far. Jeff had destroyed her ability to trust.

'I'll text you,' she said. Because that gave her wriggle room. A chance to say no when she'd had time to think about it on her own. Gabriel was charming and persuasive; Jeff had been charming and persuasive, too, and following his ideas had got her badly burned. Who was to say that this wouldn't be the same?

'Good.'

The ramp was much more manageable now the tide had turned, and this time Gabriel didn't sweep her off her feet. Nicole wasn't sure whether she was more relieved or disappointed. And he didn't suggest coffee at his place; she wasn't quite ready to offer him coffee at hers. So he merely saw her to the door of her apartment block—brushing off her protests that she was perfectly capable of seeing herself home from the car park with a blunt, 'It's basic good manners.'

And he didn't try to kiss her goodnight, not even with a peck on the cheek.

Which was a good thing, she told herself. They didn't have that kind of relationship. Besides, she wasn't good at relationships. Hadn't Jeff's mistress said that Nicole was a cold fish? So looking for anything else from this would be a huge mistake. It would be better to keep things strictly business. And, even better than that, to keep her distance from him completely.

CHAPTER SIX

'HELLO? IS ANYONE THERE?'

Nicole went in search of the voice, to discover a man standing in the entrance to the cinema, holding a metal box of tools.

'Are you Nicole Thomas?' he asked.

'Yes,' she said.

'I'm Kyle. The boss wants me to do a quick check on your wiring.'

'Boss?' Did he mean Gabriel? But she hadn't asked Gabriel for help—and this felt a bit as if he was trying to take over.

She thought quickly to find a polite way to refuse, and it clearly showed on her face because Kyle said, 'The boss said you'd tell me thank you but you don't need any help, and he says to tell you he wants me to check your wiring's OK to make sure this place doesn't burn down and set his hotel on fire.'

It was a comment that Gabriel had made before. It wasn't something she could counter easily, and this would either reassure her or be an early warning of difficulties to come. Plus it wasn't Kyle's fault that Gabriel made her antsy. She smiled at him. 'OK. Thank you. Can I offer you a coffee? I'm sorry, I don't have any milk or sugar.'

'You're all right. I just had my tea break next door.'

'Right. Um, I guess I need to show you where the fuse box is, to start with?'

'That, and I'll check a few of the sockets to be on the safe side.'

She showed him where the fuse box was, and left him to get on with it.

He came to find her when he'd finished. 'There's good news and bad,' he said.

'Tell me the bad, first,' she said.

'You've got a bit of mouse damage to some of the cabling around the fuse box, because it was an area they could get to.'

'Will it take long to fix?'

He shook his head. 'And the good news is the wiring's been redone at some point in the last thirty years. You haven't got any aluminium cable, lead-sheathed cable or the old black cables with a rubber sheath which would mean it was really old and could burn the place down. I would recommend getting a full system check, though, when you get that little bit of cabling replaced.'

'Thank you. That's good to know. I appreciate your help.'

'No worries.' He sketched a salute and left.

Nicole made a mental note to call in to the hotel later that afternoon with a tin of chocolate biscuits to say thanks. Though she knew who she really needed to thank. Strictly speaking, it was interference, but she knew Gabriel had only done it to help—and he'd dressed it in a way that meant she could accept it. She grabbed her phone and called him. 'Thank you for sending over your electrician.'

'Pleasure. So you didn't send him away with a flea in his ear?' Gabriel asked.

'You kind of pre-empted me on that.'

'Ah, the "I don't want you to set my hotel on fire" thing. And it's true. Total self-interest on my part.' He laughed. 'So how is the wiring?'

'Apparently there's a bit of mouse damage so I'll need to replace some of the cabling, but the good news is that it's modern cable so I'm not looking at a total rewire.'

'That's great. Have you sorted out a surveyor yet?'

'I have three names.' Though she knew she was working quite a way out of her experience zone. Although she wanted to keep her independence and sort out everything herself, was that really the right thing for her business? It would be sensible to ask for advice from someone who knew that area—like Gabriel—instead of being too proud and then making a mistake that could jeopardise the cinema. Asking for help would be pragmatic, not weak. Suggesting they got together to talk about it wasn't the same as suggesting a date. And it wasn't just an excuse to see him. It really wasn't, she told herself firmly. She wasn't going to let her attraction to him derail the cinema restoration project. She cleared her throat. 'I was wondering if maybe I could buy you a coffee and run the names by you.'

'Strictly speaking, I'm the one beholden to you and ought to be the one buying the coffee. You paid for dinner last night,' he reminded her.

'You paid for coffee twice. I still owe you coffee twice.'

'In which case I owe you dinner. When are you free?'

Help. That felt much more like a date. And she wasn't ready. 'Let's focus on the coffee,' she said. 'When are you at the hotel next?'

'About half-past two this afternoon.'

'The perfect time for a coffee break. See you then.'

And it was as easy as that. She knew how he liked his

coffee. She also knew he had a weakness for chocolate brownies, as long as it was dark chocolate. So, at twenty-nine minutes past two, Nicole walked in to the building site next door with two espressos, two brownies and a tin of chocolate biscuits, and asked the first person she saw to point her in the direction of Gabriel Hunter.

He was in a room which was clearly earmarked as a future office, and he was on the phone when she arrived; he lifted his hand in acknowledgement, and she waited in the corridor until he'd finished the call, to give him some privacy.

'Good to see you, Nicole,' he said.

Was that Clarence talking, or Gabriel the shark-in-a-suit? 'Coffee and a brownie,' she said, handing them over. 'And these biscuits are for Kyle, your electrician. To say thank you for checking out my wiring.'

'I'll make sure he gets them. And thank you for the coffee. Having a good day?' he asked, smiling at her.

That definitely sounded more like Clarence speaking. And the way he smiled made her stomach flip. With a real effort, Nicole forced herself to focus on business. 'Yes. How about you?'

He shrugged. 'It is as it is.'

His eyes really were beautiful. So was his mouth. It would be so very, very easy to reach out and trace his lower lip with her fingertip…

And it would also be insane. To distract herself, Nicole muttered, 'As I said, I've got to the stage where I need a surveyor and quotes from builders.'

'Obviously you know to add at least ten per cent to any quote, because with a renovation job you're always going to come across something you don't expect that will need fixing,' he said. 'And to allow extra time for unexpected delays as well. Even if you've had a survey done first, you're bound to come across something that will affect your schedule.'

'If the building is structurally sound, then I want the cinema up and running in eight weeks.'

'Eight weeks?' He looked shocked. 'Isn't that a bit fast?'

'It's the start of the school holidays,' she said. 'And it's always good to have a goal to work towards rather than being vague about things. That way you can plan and actually accomplish something instead of delivering nothing but hot air.'

'True.' He blew out a breath. 'But eight weeks is a big ask. Even if the place is structurally sound, it needs complete redecoration, you've got to sort out the fixtures and fittings, and there's no way you'll be able to do anything at all with the upstairs room until the ceiling's been sorted, not with that lead paint.' He frowned. 'I was thinking, that's probably why your grandfather used it as a storage room.'

'Because it would be too expensive to fix it, or it would take too much time?'

'Either or both,' he said. 'Just bear in mind you might not be able to have the whole building up and running at once. You might have to scale back to something more doable—say, start with the downstairs screen and kiosk refreshments only.'

Which would mean a lower income. And Nicole needed the place to make a decent profit, because she knew now that she really didn't want to go back to the bank. She wasn't afraid of hard work or long hours; she'd do whatever it took to make a go of the Electric Palace. But now she wanted to put the hours in for herself, not for a corporation that barely knew her name. 'I'm opening in eight weeks,' she said stubbornly.

'Where's your list of surveyors?' he asked.

'Here.' She flicked into the notes app on her phone and handed it to him.

He looked through the list. 'The first one's good, the second will cancel on you half a dozen times because he always overbooks himself, and the third is fine. I always like to get three quotes, so do you want the name of the guy I use, to replace the one who won't make it?'

'I'm eating humble pie already, aren't I?' she pointed out.

'Strictly speaking, you're eating a dark chocolate brownie,' he said, 'which you paid for. So no.' He sighed. 'OK. Would you have let Clarence help?'

She nodded.

'Say it out loud,' he said.

She would've done the same and made him admit it aloud, too. She gave in. 'Yes. I would've accepted help from Clarence.'

'Well, then. I thought we agreed at dinner that we're not on opposite sides?'

'We didn't really agree anything.'

'Hmm.' He added a set of contact details to her list and handed the phone back. 'I'd say from your old job that you'd be good at summing people up. Talk to all of them and go with the one your instinct tells you is right for the job.'

He wasn't pushing his guy first? So maybe he really was fair, rather than ruthless. Maybe she could trust him. 'Thank you,' she said.

'Pleasure.' He paused. 'What about builders?'

'I was going to ask the surveyor for recommendations.'

'That's a good idea.' He looked her straight in the eye. 'Though, again, I can give you contact details if you'd like them. I know you don't want to feel as if you owe me anything, but a recommendation from someone you know is worth a dozen testimonials from people you don't.'

'True.'

'And I wouldn't give you the name of someone who was unreliable or slapdash. Because that would affect my reputation,' he said.

She believed him. At least, on a business footing. Any other trust was out of her ability, right now.

'While you're here, do you want to see round the place?' he asked.

'You're going to give me a tour of the hotel?'

'Fair's fair—I made you give me a tour of the cinema,' he pointed out.

She smiled. 'That would be nice.'

The walls were made of the same mellow honey-coloured brick as her flat. She noticed that the ceilings of the rooms were all high.

'So this was an industrial complex before?' she asked.

'It was a spice warehouse,' he said, 'so we're naming all the function rooms accordingly. Cinnamon, coriander, caraway…'

'Sticking to the Cs?'

He laughed. 'I was thinking about maybe using a different letter on each floor. And I'm toying with "The Spice House" as our hotel name.'

'That might get you mixed up with a culinary supplier or an Indian restaurant,' she said.

'I'm still thinking about it,' he said.

'So this is a business hotel?'

One without the exclusive parking they'd planned originally. Instead, next door would be the cinema. And if Nicole would agree to keep the upper room as a flexible space and not just a fixed second screen, maybe there was a way they could work together. Something for the leisure side and not just the conference stuff she'd resisted earlier. Something that also might make his father finally see that Gabriel had vision and could be trusted with the future direction of the business.

'Business and leisure, mixed,' he said. 'We'll have a hundred and twenty-five bedrooms—that's twenty-five per floor on the top five floors—plus conference facilities on the first floor. We'll have meeting rooms with all the communications and connections our clients need, and a breakout area for networking or receptions. I want to be able to offer my clients everything from training and team-building events through to seminars and product launches. That's on the business side. On the leisure side, we can offer wedding receptions. I'm getting a licence so we can hold civil ceremonies here, too.' He paused. 'Though I've been thinking. Maybe you should be the one to get the wedding licence.'

'Me?' She looked surprised. 'You think people would want to get married in a cinema?'

'They'd want to get married in your upstairs room, especially if you're going to do the ceiling the way you described it to me,' he said. 'And that sweeping staircase would look amazing in wedding photos. The bride and groom, with the train of the bride's dress spread out over the stairs, or all the guests lined up on the stairs and leaning on that wrought iron banister—which would look great painted gold to match the stars on the ceiling.'

'So they'd have the wedding at the cinema, then go next door to you for the reception?'

'For the meal, yes. And then the upper room could turn back into a ballroom, if you wanted, with the bar next door or a temporary bar set up from the hotel if that's easier. Between us, we'd be able to offer a complete wedding package. The hotel has a honeymoon suite with a modern four-poster, and a health club and spa so we can offer beauty treatments. The morning of the wedding, we could do hair and make-up for the bride, attendants and anyone else in the wedding party. And maybe we could have a special movie screening, the next morning— something for the kids in the wedding party, perhaps?'

Working together.

Could it really be that easy?

'It's a possibility,' she said. 'But I want to think about it before I make any decision.'

'Fair enough.'

'So what else is in your health club and spa, apart from a hairdresser and beautician?'

'A heated pool, a gym with optional personal training packages, a sauna, steam room and whirlpool bath.' He ticked them off on his fingers. 'It's open to non-residents, like our restaurant.'

'And, being The Spice House, you'll specialise in spicy food?'

'Not necessarily, though we might have themed specials.' He smiled. 'The food will be locally sourced as far as possible, with seasonal menus. So far, it's all pretty standard stuff and I'd like to be able to offer our clients something a bit different, too, but I need to sit down and think about it.'

'If you want to brainstorm,' she said, 'and you want to bounce ideas off—well, your neighbour…' The words were out before she could stop them.

'I'd like that,' he said. 'We came up with some good

stuff between us about the cinema. And we've barely scratched the surface there.'

Georgygirl and Clarence. Their old friendship, which was in abeyance right now while she got her head round the fact that her friend was actually her business rival.

Could they transfer that friendship to a working relationship?

It would mean trusting him.

Baby steps, she reminded herself. She just needed to spend a little more time with him. Work out if he really was the same in real life as he'd been privately with her online.

He showed her round the rest of the hotel, then introduced her to his site manager. 'If anything crops up next door,' he said, 'come and see Ray.'

'If I don't know the answer myself,' Ray said, 'I'll know someone who does and can help sort it out for you.'

'Thank you,' she said, shaking Ray's hand and liking how his handshake was firm without being overbearing.

Gabriel walked her to the door. 'Well, good luck with the surveyors and what have you. Let me know how you get on.'

'I will.'

For a moment, she thought he was going to lean forward and kiss her, and her heart actually skipped a beat.

But instead he held out his hand to shake hers.

Her skin tingled where he touched her. And she didn't dare look him in the eye, because she didn't want him to know what kind of effect he had on her. Besides, hadn't Jeff's mistress called her a cold fish? And Gabriel had dated a lot of women. Beautiful women. Passionate women. Way, way out of her league. Her confidence sank that little bit more.

'See you later,' she muttered, and fled.

* * *

When Nicole spoke to the surveyors, she found that Gabriel had been right on the money. The first one was booked up for the next few weeks, the second agreed to drop round that afternoon but then texted her half an hour later to cancel, the third could make it the following week, and the guy that Gabriel had recommended was able to see her first thing the next morning. Better still, he promised to have the report ready by the end of business that day.

It suited her timescale, but Nicole had the distinct feeling that Gabriel had called in a favour or two on her behalf. She couldn't exactly ask the surveyor if that was the case, and she felt it'd be mean-spirited to ask Gabriel himself—it would sound accusatory rather than grateful.

But there was something she could do.

She texted him.

Hey. You busy tomorrow night?

Why?

She really hoped this sounded casual.

Thought I could buy you dinner.

Absolutely not. I still owe you dinner.

But this is dinner with strings.

Ah. Dinner with strings?

She backed off.

OK. Sorry I asked.

* * *

Gabriel looked at the text and sighed. He hadn't meant to sound snippy at all. He'd been teasing her. That was the thing about texting: you couldn't pick up the tone.

He flicked into his contacts screen and called her. 'What are the strings, Nicole?'

'Builder names,' she said.

'You don't have to buy me dinner for that.'

'Yes, I do.'

Was this Nicole's way of saying she wanted to spend time with him but without admitting it? he wondered. But he knew he was just as bad. He wanted to spend time with her, too, but didn't want to admit it to her. 'Dinner would be fine. What time?'

'Seven? I thought maybe we could go to the pizza place just down from the café in Challoner Road. Meet you there?'

'Fine. Want a lift?'

'I'll meet you there,' she repeated.

Nicole and her over-developed sense of independence, he thought with an inward sigh. 'OK. See you at seven.'

She was already there waiting for him when he walked into the pizzeria at precisely one minute to seven, the next evening. She was wearing a pretty, summery dress and he was tempted to tell her how nice she looked, but he didn't want to make her back away. Instead, he asked, 'How did the survey go?'

'Remarkably quickly. Considering that normally people are booked up for at least a week in advance, and it takes several days to do a survey report, it's amazing that your guy not only managed to fit me in this morning,' she said, 'he also emailed me the report at the close of business this afternoon.'

Oh. So she'd picked up the fact that he'd called in a

favour. Well, of course she would. She was bright. 'Remarkable,' he said coolly.

'*Incredibly* remarkable,' she said, 'which is why I'm buying you dinner to say thank you for whatever favours you called in on my behalf. And I've already given the waiter my card, so you can't—'

He laughed, and she stopped. 'What?'

'You're such a control freak,' he said.

'No, I'm not.' She folded her arms in the classic defensive posture. 'I just don't want to—'

'—be beholden to me,' he finished. 'Is that what your ex did?'

She flushed. 'I don't know what you're talking about.'

Something had made her super-independent, and he had a feeling that there was a man involved. A man who'd broken her trust so she didn't date any more? 'Everything came with strings?' he asked softly.

'No. I just pay my own way, that's all. Right now, I feel I owe you. And I'm not comfortable owing you.'

'Friends don't owe each other for helping,' he said gently. Perhaps it was mean of him, using insider knowledge of her family and closest friends, but how else was he going to make Nicole understand that this was OK? 'Do you insist on going halves with your mum or Jessie? Or work a strict rotation on whose turn it is to buy coffee?'

'No,' she admitted. 'And how do you know about Jessie? Is your dossier that big?'

'No. You told me about your best friend when we were talking late one night, Georgy,' he reminded her. 'And I happen to have a good memory.'

She sighed. 'I guess. Can we go back to talking about surveyors?'

'Because it's safe?'

She gave him a speaking look. 'We ought to look at the menu. They'll be over in a minute to take our order.'

Was she running scared because this felt like a date? Or was the wariness specific to him? He decided to let her off the hook. For now. 'We don't need to look at the menu. I already know you're going to order a margherita with an avocado and rocket salad,' he said instead.

She looked at him. 'And you'll pick a quattro formaggi with a tomato and basil salad.'

He could swear she'd just been about to call him 'Clarence'.

And this was what he'd fantasised about when he'd messaged her over the last few months. Going on a date just like this, where they'd talk about anything and everything and knew each other so well that they could finish each other's sentences.

Except this wasn't a date. She'd called it dinner with strings. Because she felt beholden to him. And he didn't quite know how to sort this out.

'Dough balls first?' he suggested.

'Definitely.' She looked at him. 'This is weird.'

'What is?'

'We know each other. And at the same time we don't.'

'More do than don't,' he said. But he could tell that something was holding her back. Someone, he guessed, who'd hurt her. Was that why she found it hard to trust him? The one topic they'd always shied away from was relationships. He'd stopped dating because he only seemed to attract the kind of women who wanted someone else to fund a flashy lifestyle for them, and he was tired of the superficiality. Though he knew without having to ask that Nicole wouldn't discuss whatever was holding her back. He'd just have to persuade her to tell him. Little by little.

The waiter came to take their order, breaking that little bit of awkwardness.

And then Nicole went back into business mode. 'Builders,' she said, and handed him her phone.

He looked at her list. 'They're all fine,' he said. 'It's a matter of when they can fit you in. If you get stuck, I can give you some more names.'

'Thank you.'

'So how was the survey?' he asked. 'Is there much structural stuff to do?'

'A small amount of rewiring, a damp patch that needs further investigation, a bit of work to the windows, doing what you already said to the upstairs room ceiling, and then the rest of it's cosmetic.'

'Even if you can get a builder to start straight away,' he said, 'it's still going to take a fair bit of time to do all the cosmetic stuff. If you renovate the seats in the auditorium, it'll take a while; and if you rip them out completely and replace them with the sofas you were talking about, you'll have work to do on the flooring. And there's the cost to think about. Doing something in a shorter time-scale means paying overtime or getting in extra staff—all of which costs and it'll blow your budget.'

She raised her eyebrows. 'You're telling an ex-banker to keep an eye on the budget?'

He smiled. 'I know that's ironic—but you've fallen in love with the building, and there's a danger that could blind you to the cost.'

'I guess.'

'It is—'

'—what it is,' she finished with a wry smile.

The waiter brought the dough balls and the garlic butter to dip them into, and they focused on that for a moment—but then Gabriel's fingers brushed against Nicole's when they both reached for a dough ball at the same time.

It felt like an electric shock.

He hadn't been this aware of anyone in a long, long time. And he really didn't know what to do about it. If he pushed too hard, she'd back away. If he played it cool, she'd think he wasn't interested.

This felt like being eighteen again, totally unsure of himself—and Gabriel was used to knowing what he was doing and what his next move would be.

The only safe topic of conversation was the cinema. And even that was a minefield, because she'd backed off every time he'd suggested working together.

'There is one way to get a bigger workforce without massive costs,' he said.

She frowned. 'How?'

'Remember that group on the Surrey Quays forum who said they wanted the cinema up and running again? I bet they'd offer to help.'

She shook her head. Her mother had suggested the same thing, but it felt wrong. 'I can't ask people to work for me for nothing.'

'You can if it's a community thing,' he said. 'They're interested in the building. So let them be involved in the restoration. If they don't have the expertise themselves, they'll probably know someone who does. And any retired French polisher would take a look at that countertop in your foyer and itch to get his or her hands on it.'

'Nice save, with the "or her",' she said dryly.

'I'm not sexist. Being good at your job has nothing to do with your gender,' he pointed out.

'It still feels wrong to ask people to work for free.'

'What about if you give them a public acknowledgement? You could have a plaque on the wall in the foyer with the names of everyone who's been involved.'

'I like that idea,' she said slowly. 'And they're my target audience, so it makes sense to talk to them about what I'm doing—to see whether they'd be prepared to support it and see a movie at the Electric Palace rather than going into the West End.'

'You want their views on the programming, you mean?' he asked.

She nodded. 'If I show any of say the top three block-busters, I'll have to pay the film distributors at least half the box office receipts,' she said. 'And I'll be compet-ing with the multiplexes—which we both know I can't do effectively.'

'So what's the alternative? Art-house or local film-makers? Because that'd mean a smaller potential audi-ence.'

'I need to find the right mix of commercial films, re-gional and art-house,' she said. 'Maybe I need to run it as a cinema club.'

'That might limit your audience, though,' he said. 'You could always put some polls up on the Surrey Quays website to see what kind of thing people want to see and when. And think about a loyalty scheme. Buy ten tickets and get a free coffee, that sort of thing.'

'It's a thought.'

He could tell she was backing off again, so he kept the conversation light for the rest of their meal.

'Thank you for dinner,' he said. 'Can I walk you home?'

'I live in the opposite direction to you,' she reminded him.

He shrugged. 'The walk will do me good.'

'Then, put that way, OK.'

His hand brushed against hers on the way back to her

flat, and he had to suppress the urge to curl his fingers round hers. They weren't dating.

And it was even harder to stop himself kissing her goodnight. Her mouth looked so soft, so sweet. He itched to find out how her mouth would feel against his.

But this wasn't appropriate. If he did what he really wanted to do, she'd run a mile. He took a step back. 'Well. Goodnight. And thank you again for dinner.'

'Thank you for the advice and the brainstorming,' she said, equally politely.

'Any time.' He smiled, and turned away before he did anything stupid. She still wasn't having those late-night conversations with him like they used to have. And until they'd got that easiness back, he needed to keep his distance.

The more he got to know her, the more he wanted to know her. He *liked* her. But she clearly didn't feel the same way about him.

It is what it is, he reminded himself.

Even though he really wanted to change things.

CHAPTER SEVEN

ONLY ONE OF the builders on Nicole's list could actually come to look at the cinema within the next couple of days. One was too busy to come at all and the third couldn't make it for another month. She'd already cleared out as much junk as she could from the cinema so, until she'd seen the builder's quote and agreed the terms of business, Nicole knew she couldn't do much more at the cinema. All the paperwork was up to date, too, and she was simply waiting on replies. To keep herself busy instead of fretting about the downtime, she headed for the archives.

There were newspaper reports of the opening of the Kursaal in 1911, but to her disappointment there were no photographs. There was a brief description of the outside of the building, including the arch outside which apparently had Art Deco sun rays in the brickwork, but nothing about the ceiling of stars. She carefully typed out the relevant paragraphs—the font size was too small to be easily read on a photograph—and was about to give up looking when the archivist came to see her.

'You might like to have a look through this,' she said, handing Nicole a thick album. 'They're postcards of the area, from around the early nineteen hundreds. There might be something in there.'

'Thank you,' Nicole said. 'If there is, can I take a photograph on my phone?'

'As long as you don't use flash. And if I can think of any other sources which might contain something about the cinema, I'll bring them over,' the archivist said.

Halfway through the postcard album, Nicole found a postcard of the Electric Palace; she knew that, in common with other similarly named buildings, its name had changed after the First World War, to make it sound less German. Clearly by then someone had painted the outside of the building white, because the sun rays on the arch had been covered over, as they were now.

She photographed the postcard carefully, then slipped the postcard from the little corners keeping it in place so she could read the back. The frank on the stamp told her that the card had been posted in 1934. To her delight, the inscription referred to the writer spending the previous night dancing in the ballroom—and also to seeing the film *It Happened One Night*, the previous week.

Clarence would be pleased to know there was a reference to Frank Capra, she thought as she carefully photographed the inscription.

Gabriel, she corrected herself.

And that was the problem. She really wanted to share this with Gabriel. Yet she already knew how rubbish her judgement was in men. Getting close to Gabriel Hunter would be a huge mistake.

Then again, the man she was getting to know was a decent man. Maybe he wouldn't let her down. Or maybe he would. So it would be sensible to keep it strictly business between them. Even though she was beginning to want a lot more than that.

On Saturday night, Nicole was sitting on her own in her flat. Usually by now on a Saturday she'd be talking to

Clarence online, but she hadn't messaged him since she'd found out who he really was. She hadn't spent much time on the Surrey Quays website, either; it had felt awkward. Nobody had sent her a direct message, so clearly she hadn't been missed.

Nobody had been in touch from the bank, either, to see how things were going. It had been stupid to think that the last leaving drink had been a kind of new beginning; she was most definitely out of sight and out of mind. Her best friend was away for the weekend and so was her mother, which left her pretty much on her own.

She flicked through a few channels on the television. There was nothing on that she wanted to watch. Maybe she ought to analyse her competitors and start researching cinema programming, but right at that moment she felt lonely and miserable and wished she had someone to share it with. Which was weak, feeble and totally pathetic, she told herself.

Though she might as well admit it: she missed Clarence.

Did Gabriel miss Georgygirl? she wondered.

And now she was being *really* feeble. 'Get over it, Nicole,' she told herself crossly.

She spent a while looking up the programming in various other small cinemas, to give herself a few ideas, and then her phone rang. She glanced at the screen: Gabriel. So he'd been thinking of her? Pleasure flooded through her.

Though it was probably a business call. Which was how it ought to be, and she should respond accordingly. *Sensibly.* She answered the phone. 'Good evening, Gabriel,' she said coolly.

'Good evening, Nicole. Are you busy tomorrow?' he asked.

'It's Sunday tomorrow,' she prevaricated, not wanting to admit to him that her social life was a complete desert.

'I know. But, if you're free, I'd like to take you on a re-search trip tomorrow.'

'Research trip?' Was this his way of asking her out without making it sound like a date? Her heart skipped a beat.

'To see a ceiling.'

Oh. So he really did mean just business. She did her best to suppress the disappointment. 'Where?'

'Norfolk.'

'Isn't that a couple of hours' drive away?'

'This particular bit is about two and a half hours away,' he said. 'I'll pick you up at nine tomorrow morning. Wear shorts, or jeans you can roll up to your knees, and flat shoes you can take off easily. Oh, and a hat.'

'What sort of hat?'

'Whatever keeps the sun off.'

'Why? And why do I need to take my shoes off?'

'You'll see when you get there.' And then, annoyingly, he rang off before she could ask anything else.

Shorts, a hat and flat shoes.

What did that have to do with a ceiling?

She was none the wiser when Gabriel rang the inter-com to her flat, the next morning.

'I'm on my way down,' she said.

'You look nice,' he said, smiling at her when she opened the main door to the flats. 'That's the first time I've ever seen your hair loose.'

To her horror, Nicole could feel herself blushing at the compliment. Oh, for pity's sake. She was twenty-eight, not fifteen. 'Thanks,' she mumbled. It didn't help that he was wearing faded denims and a T-shirt and he looked really *touchable*. Her fingertips actually tingled with the urge to reach out and see how soft the denim was.

And then he reached out and twirled the end of her hair round his fingers. Just briefly. 'Like silk,' he said.

She couldn't look him in the eye. She didn't want him to know that she felt as if her knees had just turned to sand. 'So what's this ceiling?' she asked.

'Tin. Like the cinema. Except restored.'

'And you know about it because…?'

'I've seen it before,' he said, and ushered her over to his car. 'This is why I said you need a hat, by the way.'

'Show-off,' she said as he put the roof of his convertible down.

He spread his hands. 'There aren't that many days in an English spring or summer when you can enjoy having the roof down. This is one of them. Got your hat?'

She grabbed the baseball cap from her bag and jammed it onto her head. 'Happy?'

'Happy. You can drive, if you want,' he said, surprising her.

She blinked. 'You'd actually trust me to drive this?'

'It's insured,' he said, 'and I know where we're going, so I can direct you.'

'I don't have a car,' she said. 'I use public transport most of the time. The only time I drive is if there's a team thing at work and I have a pool car. That doesn't happen very often.'

'But you have a licence and you can drive.' He handed her the car keys. 'Here. Knock yourself out.'

'Why?'

'Because it'll distract you and stop you asking me questions,' he said. 'And also because I think you might enjoy it. This car's a lot of fun to drive.'

He trusted her.

Maybe she needed to do the same for him.

'Thank you,' she said.

Gabriel's directions were perfect—given clearly and in plenty of time—and Nicole discovered that he was right. His car really was fun to drive. And it was the perfect day for driving a convertible, with the sun out and the lightest of breezes. Once they were on the motorway heading north-east from London, Gabriel switched the radio to a station playing retro nineties music, and she found herself singing along with him.

She couldn't remember the last time she'd enjoyed herself so much.

'Want to pull into the next lay-by and swap over?' he asked. 'Then you can just enjoy the scenery instead of concentrating on directions and worrying that you're going to take the wrong exit off a roundabout.'

'OK.'

They drove along the coast road, and she discovered that he was right; it really was gorgeous scenery.

'They found that famous hoard of Iron Age gold torcs near here, at Snettisham,' he said.

'Is that where we're going?'

'No.'

Annoyingly, he wouldn't tell her any more until he pulled in to a hotel car park.

'The Staithe Hotel,' she said, reading the sign. 'Would this place have the ceiling we're coming to see?'

'It would indeed.'

'Staithe?'

'It's an Old English word meaning "riverbank" or "landing stage",' he said. 'You see it mainly nowadays in place names in east and north-east England—the bits that were under Danelaw.'

Clearly he'd done his research. Years ago, maybe there

had been some kind of wharf here. 'Are we dressed suitably for a visit?' she asked doubtfully. 'It looks quite posh.'

'We're fine.'

Then she twigged. 'It's *yours*, isn't it?'

'The first hotel I worked on by myself,' he confirmed. 'It was pretty run-down and Dad wasn't entirely sure I was doing the right thing, when I bid for it at the auction, but I really liked the place. And the views are stunning.'

When they went in, the receptionist greeted them warmly. 'Have you booked a table?' she asked.

'No, but I'd like to see the manager—he's expecting me,' Gabriel said.

'Just a moment, sir,' the receptionist said, and disappeared into the room behind the reception desk.

The manager came out and smiled when he saw them. 'Gabriel, it's good to see you.' He shook Gabriel's hand warmly.

'You, too. Pete, this is my friend Nicole Thomas,' Gabriel said.

Friend. The word made her feel warm inside. Were they friends, now?

'Nicole, this is Pete Baines, my manager here.'

'Pleased to meet you, Mr Baines.' She shook his hand.

'Call me Pete,' the manager said. 'Any friend of Gabriel's is a friend of mine.'

'Nicole is renovating the cinema next door to the place I'm working on at the moment,' Gabriel explained, 'and her ceiling has a lot in common with the one in your restaurant.'

'I get you,' Pete said. 'Come with me, Nicole.' He ushered her into the restaurant.

The ceiling looked like elaborate plasterwork, as did the wainscoting around the fireplace.

'Believe it or not, that's tin, not carving or plaster,' Pete said. 'It's just painted to look that way. Obviously Gabriel knows a lot more than I do on that front—I just run the place and boss everyone about.'

'And very well, too. Pete, I know you're normally booked out weeks ahead,' Gabriel said.

'But you want me to squeeze you in for lunch?' Pete finished, smiling. 'I'm sure we can do something.'

'Any chance of a table on the terrace, outside?' Gabriel asked.

'Sure. I'll leave you to take a closer look at the ceiling. Can I get you both a drink?'

'Sparkling mineral water for me, please,' Nicole said.

'Make that two,' Gabriel added.

'I can't believe this isn't plasterwork,' Nicole said, looking at the ceiling and wainscoting.

'It's tin. The place was originally built in Victorian times by a local businessman. His son remodelled it to make the room look more Tudor and added the tin wainscoting and ceiling.' He flicked into his phone. 'This is what it looked like before the restoration.'

She looked at the photographs. 'It looks a mess, there—but you can't see any of the damage here.' She gestured to the wainscoting in front of her.

'I can let you have the restoration guy's name, if you'd like it. And, by the way, as you paid at La Chiatta, I'm buying lunch here. No arguments,' he said. 'Otherwise you'll just have to starve.'

'Noted,' she said. 'And thank you.'

When they sat out on the terrace and she'd read the menu, she looked at Gabriel. 'This menu's amazing. Is all the food locally sourced?' she asked.

'Yes. The locals love us, and we've had some good write-ups in the national papers as well—Pete gets foodies coming all the way from London to stay for the weekend. The chef's great and we're hoping to get a Michelin star in the next round,' Gabriel said.

'What do you recommend?'

'Start from the puddings and work backwards,' he said.

She looked at the dessert menu and smiled. 'I think I know what I'm having.'

'White chocolate and raspberry bread and butter pudding?' he asked.

At her nod, he grinned. 'Me, too.'

'Crab salad for mains, then,' she said.

'Share some sweet potato fries?' he suggested.

This felt much more like a date than the other times they'd eaten together—even though they'd officially come on a research trip to look at the tin ceiling.

The view from the terrace was really pretty across the salt marshes and then to the sea. 'I can't believe how far the sand stretches,' she said.

'That's why I said wear shoes you can take off and jeans you can roll up,' he said. 'We're going for a walk on the beach after lunch to work off the calories from the pudding, and to blow the cobwebs out.'

'I can't actually remember the last time I went to the beach,' she said.

'Me, neither. I really love this part of the coast. When the tide's out you can walk for miles across the sand, and you've got the seal colony just down the road at Blakeney.'

'You fell in love with Norfolk when you worked on the hotel, didn't you?' she asked.

'I very nearly ended up moving here,' he said, 'but London suits me better.'

'So is that your big dream? Living by the sea?'

'I love the sea, but I'm happy where I am,' he said.

She enjoyed the food, which was beautifully presented and tasted even better than it looked. Though her fingers brushed against his a couple of times when they shared the sweet potato fries, and her skin tingled where he'd touched her.

To distract herself, she said, 'There was something I wanted to show you yesterday. I found something in the archives.' She found the photographs she'd taken and handed her phone to him.

He looked at the front of the postcard, zoomed in on the script, and smiled. 'Well, how about that—a photograph of someone who danced there and saw a Capra film.'

'I thought of you,' she said. 'With the Capra stuff.'

'What a fantastic find.'

'There was a newspaper article, too.' She took the phone back to find her notes for him. 'The print's so tiny that a photograph wouldn't have helped, so I took notes. The outside of the building wasn't originally all white, and there's a sun ray on that semi-circle. Do you think I could get that back?'

'You need to talk to the builder—it depends on the condition of the brickwork underneath. But it's a possibility.' He gave her another of those knee-melting smiles. 'This is amazing. A real connection to the past. Thanks for sharing this with me.'

She almost told him that he was the one person she'd really wanted to share it with; but she knew he saw this as just business, so she'd be sensible and keep it light between them. 'I did look to see if there was a photograph of the warehouse in that scrapbook, but I'm afraid there wasn't anything.'

'I doubt there would be postcards of the warehouse.'

He shrugged. 'People didn't really pay that much attention to industrial buildings, except for things like train stations and museums.'

Once they'd said goodbye to Pete, Gabriel drove a little way down the road to the car park.

'Good—the tide's out,' he said.

'How do you know?'

'Because the car park's dry—I learned that one the hard way,' he said with a grin, 'though fortunately not in this car.'

Once they'd parked, he took a bag from the boot of the car.

'What's that?'

'Something we need to do, Georgy.'

Obviously he wasn't going to tell her until he was ready, so she let it go. She took her shoes off at the edge of the beach, as did he. As she walked along with her shoes in one hand, her other hand brushed against his a couple of times, and every single nerve-end was aware of him. With a partner, she thought, this place would be so romantic. But Gabriel wasn't her partner. Romance wasn't in the equation, not with Gabriel and not with anyone else.

'Is that a wreck out there?' she asked.

'Yes. It's not a good idea to walk out to it, though, as when the tide changes it comes in really quickly. And it comes in far enough to flood the road to the car park.' He stopped. 'Here will do nicely.'

'For what?'

'This.' He took a kite from the bag.

She burst out laughing. Now she understood why he'd called her Georgy again. 'I've never flown a kite before,' she reminded him.

'It's been a while for me,' he admitted. 'But this is the perfect place to start.'

'The wind's blowing my hair into my eyes. I need to tie my hair back,' she said, flustered. The idea of intense businessman Gabriel Hunter being carefree was something she found it hard to get her head around. She wasn't the carefree sort, either. But she was a different person when she was with him—Georgygirl. Just as she had a feeling that he was different when he was with her.

He waited while she put an elastic hairband in her hair, then handed her the kite. 'Stand with your back to the wind, hold the kite up, let out the line a little, and it will lift. Then you pull on the line so it climbs.'

She couldn't get the hang of it and the kite nosedived into the sand again and again. 'I'd better let you have this back before I wreck it,' she said eventually.

'No. Try it like this,' he said, and stood behind her with his hands over hers, guiding her so that the kite actually went up into the air, this time. He felt warm and strong, and Nicole couldn't help leaning back into him.

He tensed for a moment; then he wrapped one arm round her waist, holding her close to him.

Neither of them said a word, just concentrated on flying the kite; but Nicole was so aware of Gabriel's cheek pressed against hers, the warmth of his skin and the tiny prickle of new stubble. She could feel his heart beating against her back, firm and steady, and she was sure he could probably feel her own heart racing. Taking a risk, she laid her arm over his, curling her hand round his elbow.

They stood there for what felt like for ever, just holding each other close.

Then he slowly wound the kite in and dropped it on the sand, and twisted her round to face him.

'Nicole,' he said, and his eyes were very bright.

She couldn't help looking at his mouth.

And then he dipped his head and brushed his mouth against hers. So soft, so sweet, so gentle.

It felt as if someone had lit touch-paper inside her.

She slid her arms round his neck, drawing him closer, and let him deepen the kiss. Then she closed her eyes and completely lost herself in the way he made her feel, the warmth of his mouth moving against hers, the way he was holding her.

And then he broke the kiss.

'Nicole.' His voice was huskier, deeper. 'I'm sorry. I shouldn't have done that.'

'Neither should I.' What an idiot she'd been. Had she learned nothing from Jeff? She was a cold fish, useless at relationships.

'I... Maybe we need to get back to London,' he said.

She seized on the excuse gratefully. 'Yes. I have a lot to do for the cinema and I'm sure you're busy, too.'

No. He wasn't. He could delegate every single thing that he had on his desk for the next month and spend all his time with her.

That was what he wanted to do.

But that kiss had been a mistake. She'd backed away from him. He'd taken it too far, too fast and he knew he needed to let her regroup. He'd let himself be carried away by the fun of kite-flying. Acted on impulse. Blown it.

They walked back to the car, and he was careful this time not to let his hand brush against hers. And he kept the roof up in the car on the way back.

'No wind in your hair this time?' she asked.

He shrugged. 'It is what it is.'

'Why do you always say that?'

'It's something Vijay taught me. If you're in a situation and you can't change it, you need to accept that and make the best of it. Don't waste your energy in trying to change something that you can't change; focus instead on what you can do.'

'It's a good philosophy.'

He smiled. 'I would say it's very Zen—except he's a Hindu, not a Buddhist.'

Nicole had a feeling that Gabriel had been very lonely when he grew up and the Khans had been the first ones to make him really feel part of the family; whereas she'd always grown up knowing she was loved, by her mother and her godparents and the rest of her mother's friends. It didn't matter that she didn't have a big family by blood, or that her father had been a liar and a cheat, or that her grandparents were estranged.

She wondered how she'd moved from that to her place at the bank, where she'd never really been part of the team and had only really felt accepted on her very last day there.

It is what it is.

She couldn't change the past: but she could change her future.

So, when Gabriel parked outside her flat, she turned to face him. 'Would you like to come in for coffee?'

'Coffee?' Gabriel stared at her. 'Is that a good idea?'

'You're not a predator, Gabriel.'

'Thank you for that.' So maybe she'd forgiven him for that kiss?

'Come and have coffee,' she said.

'OK. That'd be nice.' He followed her upstairs to her

first-floor flat. The front door opened into a small lobby with five doors leading off. 'Storage cupboard, bathroom, kitchen, living room, bedroom,' she said, indicating the doors in turn. 'Do go and sit down.'

The walls in her living room were painted a pale primrose-yellow, and the floors were polished wood with a blue patterned rug in the centre. French doors at the far end of the room led onto a small balcony, and just in front of them was a glass-topped bistro table with two chairs. He was half surprised not to see a desk in the room, but assumed that was probably in her bedroom— not that he was going to ask. There were a couple of fairly anonymous framed prints on the walls, and on the mantelpiece there were a couple of framed photographs. The older woman with Nicole looked so much like her that Gabriel realised straight away she had to be Nicole's mother; the younger woman in the other photograph was wearing a bridal dress and Nicole appeared to be wearing a bridesmaid's outfit, so he assumed this was her best friend Jessie.

Looking at the photos felt a bit like spying; and he felt too awkward to sit on the sofa. In the end, he went through to the kitchen—which was as tidy and neat as her living room.

'Can I help?' he asked.

'No, you're fine. Do you want a sandwich or anything?'

He shook his head. What he really wanted was to be back on that beach with her in his arms, kissing him back. But that was a subject that could really blow up in his face. He needed to take this carefully. 'Thanks, but just coffee will do me.'

'Here.' She handed him a mug, and ushered him back into the living room. She took her laptop from a drawer and said, 'I was going to put a note on the Surrey Quays website tonight. As you're part of it, too, I thought maybe we could do this together.'

Was she suggesting that he told everyone who he was? He looked warily at her. 'I kind of like my anonymity there.'

'So be Clarence. You don't have to tell them you're Gabriel.'

'Are you going to out yourself?' he asked.

'I kind of have to, given that I've inherited the Electric Palace—but I think everyone's going to respond to me as Georgygirl. Nobody knows Nicole the banker.'

But was she Nicole, Georgy, or a mixture of the two? And could she drop the protective shell of being the hard-headed banker and become the woman he thought she really was? Because, with her, he found that he was the man he wanted to be. Not the one who kept his tongue bitten and seethed in silent frustration when he kept failing to earn his father's respect: the man who thought outside the box and saw the world in full colour.

She put her mug on the coffee table, signed into the Surrey Quays forum, and started to type.

'I guess "Electric Palace—news" is probably the best subject line to use,' she said.

'Probably,' he agreed.

She typed rapidly, then passed the laptop to him so he could see the screen properly. 'Do you think this will do?'

Sorry I've been AWOL for a bit. I've been getting my head round the fact that I'm the new owner of the Electric Palace—it was left to me in a will. It needs a bit of work, but my boss has given me a six-month sabbatical and I'm going to use it to see if I can get it up and running again.

I'm planning to start showing films in a couple of months—a mix of blockbusters, classics and art-house films, and maybe showcase the work of new local film-makers. I have a few ideas about what to do with the upper room—the old ballroom—and I really want it to be used as part of the community. If anyone's looking for a regular room for a dance class or teaching craft work or that sort of thing, give me a yell. And if anyone has photographs I can borrow to enlarge for the walls, I'd be really grateful.

Cheers, Georgygirl x

'So you're not going to ask for help restoring the place?' he asked.

She shook her head. 'That feels kind of greedy and rude.'

'There's a saying, shy bairns get naught,' he reminded her.

'And there's another saying, nobody likes pushy people. If people offer to help, that's a different thing.' She looked him straight in the eye. 'Someone fairly wise keeps telling me "it is what it is".'

'I guess.' He smiled. 'So what now?'

'We wait and see if anyone replies.'

'And you and me?' The question had to be asked. They couldn't keep pretending.

She sucked in a breath. 'I don't know. I've got a business to set up. I don't have time for a relationship. The same goes for you.'

'What if I think it's worth making time?'

She sighed. 'I'm not very good at relationships.'

'Neither am I.'

'So we ought to be sensible. Anyway, we're business rivals, so we're both off limits to each other.'

'Not so much rivals as working together. Collaborating. The wedding stuff, for starters,' he reminded her.

'We haven't agreed that.'

'I know, but it's a win for both of us, Nicole. We both get what we want. And it doesn't matter whose idea it was in the first place. It works.'

'Maybe.'

But this time there was no coolness in her voice—she sounded unsure, but he didn't think it was because she didn't trust his judgement. It felt more as if she had no confidence in herself. Hadn't she just said she wasn't good at relationships?

'You kissed me back on the beach,' he said softly. 'I think that means something.'

She flushed. 'Temporary loss of sanity. That's what kite-flying does to you.'

'We're not flying kites now. And we're back in London.' He raised an eyebrow. 'What would you do if I kissed you again?'

'Panic,' she said.

She'd been straight with him. He couldn't ask for more than that. 'Thank you for being honest.' But he needed to be sure about this. 'Is it me, or is it all men?'

'I...' She shook her head. 'I'm just not good at relationships.'

He took her hand. 'He must have really hurt you.'

'He never hit me.'

'There's more than one way to hurt someone. It could be with words, or it could be by ignoring them, or it could be by undermining their self-esteem and constantly wanting to make them into someone they're not.'

'Leave it. Please.' Her eyes shimmered, and she blinked back the tears.

'I can't promise I won't hurt you, Nicole. But I can

promise I'll try my very best not to hurt you. If I do, it definitely won't be deliberate.' He lifted her hand up to his mouth and kissed the back of her hand. 'I have no idea where this thing between us is going. And I'm not very good at relationships. But I like the way I feel when I'm with you.' He owed her some honesty, too. 'I didn't want to meet Georgygirl in case she wasn't the same in real life as she was online. I didn't want to be disappointed.'

She looked away. 'Uh-huh.'

Was that what her ex had said to her? That she disappointed him? 'When I met you, I thought you were this hard-headed businesswoman, cold and snooty.'

She still didn't meet his eyes or say a word.

'But,' he said softly, 'then I got to know you a bit better. And in real life you're the woman I've been talking to online, late at night. You're clever and you're funny and you sparkle. That's who you really are.'

This time, she looked at him. 'So are you the man I've been talking to? The one who's full of sensible advice, who makes me laugh and who seems to understand who I am?'

'I think so. Because I've been more myself with you than I've been with anyone. For years and years,' he said.

'This is a risk.'

'You took risks all the time at the bank. You're taking a risk now on the Electric Palace.'

'Those were all calculated risks,' she pointed out. 'This isn't something I can calculate.'

'Me, neither. But I like you, Nicole. I like you a lot. And I think if we're both brave we might just have the chance to have something really special.'

'I'm not sure how brave I am,' she admitted.

'It's harder to be brave on your own. But you're not on your own, Nicole. We're in this together.'

* * *

Could she believe him?

Could she trust him—and trust that he wouldn't let her down like Jeff had?

She thought about it.

Gabriel could've taken advantage of her in business. But he hadn't. He'd been scrupulously fair. Pushy, yes, but his ideas really did work for both of them.

He'd also completely fried her common sense with that kiss on the beach.

And she'd been honest about her life right now. She was going to be crazily busy with the cinema. She didn't have time for a relationship. It was the same for him, getting the hotel next door up and running.

But they could make the time.

'OK. We'll see how it goes. No promises, and we try not to hurt each other,' she said.

'Works for me.'

She looked at him. 'So does that mean you're going to kiss me now?'

'Nope.'

Had she got this wrong? Didn't he want a relationship with her after all? Confused, she stared at him.

'You're going to kiss me,' he said. 'And then I'm going to kiss you back.'

Could it really be that easy?

She's a cold fish.

Nicole shoved the thought away. She didn't feel like a cold fish with Gabriel. He made her blood heat.

Slowly, hoping that she was going to get this right, she leaned over and touched her mouth to the corner of his.

He made a small murmur of approval, and she grew braver, nibbling at his lower lip.

Then he wrapped his arms round her and opened his mouth, kissing her back.

And Nicole felt as if something had cracked in the region of her heart.

She wasn't sure how long they stayed there, just kissing, but eventually Gabriel stroked her face. 'Much as I'd like to scoop you up right now and carry you to your bed, I don't have any condoms on me.'

She felt her face flame. 'Neither do I.'

'I've dated a lot,' he said, 'but for the record I'm actually quite picky about who I sleep with. And it's not usually on a first date, either.'

'Is today our first date?'

'Maybe. Maybe not.' He stole another kiss. 'Can I see you tomorrow?'

'You work next door to me. The chances are we'll see each other.'

'Not work. After,' he corrected.

'A proper date?'

'Give me a while to think up something to impress you.'

'Clarence,' she pointed out, 'wouldn't try to impress me. He'd just be himself.'

'And if I tried to impress Georgy, she would probably be so sarcastic with me that I'd have a permanent hole in my self-esteem.' He stole another kiss. 'See what we feel like after work? Drink, dinner, or just a walk along the waterfront?'

'Sounds good to me.'

'Tomorrow,' he said. 'I'm going now while I still have a few shreds of common sense left.'

'OK. And thank you for today. For the kite and the ceiling and…everything.'

'I liked the kite. I haven't done that in years. Maybe we

could do that again—say on Parliament Hill.' He kissed her one last time. 'See you tomorrow, Nicole.'

'See you tomorrow, Gabriel.' She saw him out.

Later that evening her phone pinged with a text from him.

Sweet dreams.

They would be, she thought. Because they'd be of him.

CHAPTER EIGHT

THE NEXT MORNING, Nicole came out of the shower to find a text from Gabriel on her phone.

Good morning :) x

She smiled and called him back. 'Don't tell me you're at work already.'

'No. I hit the gym first; it clears my head for the day. I'm walking to the hotel now. What are you doing today?'

'Talking to a builder.'

'Want some back-up?' he asked.

'Thanks for the offer, but I'm fine.'

'OK. But let me look at the quote—and the contract, when you get to that stage,' he said.

Her old suspicions started to rise, but quickly deflated when he added, 'I write contracts like this all the time, so it'll take me all of ten minutes to look over them. And my rates are good—I'll work for coffee and a brownie. Maybe a kiss.'

His candour disarmed her. 'OK. Thanks. Though I saw contracts all the time in my old job, too, you know,' she pointed out.

'I know, but you were more interested in cash-flow

and gearing than anything else,' he said. 'I bet you can analyse a balance sheet in half the time that I do.'

'Says Mr MBA.'

'Yeah, well. Has anyone replied to your post, yet?'

'I don't know. Hang on a sec.' She switched on her laptop and flicked in to the site. 'Oh, my God.'

'Is everything OK?' He sounded concerned.

'There's… Gabriel, take a look for yourself. There are loads and loads and loads of replies. I can't believe this.' She scrolled through them. 'So many names I recognise, and they all want to be part of it. Some people are offering me photographs. A few want to come and have a look round, in exchange for putting a bit of paint on the walls. I've got someone who used to be a projectionist, and offers from people who want to be ushers, and there's a couple of people who say they can't manage going up a ladder or holding a paintbrush because their arthritis is too bad but they'll come and make tea for the task team and do fetching and carrying and stuff.' Tears pricked her eyes. 'I don't know if I'm more humbled or thrilled.'

'I'm not surprised you've had that kind of reaction,' he said.

'Why?'

'Because people like you,' he said. 'Your posts are always thoughtful and considered, and people respect you.'

People actually liked her? Nicole couldn't quite get her head round that. In real life, she'd tended to keep part of herself back, particularly since Jeff's betrayal; but online, behind her screen name, she'd been more who she really was.

Would they all change their minds about her when they met her? Gabriel hadn't. But the doubts still flickered through her.

'I think,' he said, 'I take it back about it being a big

ask to be open in July. I think you're going to do it, Nicole, because you've got the whole community behind you. Including me.'

'Thank you.'

'Good luck with your builder. Call me if you need back-up.'

'I will.' She had no intention of doing so, but she appreciated the offer. 'Talk to you later.'

She went onto the forum to type in a reply.

I'm overwhelmed by everyone's kindness. Thank you so much. I'm going to be at the cinema most of the time, so do drop in and say hello if you're passing. I've got power and lights working now, so I can make you a cup of tea. And thank you again—all of you.

At five to eight, Patrick, Nicole's potential builder, arrived at the cinema. She made him a cup of tea and showed him round, explaining what she wanted to do with each room.

'That roof is stunning,' he said when he was at the top of the ladder in the upper room. 'Tin. That's not very common—but I know a guy who specialises in this stuff. The bad news is that he's booked up for months in advance, so you might have to leave the upstairs for a while until he can fit us in. Until you get rid of that lead paint, you're going to fall foul of regulations if you open it to the public.'

Just as Gabriel had warned her. 'I thought you might say that,' she said. 'The plan is, I want to use this room as a multi-purpose place—I'll have a proper screen so we can have a cinema, but also I want flexible staging so I can use it for a band and as a dance hall, or as a conference hall, or hire the room out to clubs or craft teachers.'

'Sounds good. What about the downstairs? With that mouse problem…'

'I've had the pest people out already and they've been back to check—they tell me that the mice are gone now,' she said, 'so it's just a matter of fixing the damage they've already done. But I'm not going to restore the seats quite as they are.' She explained about the sofas and tables.

'That sounds great. It'll be nice to see this place looking like she did back in the old days—or even better.'

It sounded, she thought, as if Patrick had fallen as much in love with the building as she had.

'You'll need a French polisher to sort out the bar, and there's a bit of damage to the glasswork that needs sorting out.'

'But it's all fixable,' she said. 'There is one other thing. I want it up and running in eight weeks.'

Patrick blew out a breath. 'You definitely won't get the upstairs done for then. Even downstairs might be pushing it—there isn't that much structural stuff, apart from the flooring once we've taken the old seats out, but there's an awful lot of cosmetic stuff.'

'I've, um, had offers of help from people who want to see the cinema restored,' Nicole said. 'If you have a site manager in charge, can they come and help?'

'Do any of them have experience?'

She grimaced. 'Um. Pass.'

'As I said, a lot of it is cosmetic. The more hands you have on deck, more chance you have of getting it done in your timeframe—as long as they do what the site manager asks and don't think they know better, it'll be fine,' Patrick said. 'So this is going to be a bit of a community project, then?'

'It looks like it.'

'They're the ones that make this kind of job feel really

worthwhile,' he said. 'OK. I'll go and work out a schedule of works and give you a quote.'

'I hate to be pushy,' Nicole said, 'but when are you likely to be able to get back to me? This week, next week?'

'Given that you want it done yesterday—I'll try to get it to you for close of business today,' Patrick said.

She could've kissed him. 'Thank you.'

'No problem. And thanks for the tea.'

'Pleasure.'

When he'd gone, she went next door to see Gabriel.

'How did it go?' he asked.

She beamed. 'Patrick's a really nice guy and he loves the building. He's giving me a quote later today—and he's fine about everyone coming to help.'

'Sounds good.'

'I know I'm supposed to get three quotes, but I think I'd work well with him.'

'It's not always about the money. It's about quality and gut feel, too.' He gave her a hug. 'I still want to see that quote and the contract, though. Have you thought any more about furniture? The average retailer isn't going to be able to deliver you the best part of two hundred sofas in the next six weeks—they won't have enough stock. You'll need a specialist commercial furnisher.'

'I'm getting pretty used to eating humble pie around you,' she said. 'So if that was an offer of a contact name, then yes, please.'

'Better than that. If I introduce you, you'll get the same terms that Hunter Hotels do—which will reduce your costs,' Gabriel said.

'Is this how you normally do business, getting special deals for neighbours?'

'No. And it's not because you're my girlfriend, either.

If we do the weddings and conferences, together, then if you use my suppliers I know your quality's going to be the same as mine. This is total self-interest.'

She didn't believe a word of it, but it made it a little easier to accept his help. 'It's really happening, isn't it?'

'Yes, it's really happening.' He kissed her. 'This is going to be amazing.'

Nicole spent the rest of the day finalising her lists for what needed to be done next, including applying for a wedding licence. Several people from the Surrey Quays forum dropped in to see her, some bringing photographs that she could borrow to have enlarged, framed and put on the walls in the reception area. She ran out of mugs and had to go next door to borrow some more mugs and coffee, to the amusement of Gabriel's team.

'So if you inherited this place from Brian...would your mum be Susan?' Ella Jones asked.

'Yes.'

'I always liked her—she was a lovely girl,' Ella said. 'Brian wasn't the easiest man. I always thought he was too hard on Susan.'

'He was but it was his loss, because my mum's amazing,' Nicole said.

'And so are you,' Ella's husband Stephen said. 'Most people would've thrown their hands up in the air at the state of this place and sold up. I bet him next door wanted this,' Stephen added, jerking his thumb in the direction of Gabriel's hotel, 'because the space would make a good car park for the hotel.'

'Gabriel Hunter's actually been really nice,' Nicole said. And if they knew he was Clarence... But it wasn't her place to out him. 'He's been very supportive. He's got a real eye for architecture and he sees the potential of this building, so he's working with me.'

'But that company—it just guts buildings and turns them into soulless hotel blocks,' Ella said.

'No, they don't. I've seen what he's doing next door and he's trying to keep as much of the character of the building as he can in the reception area, restaurant, bar, and conference rooms.'

Gabriel overheard the last bit of the conversation as he walked into the cinema foyer. And it warmed him that Nicole was defending him.

'If anyone here wants a tour next door, I'm happy to show you round,' he said. 'Oh, and since you pinched half my mugs, Nicole, I assumed you could do with some more supplies.' He handed her a two-litre carton of milk and a couple of boxes of muffins.

She smiled at him. 'I could indeed. Thanks, Gabriel.' She introduced him to everyone. 'They've lent me some wonderful postcards and photographs.'

'That's great,' he said. 'I'll go and put the kettle on and then take a look.'

Later that evening, he said to her, 'Thanks for supporting me when the Joneses seemed a bit anti. I thought you saw me as a shark-in-a-suit.'

'I know you better now. You don't compromise on quality and I think you'd be very tough on anyone who didn't meet your standards, but you're not a shark,' Nicole said. 'Oh, talking about being tough—Patrick emailed me the quote and contract. You said you wanted to look them over. How about I order us a Chinese takeaway while you do that?'

'Great,' he said. 'Let me have the surveyor's report as

well, so I can tie them up.' He went through the documents carefully.

'What do you think?' she asked when he'd finished.

'Not the cheapest, but it's a fair price and he's been thorough. It matches what the surveyor said. And you said you felt he'd work well with you. I'd say you're good to go with your instinct.'

Once she'd signed the contract and agreed the work plan, a new phase of Nicole's life started. She ended each day covered in paint and with aching muscles, but she was happier than she could ever remember. She'd got to know more people from the Surrey Quays forum in real life, and really felt part of the community.

And then there was Gabriel.

They were still taking things relatively slowly, but she was enjoying actually dating him—everything from a simple walk, to 'research' trips trying different local ice cream specialists, through to dinner out and even dancing. If anyone had told her even six months ago that she'd be this happy, she would never have believed them.

The one sticking point was that Patrick's predictions were right and the ceiling specialist was booked up for the next few months. Gabriel had tried his contacts, too, and nobody was available: so it looked as if the grand opening of the Electric Palace was going to be the cinema only and not the room with the amazing ceiling. Weddings and conferences were off limits, too, until the room was ready. And now she'd finally decided to work with him, she wanted it all to start *now*.

'When you want something done, you want it done now, don't you?' Gabriel asked when she'd expressed her disappointment.

'You're just as bad.'

'True.' He kissed her. 'Maybe the dates will change on another project and the specialist will be able to fit us in, but even so we can still use the upstairs foyer as the café, the downstairs bar, and the cinema itself.'

'It's going to be done at some point. I just have to be patient.' Nicole stroked his face. 'You know, I'm actually working longer hours than I was at the bank.'

'But the difference is that you love every second at the cinema.'

'I love seeing the changes in the place every day,' she said. 'And really feeling part of a team.'

'Part of the community,' he agreed. 'Me, too.' Other people had chipped in with information about the spice warehouse. 'And I've noticed that everyone's the same in real life as they are online. I wasn't expecting that.'

'And there's no snarkiness, nobody competing with each other—everyone's just getting on together and fixing things,' she said. 'I'm going to thank every single person by name on the opening night, as well as unveiling the board.'

'I'll supply the champagne to go with it,' he said.

She shook her head. 'You don't have to do that.'

'I know, but I want to. It's not every day your girlfriend manages to do something as amazing as this for the community.'

Nicole's mum and Jessie helped out at weekends and evenings, when they could. One evening, it was just the three of them working together, so Nicole ordered pizza when they stopped for a break.

'So when are you going to tell us?' Jessie asked.

'Tell you what?'

'About Gabriel,' Susan said.

'He's my neighbour, in business terms, and we have

mutual interests. It's made sense for us to work together,' Nicole said.

Jessie laughed. 'And you're telling us you haven't noticed how gorgeous he is?'

Nicole couldn't help it. She blushed.

'So how long has this been going on?' Susan asked.

'Um.' She'd been thoroughly busted.

'You might as well tell us now,' Jessie said. 'You know we're going to get it out of you.'

Nicole sighed and told them about how she'd met 'Clarence' on the Surrey Quays forum and he'd turned out to be Gabriel. 'So the man I thought was my enemy was actually my friend all along.'

'But you're more than friends?' Jessie asked.

'Yes.'

'He's a nice guy. Not like Jeff,' Susan said.

'Definitely not like Jeff.' Jessie hugged her. 'You seem happier, and I thought it was more than just the job. I'm glad. You deserve life to go right for you.'

At the end of a day when Nicole had spent close to fourteen hours painting—and her arm ached so much she barely had the strength to clean her brush—Gabriel called in to the cinema.

'I wondered what you felt like doing tonight.'

'I don't think I'm fit for much more than a hot bath and then crawling into my PJs,' she said.

'I was going to suggest cooking dinner for us.' He paused. 'You could have a bath at my place while I'm cooking—and I'll drive you home afterwards.'

This felt like the next step in their relationship, and Nicole wasn't sure if she was quite ready for that. Her doubts clearly showed in her expression, because Gabriel stole a kiss. 'That wasn't a clumsy pass, by the way. It was the offer of a hot bath and cooking for you because you look wiped out.'

'Thank you—I'd appreciate that. But I'm covered in paint.'

'I could collect stuff from your place first. Or I could cook at yours, if you don't mind me taking over your kitchen,' he suggested.

'You'd do that?'

'Sure—and then you can eat dinner in your PJs. Which is again not a come-on,' he said, 'because when you and I finally decide to take the next step I'd like you to be wide awake and enjoying yourself rather than thinking, oh, please hurry up and finish so I can go to sleep.'

She laughed. 'You,' she said, 'are a much nicer person than you like the world to think.'

'Well, hey. I don't want people to think I'm a push-over, or negotiating contracts and what have you would be very tedious.'

'You're still a good man, Gabriel.' And maybe this wasn't just business to him; maybe he really did like her, she thought. He'd talked about taking the next step. It meant another layer of trust: but from what she'd seen of him she thought she could trust him. He wouldn't let her down like Jeff had.

In the end he made a chicken biryani for her in her kitchen while she soaked in the bath. 'I would normally make my own naan bread rather than buying it ready-made from the supermarket,' he said, 'but I thought in the circumstances that you might not want your kitchen being cluttered up.'

'It still tastes amazing. I don't cook much,' she admitted.

'Lack of time or lack of inclination?' he asked.

'Both,' she said.

'I love cooking,' he said. 'It relaxes me.'

She smiled. 'Are you going to tell me you bake, as well?'

He raised an eyebrow. 'I wouldn't rate my chances against a professional but I make a reasonable Victoria sponge.'

'You're full of surprises,' she said.

'Is that a bad thing?' he asked.

'No, because they're nice surprises,' she said.

Which told him that she'd had a nasty surprise from her ex at some point. She still wouldn't open up to him, but Gabriel hoped she'd realise that he wouldn't hurt her—at least not intentionally.

Georgygirl had been important to him. But Nicole was something else. The way he felt when he was with her was like nothing he'd ever experienced before.

It couldn't be love—could it?

He'd never been properly in love in his life.

But he liked being with Nicole. With her, he could be truly himself. The problem was, could she trust him enough to be completely herself with him?

'Tonight,' Gabriel said, a week later, 'we're going to see the stars.'

'That's so sweet of you, but there isn't long until the cinema opens and all the dark sky spots are way up in Scotland or near the border.' She wrinkled her nose. 'I'd love to go with you, but I can't really take that much time off.'

'Actually, there are places in London,' he said, 'right in the city centre. And tonight's the night when Mars is at opposition.'

'The closest it gets to the earth and it's illuminated fully by the sun, so it's at its brightest—hang on, did you just say there are dark sky places in the middle of London?' she asked, surprised. 'Even with all the street lights?'

'There's an astronomy group that meets in the middle of one of the parks,' Gabriel said. 'I spoke to the guy who runs it and he says we can come along—they have an old observatory and we'll get a turn looking through the telescope. So we get to see the stars tonight—but we don't have to travel for hours, first.'

'Gabriel, that's such a lovely thing to do.' She kissed him. 'Thank you.'

'You've been working really hard. You deserve a little time out and I thought you'd enjoy this,' he said.

The observatory was exactly as she'd imagined it to be, with a rotating dome and an old brass telescope. Just as Gabriel had promised, they had the chance to look through the telescope and see some of the features of Mars—and the moon, too.

Nicole loved it, and she loved walking in the park hand in hand with Gabriel afterwards. 'I'm blown away that you've taken the effort to do this for me,' she said. Jeff had never indulged her love of the stars, saying it was a bit childish. 'I feel a bit guilty that I haven't done anything for you.'

'Actually, you have,' Gabriel said. 'You've made me feel better about myself than I have in years—and I have some idea now of what I want to do in the future.'

'Such as?'

'I need to work it out in my head,' he said, 'but you're the first person I'll talk to about it.'

She grimaced. 'Sorry. I was being nosey.'

'No, you're my partner and it's nice that you're interested. Some of the women I've dated have only been interested in the depth of my bank account.'

'I hope you don't think I'm one of those.'

'Given how much hard work it is to persuade you even to let me buy you dinner,' he said, 'I know you're not.'

'So why did you date them?'

'I guess I was looking for someone who understood me. The problem was, the nice girls were wary of me—either they'd heard I was a wild child as a student, or they saw me as this ruthless businessman in the same mould my dad. And the others weren't interested in understanding me.'

'So you're a poor little rich boy?'

'Yes.' He batted his eyelashes at her. 'And I won't make a fuss if you decide to kiss me better.'

She laughed. 'That's the worst chat-up line I've ever heard.'

'It was pretty bad,' he admitted.

She smiled. 'I'll kiss you anyway.' And she did so. Lingeringly.

Over the next couple of weeks they grew closer, falling into a routine of having dinner together most nights, and then Gabriel would take Nicole home and they'd curl up on her sofa together, holding each other close and talking.

'So do I ever get to see the bat cave?' Nicole asked.

'Bat cave?' Gabriel asked, looking puzzled.

'You've been to my flat. Yours is clearly the bat cave—top secret.'

He laughed. 'Point taken. I'll make dinner there to-night.'

His flat was in a very modern development, with a balcony running along the length of the building, and all the rooms faced the river.

'Bathroom,' he said, gesturing to the various doors as

they stood in his small lobby, 'my bedroom and en-suite, main bathroom, living room, guest room.'

Like her flat, his had floor-to-ceiling windows, but his rooms were much bigger and so were the windows. Nicole adored the views.

The kitchen was just off the living room, and was about ten times the size of hers. It was clearly a cook's kitchen, with maple cupboards, worktops, and flooring. At the end of the living room, next to the kitchen, was his dining area; there was a large glass table with six comfortable-looking chairs. Three of the walls were painted cream, but the wall by the dining area was painted sky blue and held a massive painting of a stylised fish.

It looked like a show flat. And yet it also felt like home; the sofas looked comfortable, and she noticed he had the most up-to-date television.

'Home cinema?' she asked.

He nodded. 'But watching a film at home on your own isn't quite the same as going to the cinema with a group of friends. I think what you're doing to the Electric Palace is brilliant because you get the best of both worlds—all the comfort and all the social stuff as well.'

'I hope so.' The only thing Nicole couldn't see in the room was a desk. 'So you don't work at home?'

'The guest bedroom's my office,' he said. 'Though there is a sofa-bed in there if someone wants to stay over.'

He held her gaze for a moment. Would he ask her to stay over tonight? she wondered, and her heart skipped a beat.

She kept the conversation light while he cooked lemon chicken with new potatoes and she made the salad. But when they were lying on his sofa later that evening, he stroked her face. 'Stay with me tonight?'

She knew he didn't mean her to stay in the guest room. It meant spending the night in his bed. Skin to skin with him.

The next stage of their relationship.

Another layer of trust.

It was a risk. But the man she'd got to know over the last few weeks was definitely something special. Someone worth taking a risk for.

'I have a spare toothbrush,' he added.

She kissed him. 'Yes.'

And in answer he scooped her off the sofa and carried her to his bed.

A couple of days later, Nicole had some great news.

'My ceiling guy can fit us in,' Patrick said. 'The job he's working on has run into a bit of a legal wrangle, so he's got some spare time.'

'But doesn't he have a huge waiting list?' Nicole asked. 'Shouldn't he be seeing the next person on his list instead of queue-jumping me?'

'Probably,' Patrick said, 'but I've kept him up to date with what's happening here and he's seen the ceiling on your website. He says it's not a massive job—and also I think he fell in love with the stars and wants to be the one to work on it.'

'Got you,' Nicole said with a grin. 'Those stars really seem to do it for everyone.'

'I can't believe you've got all these people pitching in, too. I thought it was going to cost you an arm and a leg in overtime to get this done in your timeframe, but it's not.'

'No, but I do need to thank them. I'm going to have a board in the foyer with the names of everyone who's helped, and I'll unveil it on the opening night.'

'That's a nice idea.'

'I couldn't have done it without them,' Nicole said simply, 'so the very least they deserve is a public thank you.'

The person she most wanted to thank was Gabriel—for believing in her, and for being supportive. She just needed to work out how to do that.

'There is one thing,' Patrick said. 'Work on the ceiling means everything has to stop, because we can't do anything in that room until—'

'—the lead paint is gone,' she finished. 'Actually, that might fit in nicely.'

'Taking a holiday?'

'Sort of.'

She did some checking online, then called Gabriel. 'Is there any chance you can clear your diary for the next couple of days—preferably three?'

'Why?' he asked.

'That's on a need-to-know basis,' she said. 'I just need to know if it's possible.'

'Give me five minutes and I'll call you back.' He was as good as his word. 'OK, it's possible, but only if you tell me why.'

'It's a research trip. I could do with your views.' It wasn't strictly true, but she wanted to surprise him.

'All right. I take it that it's not in London, so do you need me to drive?'

'Nope. I'm borrowing a car. And I'll pick you up tomorrow at ten.'

It was a bright purple convertible Beetle, and Gabriel groaned when he saw it. 'You're going to tell me this is cinema-related because this is an update of Herbie, right?'

'I hadn't thought of that, but yes.' She grinned. 'Get in.'

'I thought you said my convertible was showing off?'

'Yeah, yeah.'

'So where are we going?'

'Road trip,' she said. 'Do you want to be Thelma or Louise?'

He groaned. 'This isn't going to end well.'

'Oh, it is. Trust me.'

She drove them down to Sussex, where she'd booked a couple of nights in an old fort overlooking the sea. She had a cool box in the back of the car filled with picnic food from a posh supermarket's chiller cabinet, and the weather forecast was good. This would be three days where they didn't have to worry about anything—they could just be together, relax and enjoy each other's company.

'Research?' Gabriel asked, eyeing the fort.

'Busted,' she said with a smile. 'I just wanted to take you away for a couple of days to say thanks for all you've done to help me.'

'It was pure self-interest. We have mutual business arrangements.'

'And I wanted to spend some time with you,' she said. 'Just you and me and the sea.'

'And an old fort—that's as awesome as it gets,' he said.

Three perfect days, where they explored the coast, ate at little country pubs and watched the sun setting over the sea. But best of all was waking up in his arms each morning.

Gabriel was everything Nicole wanted in a partner. He listened to her, he treated her as if her ideas mattered, he was kind and sweet and funny. And he could make her heart skip a beat with just one look.

The way she was starting to feel about him was like nothing else she'd ever known. She'd thought that she loved Jeff, but that paled into insignificance beside the way she felt about Gabriel.

But she couldn't shake the fear that it would all go wrong.

Everything had gone wrong when she'd moved in with Jeff. So, as long as they kept their separate flats and didn't say anything about how they felt, she thought, everything would be fine.

CHAPTER NINE

'I CAN'T BELIEVE how dim I am,' Gabriel said.

Nicole, curled up in bed beside him, just laughed. 'Dim is hardly the word to describe you. What brought that on?'

'The Electric Palace. We haven't looked in the film archives. And it's a *cinema*, for pity's sake. Moving pictures should've been the first place we looked.'

'Film archives? You mean, newsreels?'

'No. I was thinking of those Edwardian guys who went round the country taking films of everyday people,' he explained. 'They might have visited Surrey Quays.'

She looked at him. 'Actually, you're right, especially as your hotel was a spice warehouse—they specialised in factories, didn't they? So they're bound to have come to Docklands.'

Gabriel grabbed his phone and looked them up on the internet. 'Sagar Mitchell and James Kenyon. They made actuality films—everything from street scenes and transport through to sporting events, local industries and parades. The films used to be commissioned by travelling exhibitors, and were shown at town halls and fairgrounds.' He looked at her. 'And theatres.'

'If there aren't any films showing the warehouse or the theatre, we might still be able to find out if one of those films was shown at the Electric Palace—the Kursaal, as it was back then,' she said thoughtfully. 'That would be perfect for our opening night.'

'Have you decided what you want to show on the first night, yet?'

'I'd like one of the actuality films,' she said, 'and a classic film and a modern film, so we cover all the bases. Probably *It's A Wonderful Life.*'

'In July?' Gabriel looked surprised. 'It's a Christmas film.'

'It's brilliant at any time of year.' She punched his arm. 'Clarence, surely it'd get your vote?'

'Given your Surrey Quays forum name, what about *Mary Poppins*?' he suggested.

'We kind of did that on the beach in Norfolk,' she said.

'The first time I kissed you.' He kissed her lingeringly.

'You're an old romantic at heart,' she teased.

'Yeah.' He kissed her again.

'So, our classic film. Doesn't *Citizen Kane* top the list of the best films of all time?'

'Let's look up the list.' She did so, and grimaced. 'There are an awful lot on here I've never heard of, which is a bit pathetic for a cinema owner.'

'Let me have a look.' He glanced through them. 'I'm with you—haven't heard of most of these. And on opening night I think we need to have a broad appeal.'

'I did say I'd include some art-house evenings—I've been working on my scheduling—but I kind of want the film on the first night to be something I actually know. I'm standing by *It's a Wonderful Life.*'

'It's your show,' he said. 'And you're right. It's a good film.'

They snatched some time to visit the archives in the week. To Nicole's pleasure, there was footage of both the

Spice House and the Kursaal—and they were able to arrange to use it for the opening night. Better still, they had permission to take stills they could blow up and frame for their respective reception areas.

'Luck's definitely on our side,' Nicole said. 'I think this is going to work out.'

'I don't just think it,' Gabriel said, squeezing her hand. 'I *know* this is going to work out.'

Nicole was working on a section of wall when she heard a voice drawl, 'That's definitely not how you used to dress in the office.'

Recognising the voice, she turned round. 'Hey, Neil—nice to see you. You might like to know that wall over there is partly thanks to the office.'

'Glad to hear it—I'll tell the team.' He glanced round the foyer. 'This is really impressive, especially when you see those pictures on your website of what it looked like when you took over. So I take it you're not planning to come and claim your desk back?'

'I hope not.' She smiled at him. 'Are you enjoying the view from my desk?'

'Considering I don't have it, no.'

She stared at him in surprise. 'But you were a shoo-in to take over from me while I'm away and then permanently if I don't come back. What's happened?'

'We had a bit of a restructure and the boss headhunted this guy—and if you come back I think this guy will be *your* boss as well.' He sighed. 'I was never going to like him much anyway, because he got the job that I thought would be mine, but even without that...' He grimaced. 'I just don't like Jeff. He isn't a team player. I mean, OK, so you never came out with us on team nights out, but we all knew you had our backs in the office, whereas he'd sell us all down the river. He'd sell anything to make a profit.'

Jeff. She went cold. Surely not? 'Would that be Jeff Rumball?' she asked, trying to sound as casual as she could.

Neil looked surprised. 'Yeah—do you know him?'

'I haven't seen him for a while, but yes, I know him,' Nicole said. And the idea of failing to make the cinema a going concern and then having to go back to her old job, only to end up working for the man who'd betrayed her and left her self-esteem in tatters… Just no. It wasn't going to happen. 'My advice is to keep a low profile and to document everything. Copy things in to other people to be on the safe side, too,' she said.

'Got you.' Neil looked grim. 'We'd all rather you came back, you know.'

'Thanks for that,' she said with a smile, 'but I hope I'm going to make this place work.'

Although she chatted nicely with her former colleague and pretended to everyone else at the cinema that she was just fine, Neil's news left her feeling unsettled all day.

Jeff had used her to get ahead in his career. What was to say that Gabriel wasn't doing the same? Even though part of her knew she was being paranoid and completely ridiculous, she couldn't help the fears bubbling up—and Gabriel himself had admitted that he'd only joined the Surrey Quays forum at first to make sure he could head off any opposition to the development of the Spice House.

Eventually, sick of the thoughts whirling through her head, she left everyone working on plastering, painting, or woodwork, and walked to the café on Challoner Road to clear her head. She knew her mum was in meetings all day and Jessie was up to her eyes with her students in the middle of exam season, so she couldn't talk to them about Jeff.

Which left Gabriel.

Nicole had never actually told him about Jeff, but maybe this would be a way of laying that particular ghost to rest—and it would finally convince her that Gabriel was nothing like the man who'd let her down. She bought coffee and brownies, and headed for the Spice House.

But, as Nicole walked down the corridor to Gabriel's office, she could hear him talking. Clearly he was either in the middle of a meeting with someone or he was on the phone. What an idiot she was. She knew he was busy; she should have texted him first or called him to check when he might be free to see her for a quick chat.

She was about to turn away when she heard him say her name, almost like a question.

'Nicole? No, she's not going to give us any trouble, Dad.'

She went cold.

Jeff had used her to get on with his career. Right now, it sounded as if Gabriel was doing exactly the same. *She's not going to give us any trouble*—no, of course she wasn't, because he'd got her eating out of his hand. Over the last few months he'd grown close to her. He knew all her hopes and dreams; he'd made her feel that he supported her; and he'd made her feel that this thing between them was something special.

She'd thought he was different. After their rocky start, they'd learned to trust each other. They saw things the same way. They'd worked together to develop a conference package and a wedding package. She'd been so sure that she could trust him—with her heart as well as her business.

But that bit of conversation she'd just overhead made

it horribly clear that it had all been to keep her sweet and to make sure that, whatever he really had planned for the Spice House, she wasn't going to protest about it.

So she'd just made the same old mistake. Trusted a man who didn't love her at all and saw her as a way of getting what he wanted in business.

Sure, she could go in to his office now, all guns blazing. But it wouldn't change a thing. It wouldn't change the fact that she was stupid and trusting and naive. It wouldn't change the fact that Gabriel was a ruthless businessman who didn't let anything get in his way. So what was the point in making a fuss? It was over. Yelling at him wouldn't make her feel any better. Right now, she wanted to crawl into the nearest corner and lick her wounds—just as she had with Jeff.

She should never, ever have opened her heart like this. And she'd never, ever be stupid enough to open her heart to anyone again.

Feeling sick, she walked away, dumped the coffees and the brownies in the skip, and then sent Gabriel a text.

I can't do this any more. It's over.

Then she walked back in to the cinema and pretended that nothing was wrong. She was smiling on the outside, but on the inside she was purest ice.

She would never, ever let anyone take advantage of her like that again.

'Dad, I love you,' Gabriel said, 'but right at this moment you're driving me crazy. I know that you rescued me from the biggest mistake anyone could ever have made and I appreciate that. But it was nearly ten years ago now. I'm not the same person I was back then. And, if you can't see that, then maybe I'm in the wrong place.'

'What are you saying?' Evan demanded.

'Dad, do you really expect your hotel managers to run every single day-to-day decision past you, so your diary and your day is completely blocked up, or do you trust them to get on with the job you pay them to do and run the hotels?'

'Well, obviously I expect them to do the job I pay them to do,' Evan barked.

'Then let me do the same,' Gabriel said. 'You put me in charge of the Spice House, and I've got plans for the place. And yes, they do involve Nicole—we're doing some joint ventures with her, so we can offer something that little bit different to our clients, both business and leisure. And she's using our suppliers.'

Evan snorted in disgust. 'Using our name to get a discount.'

'Using our suppliers,' Gabriel pointed out, 'so her quality standards are the same as ours. It makes sense. And yes, she gets a discount. That way we both win, and more importantly we get to offer our customers what they want. Which means they'll stay loyal to us.'

'I suppose,' Evan said, sounding far from convinced.

Gabriel sighed. 'Look, I know I did wrong when I was nineteen. But I've spent years trying to make up for it. If you can't move past what I did and see that I'm a very different person now, then there isn't any point in me working for you. I'll step aside so you can employ the person you need to get the job done.'

'Are you resigning?' Evan asked in disbelief.

'I'm pretty close to it,' Gabriel said.

'But it's the family firm. You can't leave. What would you do? Set up in competition with me?'

'I'd work in a different sector,' Gabriel said. 'Which is actually what I'd rather talk to you about. I'd like to work with you. But it needs be on my terms now, Dad. I can't spend the rest of my life trying to do the impossible because it's making us both miserable, and Mum as well. This has to stop. Now.' His mobile phone beeped, and he glanced at the screen, intending to call whoever it was back later. But then he saw the message.

I can't do this any more. It's over.

It was from Nicole.

What? What did she mean, it was over? Had something happened at the cinema—had Patrick found something unfixable? Or did she mean *they* were over?

He didn't have a clue. As far as he knew, he hadn't done anything to hurt her. So what was going on?

'Dad, I have to go,' he said swiftly.

'Wha—?' Evan began.

'Later,' Gabriel said. 'I'll call you later, Dad. Something's come up and I need to deal with it right now.' And he put the phone down before his father could protest. This was something that was much more important than sorting out his career with his father. He had no idea what the problem was, but he needed to talk to Nicole and sort it out. *Now.*

He found her in the cinema, wielding a paintbrush. Outwardly, she was smiling, but Gabriel could see the tension in her shoulders.

'Can we have a word?' he asked.

'Why?' She looked wary.

'We need to talk.'

'I don't think so,' she said.

So she *did* mean they were over. Well, surely she didn't

think he was just going to accept that text message and roll over like a tame little lapdog? 'OK. We can do this in public, if you'd rather.'

Clearly recognising that he'd called her bluff, she shook her head. 'Come up to the office.'

He followed her upstairs, and she closed the door behind them.

'So what was that message about?' he asked.

'All deals are off,' she said, 'and I mean all of it—the conference stuff, the weddings, and us.'

'Why?'

'Because I heard you talking to your father, telling him that I wasn't going to give you any trouble.'

He frowned. 'You heard that?'

'I was coming to see you about something. I didn't realise you were on the phone and then I overheard you talking.'

'Well, it's a pity you didn't stay a bit longer and hear the rest of what I said,' he said, nettled. 'What did you think it meant?'

'That you were planning something I wouldn't like very much, but I wouldn't give you any trouble.' She gave him a cynical look. 'Because I'm your girlfriend, so of course I'll flutter my eyelashes and do everything you say. You *used* me, Gabriel.'

'Firstly,' Gabriel said, 'you only heard part of a conversation—and I have no idea how you've managed to leap to the most incredibly wrong conclusion from hearing one single sentence. And, secondly, I thought you knew me. Why on earth would you think I would use you?'

'Because my judgement in men is rubbish—and I've managed to pick yet another man who'd try to leverage our relationship for the sake of his career.'

'If anyone else had insulted me like that,' he said, 'I would be shredding them into little tiny bits right now. I've already worked out that your ex hurt you pretty badly and you won't talk about it, even to me—but now you get a choice. Either you tell me everything yourself, right now, or I'll go and talk to your mum and Jessie. And, because they love you, they will most definitely spill the beans to me.'

'So now you're throwing your weight about and threatening me?'

'No. I'm trying to find out why the hell you're acting as if you're totally deranged, and assigning motives to me that I wouldn't have in a million years,' he snapped. 'If you'd bothered to stay and overhear the rest of the conversation, Nicole, you would've heard me telling my father that we're working together on conferences and weddings, and everything's fine because we're using the same suppliers and we have the same attitudes towards our customers—and that if he can't move on from my past and see me as I am now, then maybe it's time for me to step aside and he finds the person he wants to run the show and I'll go and do something that makes me happy.'

Understanding dawned in her eyes. 'So you're not...?'

'No,' he said, 'I'm not planning to do anything underhand. That's not how I operate. I'm not planning to put sneaky clauses in our contract in such teensy, tiny print that you can't read them and then you'll be so far in debt to me that the only way out is to give me the cinema. I thought we were working together, Nicole. I thought we were friends. Lovers. I've been happier these last few weeks than I've ever been in my life—because I'm with you. So what the hell has gone wrong?'

She closed her eyes. 'I...'

'Tell me, Nicole, because I really can't see it for myself. What have I done?'

'It's not you—it's me,' she said miserably.

'And that's the coward's way out. The way the guy dumps the girl without having to tell her what the real problem is. You're not a coward, Nicole. You're brave, you're tenacious, you make things work out—so tell me the truth.'

Nicole knew she didn't have any choice now. She'd let her fears get the better of her and she'd misjudged Gabriel so badly it was untrue. And she wouldn't blame him if he didn't want anything to do with her, ever again, after this.

'It's about Jeff,' she said. 'I'm ashamed of myself.'

He said nothing, clearly not letting her off the hook. Which was what she deserved, she knew. She took a deep breath. 'I didn't often go to parties when I started work. I was focused on studying for my professional exams and doing well at my job. I wanted to get on, to make something of myself. But four years ago I gave in to someone nagging me in the office and I went to a party. And that's where I met Jeff. He was in banking, too—he worked for a different company, so I hadn't met him before. He was bright and sparkly, and I couldn't believe he could be interested in someone as boring and mousy as me. But we started dating.'

And what a fool she'd been.

'Go on,' Gabriel said. But his voice was gentler, this time. Not judging her.

Not that he needed to judge her. She'd already done that and found herself severely wanting.

'He asked me to move in with him. I loved him and I thought he loved me, so I said yes.'

'And that's when he changed?'

She shook her head. 'We moved in together and he was the same as he always was. He tended to go to parties without me, but that was fine.' She shrugged. 'I'm not really much of one for socialising. Outside work, I don't really know what to say to people.'

'You don't seem to have a problem talking to people at the cinema—and you definitely didn't seem to have a problem talking on the forum,' he pointed out.

'That's different.'

To her relief, he didn't call her on it. 'So what happened?'

'I can't even remember why, but I ended up going to this one party—and that's when I found out the truth about Jeff. I was in the toilet when this woman started talking to her friends about her boyfriend. I wasn't consciously trying to eavesdrop, but when you're in a toilet cubicle you can't really block people's words out.'

'True.'

'Anyway, this woman was saying that her boyfriend was living with someone else but didn't love her. She was a boring banker, and he was only living with her because there was going to be a promotion at work, and he knew his boss was going to give the job to someone who was settled down. The woman he was living with was the perfect banker's wife because she was a banker, too. Except the guy had bought the big diamond ring for her—for the mistress, not for the boring banker.' She grimaced. 'I felt so sorry for this poor woman who clearly thought her boyfriend loved her, but he was cheating on her and just using her to get on in her career. But then the woman in the toilets said his name. How many bankers are there called Jeff, who also happen to be living with a female banker?'

'Did you ask him about it?'

'Yes, because part of me was hoping that it was just

a horrible coincidence and there was some poor other woman out there being cheated on—not that I wanted to wish that on anyone, obviously. I just didn't want it to be true about me. But he admitted he was seeing her. He said that was the reason why he'd started dating me and the reason he'd asked me to move in, so his boss would think he was the right guy for the promotion.' She swallowed hard. 'Luckily I'd moved into his place rather than him moving into mine, so I packed my stuff and went to stay with Jessie until I could find a flat. That's when I moved here.' And she hadn't dated since.

Until Gabriel.

And she'd been so happy…but now she'd messed it up. Big time. Because she hadn't been able to trust him.

'Jeff sounds like the kind of selfish loser who needs to grow up, and I bet that promotion went to someone else,' Gabriel said.

'Actually, it didn't. He's very plausible. He got away with it. I have no idea what happened to his girlfriend, and I'm not interested in knowing.'

'So what does Jeff have to do with me?'

She bit her lip. 'You know I'm on a sabbatical?' At his nod, she continued, 'I thought my number two would take over from me in my absence, but it seems there's been a restructure in the office. Neil—my number two—came to tell me about it today. A new guy's been brought in over him and will probably be my new boss if I go back. And it's the worst coincidence in the world.'

'The new guy's Jeff?'

She nodded. 'I was coming to see you and—well, whine about it, I suppose. And then I heard what you said. And it just brought all my old doubts back. It made me think that I'd let myself be fooled all over again, by someone who was using me to get on in business.'

Gabriel took her hand. 'I'm sorry that you got blind-sided like that, but everyone makes mistakes. Just because you made a mistake trusting him, it doesn't mean that you can't trust anyone ever again.'

'I know that with my head,' she said miserably. 'But it's how I feel *here*.' She pressed one hand to her chest.

'I'm not using you to get on with business, Nicole. I never have.' He raked a hand through his hair. 'Actually I was going to talk to you tonight about the very first wedding in the Electric Palace and the Spice House. I thought it might be nice if it was ours.'

She stared at him. 'You were going to ask me to marry you?'

'You're everything I want in a partner. You make me laugh when I'm in a bad mood. You make my world a brighter place. I'm a better man when I'm with you. But...' He paused.

Yeah. She'd known there was a but. It was a million miles high.

'But?' She needed to face it.

'You need to think about it and decide if I'm what you want. If you can trust me. If you can see that I'm not like Jeff.' He gave her a sad look. 'I thought you saw me clearly, Nicole, that you were the one person in the world who knew me for exactly who I am. But you don't, do you? You're just like everyone else. You see what you want to see.' He dragged in a breath. 'Talk it over with your mum and Jessie, people you do actually trust. And come and find me when you're ready to talk. When you're ready to see me for who I am. And if you don't...' He shrugged. 'Well.'

And then he walked out of the office and closed the door quietly behind him.

CHAPTER TEN

IT WAS REALLY hard to wait and do nothing, but Gabriel knew that Nicole had to make this decision by herself. If she didn't, then at some point in the future she'd feel that he'd railroaded her into it, and it would all go pear-shaped.

Patience was a virtue and a business asset, he reminded himself. He had to stick to it. Even if it was driving him crazy.

The only way he could think of to distract himself was to bury himself in work. So he opened up a file on his computer and started outlining his proposal to take the business in a new direction. If his father wasn't prepared to let him do that, then Gabriel would leave Hunter Hotels and start up on his own. It was something he should probably have done years ago, but it was Nicole's belief in him that had helped him to take the final step and work out what he really wanted to do with his life. But did she believe in him enough to stay with him? Or had her ex destroyed her trust so thoroughly that she'd never be able to believe in anyone else?

He had no idea.

He just had to wait.

And hope.

* * *

Gabriel had walked away from her.

Nicole stared at the closed door.

Of course he'd walked away. She'd leapt to the wrong conclusions and hadn't even given him a chance to explain—she'd just thrown a hissy fit and told him it was over.

By text.

How awful was that?

He'd been the one who'd insisted on talking. He'd made her tell him about Jeff.

And he'd made it clear that she was the one letting her fears get in the way of a future. He'd said she was everything he wanted in a partner. That he wanted them to be the first people to get married in the cinema. But he hadn't tried to persuade her round to his way of thinking, or to make her feel bad about herself, the way Jeff had. He'd acknowledged that she'd been hurt in the past and she was afraid. And he'd said that she was the one who needed to think about it. To decide if he was what she wanted. If she could trust him. If she was ready to see him for who he really was.

He was giving her the choice.

And he'd advised her to talk it over with her mum and Jessie. He'd known this was something she couldn't do on her own, but he was clearly trying not to put pressure on her.

She grabbed her phone. Five minutes later, she'd arranged to meet her mother and Jessie in the park opposite Jessie's school, giving her enough time to nip home and change into clothes that weren't paint-stained and scrub her face.

Both her mum and Jessie greeted her with a hug. 'So what's happened?' Jessie asked.

Nicole explained about Neil's visit and her row with Gabriel. 'He told me to talk it over with people I trusted,' she said. 'Well, with you two.'

'So talk,' Susan said. 'How do you feel about him?'

Nicole thought about it. 'The world feels brighter when he's around.'

'Do you love him?' Jessie asked.

'Isn't that something I should say to him, first?' Nicole countered, panicking slightly.

'He told you to talk it over with us,' Susan pointed out, 'so no. Do you love him?'

Nicole took a deep breath. 'Yes.'

'And is it the same way you felt about Jeff?' Jessie asked.

Nicole shook her head. 'It's different. Gabriel sees me for who I am, not who he wants me to be. I don't worry about things when I'm with him.'

'You said he was a shark in a suit when you first met him,' Susan said thoughtfully.

'You've met him, so you know he isn't like that. He's been scrupulously fair. The problem's *me*.' She closed her eyes briefly. 'I'm too scared to trust in case I make a mistake again.'

'Everyone makes mistakes,' Jessie said.

'That's what Gabriel said. But what if I get it wrong with him?'

'OK—let's look at this the other way,' Susan said. 'Supposing you never saw him again. How would you feel?'

Like she did right now. 'There would be a massive hole in my life. He's not just my partner—he's my friend.'

'So the problem is down to Jeff—because he was a total jerk to you, you're worried that all men are like

that, and if you let them close they'll all treat you like
he did,' Jessie said.

'I guess,' Nicole said.

'Which means you're letting Jeff win,' Susan said
briskly. 'Is that what you want?'

'Of course not—and anyway, I let Gabriel close to me.'

'And did he hurt you?' Jessie asked.

Nicole sighed. 'No. But I hurt him. I overreacted.'

'Just a tad,' Susan said dryly.

'I don't know how to fix this,' Nicole said miserably.

'Yes, you do,' Jessie said. 'Talk to him. Apologise.
Tell him what you told us. Let him into your heart. And
I mean really in, not just giving a little bit of ground.'

'Supposing...?' she began, then let her voice trail off.
She knew she was finding excuses—because she was a
coward and she couldn't believe that Gabriel felt the same
way about her as she did about him.

'Supposing nothing,' Susan said. 'That's your only option, if you really want him in your life. Total honesty.'

'You're right,' she said finally. 'I need to apologise and
tell him how I really feel about him.' And she'd have to
make that leap of faith and trust that it wasn't too late.

Gabriel looked up when he heard the knock on his office door, hoping it was Nicole, and tried not to let the
disappointment show on his face when he saw his father
standing in the doorway.

'I didn't expect to see you,' he said.

Evan scowled. 'You said you'd call me back, and you
didn't.'

The last thing Gabriel wanted right now was a fight.
'I'm sorry,' he said tiredly, and raked a hand through his
hair. 'I got caught up in something.'

'I'm not criticising you,' Evan said, surprising him. 'I

was thinking I'd pushed you too far.' He looked Gabriel straight in the eye. 'We need to talk.'

'Yes, we do.' And this conversation had been a very long time coming. Gabriel paused. 'Do you want a coffee or something?'

'No.'

'OK. I'll tell Janey to hold my calls and I'm not interruptible for the time being.'

When Gabriel came back from seeing his PA, his father was staring out of the window. 'I see the cinema's nearly finished,' Evan remarked.

'Yes. It's a matter of restoring the sun ray on the half-moon outside and redoing the sign and that's it. It's pretty much done indoors, too.' He looked at his father. 'So what's this really about, Dad?'

'Sit down.'

Gabriel compromised by leaning against the edge of his desk.

'I owe you an apology.'

Now he knew why his father had told him to sit down—not to be bossy but to save him from falling over in shock. 'An apology?' He kept his voice very bland so he didn't start another row.

'What you said on the phone—you were right. Your mistake was nearly ten years ago and you're not the same person you were back then. You've grown up.'

'I'm glad you can see that now.'

Evan grimaced. 'I had you on speakerphone at the time. Your mother might have overheard some of what you said.'

Gabriel hid a smile. 'Mum nagged you into apologising?'

'Your mother doesn't nag. She just pointed a few things out to me. All the decisions you've made—some of them I wasn't so sure about at the time, but they've all come good. You have an astute business mind.'

Compliments from his father? Maybe he was dreaming. Surreptitiously, he pinched himself; it hurt, so he knew he really was awake.

'I saw that,' Evan said. 'Am I that much of a monster?'

'As a boss or as a father? And do you really have to ask?'

Evan sighed. 'I just worried about you, that if I wasn't on your case you might slip back into your old ways.'

'Maybe that was a possibility when I was twenty, but I'm not that far off thirty now—so it's not going to happen. I've grown up.'

'I guess I need to stop being a helicopter parent.'

'That,' Gabriel said, 'would be nice, but I guess it'd be hard to change a lifetime's habits.'

'Are you really going to leave the company?'

'Right now, I can't answer that,' Gabriel said. 'It might be better for both of us if I did. Then I can concentrate on being your son instead of having to prove myself to you over and over again at work.'

'You said about taking the business in a new direction. What did you have in mind?' Evan asked.

'We already have the hotels,' Gabriel said, 'for both business and leisure. The logical next step would be to offer holiday stays with a difference.'

'What sort of difference?'

'Quirky properties. Lighthouses, follies, water towers—places with heritage. Think somewhere like Lundy Island.'

'Old places that need restoring carefully?'

Gabriel nodded. 'That's what really interests me. I first started to feel that way when I did the Staithe Hotel, but working on this place and the cinema crystallised it for me.'

'Yes, I noticed you in a few of the photographs on the Electric Palace's website.'

Gabriel let that pass. 'This is what I really want to do. The way I want to take the company for the future. I like the research, looking up all the old documents and then trying to keep the heritage as intact as possible while making the building function well in modern terms. Fitting it all together.' He smiled. 'Hunters' Heritage Holidays. It's not the best title, but it'll do as a working one.'

'You've done a proposal with full costings?'

'Most of it's in my head at the moment,' Gabriel admitted, 'but I've made a start on typing it up.'

'You see things clearly,' Evan said. 'That's a good skill to have. I'd be very stupid to let that skill go elsewhere. And diversification is always a good business strategy.'

'So you'll consider it?'

'Make the case,' Evan said.

But this time Gabriel knew he'd only have to make the case once. He wouldn't have to prove it over and over again, the way he'd had to prove himself ever since university. 'Thanks, Dad. I won't let you down.'

'I know, son.' Evan paused. 'So do I get a guided tour of the cinema?'

'Not today,' Gabriel said. 'I have a few things to sort out with Nicole. But soon.'

Evan actually hugged him. 'Your mother wants you to come to dinner. Soon.'

'I'll call her later today,' Gabriel promised. With luck, by then Nicole would've had enough time to think about it—and with a little more luck he'd be able to take her home and introduce her to his family. As his equal.

After Evan left, Gabriel spent the afternoon working on his proposal. The longer it took Nicole to contact him, the more sure he was that she was going to call everything off.

Or maybe a watched phone never beeped with a text, in the same way that the proverbial watched pot never boiled.

He was called to deal with an issue over the spa and accidentally left his phone on his desk. He came back to find a text from Nicole.

I'm ready to talk. Can we meet in the park by the observatory at half-past five?

Please let this be a good sign, Gabriel thought, and texted her back.

Yes.

Nicole sat on the bench near the observatory, trying to look cool and calm and collected. Inside, she was panicking. Should she have planned some grand gesture to sweep Gabriel off his feet? Should she have spelled out 'sorry' in rose petals, or bought some posh chocolates with a letter piped on each one to spell out a message? Should she have organised a helicopter to whisk them away somewhere for a sumptuous picnic on a deserted beach, or—

And then all the words fell out of her head when she saw Gabriel walking up the path towards her.

He was still wearing a business suit, but he was wearing sunglasses in concession to the brightness of the afternoon. And his expression was absolutely unreadable.

He'd given her nothing to work on with his text reply, either. Just the single word 'yes'.

Help.

This could go so, so wrong.

'Hi.' He stood in front of the bench and gestured to it. 'May I?'

'Sure.' She took a deep breath. 'Gabriel. I'm sorry I hurt you.'

'Uh-huh.'

'I've been an idiot. A huge idiot. Because I was scared. I got spooked, and I should have trusted my instincts. I know you're not like Jeff. I know you're not a cheat or a liar. I know you have integrity.'

'Thank you.'

She still couldn't read his expression. Was he going to forgive her? Or had he, too, spent the time apart thinking about things and decided that she wasn't what he wanted after all?

All she could do now was be honest with him and tell him how she really felt.

'You've been there for me every step of the way. Firstly as Clarence and then as—well, once we realised who each other was in real life, and you made me see that you're not a shark in a suit. And ever since I first met you online, you've become important to me. Really important. I know I've behaved badly. And I'll understand if you don't want anything to do with me any more. But I think the Electric Palace and the Spice House have a lot to offer each other, and we've done so much work on our joint plans—it'd be a shame to abandon them.' She took a deep breath. 'But, most of all, Gabriel, I want you to forgive me and give me a chance to make it up to you. I have to be honest with you—I can't promise that I won't panic ever again. The hurt from what Jeff did went pretty deep. It shattered my confidence in me. I find it hard to believe that anyone can even like me for myself, let alone anything more. But I can promise you that, next time I have a wobble, I'll talk to you about it instead of over-reacting and doing something stupid.'

Still he said nothing.

'I love you, Gabriel,' she said quietly. 'And I don't know what to do about it. I can't turn it into a balance sheet or a schedule or a timetable. It's just there. All the time. I want to be with you. I know you've dated women who just saw you in terms of your bank account, but that's not how I see you. I don't need a huge rock on my finger or a mansion or a flashy car. I just want you. Gabriel Hunter, the man who loves the sea and the stars and very bad puns, who makes my heart beat faster every time he smiles, and who makes even a rough day better because he's *there*.'

'That's what you *really* want?' he asked.

She nodded. 'You told me to think about it, to talk it over with Mum and Jessie, and I have. You're what I want, Gabriel. You and only you. I trust you. And I see you for who you are—the man I want to spend the rest of my life with. If you'll have me. And you're right—it would be pretty cool if the first wedding at the Electric Palace and the Spice House was ours.'

He removed his sunglasses so she could actually see his eyes properly. 'Are you suggesting marriage?'

'Strictly speaking, you suggested it first,' she said. 'But a merger sounds good.'

'Hunter Hotels is my dad's business, not mine. We won't be going into this as equal partners,' he warned.

'Yes, we will. Because this isn't about money or property or business. It's about you and me. That's all that matters. I want to be with you, Gabriel. You make my world a better place and I'm miserable without you.'

'Same here,' he said, and finally he put his arms round

her. 'I love you, Nicole. I think I fell for you when I read that first message on the Surrey Quays forum. I was horrified when I met you and realised that my private friend was my business rival.'

'Except we're not rivals. We're on the same side.'

'Definitely.' He kissed her. 'So will you marry me?'

There was only one thing she could say. 'Yes.'

EPILOGUE

Three months later

GABRIEL, DRESSED IN top hat and tails, walked out of the honeymoon suite at the Spice House Hotel. The suite he'd be sharing with his bride, later tonight.

Everything was ready in the Coriander Suite—the tables were beautifully laid out and decorated for the wedding breakfast.

The Electric Palace was all decked out for a wedding, too. The old cinema was bright and gleaming, the bar in the downstairs foyer perfectly polished with trays of glasses waiting to be filled with champagne, and the Art Deco windows restored to their full splendour. On the walls were the plaque Nicole had unveiled on the opening night—thanking every single member of the Surrey Quays forum who'd helped to restore the cinema—along with framed enlargements of the Kursaal in its heyday and framed posters for *It's a Wonderful Life* and *Mary Poppins*.

There was a garland of ivory roses wound round the bars of the sweeping staircase to the upper floor, and when Gabriel glanced inside the upper room he could see that all the chairs were filled apart from the front row, which was reserved for his parents, Nicole's mother, and the bridesmaid.

The ceiling looked amazing. Just as Nicole had imagined it, the tin was painted dark blue and the stars were picked out in gold. There was an arch in front of the cinema screen, decorated with ivory roses and fairy lights.

All he needed now was to wait for his bride to arrive.

He glanced at his watch. He knew she wouldn't be late—that particular tradition was one that annoyed her hugely. But he was pretty sure she'd arrive exactly one minute early. Just because that was who she was.

The very first wedding in the Electric Palace and the Spice House.

Not because they were using their wedding as a trial run for their businesses, but because the buildings had brought them both together and there wasn't anywhere else in the world that would've been more perfect as their wedding venue.

And at precisely one minute to two the wedding march from Mendelssohn's *A Midsummer Night's Dream* began playing, and Gabriel turned round to watch his bride walking down the aisle towards him, on her mother's arm.

Her hair was up in the Audrey Hepburnesque style she'd worn the night he'd first taken her out to dinner, and the dress had a simple sweetheart neckline with a mermaid train that would look spectacular spread over the staircase. She looked stunning.

But most of all he noticed the expression in her eyes—the sheer, deep love for him. The same love he had for her.

'I love you,' he whispered as she came to stand beside him.

'I love you, too,' she whispered, and they joined hands, ready to join their lives together.

* * * * *

"Johnny talked about you from time to time, but I gather he said little about me."

"He mentioned R.T. a couple of times but no, he didn't say much. But then he didn't talk much about his friends in the Rangers or later. It was like when he came home, he turned all that off."

"Probably wise," Ryker said. He washed down a mouthful of bagel with some coffee. "Compart-mentalizing, we call it. Keeping things separate. Why would he want to bring any of that home to you?"

"But he talked about me," she argued.

"Once in a while. Sometimes everyone talked about home. Sometimes we needed to remember that there was a place or a person we wanted to get back to. The rest of the time we couldn't afford the luxury."

That hit her hard, but she faced it head-on. Remembering home had been a luxury? That might have been the most important thing anyone had told her about what Johnny had faced and done.

"I didn't know him at all," she whispered, squeezing her eyes shut, once again feeling the shaft of pain.

"You knew the best part of him. That mattered to him, Marisa. You gave him a place where that part could flourish."

* * *

Conard County:
The Next Generation

AN UNLIKELY DADDY

BY
RACHEL LEE

First Published in Great Britain 2016
By Mills & Boon, an imprint of HarperCollins*Publishers*
1 London Bridge Street, London, SE1 9GF

© 2016 Susan Civil Brown

ISBN: 978-0-263-92008-6

23-0816

Rachel Lee was hooked on writing by the age of twelve and practiced her craft as she moved from place to place all over the United States. This *New York Times* best-selling author now resides in Florida and has the joy of writing full-time.

To all the heroes whose stories will never be told.

Prologue

Marisa Hayes stood atop a hill in the Good Shepherd Cemetery in Conard County, Wyoming. The ceaseless spring wind seemed to blow through her hollow heart, sweeping away her life. Johnny's coffin, wood and brass, sat atop the bier, ready to be lowered. Beneath it a strip of artificial turf covered the gaping hole in the ground that would soon contain him. The green swatch was an affront to the brown ground all around.

She couldn't move. Pain so strong it was almost beyond feeling, a strange kind of agonized numbness, filled her. Several men were waiting to lower the casket. A few of her friends waited behind her, giving her space and time. Dimly she realized they must be growing impatient as time continued its inexorable march into a future she wished would go away.

Beyond the coffin she saw the tombstones of others

who had left this life before Johnny, generations of markers, some newer, some so old they tilted. Plastic flowers brought artificial color here and there to a comfortless landscape. No well-tended ground, this. No neatly trimmed lawns and shrubs trying to create an impression of life amidst death. Just the scrubby natural countryside, tamed to a level one could walk through, but no more. A couple of tumbleweeds had rolled in and hung up just since she arrived here. They'd move on soon. Everything moved on. Time stole everything, one way or another.

Her hand rested against her still-flat belly. She'd never had a chance to tell Johnny. If she believed the pastor, her husband knew. She wasn't sure if she believed the pastor. Right now she didn't know if she believed in afterlife, God or anything at all.

What she believed in was her pain. What she believed in was that she was carrying Johnny's baby. What she believed was that when she had tried to Skype him, to tell him, she had been told he was out, they'd give him a message. What she believed was that the next thing she heard was that Johnny was dead.

No open coffin. They'd warned against it. The funeral director had practically fallen on his knees, begging her not to demand it. Telling her that some images were best not remembered. Telling her to remember Johnny alive.

If the funeral director couldn't pretty it up…

But, no, she refused to go there. It was the one piece of advice she had taken. Holding the folded flag in her arms, against her baby, she could still hear the ring of "Taps" on the desolate air, could still feel the moment she had accepted that flag, as if it were the moment she had accepted Johnny's death. Then the man, someone she didn't know, a State Department official who had given his name, as if she cared, had said, "John was a true hero."

So? He was a dead hero, and his widow just wanted to climb into that hole beside him.

She lifted her gaze to the insensitive blue sky, wondering why it wasn't gray and weeping, the way her heart wept. Why thunder and lightning weren't rending the heavens the way her heart was rent.

She thought about burying the flag with Johnny. Just marching the four steps and placing it on the coffin. He'd earned that flag, not her, and right now it felt almost like an insult, not an honor. But she didn't do it. The baby. Someday the child within her might want this flag, all it would ever have of its father except a few photographs. Maybe someday it would even mean something to *her*.

"Marisa." Julie's quiet voice, near her. A touch on her arm. "We need to go."

"Then go."

"I think I was including you in that."

She turned her head, her neck feeling stiff, and looked straight into Julie's worried face. "I…can't."

"Yes, you can. Come on, hon. You can come back tomorrow if you want. You can come every single day. But right now…"

Right now people were waiting for her, waiting to take her home, waiting to put Johnny in the ground. When she came back tomorrow, the turf would still be there, covering the bare, freshly turned earth. But Johnny's coffin wouldn't be where she could see it. His final home.

Numbly she nodded, facing the inevitable. Everything seemed inevitable now. She felt like a leaf caught in a rushing river's grip, unable to stop anything, unable to catch her breath, unable find the shore. Adrift, banging from one rock to the next, helpless.

Despite Julie's entreaties, she walked up to the coffin and laid her hand on the cold, polished wood. "I love you," she whispered, hoping he could hear, fearing he couldn't.

Then, jerking with every single movement as if her body belonged to someone else, she allowed Julie to lead her back to her friends and the row of cars.

It was over. Tomorrow loomed like a devouring dragon. She hoped it devoured her.

Chapter One

Ryker Tremaine pulled up to the Hayes house on a frigid November night and looked at it from within the warm confines of his car. He needed to go in there, introduce himself to John's widow and start making amends. He suspected what John's death had cost Marisa, but it was only when word had sifted back to him that she was pregnant that he realized he had a whole hell of a lot of atoning to do. Because of him there was not only a widow, but a fatherless child.

He had some stains on his soul, but this one felt bigger than most, and some were pretty big.

It was a large house. He knew it had been in John's family for generations, because John had told him. It was, in John's mind, a safe place for Marisa to stay. She had grown up around here, too. She had a job at the community college, she had friends to look after her when her husband was away. And neither of them had any family left, odd as that seemed. Even Ryker, at almost forty, had parents who had retired to New Mexico and a sister who had married a sheep rancher from New Zealand. Somehow Marisa and John, through the vicissitudes of illness and life, had been left alone.

And now Marisa had no one but friends. Had she been blessed with a big family, he'd have felt his mission of repentance was pointless. But there was a woman and a baby who John Hayes couldn't look after. He owed something to John, to that woman and to that baby.

Just what, he wasn't sure. Conscience and a vague promise to John had driven him here, and now conscience kept him inside the car when he should have just strode up to the door and introduced himself.

She'd had nearly six months. Maybe someone out of her husband's past would only refresh her grief. And maybe he was making excuses because he dreaded this whole thing.

He wasn't a chicken by nature.

Sighing, he glanced in the rearview mirror, taking stock as much as he could. He'd ditched the suit because it was too much around here, and had settled on a sweater, jeans and a jacket. He didn't want this to look official, or remind her of bad things more than necessary.

But he continued to sit in the car a little while longer, wondering if this was just a huge act of selfishness on his part. He'd been wrestling with that since the thought of coming here had first begun goading him.

Penance was fine, as long as it didn't inflict pain on someone else. Atonement should make things better, not worse. He shouldn't salve his own guilt by worsening her pain.

He'd finally gotten to the point where he could no longer tell what was right or wrong, whether he was being selfish or paying a debt he owed a friend.

There was only one way to find out. That was to knock on the door and introduce himself. If she told him to go to hell, he'd have his answer. And maybe that wouldn't freshen her grief too much, just to hear someone say, "John was my friend."

Finally, he climbed out of the car, crunched his way across a sidewalk covered with rock salt and went up the porch steps. Icicles hung from the eaves, probably from a recent, brief thaw. If she didn't tell him to get out of her life immediately, he should knock them down. They weren't huge, but they could be dangerous, and she shouldn't do it herself in her condition.

At last he could avoid the moment no longer. The doorbell glowed, demanding he punch it and then face whatever came. Usually that wasn't a problem for him. Most things in his life had come at him the hard way. But this time…well, this time was different.

He rang the bell. He waited as the winter night deepened. She must be gone. Well, he'd come back tomorrow.

Then he heard the doorknob turn and the door opened. He recognized her instantly from photos John had shown him. Long ash-blond hair, eyes that were shaded somewhere between blue and lavender, set in a heart-shaped face. Her lips, soft and just full enough, framed the faintest of quizzical smiles. And her belly… He couldn't help but look at the mound. John's baby, due in a few months.

"May I help you?" Her voice was light, pleasant, but cautious.

He dragged his gaze to her face, understanding in an instant what had drawn John to her. Surprise shook him as attraction gut-punched him. He figured he must be plumbing new depths of ugliness. His friend's pregnant widow? Off-limits. He cleared his throat. "Hi," he said. "My name's Ryker Tremaine."

If he expected her to recognize it, he was disappointed. Her brow creased slightly. "Yes?" No recognition, nothing.

"I was John's friend," he announced baldly. "We worked together at…State. Before that, a few times when he was in the Rangers."

Her smile faded, but at least she didn't pale. "He never mentioned you."

He'd anticipated this possibility. The question was whether he should just walk away or press. He nodded. "He used to call me R.T."

"R.T.?" The furrow deepened, and then recognition dawned. "Oh. Oh! I thought he was saying Artie. Short for…" She clapped her hand to her mouth, as if containing something, and her face paled a little. "You were with him."

"Not that day," he said evenly. This wasn't going the way he'd imagined, good or bad. "I'm sorry. I'll leave you alone. I just…when I heard you were…" He glanced down.

Her hand dropped from her mouth to the mound of her belly. "Oh." She sounded faint and closed her eyes. Then they opened, blue fire. "Is there a reason for this visit after all this time?"

"I couldn't get away when…" He didn't want to say funeral. "Then I thought it was too late. And then I heard about… Maybe you have some questions I can answer."

At once he wanted to kick himself, because those were questions he mostly couldn't answer. He was usually better than this. Smoother. This was turning into a hash. "I've been out of the country," he finished finally. That was absolutely true.

She looked down. He braced for her to tell him to go to hell, a place he was intimately familiar with. But then, with a visible shake, she said, "Come in. I'm going to freeze standing here." She stepped back, allowing him to pass.

The house was warm and quiet except for the laboring forced air heat. A pleasantly sized foyer welcomed him, speaking of age and care. She pointed to his right. "Get yourself a seat in there. Do you want a hot drink?"

"I'm fine, Mrs. Hayes. If you want something, don't mind me. I'm not trying to impose."

But that was exactly what he was doing, he thought as he watched her walk away toward what was presumably a kitchen. She wore jeans and a bulky blue sweatshirt that reached to her hips, with the sleeves pushed up. He would have bet that sweatshirt had belonged to John, and now it was doing double duty as a maternity top.

He stepped into a cozy living room, a collection of aging and mismatched pieces that somehow came together to create a quietly colorful charm. He settled on a goosenecked chair covered with worn burgundy damask, only to pop to his feet again as she returned carrying a glass of milk. She took the other chair, a rocker, probably easier for her to get in and out of these days than the sofa across from them. He sat when she did.

Then the silence grew almost leaden. He let her study him while trying not to return her stare. She hadn't suggested he remove his jacket, so she wanted to keep this short. Fine by him. He could come back tomorrow.

She broke the silence. "You got him the job with the State Department."

If she'd etched the words with acid, they couldn't have stung anymore. "Guilty," he admitted. And of a whole lot more besides.

"Did he know?" she asked.

"Know what?"

"How dangerous it might be?"

God in heaven, that was a question with no right answer. Truth, he decided. As much truth as he could offer. "Yes."

"As dangerous as being in the Rangers?"

Again he offered the truth. "It wasn't supposed to be."

She closed her eyes again, and he noted that she was rocking a little faster. "They won't tell me the truth," she murmured. "They said it was a mugging." Her eyes snapped open. "I know Johnny. No mugger could have taken him."

It was true. But it was equally true that they'd given him the same story. "They told me the same thing. A street mugging." Initially. Unfortunately, he couldn't reveal the little he'd learned later without revealing operational secrets. God, he'd been a fool not to have considered all the secrets he'd have to continue to keep. But still, he owed this woman and her child something.

Her gaze bored into him. "Do you believe it?"

"I...found it difficult. But..." He hesitated, choosing his words carefully. Some things he knew couldn't be shared. Other than that, he knew almost nothing. "Muggings, street violence, in other places...well, they aren't what we know here. And it's pretty bad in some places here."

Her rocking slowed, and he watched tension seep out of her. At last she lifted her milk and sipped it. "So you're as much in the dark as I am."

He chose not to answer.

Then she smiled faintly. "So you're R.T. And here I thought you were an Arthur. Why didn't you ever visit when he was home?"

"Because," he said with perfect truth, "when John came home, all he wanted to do was be with you. I wouldn't have intruded even if he had asked me."

Marisa felt the words burrow straight to her heart like a spike. Reminding her of her loss, a loss that walked beside her every waking minute and during sleep sometimes, as well. But she heard the truth in them. He *had* known Johnny, because once she had suggested that he bring home some of his friends to visit. His answer had been, "I'm selfish. When I'm home I want you all to myself."

She studied this Ryker Tremaine, this ghost out of John's past. She saw in him the same hardness that she had sometimes seen in Johnny. Men who had faced death in the service of a cause. It changed them, gave them an edge.

A tall man, solid, with a face etched by many suns and hardships into a near rocky definition. A square face, with eyes almost like midnight and a strong jaw. He had been pared, the way she had watched Johnny get pared by his experiences. Honed, like fine knives.

Seeing Johnny in him, seeing a resemblance in their characters, eased her doubts even more. She'd invited a stranger in, and now she recognized him. Johnny's ilk. Johnny's friend. Certainly someone who had walked the same difficult, secretive paths.

"Why are you here?" she asked.

"John wanted it. Because…" She watched him hesitate, wondering what he was withholding. "Because I care." That at least sounded true.

"Did he ask you to come?"

Ryker shook his head. "Not exactly. This wasn't supposed to happen. But after he started working at State, yes, he did ask me to check on you. I wasn't sure if he wanted me to come or just call you."

She could believe that. The fist that had been clenching her heart, since she'd realized Ryker was part of Johnny's history, loosened its grip a bit. "I'm sorry," she said. "I don't mean to be cold. It must be hard for you, too."

Something passed quickly over his face, then he said bluntly, "It's been hell. Not your kind of hell, I'm sure, but it's been hell."

She felt a little warmth for him then. Though she hadn't thought much about it, Johnny must have left other people grieving, too. Like an old friend named Ryker Tremaine. "You want to talk about him?"

"If you want to."

"I have some gaps I'd like filled in."

Again that odd hesitation from him, but then he explained, "Within the bounds of operational secrecy. You must have heard that from John."

Words she had come to hate, because they had left her with huge holes in her memory of Johnny. Things she would never know, things he couldn't share. Maybe even some things he didn't want to share, which she could understand. But now, with an empty future in front of her, she was hungry to fill in that unknown past. Things he had done and seen but had never mentioned.

She rocked a little more, feeling her child stirring inside her. She laid her hand over her belly, feeling the active little pokes. A girl. She'd kept that to herself, as well.

"Johnny didn't know we were going to have a baby," she said. One of her greatest pains, laid bare now to a stranger. "I called to tell him, but he wasn't there, and then…"

"I just heard about it recently. Evidently John wasn't the only one who didn't know."

She nodded, absorbing the betrayal again. He should have at least known about his baby before he was killed. It seemed so wrong that he didn't.

"He'd have been happy," Ryker offered.

"I suppose." Another resentment bubbled up inside her, one she tried to bury, but one she couldn't quite quell. "He was gone a lot. Did he tell you how we met?"

"You grew up together."

"Not quite. He was older. A senior in high school when I was in seventh grade. I had a crush on him, but he didn't know it until much, much later. I was in my last year of college when he came home on a visit and noticed me. Really noticed me. We were married the day after I graduated. Then he was off again."

"It was hard on you." It didn't sound like a question.

"Of course. But he laid it all out. I knew what it would be like. What mattered was that we loved each other."

Ryker nodded. "Of course. I know he loved you more than anything on this earth."

She felt her mouth twist. "Not quite. The Rangers were his first love. No competition there."

Ryker surprised her then. He leaned forward, putting his elbows on his knees. "I wouldn't say that. I listened to him talk about you. Man, did he brag when you got your master's degree. When you started teaching at the college here. He was so proud of you."

"I was proud of him, too," she answered simply. "I still am." Then the grief speared her again. "When he took the job with the State Department, I thought he'd be safer!"

"He should have been, Marisa."

Anguish twisted her gut. The baby reacted, kicking hard. "Well, he wasn't."

Ryker didn't answer, not that she could blame him. How did you respond to that? She had no answers for herself, so how could anyone else? She leaned back in the rocker, giving her lungs a little more room, feeling the baby's agitation like scalding criticism. She had to remain calm for her daughter.

Ryker remained silent, a sphinx full of secrets he was no more likely to share than Johnny had been. Why had he come? Because of Johnny? Probably. But to what purpose? What could he possibly do to make any of this better? "I don't see the point of you coming."

"To help in whatever way I can. Just to talk if that's all you want from me. But I'm going to stay in town for a while, Marisa. I know my arrival is a shock, and I'm sorry. But I owe something to John."

"John's past caring," she said bitterly.

"Not for me he isn't. And if there's anything I can do for you, I'll do it, even if it's just knocking down the icicles out front."

She looked at him again and couldn't mistake his determination. Wherever Johnny's loss had forced her, it was clearly pushing this man, too. So they had something in common. Little enough.

She closed her eyes again, rocking gently, feeling her baby settle down, the pokes lessening. Peace returning. A hard-won peace. Acceptance hadn't come easily, but it had come, although it hadn't eased her grief one bit yet.

If there was any blessing in all of this, it was that during her marriage she'd grown accustomed to Johnny's long absences. She didn't expect to see him around every corner, didn't expect to wake to find him beside her in bed, didn't keep listening for the sound of his voice. Not every waking moment prodded her with reminders of his absence.

But the grief, anger and sometimes even despair often rolled over her like a tsunami, irresistible and agonizing. For all the holes in the past, there was a bigger one in the present.

Let it go, just let it go. The man nearby was grieving, too. Maybe together they could find some answers for each other. Not that life offered many answers. Things just seemed to happen.

She looked at Ryker again. He studied his hands, or maybe the floor. She couldn't tell which. "How long will you be in town?"

"I don't know. I *do* know that I'm not leaving immediately. And I have quite a bit of time."

Meaning what, exactly? "So you were with Johnny in the Rangers, too?"

"We worked together on a number of missions."

She accepted that, for now at least. "When he joined the State Department, I thought we'd be traveling a lot. I was looking forward to it. Only he got sent somewhere families can't go."

"I know. There are a lot of those places, unfortunately."

"So what do you do?"

His smile was almost crooked. "Security. Keeping the embassy or consulates safe, and most especially the people who work there."

"Johnny was a translator." But of course he knew that. Her husband had a gift for languages. He soaked them up the way the grass soaked up the rain. She'd never found out exactly how many of them he knew. But then she'd never asked him to count them for her. When they'd been together, other things had seemed so much more important, the sharing and caring and lovemaking. The occasional time with old friends, but mostly... She lifted her head. "Our marriage was like one long honeymoon. When he was home we might as well have been on our own planet."

Ryker's face shadowed. "That's wonderful."

"I thought so. We never had enough time to take one another for granted." Why was she telling him this? Was she reminding herself? Was it important somehow? "But one thing I took for granted was that we'd have a future. No matter where he went, I always believed he'd come home. I was a fool."

"You were an optimist," he corrected firmly. "How else could you do it?"

Good question, she supposed. No answer, but still a good question.

He spoke again. "Some of us do things with our lives that are very unfair to the people we love."

"Are you married?"

He shook his head. "I envied John. He was happy with you, he trusted that you were strong enough to handle all this. I could never trust that much."

"Maybe you were kinder." She hated herself for saying it, but there it was. Johnny had trusted her to be able to handle *this*?

"No, I wasn't kinder," he said. "More selfish. Love 'em and leave 'em, that was me. My romantic past is strewn with ugliness. John at least made a commitment, tried to build something good. I not only envied him, I admired him for it." Then he offered her something approximating a smile. "But then I never met a woman like you."

"Meaning?"

"One who could put up with this. They always wanted me to change. You didn't try to change John. Pretty special."

"Trying to change someone is pointless." Of this she was certain. "We are who we are, and if you can't love someone just the way they are, then you don't love them."

"There's a lot of wisdom in that."

"Just truth." She sighed. Facing up to reality again. Always painful these days. "So you weren't with John when this happened?"

"I was in another country. A little far away to be of any use."

"Johnny could take care of himself," she said. "I guess that's what's bugging me as much as anything. He could take care of himself. This shouldn't have happened."

Ryker stirred. "No, it shouldn't have. But a lot of things shouldn't happen. I live in a world where things that shouldn't happen often do. I'm just sorry you got dragged into it. I'm sorry John didn't make it. I'm sorry as hell I got him the job. And I wish it had been my funeral, not his."

She couldn't doubt him, but this wasn't right. She

felt a stirring of self-disgust. All her dumping had done was make this man feel worse about something that had been out of his control. What kind of shrew was she becoming?

"Don't say that, Ryker. Please. I'm not attacking you."

"Why not? I deserve it. I saw my good friend talking about changing careers, and I found him a job. It's my fault you're grieving, and I know it. I should have just told him to come home to you and become a shopkeeper or something."

That had the oddest effect on her. It booted her right out of her misery to a place where she could actually see some humor. The shift was instantaneous and shocking. She actually laughed. It sounded rusty, but it was real. "Tell me," she said, "do you really think Johnny would have done that? Do you think he'd have taken that job you got him if it wasn't what he really wanted to do? Come on, Ryker. Let's be honest here. Johnny was Johnny, and he'd have made a lousy shopkeeper."

Astonishingly, he smiled. It was a beautiful expression, erasing all the hardness from his face, nearly lighting up the room. Her heart quickened, but she barely noticed. "You're right," he said.

"Of course I'm right. He was an adventurer at heart. I knew it. I walked into it with my eyes open. That's not making this hurt any less, but there was no way I was going to keep him stapled to my side for fifty years. If not this, then something else."

He sat up, half nodding, half shaking his head. "Probably," he agreed, then made an effort to change the subject. "Are you still teaching?"

"I'm on sabbatical until next fall." She paused, then decided her reasoning needn't be kept private. "It felt like too much to deal with—the baby, Johnny's death. I couldn't have focused on teaching. So I decided to focus on getting through this year, having the baby and taking some time to be a mother. Fall will be soon enough."

Soon enough to try to resume a full life. Right now she wanted no part of it. Her life was all in a shambles, and she felt like she had to glue some of the pieces back together before she'd be any use to anyone. She tried to think of it as convalescence. Maybe it was sheer cowardice. An unwillingness to face more of the world than she had to, to deal with constant reminders that life went on. To deal with students who were young enough to be cheerfully falling in love or agonizing over not being asked for a date. For young people, even minor things were magnified. For her, she didn't need a magnifying glass. She doubted she'd have patience for all that. She even doubted whether she'd be focused enough to be a good teacher.

Life had become an unending blur of pain punctuated by moments when she felt the joy of the coming child. A stark contrast that left her feeling continually off balance.

Ryker drew her attention back to him by rising. "I didn't mean to intrude for so long. I just wanted you to know that I'm here. If it's okay, I'll stop by again in the morning."

She didn't move. "Where are you staying?"

"At the motel."

She sighed. "Lovely place."

"I've stayed in worse." He moved toward the door. "Don't see me out. And like I said, I'll stop by in the morning. I don't know about you, but I need some rest. Still adjusting to a major clock change. Jet lag."

She looked up at him. "Where did you fly in from?"

A half smile. "Quite a few time zones to the east. Even more if you count to the west."

A pang struck her. "Johnny used to say something like that. Really helpful."

"I told you…"

She waved a hand. "I get it. Operational security."

He paused and offered his hand. Reluctantly she took it, feeling warm, work-hardened skin. So familiar, but from a stranger. "Ryker…"

"We can talk more tomorrow." He gave her hand a squeeze, then let himself out.

When Marisa heard the front door close, she felt at once a sense of relief and one of disappointment. There was more she wanted to ask. A lot more.

Well, he said he'd come back. Then she sat rocking and thinking about Ryker Tremaine. She didn't quite trust him, even if he had been Johnny's friend. How could she? He wouldn't give her any more answers than her husband had.

Men who lived in the shadows, both of them. After all these years she was just beginning to understand how much.

Finally she rose, rubbing her back a bit, and went to lock the front door, something she didn't usually do.

But the simple fact was, a stranger had come to her door, claiming to know Johnny. Maybe he did, but that alone didn't make him trustworthy.

In all, the situation felt wrong. After all these months? Out of the blue without warning? Not even a condolence card? While she wasn't yet prepared to reject the possibility that he was the "Artie" Johnny had sometimes mentioned, even that alone wasn't enough to create trust.

He was a stranger. And while she might not care all that much about her own life, she *did* care about her baby.

When at last she went to bed, she rested on her side, feeling her daughter's gentle stirrings, and staring into the darkness. She thought of Johnny, which was slowly growing easier, she thought about the child who would soon join her in this world and she thought about Ryker Tremaine.

Her sense of him was that he was a lot like Johnny in some ways. But different, too. Maybe even harder.

Or maybe this visit had been as difficult for him as it had been for her. She couldn't imagine why he was planning to stay, was troubled by the fact that he wouldn't say for how long, and realized that another box of secrets had just walked into her life.

Like she needed more of that. At last sleep freed her, giving her gentle dreams for a change, offering escape from a world that had too many hard edges.

Morning would come. Somehow, to her everlasting sorrow, it always did.

Chapter Two

Rising before the sun. The phrase had amused Marisa since childhood, especially since she was climbing out of bed at the same time as usual. The sun's winter-delayed arrival always made her feel cozy somehow, and this morning was no different. By the time she finished showering and dressing in one of Johnny's old flannel shirts and maternity jeans, faint gray light began to appear around the edges of the curtains.

In the kitchen she made her allotted few cups of coffee and decided to eat cinnamon oatmeal for breakfast. With a glass of milk, she swallowed her prenatal vitamin while she stirred the oatmeal.

She had just poured the oatmeal from the pan into the bowl when she heard a knock at her side door. Looking over, she saw Julie standing there and waving. Immediately she went to let her in.

"Gawd, it's cold out there this morning," Julie said, pulling back her hood and shaking out her long auburn hair. Green eyes danced. "Be glad you don't have to be anywhere. After that thaw last week, it feels like an insult. Oatmeal, huh?"

"Want me to make you some?"

"Sweetie, I already gorged on Danish and coffee. Unlike you, I don't have to worry about healthy eating."

Marisa laughed lightly. "Not yet, anyway."

"I know, I know, it'll catch up with me. All our sins do. So, dish."

"Dish?"

Julie pulled out a chair without unzipping her jacket and sat, arching a brow at her. "Did you really think a mysterious man could show up on your doorstep last evening and that your neighbor Fiona would miss it? Or that she wouldn't call me and probably half the rest of the town? Sit, eat."

Marisa brought the bowl of oatmeal and a milky mug of coffee to the table. Julie eyed the coffee. "Still on restriction?"

Marisa shook her head. "Not now. The doc says I can have more, it's not risky. But now…I don't want any more."

"Hah. They retrain us. Anyway, the guy last night."

"Fiona. Does she report on every breath I take?"

"You know her better than that. But last night was something new. Everyone needs something new to talk about. So, who was he?" Julie waited eagerly.

"He says he worked with Johnny for years."

Julie's smile faded. "What's wrong, Marisa? Did he scare you?"

"I don't know what to make of him, that's all. He said

a few things, so yes he knew Johnny but…it seems kind of late to be making a social call. He certainly doesn't know me. And he's talking about Johnny wanting him to check on me."

"Well, that sounds like Johnny."

Marisa's head popped up, a spoonful of oatmeal in her hand. "What do you mean by that?"

Julie bit her lip, finally shrugged and said, "Johnny asked me to keep an eye on you if… Well, you get it."

"He did?" Anger billowed in Marisa. "He asked you that, and you never told me?"

Julie put up a hand. "He asked me not to. Don't bite my head off. But, frankly, I could see his point."

Marisa put down her spoon and gripped the edge of the table. "See what point?"

"The point that he was going away for months at a time to do a dangerous job, and sometimes his feet touched ground long enough to worry about *you*. He didn't want to share that with you because you might worry about him more. It was always understood, wasn't it, that Johnny would come home?"

The oatmeal was beginning to congeal. Marisa pushed it to the side, her appetite utterly gone. More secrets, now one that had been shared with her best friend. What else hadn't Johnny told her? She guessed at some of it, but now she wondered. "What else?"

"That was it," Julie answered quietly. "You know Johnny. He made light of it when he asked me, but I could tell he was serious. I'd have looked after you, anyway. You're my best friend."

Numbness was slowly replacing anger. Julie popped up. "Let me make you some fresh oatmeal."

"I don't want it anymore. Maybe I'll make some later."

Julie paused beside her, squeezing her shoulder. "I didn't mean to upset you. I honestly didn't think that telling you that would."

"No?" Craning her neck, Marisa looked up at her. "How many other things didn't he tell me?"

"God," Julie breathed. Slowly she returned to her chair. "Don't take it like that. We all know he couldn't talk about his work. It wasn't like he was running around confiding in everyone except you. That was it, Marisa, I swear. Given that he had a dangerous job, why should it surprise anyone that he asked a handful of close people to help you out if something went wrong? Seems more thoughtful than secretive to me."

Maybe Julie was right. Gripping her mug in both hands, Marisa tried to swallow the coffee before it cooled down too much and warmed her not at all. But this on the heels of last night…she felt alarm flags popping up inside her. Had she ever known her husband at all?

"Damn it," Julie muttered. "The last thing on earth I wanted to do was make you feel bad. I just came over to hear about Mr. Mysterious, and look what I've done."

Marisa didn't answer immediately. Julie had been her friend since kindergarten, and she had to believe her. So Johnny had been worried. Well, he'd kind of explained the possibility when they were dating. He'd been in the Rangers, after all. Going into combat and who knew what else. She certainly didn't. How would anything have changed if he'd told her he'd asked friends to check on her if something happened? Not at all. She would still have moved forward with the certainty that he would always return, because any other possibility was unthinkable. Johnny had seemed to believe that himself. Maybe she was more troubled by the realization that he'd been acutely aware that he might not come back. If so, he hadn't shared that with her. Another in his long line of omissions, most of which hadn't bothered her. So why was this getting to her?

"So," Julie said eventually, "I've got only a few minutes before I have to get to work. I want to hear about this friend of Johnny's."

Marisa struggled back to the present moment. "Not much to say. He's in town for a few days. He wanted to see how I was doing mainly because Johnny asked him to at one time or another."

"But it took him six months to get here?"

Marisa nodded. "Same kind of job as Johnny's. Anyway, I gather from what he said that he heard I was pregnant and that galvanized him to get here. He said something about how Johnny had mentioned that I was safe here, among friends. So maybe it didn't seem all that critical."

"Or," Julie said fairly, "he simply couldn't get away."

"Maybe."

"So…" Julie grinned. "Is he gorgeous?"

"Julie!" Marisa's shock caused her to gasp. "Are you kidding?"

"No, perfectly serious. Johnny wouldn't want you to bury yourself, and a calendar is a poor way to measure grief. I always thought that old thing about wearing widows weeds for a year was a bit over the top. I mean, you grieve however long you grieve. There's not some magic date when it stops. As for everything else—" she pushed back from the table and stood "—you're still here, hon. You should snap at anything good that happens by, or the next fifty years are going to be awful. At least enjoy having a new face around for a few days. I'm off!"

Anything good that happens by? Really? Emotionally she still felt like a train wreck most of the time. Snap at life? The only snapping she'd like to do was angry.

Then her baby stirred again, reminding her she did indeed have to carry on. She scraped the oatmeal into the trash and made herself a fresh bowl to eat with her second cup of coffee.

Slowly, as the warm oatmeal and coffee hit her system, calm began to settle over her. When she was done eating, she sat for a while with her eyes closed, her hands on her belly, and concentrated on the new life growing inside her.

She already loved her child. It hadn't taken long for that to happen. At first, during the darkest days, she'd hated her pregnancy almost as if it were a promise that would never be fulfilled. She'd gone through the motions of taking care of herself only because she had to. But then had come the day when she had felt the first movement. Even in the midnight of her soul, she'd felt an incredible burst of joy, a connection she had never imagined possible before she even saw the child. Her baby was growing inside her, and it was indeed a promise. Her child, her love. An unbreakable link was forged with those first tiny, almost bubble-like movements.

The future *did* hold something good, she reminded herself. It held this baby, Johnny's final gift, a new life she needed to live for and work for. A purpose, a joy, a journey. Her imaginings might have turned to dust with Johnny, but now there were new imaginings. Maybe it was time to quit fighting with herself and just get on with setting up the nursery, making sure she had everything a baby would need. Maybe it was time to accept Julie's repeated offer of a baby shower. Time to stiffen her spine and start taking steps of her own choice into all the tomorrows to come.

Because if she was sure of anything, it was that she couldn't remain like this, paralyzed and hunkered down. If she didn't change it now, she'd be changing it in a few months because life would force it on her.

Maybe it was time to stop being a victim.

The doorbell rang shortly after she finished washing her breakfast dishes and absently wiping the counters clean. Ryker, she thought. No one else she knew in Conard City would come by at this time of day. She'd half expected never to see him again. She hadn't been exactly welcoming last night, and he could have called his duty to Johnny done. He'd checked on her. What more could Johnny have expected of him, of a man who was a stranger to her?

She dried her hands on a towel, smoothed her still-damp hair back quickly, then went to answer the door. She half hoped it was Fiona, who lived next door, coming to try to pry some more gossip out of her. Fiona, she often thought, needed to get a job now that her two children spent all day in school. She clearly didn't have enough to do with her time. Of course, who was Marisa to criticize anyone else for that?

But as she had half feared, she opened the door to see Ryker. He looked more rested, his face less like granite this morning. Sunlight reflected almost blindingly off the snow.

"Good morning," he said pleasantly. He offered a small white bag. "Bagels from your local bakery. I figured they couldn't be too bad for you. Want me to knock down those icicles?"

She felt as if a whirlwind had just blown into her quiet life. "The icicles are really bothering you," she remarked, suddenly remembering that he'd mentioned them last night.

He glanced over his shoulder. "Most of them aren't too dangerous, but why let them grow? Got a broomstick?"

Arguing seemed utterly pointless. She gave him her broom, then listened to the dull thuds from the porch as he took down the icicles. In the kitchen, she opened the bag he'd brought, and her nose immediately filled with the amazing smell of oven-fresh bagels. For the first time that morning, she became genuinely hungry. Melinda, the bakery owner, had also tossed in a few small containers of cream cheese. At that point it seemed churlish not to set out a couple of plates and make some fresh coffee.

Ryker came in, bringing the cold and the broom with him. "All done. Where should I put this?"

She pointed to the pantry door at the back of the kitchen. "Just inside there. Thank you."

"Safety, that's my thing," he said as he put the broom away and shucked his jacket, revealing a gray flannel shirt that made his eyes and hair look even darker. "How are you this morning?"

"I'm okay." It was the best she could say. "I made coffee to go with the bagels. Do you drink it?"

"By the gallon. But you don't have to feed me just because—"

She interrupted him, feeling a sense of desperation. "Let's get past this, okay? Maybe you showed up out of nowhere without any warning. Maybe I don't know you from Adam, but you're here because of Johnny. One way or another we should both respect his wishes. He wanted you to check on me. I'm not going to tell you to get lost, at least not right away. You brought breakfast, which was nice, and I do have enough manners left to invite you to enjoy it with me. Okay?"

For a couple of seconds he didn't move, then a smile spread slowly. "Cutting to the chase, huh?"

"As much as I can. We can spend the next few hours fencing around, but honestly, I hate wasting time like that. Especially now. Sit down. Eat. I'll join you. Thank you for the bagels."

With a snort like a laugh, he took the chair she indicated at the kitchen table. The bagels were already sliced, so all they had to do was spread the cream cheese. Melinda, the bakery owner, had remembered that Marisa liked hers with chives. She hadn't had room to feel much outside her own pained universe for the past few months, but she was touched now by Melinda's thoughtfulness. So many good people around here, and she'd been avoiding most of them.

Maybe Ryker's arrival had jarred her out of her self-preoccupation. Was grief selfish? She supposed it was.

At least he didn't tell her to sit while he got the coffee, or otherwise imply that she wasn't perfectly healthy. Lately, on the rare occasions she visited with her friends, they wanted her to let them take care of everything, as if she were an invalid. She understood they felt helpless to do much about anything else, but really, she was in good health and capable of getting a cup of coffee for someone.

But then the awkwardness returned. Ryker decided to pierce it. "I probably know more about you than you do about me," he remarked. "Johnny talked about you from time to time, but I gather he said little about me."

"He mentioned R.T. a couple of times, but, no, he didn't say much. But then he didn't talk much about his friends in the Rangers or later. It was like when he came home, he turned all that off."

"Probably wise," Ryker said. He washed down a mouthful of bagel with some coffee. "Compartmentalizing, we call it. Keeping things separate. Why would he want to bring any of that home to you?"

"But he talked about me," she argued.

"Once in a while. Sometimes everyone talked about home. Sometimes we needed to remember that there was a place or a person we wanted to get back to. The rest of the time we couldn't afford the luxury."

That hit her hard, but she faced it head-on. Remembering home had been a luxury? That might have been the most important thing anyone had told her about what Johnny had faced and done.

"I didn't know him at all," she whispered, squeezing her eyes shut, once again feeling the shaft of pain.

"You knew the best part of him. That mattered to him, Marisa. You gave him a place where that part could flourish."

"But why?" she asked, opening her eyes. "Why do you get into this? This kind of life?"

"I can't speak for Johnny. Only for myself."

"Then tell me."

"I was young, hotheaded and determined to do something important with my life. And in case you start to wonder, Johnny did a lot of very important things. But we don't know what it'll cost when we cross the line and take up the work. We have no idea in hell what we're getting into. No one can."

She managed a stiff nod and tried to eat some more

bagel. The baby kicked, then she felt a little foot or hand trail slowly along her side.

"Anyway," Ryker continued after finishing half a bagel, "we do it for a variety of reasons. I wanted excitement. Exotic places. A sense of mission and purpose. Adrenaline junkie, I guess."

"And Johnny?"

Ryker spread his hand. "By the time I met him, I couldn't have guessed a thing about why. By then he was one of us. And as you so correctly said last night, by then he wouldn't have been happy with a tamer life. Somehow, I guess that's how we're built." He frowned faintly and looked past her. "I don't know if I can make you understand, or even find the right words. But there's a point where the mission becomes everything. It motivates every breath we take. Not for everyone, mind you. But for some of us…well, we get hooked. We don't just carry the sword, we *are* the sword." He shrugged and picked up another piece of bagel. "Unfortunately, the world needs swords. I'd have made a lousy plowshare, I guess."

The reference didn't escape her. Her stomach turned over, and for a few seconds she felt so nauseated she wondered if she'd have to run to the bathroom.

But memories floated back, instants out of time, just brief things she had heard or seen with Johnny, moments when he had seemed almost like someone else. Moments when she glimpsed the sword. They always passed swiftly, wiped away by a ready smile, but she'd seen them. She just hadn't wanted to remember them.

But recalling them now, she felt just awful that Johnny had felt the need to hide a very big part of himself from her. She'd have loved him no matter what. Hadn't he trusted her?

"We also get older," Ryker continued. "So we change some more. I'm nearly forty. Too damn old for this business. Johnny was starting to feel the same way. So after I moved over to State, he asked me to let him know if something opened up."

"How could you give up the rush?"

Another faint smile. Her insides prickled with unwanted awareness of him as a man. She shoved it quickly aside, and guilt replaced it. At least he was speaking.

"It's possible to get one without being the pointy tip of the sword. Besides, it's important to know when the time has come. You can shift without giving up the mission or your sense of purpose. It's safer for everyone. Johnny had started to think more about you, about being with you more."

Her breath caught. "He told you that?"

"Actually, yes. When he asked me to let him know if there was a position for him, he said it, Marisa. He said he was thinking about all the time he'd missed being with you, and that he was ready to start down a different road. Unfortunately…"

"Yes," she said tightly. Unfortunately. Johnny had said the same thing when he told her was trying to get a job with the State Department. *We'll have more time together. We'll even be able to travel together once in a while. I'll need to work my way up a little higher on the food chain, but think of the places we could visit.*

How much of that had been real? "Just last night you said he knew it could be dangerous."

"It's always dangerous," Ryker said bluntly. "Always. But I didn't think it would get him killed."

Nor had she. In her blissful ignorance, she had forgotten all the places in the world where a State Department employee would be unwelcome. No, she'd been thinking of London, Paris, Tokyo...not little out-of-the-way consulates in dangerous countries. But of course Johnny wouldn't shy away from the dangers. He never had.

She needed to get away from this, at least for now. Ryker was shifting her mental images around like a puzzle, and she wasn't sure she would like the new picture. "So, more about you," she said.

"I was born," he said.

Despite everything, she felt her mood rising to a much lighter place, and realized she desperately needed it. "That's it?" she asked, surprised to hear a tremor of humor in her voice.

"No, of course that's not it. I had, still have, family. I grew up like a normal kid, two parents and a sister. My parents are retired now, and my sister lives in New Zealand. I get to see her once every few years. And that's where normal ended, I guess. The military called to me like a siren. My imaginings were very different from reality. But I think I mentioned that. Anyway, since then my home has been my job."

None of that told her very much, but what had she been expecting? "That could be lonely."

"I haven't noticed it, except occasionally." The way he spoke led her to believe there had been times when it had been incredibly lonely. She wondered if Johnny had felt that way sometimes, too. And why.

"So you're going back to teaching in the fall?"

She nodded. "I hope I'm ready by then. I'd be a lousy teacher right now."

"How are you filling your days?"

"Trying to get through them."

The words lay there, stark and revealing. More than she had wanted to say to this stranger, more than she had even said to her friends. The fact that hell lived inside her was not something she felt compelled to inflict on her friends. She tried to keep it to herself as much as humanly possible. She knew she didn't do the best job of it, but she still made the effort.

"Everything's okay with the baby, though?"

"Fine." It wasn't really his business.

"And a nursery? Have you put one together?"

She felt a prickle of guilt. Her pregnant friends had usually attacked the nursery business early and had things ready months in advance. For some reason she had been postponing it, as if she could stay in this state of stasis forever. Unrealistic. Ducking. Evading what she couldn't have said. "No. There's a crib in the basement that was Johnny's. I thought I'd use that."

"Need help getting it up here?"

It was clear he wanted to do something more than knock down a few icicles. Well, this was one task where help would be welcome. "Yes, actually I do."

She had just given him a wedge to drive farther into her life. She hoped like hell she didn't regret it.

Glad of a useful job to do, Ryker headed downstairs to the basement. Marisa had told him where to find the crib, and he didn't have any trouble locating it. The basement was clean, scrupulously organized and stocked with every tool a man could wish for. The only thing that bothered him was that the laundry machines were down here. That meant Marisa was going up and down those narrow steps at least once a week, and when the baby came she'd have to do them even more often. He didn't like it. The railing didn't seem stout enough; the steps were too narrow. How often would she attempt them with a baby in her arms? He hated to think.

But as he carried the awkwardly sized pieces of the crib frame up one by one, he had the opportunity to think about Johnny and Marisa, and his opinion was changing.

Had Johnny even once considered how his death would gut his wife? Had he ever looked at her and wondered what would become of her? In just a short time Ryker had gleaned a decent impression of the price Marisa was paying, a price compounded by the impending arrival of a child she would now have to care for on her own. He had no doubt she could do it, but there'd be no handy dad to spell her when she got tired or needed a break.

Lots of women did it. He got it. But Marisa should have had Johnny to lean on. Of course, Johnny had been so busy pursuing his new goals that maybe he'd have been no help at all.

Thoughts such as these had been one of the main reasons Ryker had avoided every opportunity to settle down. It wasn't just that women wanted to change him. No, they had a right to expect certain things from a husband, things he couldn't provide.

And the lie. The big lie. That they would travel together? Johnny would likely have never been assigned to any station where he could take his family. Not with his skills.

And another lie, his own. He and Johnny didn't work for the State Department. They worked for the CIA. State was their cover. He hated having to perpetuate that with Marisa. At this point she deserved something better than lies. She certainly deserved to know about a black star on a marble wall at Langley that would never bear Johnny's name.

But the simple fact was, the agency would put up the star, but it might never acknowledge that John had been one of them. It had happened before and would happen again, and setting Marisa on a quest to break through that huge barrier to truth seemed fruitless. Some names were never inscribed in the book, which was guarded as well as the crown jewels. Some families were never invited to the annual memorial ceremony. Some were never told what their loved ones had done. Some were left forever with stories such as those Marisa had been told because even one slip might cause an irreparable harm.

He didn't even know himself exactly what had happened to John. He'd never know. But he didn't like giving her the cover story when she deserved the truth.

But maybe the truth would upset her more. Maybe knowing that all that talk about exotic travel had been most likely lies would only compound sins that never seemed to stop compounding.

He'd been at this business longer than John had; he was more used to deceptions that went with it. But he found himself getting sick to the gills of it. That woman up there reminded him that secrecy had repercussions. Horrible repercussions. At least if John had been killed in a combat mission with the Rangers, she'd have been given some information about where, when and how that was truthful. Instead, she'd been given a lie. A street mugging?

Not much closure, especially when she was right that John could have taken care of himself.

He brought the springs up to the bedroom she had indicated. Her room, he guessed, at the back of the house. She wanted the child near. She was already working over the wood with a damp rag. He looked at the springs, though, and wondered if they should be replaced. A few rusty spots marred them.

"Can we get new springs for the crib?" We, as if he belonged.

She let it pass, though, and stepped over to look. "Maybe I should."

"Can you get them in town?"

"I can order them. I know I need to order a mattress."

But not a whole new crib. He didn't need brilliant insight to understand that. "Let me measure them, then. Can you just call to order them?"

"Freitag's?" She smiled faintly. "They'll order anything anyone around here wants. We used to have a catalog store, but that closed. Miracle of the internet."

"Where do I find a tape measure?"

He found it in the kitchen drawer she had directed him to and returned with it and the memo pad and pen from the fridge. He measured the frame, made notes about how it bolted to the bed, then joined her in wiping down the wood. At last she sat on the edge of her bed, holding her stomach and laughed. "That felt good!"

"Yeah? Somehow I think you need to tell that to your back."

"How did you guess?"

"Because mine would have been aching after being bent over all that time." He stepped back and looked at the crib. "It's a very nice piece of furniture."

"Johnny's grandfather built it for him. Carpentry was his hobby."

"A great heirloom then." He looked again at the springs. "You know, I should probably take this back downstairs and work on it with some oil and rust remover. Maybe it doesn't need to be replaced."

She shook her head. "I want new springs if I can get them. Babies bounce when they get old enough to stand. I wouldn't trust it."

"Fair enough," he agreed, and carted it back down to the basement. He could also put some wood slats in place to replace the springs, he thought. Peg them in so they couldn't slip out.

But why was he even thinking of such things? He had no place here, and no sense of how long Marisa would tolerate him. Worse, with every passing hour he was building the wall of lies higher.

Sometimes he just hated himself.

When he got back upstairs, he found Marisa in the kitchen. She was nibbling on some carrots, and a plate of them sat at the center of the table as if in invitation to him.

"Mind if I get some coffee?" he asked.

"Help yourself. Make fresh if you want. And thanks for your help with the crib."

"No big deal." He filled a mug and sat across from her. She appeared pensive, so he waited for her to speak.

"You know, I don't want to use springs in that crib at all. I shouldn't need them. They look dangerous to me, and my friends all have mattresses that just sit on brackets around the outside of the crib."

He summoned a mental picture. "That would work.

I could add some more brackets for you easily enough. The way it looks now, you only have four of them."

She nodded thoughtfully. "I'd need them all the way around so the mattress is higher. You know, so fingers or hands couldn't poke out."

"Easy enough."

Then she smiled faintly. "And that's part of the reason for crib bumpers, I guess." A little shake of her head. "I need to get on the stick about this, don't I?"

"You've got a little time."

"Not a whole lot." She held out her hand. "Pad? Pen?"

He'd forgotten he'd tucked them into his breast pocket and turned them over immediately.

"So, hardware for angle brackets and screws, right? Say eight of them?"

"Maybe twelve. And they should be wide, not too narrow."

She wrote. "Then mattress, bumpers, sheets, blankets…" Her voice trailed off. "I let this go too long."

"You've still got time, right?"

"Another ten weeks."

"That's plenty," he said bracingly. "Your friends and I will help if you let us." Then he took a leap into a potential briar patch. "I don't like those basement stairs of yours."

She looked up from her writing. "Why?"

"Too narrow, and the railing isn't sturdy enough. "You shouldn't be climbing them right now, but with a baby in your arms or on your hip…" He let it hang, and braced for her justifiable anger. Just who the hell did he think he was? She'd have every right to demand that of him.

She frowned, then sighed. "You're right. I hate those stairs."

"I can fix them."

At that her head jerked back. "Ryker, you just dropped by to do your duty to Johnny. You checked on me. Are you planning to move in?"

A justified question. But he was feeling a need, a strong need to atone and make up for things, including the lies he kept telling by omission as much as anything. His answer, though, surprised even him. "For a change I'd like to actually build something."

Something passed over her face—whether sorrow or something else, he wasn't sure. "Why should I trust you?" she asked finally. "You think I can't tell you're keeping secrets?"

"John kept secrets, too," he said. "And by the way, John trusted me, or I wouldn't be here now."

She debated. He could see it. He wondered how much faith she'd lost in her husband just by the few things he'd told her. He'd certainly tried to avoid telling her that she'd been fed some outright lies. He didn't feel good about it, but that was the job. Besides, he owed it to John to protect her from the ugly truths.

"What would you do to the stairs?" she asked.

"For one thing, the steps need to be wider. So it'll stretch farther into the basement, but there's room. And I'd give you a rail on both sides strong enough that if you grab or fall against them, they won't collapse."

She nodded slowly, giving him his first sense that he might actually be getting somewhere with her. "I'd like that," she admitted.

He rose and reached for the jacket he'd slung over the

back of the chair earlier. "I've imposed too much. See you tomorrow."

Before she could answer, he headed for the door. Coming here hadn't eased his sense of guilt in the least. He'd better watch his step before he carried that woman into another thicket of lies, a thicket worse than the one left to her by John.

He was, after all, still CIA. And while he might have a few months off, that didn't mean he should spend them weaving another trap for an innocent woman. She'd paid a high enough price already for loving the wrong man.

Chapter Three

Ryker's departure left Marisa feeling adrift again. Maybe she'd been too quick to take such a long sabbatical. No, she couldn't have handled teaching in the fall, but now that months had passed, she itched at times to have a schedule, to have things that needed doing. A point, a purpose, beyond wallowing in grief and taking care of her health and the child in her womb.

Johnny's death had inalterably changed her life, but she had managed his absences before by keeping a busy, full life. These days she'd all but cut off her friends.

And Ryker. He intrigued her. She felt the hardness in him at times, but she felt more there. As if he were reaching out for something, too. He'd helped her with the crib, and he said he wanted to fix her basement stairs. God, she hated those stairs. For years now she'd stood at the top of them and thrown her laundry down because she couldn't safely carry it.

It would be nice to get them fixed, but his words had struck her even more: Ryker had said he wanted to *build something for a change.* If that wasn't one of the saddest statements she'd ever heard...

He'd said he handled security for the State Department. She wondered if that job was even more dangerous than Johnny's. Johnny, after all, had gone as a translator. But Ryker being involved in security sounded even more hazardous. Yet he seemed to accept those kinds of risks casually, which was chilling, in a way.

But then, hadn't Johnny done the same?

She tried to fight the downward spiral her thoughts were taking again. Reality decreed she had to carry on. Indulging a grief that would never leave her didn't seem to get her anywhere. One foot in front of the other. How many times had she reminded herself of that?

Julie showed up again in the late afternoon, an unusual number of visits for one day. Apparently Julie was concerned about something. Her? Ryker's presence?

Anyway, it was a relief to see her cheerful face breeze into the house. Julie had apparently taken the bit between her teeth. While she gabbed humorously about her day with "those imps," as she sometimes referred to her kindergarten class, she dove into the refrigerator and started pulling out food.

"I didn't want to eat alone," she remarked. "You up to a chicken casserole?"

"Absolutely." Marisa sat back, enjoying Julie's minor whirlwind.

"Just us, or will your new friend be here?"

"I'm not expecting him."

Julie paused, package of skinless chicken breasts in hand. "Why not? Did he leave?"

"I doubt it. He wants to rebuild my basement stairs."

"I love him already. Those things have been worrying me. So call him."

"Call him? Why?"

"Because in this case three might be company. I mean, sheesh, Marisa, the guy came to look you up because of Johnny. How rude do you want to be?"

Marisa felt her stomach lurch. What was Julie doing? Was she being rude? She hadn't asked Ryker to come visit; he'd just arrived without warning. She didn't owe him a thing…or did she?

"He helped bring the crib upstairs," she said slowly.

"Good man. So you're finally facing the inevitability. Great. And that means we can throw a baby shower for you. My gosh, girl, the presents have already been bought. We've just been waiting for you to agree. And if you don't, you're going to have the shower around your hospital bed. So don't you think it'd be best to know what you already have before you start shopping?"

Marisa felt an urge to giggle rising in the pit of her stomach. "You sound manic."

"Comes from dealing with five-year-olds. Can't keep their attention for long. Talking rapidly is necessary. You never noticed before?"

"I guess not."

Julie rolled her eyes. "Call the man. He must be at the motel. Besides, I want to size him up. Protective urges also go with being a teacher."

And a friend, Marisa thought. But Julie had leavened her mood, and she decided she wouldn't at all mind hearing Julie's opinion of Ryker. Right now she herself couldn't make up her mind about the man. He'd zoomed in from nowhere, and experience with Johnny had taught her that he'd zoom away again just as unexpectedly, and probably without any explanation except he had to return to work. She also wondered if Julie would sense the secretiveness in him, would also feel that Ryker was withholding important information.

Because, honestly, she didn't quite trust the man, whatever his association with Johnny.

Julie left the food on the counter and got them both some coffee. Sitting at the table with her felt good and familiar. "Call him," she said more gently. "A second opinion is good and, frankly, I've been wondering about him all day. Strangers make me uneasy. So let's sort it out."

With an almost leaden hand, Marisa reached for the wall phone and called the motel. One click, and then a voice answered. "Ryker Tremaine."

"Ryker, it's Marisa. My friend Julie and I wondered if you want to join us at my house for dinner. Nothing fancy, just chicken casserole."

Julie grabbed the phone from her hand. "Hi, Ryker, this is Julie. Believe me, my chicken casserole is fancy. Say an hour? We can chat while it cooks. Thanks. Looking forward to it."

Then Julie hung up the phone.

"Why did you do that?" Marisa demanded. She may have been living in a state of near paralysis for months now, but she was still capable of making a phone call.

"Because," Julie said frankly, "you sounded like you didn't want him to come."

"Maybe I don't!"

"Too late now." Julie grinned. "I'm going to get you out of that shell before it hardens into an unbreakable habit. Anyway, I need to start cubing the chicken."

Marisa's curiosity overwhelmed her irritation. It always did with Julie. "What did he say? Did he hesitate?"

"No hesitation. Just asked for time to shower since he was out running."

Marisa's gaze drifted to the window, still frosty in many places. "In this?"

"The tough get going," Julie tossed back as she rose and pulled out the cutting board. "Did you exercise today?"

"I forgot." The realization shocked her. What had happened to the entire day? Had she just sat here brooding for all these hours?

"Bad girl. If you want to ride your exercise bike while I cook, go for it."

Marisa had a recumbent bike to ride every day. It had become too risky to walk outside with patches of ice scattered everywhere, and the bike was designed so that she could lean back and leave plenty of room for her belly. "No. One day off won't kill me."

"Probably not, but you know what the doc said. More exercise means easier labor."

"Like he knows for sure."

Julie giggled. "It's got to be better, and you know it. For bunches of reasons. But you're right, one day off won't kill you. Now enjoy your cup of coffee and watch me slave after a long day of sitting in chairs that are way too small for me and listening to piping voices that never quiet down unless I roll out the nap mats."

However Julie talked about it, Marisa was certain that she loved teaching kindergarten. She'd had a chance to change grades more than once, but she stuck with her five-year-olds.

"Formative years," Julie had explained once, but

Marisa had always believed that Julie got a kick out of the little ones. She also believed that getting them young gave her the best chance to instill a joy in learning. "Not that some other teacher won't knock it out of them," she had added wryly. "But I can't do anything about that. All I can do is give them the best start."

"Well, they've sure lost their interest by the time they get to me," Marisa had retorted.

"That's your fault," Julie had answered. "You should have majored in something besides the classics and dead gods."

Much to her surprise, Marisa felt her mood elevating. Having dinner with Julie and Ryker might well be enjoyable, especially since Julie never pulled her punches.

But the instant she felt her spirits improve, she felt guilty, and her thoughts tried to return to Johnny and his death. For the first time, it occurred to her that she shouldn't feel guilty every time she enjoyed something. In her heart of hearts, she knew Johnny wouldn't have wanted that. She shouldn't want it, either. Grieving was hard enough without adding guilt to the mix every time she knew a few moments of respite from the loss. Julie was right, fifty years was too long to waste.

So she pushed the guilt down and focused instead on the here and now. Julie been trying to tell her for some time that there was no proper way to grieve, no set of requirements to be met. Her heart had been ripped wide open, but that didn't mean she couldn't allow herself to heal.

Locking herself in a permanent purgatory helped no one. It didn't bring Johnny back, and it wouldn't be fair to her baby. Time for some stiff upper lip.

"I was thinking it's time to shop for the baby," she remarked as Julie began to scoop chicken and vegetables into the casserole.

"I saw the list on the fridge. About time, kiddo. But first we'll have the shower. Friday evening. Then I can go shopping with you on Saturday. Or if you really want to splurge, we can go to Casper or Denver. It might do you some good to get away."

Indeed it might. "You're the best, Julie."

"I know." Julie flashed a grin over her shoulder. "The world spins because of me."

Marisa actually laughed. That made two laughs in one day. Maybe she was improving.

Ryker arrived just as Julie was popping the casserole into the oven and setting a timer. "I'll get it," she said when the bell rang. "I want a first view all to myself."

"Do you want a spear and shield, too?" Marisa tried to joke.

"My tongue can take care of all that. Just relax."

Marisa listened to the greetings at the door and thought it all sounded pleasant enough. Julie apparently gave Ryker time to doff his jacket and gloves in the hall, then the two of them returned to the kitchen. She didn't feel tension between them, but somehow she didn't think that would last. She knew Julie too well.

Once they were all seated around the wooden table, Julie plunged right into the inquisition. "So what took you so long to get here?"

Ryker arched one brow. "Meaning?"

"Well, the funeral was nearly six months ago. Most planes are faster than that."

Marisa battled an urge to quell Julie, realizing that she needed to hear some of this, too. And count on Julie to address it baldly.

Ryker rested his arms on the table. He wore a gray Yale sweatshirt that looked as if it had seen a lot of washings. "It depends on whether we can take a break," he answered. "I couldn't get away. Not then."

"But six months?"

Marisa felt this was a bit unfair. She opened her mouth to say so, but Ryker spoke first. "Sometimes one is in a situation that one can't walk away from. Not even for the death of a family member."

"Now that's mysterious," Julie popped back. "I guess it'll stay that way, won't it?"

"I'm afraid so. There are things I can't talk about. Marisa knows that. There were things Johnny couldn't talk about, either."

"I get it," Julie said pleasantly enough. "So, what happened to Johnny? And how about a truthful version?"

Relax? Julie had told her to relax and now she was delving into this? Marisa wanted to get up and leave, but Julie had arranged her chair so that Marisa couldn't. Damn!

"I was told the same thing Marisa was. That's all I know."

"Officially, anyway," Julie said bluntly. "I guess that's all anyone will know."

Then Ryker surprised Marisa by getting angry. He'd seemed so self-contained until that moment, but a definite edge crept into his voice, and his dark eyes sparked. "That's more than some people get, Julie. Some never know anything at all." He started to push back from the table, but Julie's hand shot out and caught him by the arm. He looked at her grip on him, and Marisa was sure he could have shaken it away like a fly.

"I'm sorry," Julie said. "I'm worried about Marisa.

She's my friend, and you popped up out of nowhere at a very late date."

Ryker turned his gaze on Marisa. "You couldn't have asked me this yourself? You needed someone else to speak for you?"

"I asked you last night," she reminded him, her heart thumping. He appeared to relax a hair, and Julie released his arm.

"Look," he said, "I didn't come here to make your life harder. I came because John asked me to. I came as soon as I could get away. But if it'll save you problems, I can leave right now. I'd feel bad about it, because I said I'd be here for you, but if you don't want me around, then it hardly matters what I promised."

Before Marisa decided how to answer, Julie looked between them, then said, "We're throwing Marisa a baby shower on Friday night. You can crash it if you want. Of course you might get nauseated looking at tiny clothes and booties."

Several noticeable seconds passed before Ryker answered. Marisa got the distinct impression that he was putting a lid on something inside himself, although she couldn't imagine whether it was anger or sorrow.

"It won't nauseate me," he said. "But it's up to Marisa." He gave her a crooked smile. "I'm totally out of my depth here. I know nothing about baby showers, and I just spent eighteen months in a country very different from this. Help me out here."

"You can come," Marisa said impulsively. "And you don't have to bring anything."

All of a sudden his eyes widened. "I picked up dessert at the bakery, and it's out in my car freezing." Without another word, he jumped up. An instant later they heard the door slam behind him.

Marisa and Julie shared a look. "I think he's okay," Julie said finally. "Sorry if I upset you."

"I think he's okay, too," Marisa agreed. "But he's a box full of secrets." She didn't want to admit how much that disturbed her.

"Just like another man we both knew and loved. Say, Marisa?"

"Yeah?"

"If you ever fall in love again, find someone uncomplicated. I know a teacher or two. You know, someone without secrets?"

Another laugh escaped Marisa as they heard Ryker come back in. "Yeah," she agreed. But she doubted that would ever happen. Losing one love had been enough for her lifetime.

And while Ryker was an attractive, sexy man, her response to that had been muted. She hoped it stayed that way.

Ryker left early, after dinner and a piece of the cake he had brought, and after insisting on doing the dishes. He was a man who was used to taking care of himself under far worse conditions. Washing dishes with running water felt like a luxury, although looking around the kitchen and thinking of the baby to come, he wondered if they could install a dishwasher in there. There seemed to be room.

But first the basement steps, he decided. Marisa hadn't refused his offer, so he supposed he ought to hit the lumberyard in the morning and buy what he'd need, as well as the angle brackets to attach to the crib. At least then he'd feel like he'd done more for John's wife than freshen her grief.

Marisa was a pretty armful. He could understand what John had seen in her, despite the grief that weighed her down now. If anything, pregnancy had made her blossom, although maybe the pictures John had shown him once hadn't done her justice.

And that Julie! The woman was something else, and he suspected that under better circumstances Marisa could be every bit as pointed and outspoken. Julie was protecting her friend from the possible threat he posed, and he approved of that, even though it had annoyed him a bit.

He was, after all, a stranger to them both, and John certainly hadn't been mistaken when he felt Marisa was safe here in the cradle of people who knew her. A very different life from his own, and he couldn't quite smother a flicker of envy.

It wasn't that he hadn't had decent friends over the years, John among them. But forged in the heat of a mission, they tended to be intense and brief. If you worked with the same guys repeatedly, as he had with John a number of times, something more enduring resulted. But with too many, the friendships had evaporated, either through death or dispersal.

Secrets weighted his soul the way grief weighted Marisa's. He'd never been a Ranger with John, although he let Marisa believe it. No, he'd always been an operative on the outside, working for the agency after his initial special ops training with the military. She, of course, had no idea what kind of missions John and his fellow soldiers had been sent on, dangerous missions behind the lines, in disguise, spying, gathering intelligence, always risking execution if they were discovered.

And deep in his heart he suspected John had been executed.

Marisa didn't need to know that, and without proof he was forced to doubt it himself. But she was right: A street mugging? He didn't believe it, and his web of contacts within the agency had quivered a little, letting him know that secrets were running around again, secrets about John's death.

He'd lived his whole life with secrecy, but lately he was coming to hate it. Having met Marisa, he hated it even more. He understood that the truth would probably serve no one in this case, but he was still distressed to know that Marisa didn't believe the cover story she'd been given. What would that do to her over time? Kill her ability to trust and believe?

He'd pretty much left his own behind.

He took a long run in the cold night air along the quiet streets of Conard City. The elements never bothered him, and he paid them only as much mind as he needed to for safety. A ski mask protected his nose, gloves protected his fingers and the rest of him stayed plenty warm from running.

He ran into the truck stop across from the motel just long enough to buy a couple of strong coffees, then headed back to his room. Not the Ritz, but he'd never stayed anywhere fancy. He was used to far worse and had learned to bed down just about anywhere he felt safe.

It was not a life he wanted to drag a woman into, even at long distance. John had managed it, but if Ryker had needed a reminder, Marisa had provided it. Some guys didn't worry about such things. They felt they could bal-

ance the two ends of the spectrum, but finally it came
down to fairness, at least to his way of thinking. John
might have loved Marisa completely, but as he'd thought
before, there was something John had loved more than
her.

As crazy as it might sound, John had been cheating
on his wife with his job. Ryker preferred to just let it
be known up front: he had one love and one love only.

He downed one of the coffees, took a hot shower, then
flopped on the bed in a fresh set of sweats and stared at
the ceiling while drinking his second coffee.

He might be used to being alone, but solitude wasn't
always a good thing. He had no mission right now, other
than to do whatever little things he could for Marisa,
and more time on his hands than he wanted. Whenever
he came home from an extended assignment, they gave
him time to repatriate.

Funny word, but he understood it. Adapting to a for-
eign culture was somehow easier than coming home.
Call it a mental health break or whatever, but they were
giving him time to remember that he was all-American,
apple pie, football-loving and all the rest of it. Making
sure he had come fully home.

Regardless, time and guilt hung heavily on his hands.
Something else, too, was creeping into his thoughts:
awareness of Marisa as a woman. Neither of them needed
that, and she sure as hell wouldn't want it.

But she was attractive as hell, even in her gravid
state. Being around her was wakening the man in him
in a totally unwelcome way. Man! He sat up and tried
to shake it off.

Of all the unwelcome things he could feel. She was
still deep in grief, pregnant with her dead husband's

child, and he'd helped lead John to his death by getting him the damn job. It was a wonder she hadn't sent him on his way for that sin alone.

He took another swig of cooling coffee and reached for the self-control that locked away everything else inside him when he was on a mission. But that wasn't working now for some reason. He was drawn to Marisa, like it or not, and his mental shovel couldn't seem to bury it.

Maybe his bosses were right. Maybe they'd sensed something in him that had made them put him on enforced inactivity for longer than usual. Maybe John's death had hit him harder than he thought.

Death was his constant companion. He'd lost buddies before. Why should John be different? But somehow, in some deep way, he was. He had been, even before Ryker had decided to use this enforced break to keep his promise about Marisa. Why?

He racked his brains, trying to get at it. Compartmentalizing wasn't working. Nothing was working. John's death had struck him hard, harder than others. Maybe he felt personally responsible? But that was ridiculous. Men who took these jobs took them willingly. Nobody lied about the risks, ever. They might lie and conceal everything else, but not the risks. Once you were in the field, it was a very bad time to discover you couldn't handle the danger. And John had had plenty of previous experience. Some of the missions that Marisa would never know about had been CIA ones that used the Rangers, and John had known it.

He rubbed his hand over his face, feeling a day's stubble. Weird to be clean-shaven again. He still wasn't used to it. He wondered if he could go for that two-day's growth look that seemed so popular now.

He wondered if Marisa would like it.

Which brought him back to the guilt trip. He flopped back on the bed, telling himself not to be an idiot. Maybe he should just take care of those stairs, so she didn't hurt herself and the baby, and then clear out. It'd be safer.

But safer for whom? Himself? Marisa was so lost in grief and pregnancy that he was probably peripheral to her awareness of anything. So what if he wanted her? He could be certain she wouldn't feel the same about him.

Atonement, he reminded himself. Penance. Maybe hanging around and enduring his burgeoning desire for her was just part of the price he needed to pay. He'd already reopened her wounds. Who cared how uncomfortable this might be for him?

He'd withstood more in his life. Far worse than a little self-denial when it came to sex. Although sex was one place he hadn't practiced a whole lot of self-denial, except when on a mission.

Love, he realized, was the one thing he'd never allowed to blossom in his heart. He preferred it that way. He'd leave no one behind to grieve him. If he needed proof that he was being wise, there was a woman right across town.

A woman expecting a baby who'd never know its daddy. He never wanted to be responsible for that.

But in a different way, he was accepting responsibility for it. It hadn't been his choice, but it was still his responsibility. He owed that woman and child something. Hell, the whole damn agency did, but the most they ever managed was a letter and a star, and Marisa would never get those. If they had intended to tell her, she'd already know.

The secrets must be kept.

And suddenly, he hated them with every bit of passion he owned.

"Well, he was certainly interesting," Julie remarked later as she and Marisa curled up in the living room with some hot chocolate. "Did you see that flash of anger?"

"Yeah."

"All I did was ask him what took him so long to get here. You want my guess?"

"About why?"

Julie nodded. "I wish I had some marshmallows for this cocoa. My students have ruined me. I used to hate them. Anyway, he got mad because he felt bad about taking so long to get here. You must have noticed. Men get mad because it's easier for them than dealing with other emotional stuff."

Marisa gave a little laugh. "Sometimes, anyway."

"Well, that's my theory, and I'm sticking to it. They can't cry, so they throw things or punch something. They could learn from us. Anyway, he's an intriguing character. Attractive, too. He fluttered my little heart."

Now Marisa *did* laugh. "I thought you were recommending men without secrets. Like a teacher."

"Oh, definitely. If you want stability, avoid the bad boys." Then she caught herself and frowned. "Sorry, I wasn't including Johnny in that."

Marisa glanced down, eyeing her stomach, watching a small ripple pass across it. Her baby. Her touchstone. "Why not?" she asked finally. "Johnny was a bad boy. He liked danger. But he wasn't bad with me, or at home."

"Nope. Definitely not. He definitely worshipped you."

But not enough to give up the danger. The thought slammed into Marisa's mind, and a tiny gasp escaped her. No, she didn't want to think that way. Not about Johnny.

"Are you okay?" Julie asked swiftly.

"Just a little foot poking a rib. I'm fine." And now she was lying to her best friend, keeping her secrets. But she sure as heck didn't want to get into this with Julie. Not ever. In fact, she didn't even want to think it.

But the thought stayed in the back of her mind, refusing to go away.

"So," Julie went on, "are you going to let him work on the basement steps? He seems to want to."

"I think so," Marisa answered slowly. "They've been worrying me more and more often. Especially as ungainly as I am right now. One slip could be catastrophic." She paused. "Funny how things change. When I first married Johnny, I charged up and down those steps without a thought. But over the last few months—well, I guess I no longer feel indestructible or immortal."

"Actually," Julie said gently, "when you married Johnny a fall might have meant a broken bone. A fall when you're pregnant is a whole different thing."

"It feels like it."

"It's curious, though," Julie mused. "Ryker doesn't hang for long, does he? He came over, then vanished as soon as he'd finished cleaning up."

"He keeps saying he doesn't want to impose too much." She sighed and sipped cocoa. "Frankly, I don't think he's comfortable. When he walks in here, I get the sense that he feels like he's walking into an alien world."

"Probably is. Which I guess makes him sad in a way. Where the hell does a man like that belong?"

For once Marisa had no answer, because she had begun to wonder if Johnny had really felt he belonged with her. Oh, he'd loved her; he'd always come home to her. But belonging? Maybe it was different for him. He wasn't just coming back to her, but to the town he grew up in. Ryker didn't have that, not here. Maybe not anywhere.

Julie was right. That made him sad, no matter how strong, dangerous or driven he might be.

Chapter Four

This time Ryker called before he showed up. Marisa appreciated the gesture but was a little surprised by her reaction. Now that her first shock and discomfort had passed, she was looking forward to seeing him again.

A major change of pace, she assured herself. That was all it was. At this point she still distrusted him. Oh, she didn't fear he might hurt her or threaten her in any real way, but as she had phrased it to Julie, he was another box of secrets. If she hadn't known Johnny for so many years, she might not have been able to trust him enough to marry.

Because when you felt that there were large parts of a person you could never know, how did you offer them trust?

Not that that was an issue here. He'd stay for a little while, then go back to his secret world, and her life would resume.

Sometimes bitterness overtook her, and she wondered
what life, what future, but the baby never missed an opportunity to remind her. Little Jonni, as she had started
to think of the child, *was* her future, and all that mattered right now. The important thing was taking care of
Johnny's final gift to her. Raising a daughter he would
have been proud of. But sometimes she wondered if
things might have been different if she'd been able to
tell him she was expecting.

What would have been different? Would he have quit
his job and settled into some boring path doing something he didn't love because he had a responsibility?

She wasn't sure that would have happened or worked
out if it had. She'd bravely told Ryker that loving someone meant loving them just as they were, not trying to
change them. She had done that with Johnny, so why
even harbor any too-late hope that her pregnancy would
have changed a thing?

Life had gutted her, and sometimes she grew angry.
Extremely angry—a state that hadn't been familiar to
her before. Sometimes she wanted to smash something.
Throw something. Get even somehow. But none of that
would have helped, and she knew it. Sometimes she
wondered why life was so unfair, but even in the depths
of misery she could look around and see that life was
unfair to everyone. Fairness didn't even enter into it.

Since Ryker was coming and seemed to enjoy coffee, she made a fresh pot. Back in the early days of her
pregnancy, when her doctor had limited her to two cups
a day, she thought she was going be miserable forever.
Now here she was six months later, and her two cups
seemed more than ample.

Until right now. The brewing coffee smelled so good, she decided she might indulge. At this point, the restriction had been removed, but she had lost her old urge to drink the brew all day long. Right now, however, the aroma made her mouth water.

But as she waited for Ryker, some old, nearly forgotten instincts began to arise. She ought to be able to offer him something to eat. God, she hadn't done that even for her friends since word of Johnny's death. Not even now. Instead, Julie came over and cooked a meal for her, or her other friends dropped by with some tidbit and conversation. She'd become an ungracious mole.

It was a wonder she still had any friends, given how self-absorbed she'd become. She didn't laugh much, didn't say much and couldn't even welcome a guest with a cookie. She took, but she didn't give.

A new kind of guilt speared her, one she hadn't had room for since the funeral. Time, she guessed, to start dusting off her social skills again. Time to make an effort to participate, at least a little. The shower on Friday would be a good start. She hadn't wanted it, but she was getting it, and the girls were going to do it right here in her cave. She wouldn't even have to set foot out into the icy night; the party would come to her.

She made up her mind right then that she was going to enjoy it. Failing that, she'd make every effort to appear to be enjoying it. God, their patience with her was amazing, because being around her had to have been a serious downer all these months.

The doorbell rang, and she went to let Ryker in. Evidently the winter cold had returned in force. He stomped his feet as if to get blood flowing to them again, and pulled off his ski mask to give her a smile. "I've been to cold places before, but this one is heading to the top of my list."

"I haven't been paying attention." Sadly true.

"Take my word for it. It's beginning to feel like Antarctica."

She had started toward the kitchen but swung around instantly. "Was that hyperbole, or have you been there?"

She saw him hesitate. More secrets. Smothering a sigh, she started for the kitchen again. "I made a fresh pot of coffee for you. How are you managing at the motel?"

"The motel's fine. So is the truck stop diner."

"Try the City Diner sometime. Ask for it as Maude's diner, which is what everyone calls it. The service may be less friendly, but the food is fabulous."

"I'll remember that." As she entered the kitchen, with him following, he added, "Yes, I've been to Antarctica."

She froze, then turned to face him. He was shucking his jacket, hanging it over the back of one of the kitchen chairs. For an instant, just an instant, she thought that he looked like a hunk in flannel and jeans. She pulled herself back quickly, returning to curiosity. "For real? Are you allowed to tell me that?"

"I just did. Training exercise years ago."

"Wow," she said slowly. Not that she believed that was the whole story, but she decided to accept it. "I used to want to go there."

"What in the world for?" He sounded astonished.

A half smile tipped up one corner of her mouth. "I hear there are more shades of blue in the ice than we can imagine. And penguins. But I was thinking of a cruise."

"Ah." His smile returned. "Well, there *are* more shades of blue than you can imagine, if you have time to look at them. The penguins are smaller than you'd think, the seals more dangerous and the terrain and weather totally unforgiving. Which probably explains why no one except crazy scientists and crazy military people try to hang out there for long."

To her surprise, he drew a small laugh from her. Now, that wasn't so hard, was it? As she poured two mugs of coffee she said, "So, have you been on every continent?"

Again he didn't answer immediately. When she sat at the table, he sat, too. "No," he said finally. "And to answer the question you haven't asked, neither had John. And no, he didn't go to Antarctica as far as I know."

"That probably explains why he didn't quash my dream of taking that cruise someday." She stared into her coffee for a few seconds, thinking that it might be wise to back off this. This man was no more free to talk than Johnny had been. "So, what brought you today?"

"Well, I wanted a good look at those stairs to see what I'll need and figure out how to make them safer without taking over your entire basement. Measurements, mostly. Do you mind?"

She felt a flicker of warmth toward him, although she wasn't sure it was wise. "I really appreciate this. I'll pay for the materials."

He shook his head. "Call it my shower gift. It will probably take me a few days, though. Can you handle it?"

She decided she could. Internally, she'd made some kind of shift, she realized. She would never fully trust this man. She would always suspect he knew more about what had happened to Johnny than he would say, but she appreciated his willingness to deal with a problem for her.

"Are you a carpenter?" she asked.

"It used to be one of my hobbies. I can do stairs. Don't ask me to do any cabinetmaking. I don't have that level of skill."

"When did you learn?"

"My dad and I used to spend a lot of time in his shop. It was his hobby, too."

At last, something truly personal. That seemed important. She wondered where else she could safely wander. Then, an unexpected wave of resistance hit her. "I can hire someone to do it."

"All right." He sipped coffee before putting his mug down. "But you're not going to get rid of me that easily."

"Is that a threat?" Her heart slammed as she wondered if she had totally misjudged him.

"No, not at all." He shook his head. "I don't expect my feelings to matter to you, Marisa. Why should they? But understand this. I promised something to Johnny. You're going to find me as tough to get rid of as gum on the sole of your shoe."

"But why?" she demanded again. "Just tell me why, and don't tell me about promises. Just coming here fulfilled your promise. If I want you to go…"

"It's not just about promises. It's about debts. Guilt. Whatever you want to call it. I should never have gotten John that job. Never. I have to live with that." He sat there pinning her with his hard, dark gaze. "We all have our griefs and guilts, Marisa. All of us."

The raw honesty of that gripped her hard. Her lungs felt squeezed. "I don't want to be anyone's penance!"

"You're not my penance, believe me. You couldn't be if you tried. These are things I need to deal with myself. In the process, if I can help you out a little bit, it would be nice."

Understanding shook her. She wrapped her arms around herself. She could barely whisper. "You feel like you killed Johnny."

His face darkened until it looked like a winter sky, threatening, harsh.

"Did you?" she asked with the last bit of breath she could summon.

"I wasn't lying when I said I was in a different country." Without another word, he rose and left the kitchen. She half expected him to leave the house until she saw that his jacket was still there. She sucked air and rocked a bit, dealing with a blow she couldn't quite explain to herself. He felt responsible for Johnny's death, but in a way that went far past simply getting him a job. But why? What the hell was involved in that job? Translating shouldn't have been a deadly occupation.

Something was being withheld. The feeling that had overwhelmed her from the start battered at her again. She didn't know, she might never know, what had really happened, what Johnny had really been doing.

She listened to Ryker pace, felt her baby's stirrings as if they came from another world, and wondered how she was ever going to deal with any of this.

But oddly, as complicating as Ryker's presence was, even though she couldn't decide if she loathed him, and certainly knew that she didn't trust him, she felt a burgeoning seed of sympathy for him. She'd been so lost in her misery that she had forgotten that others had lost someone, too. That Ryker had not only lost a friend, but even felt responsible for it. The responsibility wasn't his. Even she knew that. The responsibility lay with Johnny's choices and whoever had attacked him. Ryker shouldn't have to shoulder that on top of anything else.

She had to live with loss and endless questions, but at least she didn't feel responsible. She couldn't imagine the weight of responsibility being added to all this hell.

For the first time since she got the news, she honestly thought about what someone else might be feeling. Actually cared that someone else was hurting, too. God, how utterly selfish she had become.

Standing back, for just a few seconds, she looked at herself and didn't like what she saw. Yes, grief was consuming, but it needn't rule out every other human feeling on the planet. In fact, she thought she might have been incredibly self-indulgent. Other people had to pick up the pieces after a death. They couldn't just withdraw into a private cocoon of hell, even if they wanted to. They had jobs and others they couldn't afford to forget.

"I'm weak," she announced.

Ryker's pacing in the foyer stopped. A moment later he appeared in the doorway. "You said something?"

"I'm just thinking about how weak I am." Might as well be truthful about something, and a near stranger seemed like a safer ear than even Julie right now.

"You're not weak," he said quietly.

"I disagree. I dropped out of everything. I put everything else on hold so I could curl up in a ball and feel sorry for myself."

"Grieving is not self-pity."

"Depends on how you do it, don't you think?" For the second time that morning, she felt scalded by understanding. Then she remembered something else. "You didn't kill Johnny. If there was one thing I learned as his wife, it's that he made his own decisions. If you hadn't found him that job, he'd have found another. It's how he was. How *you* are. You, of all people, should understand that."

Ryker visibly hesitated, shifting back and forth on his feet, as if he wasn't quite sure how to respond. She waved a hand. "You don't have to answer me," she told him. "Secrets. I get that part very clearly."

Slowly he came back to the table, as if he were dragging something heavy. He poured them both fresh coffee, then sat again. "Can we talk about John?"

She drew a long breath. "I guess we need to. He's here right now, right between us, still full of secrets I'll never know. Things I'll never understand. So go for it."

"I don't want to rip you up."

She swallowed hard. "I don't think anything can rip me up more than I already have been."

He nodded slowly. "Over the years John and I worked on a number of missions together. Not every one, but enough. The thing about me, about people like me, is that after a while you start to know exactly what you're capable of. Good and bad. What you can endure."

She nodded slowly. She guessed she could understand that.

"It doesn't usually take long for the brass to come off."

"Meaning?"

"You get to the point where you know you have nothing to prove to anyone, not to yourself, not to others. You've proven it already. So you kind of quiet down. That's what I meant about the brass going away."

"Okay." She sipped coffee, trying to wet a mouth that was turning dry. Somehow she knew she wasn't going to like this.

"John was different. I should have faced that difference more squarely. More honestly."

"How so?" She closed her eyes.

"He never stopped feeling he had something to prove. To whom or what I don't know. He rode himself hard. And—I'm sorry, Marisa—I wouldn't have taken that last post he took. If I had known, I'd have done my level best to talk him out of it. But he had something to prove. I knew that, and I should never have gotten him the job."

His words dropped into her heart like heavy stones of ice. She knew he was right but didn't know how to explain how she knew. John had always been involved in some kind of private competition. She'd always assumed it was with himself. "You're right about him," she admitted hoarsely. "I saw it sometimes."

"So that's where I failed you both. I knew he had a dangerous attitude, but I didn't act on that knowledge because I also knew he wasn't stupid. But more than once I had to remind him we were flesh and blood, not superheroes."

"Really?" Surprise opened her eyes. Amazingly, she could almost hear the conversation in her head. "I can believe that," she admitted. "Oh, I can believe that."

"Anyway, I'm not saying he did something stupid that got him killed. I know what you know. But I kind of feel like I should have guessed this might…happen."

The words emerged stiffly from her mouth. "You weren't his caretaker."

"No, but I evidently wasn't a very good friend, either."

Irritation sparked in her. "Do you really think he'd have listened to you? I know what he was like when he decided to do something. Wild horses couldn't stop him.

And if he felt he had something to prove, then that last job may have attracted him for that very reason."

His face softened a shade. "You're being very kind to me."

"No," she said, her tone sharpening. "I'm being brutally honest here. Maybe it's time I was. I loved him. I loved him with my whole being. But do you think he ever thought of that when he went away? When he made his decisions? No. I know he didn't. He always promised to come home, and I think he believed he always would. Maybe that's a dangerous way to live. But he sure didn't wonder about leaving me as a widow, or about the possibility of a child. I know because he *never once mentioned it to me*. I'm surprised he even thought about it enough to ask you to check on me."

"Marisa…"

"No." She silenced him. "He was a good man. He was always good to me. But there was a part of Johnny no one could ever tame. And I knew it, too."

Ryker closed his hands around his mug and looked down into it. "Maybe," he said finally. "But don't take it on yourself."

"I could no more take it on myself than I could control a wild mustang. He was who he was. We all are."

She put her hand to her forehead, then started to rise. "I need ice water. Enough coffee."

"Let me get it."

She let him do it because he seemed to need to do something, but as she watched him pull out the glass and deal with the ice dispenser on her fridge, she realized that she needed to do something, too. She was half ready to crawl out of her skin.

He placed a tall glass of ice water in front of her, and

she downed half of it immediately. Coffee, she had discovered, only made her thirstier.

He sat again, pushing the chair back and crossing his legs, one ankle on his knee. Leaning back, he cradled his coffee. "I didn't want to bash John. Don't take it that way. I wasn't saying he was reckless."

"Not exactly," she qualified. But in the deepest recesses of her being, she knew Johnny *had* been reckless. Not stupidly so, but she had taken some motorcycle rides with him in the mountains that had left her scared to death. He loved the adrenaline rush and kept on doing it even after she refused to go with him again. No sedate weekend drives for him. Nothing sedate about Johnny.

She looked at Ryker, who was studying the mug in his hands, and wondered how much like Johnny he was. He kept secrets, obviously, but he'd said he wouldn't have taken that last assignment that Johnny took. She desperately wanted to know why. But she knew the wall would slam in place again. Still, she had to ask.

"Ryker?"

"Yeah?"

"Why wouldn't you have taken that assignment?"

He glanced at her, those dark eyes drawing her in for just a moment before he returned his gaze to his mug. "Some situations," he said slowly, "are inherently unstable. Even a local lives in constant danger. So the key is to evaluate the situation. How much can I do? How helpful will I be? Or will I just be putting my head in a noose for no good reason? John and I had slightly different standards, I guess. If some good can be served, I'll go. If I judge that it can't…well, I've turned down a few postings. Not many, but a few."

"So you would have judged this one to be pointless?"

"Maybe not," he said quietly. "It's easy to judge in ret-rospect. John must have felt he could accomplish some-thing while he was there. I shouldn't second-guess him now."

She reached out desperately for just another kernel. "But how much can a translator do?"

"Negotiate." One word, edged with warnings not to pursue it.

Unstable situation. Negotiation. She guessed he didn't mean the kind of negotiations she saw on TV with con-ference tables surrounded by serious men and women in business suits. She could imagine another kind, though, a much more dangerous kind. She didn't want to go there, but she suspected her late husband had done ex-actly that. And Ryker had just told her more than she had believed she could possibly learn. "Thank you," she said.

"Don't thank me. I'm not even sure I'm right. Like I said, I heard the same thing they told you. And that could be the truth, Marisa. I'm not saying it isn't. It could have been a random street attack, nothing to do with his job at all. Maybe someone thought he had money."

But she didn't believe it, and she suspected he didn't, either. He was as much in the dark as she was, and given that those walls of secrets that kept her out also kept him on the inside, it probably bothered him even more than it bothered her.

She drew a long breath, finally accepting that she would never know exactly what had happened. It was even possible that no one knew any more than they'd told her. Much as she hated the idea, it was possible, and she was going to have to live with it.

Studying Ryker, surprised by how much he had found a way to share with her, she noticed again how attractive

he was. She'd felt the instant of recognition on their first
meeting, but with him sitting there looking so relaxed,
she let herself absorb it, this time without guilt. Maybe
it was a good sign that she even noticed.

But he was so different from Johnny in appearance.
Johnny had had a fresh-faced look to him, even when he
came home after a long stint overseas. All-American guy
looks. Ryker had a totally different impact. His black
hair and eyes looked almost exotic, as if he had some
Native American in him, and his skin was a few shades
darker. His face had been chiseled into harsh lines, and
today he apparently hadn't shaved, because dark beard
growth shadowed his chin and cheeks. He was larger
than Johnny, a few inches taller and a bit broader. Johnny
had been solidly built, but this guy gave new meaning
to the words. He might have been carved from granite.
Appealing in a very different way.

But this was a path she didn't want to wander. It felt
somehow like cheating on Johnny, although cheating
on him was at least six months in her past. Not possible
anymore, but a pang of guilt struck her again, anyway.
Noticing another man with Johnny's baby in her belly.
Betrayal.

"So," she asked, "do you prefer to be called R.T. or
Ryker?"

He lifted his head, her words drawing a smile from
him. "Ryker. It reminds me I'm home."

"It's an unusual name."

"Dutch. My mother's family had a few Rykers in the
past. She dusted it off for me."

Marisa gave a little laugh. "Dusted it off?"

"Well, I think it skipped a few generations. My sister
lucked out with Lila." Leaning forward, he put his cup

on the table. "I need to go do my inspection and measuring. It looked like the tool shop downstairs was pretty well equipped. Mind if I explore it?"

"Help yourself." About the only things she was familiar with down there were the water heater, the heater, the humidifier and the washer and dryer. Other than to grab a wrench or a screwdriver from time to time, she really had no idea what wonders might be in the workshop area.

She needed to put her feet up for a while. She could feel her shoes growing tighter, so it was a relief when Ryker smiled, nodded and left the kitchen. Then, with another glass of water, she went into the living room where she could put her feet up on a hassock. Amazingly, it wasn't long before she fell asleep.

Ryker found some good work lights in the basement and positioned them so he could see the stairway clearly. He had plenty to think about as he used various measuring tools and a pencil and pad for note-taking.

He wondered if he'd spoken too harshly about John. The man had been a good friend for many years, but that didn't mean he couldn't see him clearly. John had not only kept his brass, but he'd remained unusually gung ho. His edge had grown harder with time, but it had never seemed to temper the way it did for most of them. If John had been brash when he'd come out of his Rangers training, he'd been just as brash the last time Ryker had seen him, nearly two years ago.

Turning down assignments wasn't something anyone did often, but they were allowed to. Not even the CIA wanted to send someone into a situation they didn't think they could survive. It wasn't like being in the army. You didn't have to salute sharply, then march up the hill into a hail of certain gunfire.

But given the country John had been sent to, Ryker was fairly certain he would have turned it down himself, maybe only the third time in his long career. It wasn't a job for cowards, but it was also a job that required a lot of smarts and street savvy. Clearly John had viewed his last assignment differently, but John had been a born risk-taker. They all were to a large extent, but John more than most.

He should have kept his mouth shut about that, even though Marisa had seemed to know the truth of it. The other stuff he'd told her, that was okay. No violation of operational secrecy. But being a translator? He had no difficulty imagining what Marisa had believed the job would be. It certainly wasn't standing as the lone man in a torn area of the world, probably trying to negotiate a prisoner release, or maybe a temporary cease-fire, or even to glean intelligence from dangerous sources. She had no idea of a world run by people who actually *liked* being at war, and to hell with everyone else. Nor would she even conceive that he might have been trying to infiltrate some subversive group.

But John had known. He had still walked in.

He admired John's guts. Someone had to do it. Once he'd been willing, but as he'd said, the years had taken some of the brass off him. These days it wasn't enough that a job needed doing. No, these days he calculated the likelihood of success versus failure...failure meaning death.

He wasn't afraid to die, but damned if he'd throw his life away in a pointless venture anymore. It all depended on what was on the line.

Maybe John's assignment had seemed important enough to take the risks. Maybe he'd judged that the value outweighed his own life. Well, of course he had. The question that would always hang over him was if John had misjudged. The world needed men like John, the ones who didn't count the cost.

But hell, when you had a wife… Ryker just shook his head. He and Marisa's husband were very different in one respect: Ryker had never let a woman get close enough to be singed by the fire. John had wanted it all.

And this was the end result. Ryker swore quietly under his breath, then switched off the lights and headed up the stairs to do some calculations at the kitchen table. He found Marisa dozing in the living room and couldn't quite suppress a smile. Remarkable woman. And in her late pregnancy, beautiful. An earth goddess, a vessel of life. Unlike him and John, who had been vessels of death all too often.

He'd never before noticed how sexy a pregnant woman could be, but this one had shown him. Lost as she was in the midst of her grief, something about her reached out to the man in him. He wanted her. Not wise. Her life had been shattered, and he didn't want to add to it.

Scolding himself, he went to the kitchen, filled a mug with the dregs from the coffeepot and sat down to figure out just how much lumber he was going to need. Minutes later, he was lost in sketching a diagram of the work ahead of him.

Marisa awoke to find the house empty, and relief flooded her along with a tide of shame. Thank God he wasn't here. She felt horrified by the vivid dream that had startled her into consciousness, a dream of making love with Ryker. How could she even…?

She guessed her somnolent libido was reawakening, but did it have to be Ryker? A real man who was in her life right now?

No gauze covered the memory of the dream. No symbolism had filled it, making it hard to be sure what she had dreamt. It had been as vivid, as detailed, as real as a pornographic film. She couldn't remember ever having a dream like that.

It had left her aching with desire. The longing throb between her thighs followed her into the real world, holding her frozen in her seat despite being able to see that Ryker's car was gone. Despite knowing she was alone and no one could possibly see the heat in her cheeks.

But the feeling…it shamed her, but she wanted to hang on to it. It had been so long since her body had cried out for a man's touches, but it was crying now. *Love me. Fill me. Take me.*

It pounded through her blood like a song that wouldn't quit. What the heck was happening to her? She didn't have feelings for Ryker. Sometimes she wished he'd never shown up. She even occasionally wished he'd just go away.

What had she been thinking to agree to allow him to fix the stairs? Now he'd be around longer. Now he'd even attend her baby shower, a man in place of her husband.

She didn't want to replace Johnny. Hell, she never wanted to walk that road again.

Ryker?

But her subconscious had launched it into her awareness, and no amount of mental shoveling could make it go away. Okay, so she'd had a dream. A delicious dream.

But just a dream and she didn't have to tell anyone, nor did she have to act on it.

Guilt grabbed her again, the feeling that she might betray Johnny. But even as it did, she heard Johnny's old familiar laugh in her head. *Just go for it.* How many times had he told her that? How many times had Johnny done exactly that? He believed in going for what you wanted. If he'd ever felt guilt about anything, she didn't know it.

Johnny-in-the-moment. Always in the here and now. Hell, he'd be egging her on, she thought grumpily. He often had.

The remembered dream clung and, with it, physical sensations almost as if Ryker really had touched her, and her cells remembered each caress. Finally, she glanced down at her ankles and saw the swelling had subsided. Time to get up, get some water and think about dinner.

When she meandered into the kitchen, she saw papers scattered on the table. Taking a look at them, she realized Ryker had been doing calculations and drawings for the staircase. As she scanned them, she decided he did seem to know what he was doing.

Good, because she'd be in a mess if she couldn't reach the basement. The forced air heat kicked on, stirring the air and, for just a moment, letting her feel a chill.

Dinner, she reminded herself. But for how many?

The question almost overwhelmed her. For the first time in ages, she needed to consider it, and she didn't even know if Ryker would be there. She could have laughed, had she felt more like it. But the dream haunted her, making laughter seem almost criminal.

Peering into her freezer, she wondered if she had enough of anything to make a meal for two. She didn't even know what Ryker liked or how much he ate. Johnny had always had a huge appetite, but considering how in shape he always was, and that he invariably came home from every mission looking as if he'd lost ten pounds or more, of course he'd been a heavy hitter. One of the hardest things she'd always had to deal with was making the mental shift from cooking for two to cooking for one. Although now she wondered how she could ever have thought that hard. Life had shown her just how sheltered she had been until recently.

Now her brain didn't seem to want to shift in another direction. She peered into her freezer, looking for something she had time to thaw that she might adequately turn into a meal for two. The pickings were slim, however, so she headed to the pantry. She always kept broth on hand, and it could readily be turned into a soup with some noodles and vegetables. At least if she ate alone tonight, the soup would still be good tomorrow.

Just as she was reaching for the carton of chicken broth, she heard the front door open and close. Ryker?

"Marisa?" she heard him call.

"In the kitchen."

She heard his steps cross the foyer and turned from the pantry in time to see him carry in a large paper bag. "I found Maude's," he said with a smile. "You were right about the service."

"Everyone's used to it."

"Anyway, I took a chance and brought something for us to eat. Interesting thing happened."

She realized she was devouring him with her eyes and fought to drag her gaze to the bag. "What?"

"The incredibly angry woman who runs the place asked if I was buying dinner for you, too. I said I was. She picked out your meal for tonight."

Despite everything, a laugh overtook Marisa, and she had to grab the back of a chair and hold her side. "Oh, that's Maude," she said breathlessly.

"So I gathered. I also gathered at least half the town knows I'm here to see you. Great intelligence network."

"Fiona," she answered.

"Fiona?"

"My next-door neighbor. I'm surprised she hasn't come over here to give you the third degree. Anyway, she was the first to see you, and the entire reason Julie came to check you out. If you want secrecy, you won't find it in this town."

He flashed a smile. "I'm already discovering the usefulness of that. I ordered supplies at the lumberyard, and they'll be delivered tomorrow. Two guys are going to help get them down your stairs, and I'm reliably informed by one of them—Hank, I think it was—"

"That'd be Kelly's husband. You'll meet him Friday night."

He absorbed that. "Okay, then. Anyway, he says more than one person has lately been worrying about you on those stairs, so it seems I'm going to have some help."

She gripped the chair with her other hand. "Heavens!"

He shrugged and started pulling foam containers and beverages out of the bag. "I think it's great. We'll make short work of it this way and cause you less commotion." He raised his gaze as he put the last beverage container on the table. "I can see why Johnny believed you were safe here. The gargoyle at the diner knew what you'd want to eat, and three guys at the lumberyard couldn't wait to help with your stairs. That's special."

She nodded, admitting it. People around here could be very special, yet she'd been avoiding them like the

plague. What did that make her? "I never even mentioned the stairs," she said, lacking a more appropriate
response.

"Well, according to Hank, his wife went down them
once after...the funeral, to help you out with the wash,
and she's been muttering ever since. He said, unfortunately, he couldn't afford to do it himself."

She shook her head. "Hank and Kelly have a lean
budget."

"Well, I don't. I suspect from the way they were talking there was some discussion of trying to get a pool
going to fund the supplies. So we'll start on Saturday."

"Wow," she whispered. She paused just long enough
to get her glass of ice water, then slid into a chair at the
table.

"Maude sent you hot cocoa," he said, pushing a foam
cup her way. "Something about you being restricted on
coffee?"

A surprised laugh escaped her. "You know, Johnny
kept his secrets, but I guess I don't have any."

Ryker slid into a seat across from her. "I like it here,"
he announced. "I've seen other close-knit places like this
all over the world, but I was always the outsider. You're
fortunate to have these people."

She thought then about the amazing loneliness he
must live with and felt a pang. Not knowing what she
could say without offering offense in some way, she
opened the foam container and found that Maude had
sent her a Cobb salad loaded with turkey and conspicu-
ously lacking bacon. She smiled as she looked at it. Caring even from Maude, who rarely showed any.

"I liked the guys I met," he remarked. "They all seem
like good sorts."

A few minutes later, as they ate, he spoke again. "You've grown awfully quiet. Are you okay?"

"I'm fine. It's just that you reminded me of something I lost track of after Johnny. How good my friends are. How lucky I am to have them."

He swallowed another bite of his sandwich before replying. She watched him wash it down with his own drink, which appeared to be coffee. "You know," he said, "I can see why John could leave you behind, knowing you had these people around you. He relied on them. And I can also understand why you've lost sight of them since John died. Some things are so huge they don't leave room for much else."

"Grief," she replied, "is totally selfish, as I've just begun to realize."

"It's also overwhelming. Cut yourself some slack."

She raised her gaze to his face. "How much slack do you cut yourself?"

He didn't answer, which she decided meant he didn't cut himself much slack. He was here, wasn't he? Keeping a sort-of promise he'd made to Johnny back when. She hadn't exactly given him a gracious welcome, but he had told her that he was stuck to her like gum to the sole of a shoe—apparently until he decided he'd kept his word.

"So when's your due date?" he asked.

"Two and a half months, give or take."

"You don't look that far along…not that I'm a great judge."

"Well, I am. I expect I'll get really big soon. But not everyone does, I guess."

"Girl or boy?"

"Girl."

She caught sight of his smile. "It's been a long time

since anyone had to wonder. Must have been very different when you didn't know whether to get blue or pink."

She managed a laugh. "Like the baby would care."

He joined her laugh. "Probably not. But isn't that designed to avoid all those mistaken comments about the baby's sex?"

"Maybe. I don't know. What's the point of getting bothered by that? I can't imagine getting offended by a pronoun."

He laughed again. "You might feel differently after the hundredth time. But then I guess around here word will travel fast. Probably won't be a problem if you dress the girl in orange."

She smiled but then realized she was getting tired again. Having someone around so much had become taxing. And Ryker, though he didn't mean to be, was especially taxing. He was wakening feelings in her she didn't want and making her think about how she had changed in ways she didn't like.

As if he sensed her fatigue, he left as soon as he finished eating, promising to see her tomorrow night at the shower.

She was relieved that he was gone and strangely disappointed that he didn't intend to come back until the shower. She guessed the lumberyard would deliver without his supervision.

That was for the best, wasn't it? She didn't need to cultivate a relationship with him. He was part of Johnny's past, and she didn't want him to be part of her future.

At some deep level, she still felt distrusting. They'd get through the baby shower and then the stairs, and then she'd try to send him on his way.

Because she absolutely didn't like the painful awakening he stirred inside her, and she didn't want to emerge from her cave just yet. Her desire for him felt like a betrayal, and he wasn't the staying kind, anyway.

So even if she hadn't felt that he was still guarding secrets and keeping her in the dark, she would have still wanted him gone.

Ryker Tremaine was trouble. He had to leave.

Chapter Five

Ryker attended the baby shower but left as early as he could. All the oohing and aahing over tiny clothes in every color of the rainbow and over a ton of other baby supplies didn't interest him.

Well, it didn't exactly repel him, but it reminded him of how empty his own life had been except for work. He was nearly forty and had just discovered the whole concept of baby showers. There was something wrong with the way he lived his life.

By choice, he reminded himself as his feet pounded cold pavement. In his motel room, he did endless sit-ups and push-ups and wished for a gym.

Then they went to work on the staircase. He liked the three other guys well enough, Hank and his cohorts, but they were as far from his world as it was possible to be. He listened to their conversation, occasionally managed to join in some of the joking, but mostly just kept his mouth shut. They had the new stairs done by Sunday night and watched Marisa try them out. She smiled hugely and thanked them repeatedly...and once again he exited as quickly as he decently could.

One of his greatest survival mechanisms was being able to read people, and he was reading Marisa. She was uncomfortable around him. She didn't trust him much, justifiably so. And judging by the way her gaze skated past him so often, she didn't really want him there.

So he stayed away. He should have left town, but something made him hang around, anyway. He'd made a promise of sorts, and somehow sticking his nose in the front door and helping build some stairs didn't leave him feeling as if he was done with it.

But what could Marisa need him for? She had an ample number of concerned friends. He was no one to her, except possibly the man who had gotten her husband into a deadly situation.

He sent out some feelers, trying to get more information about what had happened to John Hayes, wondering at himself even as he did so. Did he really need any more secrets to conceal from a grieving widow? But he still wanted to know, and he still didn't learn a thing. The cloak of secrecy that had been thrown over John's final activities was as impenetrable as steel.

That bothered him, too. He was beginning to see the organization he worked for in a new light, one shone on it by Marisa's loss. The agency was built on secrets, swamped in them, but for someone supposedly on the inside to be unable to learn even something small? Whatever they had asked of John, they didn't want anyone to know. The secrecy was so deep they didn't even have a decent cover story to share in-house. It was as if John had never existed, except for one anonymous black star on a wall.

Then, a few weeks later, while still wrestling with his own demons and trying to ignore the Christmas decorations that had popped up everywhere, he ran into Marisa and almost didn't recognize her. She was coming out of a doctor's office, and her belly had ballooned. Late pregnancy was truly on her. He wondered if she was nearing term, despite what she'd told him.

She saw him and froze mid-step.

"Hi," he said, slowing his jog and stopping. "How are you?"

"I'm fine," she said hesitantly. "I didn't know you were still in town."

He doubted that. "Well, I don't need to go back, and I kind of like the place."

"Like gum on my shoe," she remarked.

"Hey, I've been staying away. I know you don't like me being around."

A frown trembled around her mouth, though he could see she was making a valiant attempt to smile. "It's true," she admitted finally. "Go home, Ryker."

Wind cut through his jogging clothes, despite the jacket and gloves. "Where's that?" he asked rhetorically, starting to run in place.

"This is creepy. I feel stalked."

"I haven't bothered you anymore," he argued, keeping his tone level. "I got the message."

"And it's a free country," she said sharply.

"Last I heard. Look, I don't want to fight with you. I'm staying out of your way. Let's just leave it, okay?"

He started to pass her, but her voice stopped him.

"You don't have a home?"

He hesitated. "Depends on what you mean by that."

"Oh, for the love of…" She broke off. Then, almost a command, she said, "Follow me home."

"Why?"

"Because I want to talk."

"You've got plenty of friends."

She drew a breath. "But they're not you." Without another word, she walked around a car and climbed in behind the wheel.

"Should you be driving?" he called after her.

"Who else will do it for me?" She revved the engine and drove away, leaving him somewhere near hell's door as he wondered if he should follow her or ignore her. He certainly hadn't come here to make her life harder.

But his feet seemed to have a mind of their own and carried him toward Marisa's place. He guessed they were going to have it out. Maybe then he'd be free to leave.

She opened the door to him, and he stepped in from the cold. Odd how symbolic that suddenly seemed. "I made you coffee. I need to get my feet up."

"Something wrong?"

"Pregnancy. Nothing's wrong."

"You want coffee, too?"

"Sure, why not?"

Hardly inviting, but she'd seldom been inviting toward him. He was like a mess she didn't know how to clean up. He got it. He just wished he could explain what kept him stapled here when he was clearly so unwanted.

He brought coffee into the living room and found her in the rocker with her feet up on the hassock. "Badly swollen?" he asked, trying to be polite.

"It's becoming more common, but the doc isn't too

worried. Just spend a little less time on my feet and put them up when I can."

Well, that was more than she'd been sharing since their first meeting. Was that good or bad? "So, what's been keeping you on your feet?"

She surprised him then, laughing softly. "Nesting."

"Nesting?"

"I was warned this would happen toward the end of my term. Cleaning binge. Getting everything ready."

"The crib is sorted out?" He'd managed to put those brackets in for her in the midst of handling the staircase.

"Go look," she said, waving her hand.

So he did. The crib was at the foot of her bed, a mattress in place, the bedding all made up, pads around the entire thing for protection, he supposed. He had to do a lot of guessing when it came to babies. He'd learned some things after his sister was born, but a ten-year-old boy didn't pay attention to many of the details. A mobile hung from the ceiling, and he imagined one of her friends had done that for her. Soft cartoon characters hung from it. The top of her dresser looked ready to be a changing table.

He returned to the living room feeling odd in some way. Preparation for a new life. Never had he felt more out in the cold. He perched on the edge of the couch, alert, ready to leave as quickly as necessary. Hell, he lived most of his life that way.

"So you don't have a home?" she said.

"Not really. I'm gone too much."

She nodded. "Johnny was, too." Then she surprised him. "I've been rude to you."

"No—"

"Yes," she interrupted. "Rude. You were Johnny's

friend. Apparently, a good enough friend to come to the back of beyond to check on his wife. I've treated you exactly like that gum on my shoe."

"It's okay."

"No," she said hotly, "it's not okay. You were my husband's friend, one of the best he had, and I've treated you poorly. I didn't want you here."

There, she'd said it. He edged forward, ready to leave.

"But the thing is," she continued, "I didn't want you here for reasons that weren't fair to you."

He hesitated, wondering if he should speak at all.

"You reminded me, not just of Johnny, but of the person I used to be. I'd become something awful, and I had some time to think about it. *You* made me think about it. I'd become a hermit. I'm surprised all my friends didn't abandon me, and then you…you got me thinking about what I was doing. Grief *is* selfish, but it doesn't have to be this selfish. I didn't want you here because you made me see myself. It wasn't a pretty picture."

"But an understandable one," he said in what he hoped was a kind voice. It was a voice he didn't get to use often.

"Maybe or maybe not. The point is, I woke up to the fact that I was making things worse for everyone around me, and I wasn't dealing. Not really. I was hiding in my misery. Then it struck me that misery is, if not comfortable, at least a safe place to stay. It takes no risks."

He tried to sort thought all this, to understand what she was driving at, but he wasn't at all sure.

"Anyway, you made me uncomfortable, and a lot of it had to do with me. I have a right to grieve, but not to wallow in self-pity and to hurt my friends because it hurt me to see them."

He grasped that. "It hurts to see others happy when you're not."

"So what? They have a right to be happy, and I should be happy for them, not hating them for it. Loss comes to everyone, Ryker. I tried to remind myself that you'd lost Johnny, too, but…well, maybe that was the first thing that made me look harder at myself."

His chest tightened for her. God, all the things this woman had to deal with. He was amazed that she could even find concern for others with all that had happened. "Don't be hard on yourself."

"Why not? I'm not the only widow in the world. It happens to thousands every single day. I just let it suck me down like quicksand. I shut out everything and everyone. I'm not very proud of it. Anyway, get your stuff from the motel. You can stay in one of the spare rooms."

He felt he'd just been gut-punched. Was she having some kind of break? A moment of insanity? Stay in this house with a woman he'd bed in an instant if she crooked a finger his way?

"No, really…"

"I'm serious. You may not be a talker, but I'd like to know you better."

"Because of Johnny?" He was definitely wrestling with this.

"Not just that. For me, too. And anyway, I need someone around. You want to help, I need help. Right?"

"Yes," he answered promptly, although the request for help left him feeling a little deflated. For the last few weeks, despite all the time he'd spent trying to cut Marisa out of his thoughts, she'd simply taken up firmer residence there. He'd have liked it if she just wanted him around. Not that that was ever going to happen. Was he losing his mind? He usually met life with more clarity than this. "What kind of help?"

"A little of everything, but mainly I need someone around because the doctor told me he thinks I'm farther along than he originally thought. I may need someone to drive me to the hospital all of a sudden."

"Farther along?" Now he was in the weeds in a swamp he didn't begin to understand. Pregnancy had not been a part of his life. "How is that possible?"

"It's possible. Johnny was home for a little over two months. I could have been pregnant the first two months without even knowing it."

He sensed the details of that were something he should leave alone. "So is he sure?"

"Pretty much. He judges the baby to be over seven pounds right now. Either I'm going to have an elephant or I'm getting close to term. I'd rather not have an elephant."

That surprised a crack of laughter from him. "I read you."

She smiled faintly. "Given the range of time…well, we're just hoping that her lungs are fully developed when she arrives. That's why I don't want to be early. But if he's right…Jonni could be here in the next few weeks."

"I like the name," he offered.

"It seemed to have stuck without me even thinking about it. Not really. I didn't even indulge in looking up baby's names. So she's probably going to be Johnna, Jonni for short."

"Pretty. So this nesting thing? It's for real?" He was surprisingly curious about all this. Something totally new in his life, and he evidently needed it. Great big gaping holes in his experience stared him in the face. Sometimes he felt as if he'd become a one-dimensional man.

"My friends tell me it means I'm getting close, maybe in the last month. Connie loves to talk about moving a two-hundred-pound couch all by herself because she simply had to rearrange the living room. And I've certainly been on a cleaning binge. Even the insides of my kitchen cabinets are sparkling."

"I could have helped with that." Lame, but all he could think of when he was still trying to wend his way through this, trying to figure out what this woman was really saying.

"I'm sure. And if I get an urge to wash windows, I'll put you to work."

For the first time, he relaxed. Some kind of relationship was being laid out here, and so far he didn't have any problems with it. "Fair enough. I need the workout."

Was he really agreeing to move into this woman's house? He guessed he was, which was sure going to make life difficult.

Marisa sighed and put her cup aside. "I'm perfectly healthy, the baby is doing great, I just get tired more easily. Normal activities are all allowed."

Meaning? He didn't know if he should ask. But then a thought struck him, a thought so alien to him that he had to digest it before speaking. This woman had a big hole in her life, yes, but there was an even bigger hole. She didn't have a husband to share this experience with, to talk about her baby with, to discuss each development along the way. He might not know a lot about it, but he suspected pregnancy was a huge deal for a woman, and she ought to have someone to share it with. Marisa had been missing the most important part of that.

He asked carefully, "Do you talk to your friends about your pregnancy?"

"Sometimes. Well, rarely. It's not like it's a big thing for them the way it is for me. Besides, like I said, I've been hiding away. Staying inside myself."

"Well, I don't know squat about it," he said truthfully. Rising, he put his own cup down and crossed the room. He lifted her ankles from the hassock, feeling that simple touch like an electrical shock, and sat with her feet on his thighs. Gently he started rubbing her ankles. "I'd like to know," he said quietly. "Tell me about it."

The frozen way she looked at his hands, he expected her to tell him to keep his mitts to himself. But then she astonished him. With a smile, she said, "That feels so good."

"Then I'll keep it up." Carefully he removed her jogging shoes, leaving her socks in place, and began to rub her feet, as well. It felt like sparks were shooting from his hands, or from her feet to his hands. "So talk to me. Despite everything, you must have had some special moments after you learned you were expecting."

"I did." Utter relaxation appeared to pass through her, and she let her head fall back and her eyes close. "There was the first time I felt movement. It was…amazing. All of a sudden this baby was real, totally real to me. It changed everything."

"What did it feel like?"

"At first almost like small bubbles moving. Now it's stronger. I get definite pokes and kicks."

"Can you see them?"

"I sure can. Sometimes I think I can even make out a foot, just this tiny little wedge, but I'm not sure. As the doc said, the baby's inside a pillow which is inside another pillow."

"But you've seen an ultrasound?"

"This morning." Her eyes didn't open, but a smile came to her face. "She's so perfect."

"Did you get to keep a picture?"

"It's in my purse."

"I'd like to see it later."

Her eyes opened. "Ryker? Why are you doing this? You don't need to get involved with the baby."

He thought about that before answering. "I've led an active life, but there are lots of things I've missed. This is one of them. And besides, the baby is John's legacy."

"Legacy," she repeated the word. "I like that."

He rubbed her feet, extending her toes, massaging the muscles along her arches, then returning to her ankles, rubbing gently to move the fluid upward. "We're different in a very important way."

"What's that?"

"You create life. You bring something wonderful into the world."

She tilted her head. "And you don't?"

"I try to save lives, yeah. But it's not always possible."

Another sigh escaped her, and her eyes closed. "That's sad. And I could sleep."

"You just do that. While you nap, I'll get my belongings from the motel."

She nodded slightly, and he watched with a faint smile as she dozed off. Only when he was sure she slept did he stop massaging her.

She was giving him a totally different perspective on life, he thought as he grabbed his coat and headed out. That could be a good thing or a very bad thing.

One thing for sure. He was beginning to wonder how John could have ever left this woman's side.

After he'd filled his duffel and backpack, which pretty much contained his whole life except for some items in storage in Virginia, he headed for the diner. He was recognized when he entered and greeted by some of the folks having lunch there. While he didn't feel as if he were part of their community, he guessed they were letting him know that they'd decided he was okay.

Even irascible Maude gave him a nod and asked what he wanted. As soon as she heard he was buying for two, she asked if it was for Marisa. When he answered yes, Maude went to work making a meal.

"She swelling any?" Maude asked.

"Her ankles and feet."

"I'll leave off the salt, then. I swear that woman looks ready to pop any day."

Ryker didn't offer any gossip. Keeping secrets was nearly automatic.

"She needs someone looking after her now." Maude glared at him. "Any volunteers?"

He almost laughed at her pointedness. He'd known gunnery sergeants who didn't hold a candle to this woman. "Yes, ma'am. Me."

"About time," Maude grunted, then went back to work. Quite soon she had a paper bag full of foam containers and beverages. Ryker stepped out into the bracing cold and found himself face-to-face with a guy in a sheriff's uniform. One side of his face was burn-scarred, and his badge said "Dalton."

So this was the sheriff he'd heard about a couple of

times. "Put that food in the car," the man said. "Let it keep warm. I just want a word."

Ryker nodded, put the bag on the passenger seat, then faced the man. He wore a heavy shearling coat, but the badge and name tag were still prominent, as were patches on the shoulder. He offered his hand.

"Gage Dalton, sheriff," he said. "And you're Ryker Tremaine."

"Yes."

"I got word you checked out of the motel. Leaving town?"

"Marisa Hayes asked me to stay with her."

Dalton nodded slowly. "I checked up on you. I still have some pretty good contacts from my days with the DEA."

Ryker tensed. What was this about?

"You have an amazingly bland background," Dalton remarked. "Which tells me a whole lot. The absence of information is often very informative."

Ryker waited, vigilant, for whatever was to come.

"Just be careful," Dalton said. "I don't think Marisa could handle another John, if you get my drift."

"Perfectly."

Dalton nodded and walked back toward his office up the street. Ryker stood there for a minute. The man was right. Marisa couldn't handle it again. But he already knew that. What struck him was the way this town kept trying to protect her. Even the damn sheriff.

He figured that living here could either make a person claustrophobic or very grateful. So far he didn't feel claustrophobic, but then he wasn't trying to put down roots here. Maybe folks were pretty much leaving him alone.

He took the warning in good part, even though he didn't need it. He knew he was poison. That was why he'd never stayed long enough to get attached. This was different, however. Between repatriation time after his last mission and having a whole lot of built-up vacation time, he could stay as long as he wanted.

But only if he didn't feel he was hurting anyone. Marisa had her doubts about him, justifiably so. He might want to take her to bed, maybe even indulge in a little fantasy about a life with her, but that was all it would ever be: fantasy.

Because Marisa carried a price tag. He'd have to give up his job to be what she needed, to spare her another loss. The thought was so impossible that he'd never considered it.

Not before Marisa, anyway.

Crap, he was a mess. He needed to square his head away, and he needed to do it soon.

When he got back to the house, he left his bags in the car and went inside with the food. She was gone from her rocker, evidently done with her nap.

"Marisa?"

"In the kitchen."

He walked through the door and froze. She was standing on the top of a three-step stool, reaching for something well above her head.

"My God, woman! What the hell…?"

"I wanted that casserole dish from up there," she said. "It didn't use to be so high."

He saw her teeter a bit. He moved in a flash, dropping the bag on the table as he passed it and catching her by the hips, steadying her. "Are you out of your mind?"

"Oh, hush, Ryker. I've done this a million times."

"Probably not with about twenty pounds hanging off your front affecting your balance. Down. Now. I'll get the damn dish."

"Sheesh," she said, but a little giggle escaped her. "I think the nesting hit again."

"I think you're out of your mind. Step down. Easy now. I've got you."

With each step down, her back brushed the front of his body, stoking fires he'd been trying to put out almost from the first instant he saw her. "You know," he muttered, "this sucks. And you shouldn't be allowed to be alone for even ten minutes if you're going to pull stunts like this."

"Maybe not," she said quietly, then astonished him by leaning back into him as her feet settled on the floor. His hands remained on her hips, and he stopped breathing as she covered them with her own.

What was the she up to?

"You have big hands," she remarked. "Strong." Her fingers curled briefly around his and squeezed. "Thanks. Forget the casserole. I have others."

"But you wanted this one enough to risk your neck."

"It was my grandmother's. I mainly wanted it down where I could see it. Pure decoration. Ryker? I think my back hurts a bit."

Well, he could sure understand why, given the way she had been reaching and that twist to look at him when he first arrived. "Where?" he asked.

"High up. Not low. Don't panic, it's not labor."

Panicking wasn't usually in his nature, although he supposed anything was possible. But he didn't want to let go of this moment of intimacy, however pointless and brief it was. He had begun to crave this woman, and a stupider thing he'd never done.

Slowly she released his hands. Taking it as a sign, he stepped back. He cleared his throat, feeling uncharacteristically awkward. "I brought food from the diner. A warning, though. Maude left the salt off yours."

She turned slowly, her cheeks flushed. "Nice of her."

He guided her to her chair and began pulling items out of the bag. His groin throbbed, and he hoped she couldn't see it. His jeans weren't that tight, he assured himself, and his black sweatshirt was extra long, providing a little more camouflage.

"Ryker?" She sounded breathless. Concerned, he looked up from the bag.

"What?"

"Am I awful?"

"Awful? What in the world would make you think that?"

"Because…because…" She put her face in her hands.

At once he squatted beside her, worried, touching her arm. "Marisa? What's wrong?"

"Nothing. It's just…I shouldn't be having these feelings."

"What feelings?" Suicidal thoughts? Urges to kill someone? Fear? The whole palette of emotions lay there waiting for her to choose one.

She kept her face covered. "I have dreams about you."

His entire body leaped. He had dreams about her, too, and not only when he was sleeping. "And?"

"I want you. Is that wrong? I mean…it hasn't been that long…"

Her words deprived him of breath. He could have lifted her right then and carried her to her bed. He'd have done so joyfully. But caution and maybe even some wisdom held him back.

"I want you, too," he said huskily.

She dropped her hands, her wondering eyes meeting his almost shyly. "Really? Looking like this?"

"You're beautiful looking just like that. But…"

"But?" She seized on the word, some of the wonder leaving her face.

"I don't want you to regret it. So how about we spend more time talking to each other? Give yourself some time to be sure. Hell, it probably wouldn't be safe, anyway."

"My doc says it would."

She'd asked her doctor? A thousand explosions went off in his head, leaving him almost blind. He cleared his throat. "Uh…I could take you right now. I want to. So, please, don't be embarrassed. I don't think you're awful. But…please…get to know me a bit better. I want to know you better. I want you to be sure."

"I feel guilty," she admitted. "It's been driving me nuts. Am I betraying Johnny?"

"I don't believe he'd think so. But that's a question only you can answer, and you need to do that for yourself. Then there's me."

"You?" She studied him.

"I don't exactly feel right about this. After what you've already been through, I shouldn't have to explain that. I'm another John, Marisa. Why in the world would you want to risk that again?" And now that he knew the real reason she'd been trying to avoid him, he felt like crap. He'd read her all right. She wanted him gone. But only because she wanted *him*, and it made her feel guilty. Could it get any messier?

She nodded slowly, looking down at where her fingertips pressed into the wooden table. "I don't know," she finally said quietly. "Not that it'd be a risk. You already said you don't commit."

At a rather advanced stage of life, he was discovering how fast feelings could grow. It was as if he'd let something off his internal leash, and now he hurt to hear himself described in his own terms. "Think about it," he said. "Just think about it. I'll be living here for a while, so you can find out if this is what you really want. In the meantime, let's chow down before the food gets cold."

He hated to remove his hand from her arm, to withdraw to a safer distance. Food held little appeal now, because he knew he didn't just need her to evaluate her feelings, but he needed to evaluate his whole damn life.

Later, after he'd cleaned up and put half her salad in the fridge for later, he retrieved her casserole dish for her. "It's pretty," he said. It was cobalt blue, with pink flowers and gold scrolling.

"I always thought so." Then she shook him to the core. "You know I've been avoiding you."

"I know. Same here. I could tell you didn't want me around, so I stayed away."

"But do you know why I felt that way?"

"Tell me." So it wasn't all about illicit feelings of desire. He didn't know whether to be relieved.

She hesitated while he set the casserole dish on the counter and put the stool away. "I didn't trust you. Too many secrets. And then I wanted you, and I felt guilty. Did I upset you by telling you that?"

He faced her squarely. "Truth is always welcome in my life." A rare commodity, if he were to be honest. "No, you didn't upset me. Why should you trust me? But you shouldn't feel guilty."

"But I hate that you know things about Johnny I can never know."

Ouch. His mind raced, seeking adequate words to give her. There were none. There would never be any. "I can't tell you," he said finally.

"I know. But why do I think there are things I wouldn't want to know even if you could?"

"Because you're probably right," he said brutally. "What we did…what we sometimes had to do…you don't need to know about it."

She nodded, drawing a shaky breath. "I suspected. I didn't want to think about it, but I suspected. Someone has to do the world's dirty work."

Then she left the kitchen. He found her a few minutes later in the living room with her feet up, staring into space.

Before he could sit or speak a single word, she began to talk. "Johnny had trouble with it sometimes. I could tell. Nightmares, mostly. Sometimes he'd just withdraw and not even want to be touched. It didn't happen often, but I could sense…changes. But it always passed quickly and then he'd be the old Johnny again." She turned her head toward him. "Every time he came back, I could feel that he'd changed some more. Life changes us all over time, but this was…different."

"It worried you?"

"Not exactly. It troubled me. Since he was killed, all I could remember were the good things. But they weren't always good, Ryker. God, I loved him, but I sometimes wondered what he was becoming."

He knew exactly what she meant. He could reach

back in his own mind and remember a young man who
didn't carry so many dark secrets and stains on his soul.
John had picked up those stains, too, and like acid they
sometimes ate away at the soul.

He wished he knew what to tell her. He finally settled
on, "Remember the good things, Marisa." Desperation
struck him then. He didn't know where this was going,
didn't know if he should clear out before it went any further. Wanting this woman wasn't enough. The question
was if he had enough to give her.

When he saw her eyelids drooping again, he took advantage of it. "Take a nap. I'm going out for another run."

"Okay," she said drowsily. Then, "What are you running from, Ryker?"

He froze, but she was already asleep. He grabbed
his jacket and left. What was he running from? Marisa
Hayes and a future he didn't believe he had a right to.

Wasn't that enough?

Chapter Six

Ryker was doing laundry for Marisa. Much to her amazement, he not only knew how to do it, but he folded it beautifully. She'd let it go until she was down to her last clean underwear, and while it made her flush a little to think of him handling her intimate apparel, she had to admit she appreciated the help. Lately she'd been getting tired more often and napping more often, and the laundry looked like a daunting task.

It was Saturday morning, the day after Ryker had moved in, when Julie showed up unannounced.

"You need a change of scenery," Julie said. "We're going to my place, where I'm going to ply you with conversation and sinful food." She paused. "Is that Ryker in the basement? I saw his car out front."

"I asked him to move in. It was rude of me to keep him at the motel. Anyway, he's doing my laundry." She pointed to the basket on the floor beside the couch.

"You found a man who does laundry? Oh, be still, my beating heart!"

Marisa laughed.

"Just a sec." Julie went to the head of the stairs and called down. "Ryker?"

"Yo."

"I'm taking Marisa to my place for a change of scene."

"Go for it," came the answer. "When I'm through washing her stuff, I'm going to get to my own. She needs some time out of here."

"Don't I know it. Back in a few hours."

Ryker had freshly salted the porch and sidewalk, so the trip to Julie's car was safe enough. When they were inside, the engine running and the heater blowing, Julie asked, "Need to pick up anything while we're out?"

"I don't know. The guy moved in yesterday, he went grocery shopping, and I'm not even sure what he got, and he bought us dinner last night."

"Okay then." Julie smiled. "We'll call him before we come back to see if *he* needs anything. First, let's get to my place."

Julie had taken a ground floor apartment in one of the relatively new complexes that had been built during the brief boom of the semiconductor plant. The plant now sat sadly empty, the jobs had gone away, but the apartments remained.

She had a cheerful place, full of bright colors, impeccably clean except for stacks of papers and books on her coffee table and small desk from her teaching. She brewed a pot of tea after Marisa settled on an armchair, and brought it with some shortbread cookies.

"Now, dish," she said, her favorite line. "What did the doc say, and what is Ryker up to?"

"The doc says I'm nearly due."

Julie clattered the teapot as she put it down. "What?"

"You heard me. He thinks I got pregnant before my last period."

Julie sat down slowly. "Wow. Is that possible?"

"He says sometimes women have a light period when they first become pregnant. Well, it was light. And he added that he'd suspected when I first came to see him that I was farther along. I thought two months, he thought three. But he didn't say anything, because as he put it, it's hard to be sure. But now he thinks I'm getting pretty close."

Julie laughed. "Imagine the other girls dying of envy. Especially Connie. Her pregnancies always lasted ten months."

Marisa had to laugh, too. "I'd forgotten. Anyway, he said it's far from an exact science, that nine months is an approximation, but…he said there are signs. He's guessing just a few more weeks."

"How do you feel about it?" Julie settled and tucked her legs under her.

"I guess it's okay. I've been in stasis so long… God, Julie, I've been awful to everyone, and I'm so sorry."

"Cut it out," Julie said firmly. "You've been through a lot, and what kind of friends would we be if we didn't understand? Is that why you had Ryker move in?"

"Well, he'd be right there to drive me to the hospital."

Julie sipped her tea. "Have a cookie. Can I be perfectly frank?"

"Aren't you always?"

Julie sighed. "No. You know that. But I'm wondering about something."

Marisa tensed a little, but reached for a cookie. It gave

her something to occupy her hand and her mouth. Her heart thudded a bit as she wondered what was coming.

"This Ryker guy," Julie said. "A few weeks ago, you pushed him away. The *Do Not Disturb* signs were practically neon."

Marisa opened her mouth to explain, but Julie spoke first.

"The thing is, Marisa, maybe you don't know it, but I saw you eating him up with your eyes. You wanted that man."

"Oh, God." Marisa dropped the cookie on her saucer and felt a tear leak from one eye. She wanted to run and hide. "I'm awful."

"Awful?" Julie sounded startled. "What was awful? My God, I was so happy to see a stirring of life in you. I thought it was wonderful. Then you just shoved him away. Why?"

Marisa could barely shove the words out through her tightening throat. "It was wrong. Johnny..."

"Oh, to hell with that. You were grieving, sure. But that doesn't mean you can't live. You didn't have to crawl into that coffin with Johnny. Hell, none of us wanted to see that. We were worried about you. You just went into a cocoon and barely poked your nose out. So I got happy for you when you...showed some interest in something. A man. That's not a freaking crime!"

More tears rolled down Marisa's face, and she began to have trouble breathing. "I felt like it was."

"Well, it's not. And while we're on the subject, I want to remind you of something."

Marisa closed her eyes and nodded. Once Julie was on a roll, there was no stopping her. Even when it felt like taking it on the chin.

"Johnny was the one who left you. Over and over again he left you. Try to remember that. Then there's just one other thing before I shut my mouth. Go ahead and have a fling with Ryker if he's interested. You're entitled to some pleasure in your life. But damn it, just a fling, because he's another Johnny."

Ryker couldn't put Marisa's clothes away, so he left the basket beside her bed, awaiting her directions when she got home. Then he headed into the kitchen to start dinner for them, wondering if he should cook for Julie, as well.

But mostly he was wondering about himself. He felt yearnings he'd never felt before. Yearnings for a home, a family, all those ordinary things his life had kept from him. But unless he changed himself, he couldn't have any of them.

Quite a conundrum, he thought with bitter amusement. For years he'd been amazed that John had managed both, but then he'd been faced with Marisa. That was the price of his kind of life. Dying didn't begin to touch it. John had left devastation behind him in the life of a woman he loved. Maybe he'd never really thought it would happen. Or maybe he'd been so addicted to danger he simply couldn't quit.

But faced with the wreckage, Ryker couldn't consider adding any of those missing things to his life unless he was prepared to carve out a piece of himself. It just wouldn't be fair.

But when he tried to visualize himself in any other role, he faced a blank wall. He'd never been anything else. What would he replace it with? He couldn't imagine.

He'd never been given to a lot of self-reflection. As

a rule he was too busy, either on an assignment that took his full attention, or getting ready for one or coming back from one. Total job absorption. But since he'd learned about John, and mostly since he'd met John's wife, he had a hell of a lot to think about. Reevaluating himself proved to be an uncomfortable place to be.

Thus he was glad when he heard the front door open, heard Marisa's and Julie's voices.

"Welcome back," he called out.

But only Marisa came into the kitchen. She looked worn out, and he felt a spark of instant concern. "Something wrong? Where's Julie?"

"She had a meeting. I'm fine."

"Well, you don't look it," he said bluntly. "Go put your feet up. Want a glass of milk or something?"

She didn't answer, so he got her one, anyway. He found her in her bedroom, curled up on her bed. She hadn't even removed her jacket, although her gloves and scarf lay on the floor. The rules he had set for himself dictated that he just leave her alone. Well, to hell with the rules.

He entered the room, put the milk on her nightstand, then sat beside her. After a moment he caressed her arm. "Marisa? What happened? I thought you two were going to have fun."

"We did," she mumbled.

"Then what happened to fun?"

She didn't answer. He kept stroking her arm, hoping his touch felt soothing. Just as he was about to give up and leave her alone, she spoke.

"Julie said something that shook me up."

"What was that?"

"She pointed out to me that I had nothing to feel

guilty about. That I didn't leave Johnny, that he left me. That he was always leaving me."

He felt those words like a blow to his chest. They were painful to hear, and saying things about how it was John's job didn't take the sting out. He knew it. John had left her repeatedly, and not just to go to the corner store.

He continued to massage her arm gently, then did something totally uncharacteristic. He stretched out behind her and wrapped his arm around her. He wasn't accustomed to offering comfort, but strange as if felt, it was good. He just hoped it helped her in some small way. He also wondered if there was any way to convince her that John hadn't been leaving her. Because the truth was, year after year, John had gone away for months at a time, and he kept going away until he was unable to come home anymore.

Ryker was just the same. He had no business inserting himself into this woman's life, maybe giving her something else to worry about. Certainly no business holding her like this as if he could offer comfort when he was himself no comfort at all. Regardless of their earlier conversation, he needed to keep his distance. Protect her from a relationship of any kind that could leave her in the straits John had. Even friendship might be a danger to her.

But his world had been shaken, too. Here he was, holding a woman simply to offer comfort, and it felt magical. The lacks in is own life jolted his perspective, and he stared into emptiness over Marisa's head.

He felt her beginning to relax. Falling asleep? Maybe. He wondered if he should move anyway, get the hell out of this house and town.

Then she surprised him by murmuring, "I knew the

rules going in. Why did I let what Julie said upset me so much? It's not fair to John."

Now, that was a question indeed. His understanding of human nature was large but limited in scope. He wasn't used to dealing with the tenderer emotions. Not with things like this, and yet, here he was, comforting this woman with a hug, aware that lies would always stand between them and absolutely no understanding of what she was going through. He stifled a sigh and tried to think of one useful thing to offer. Some way to ease her. Because she didn't deserve this.

"Julie didn't mean it the way I took it," Marisa said after a short while. "I think she was encouraging me to get on with my own life. But…it hit me hard, Ryker. It was like looking at everything from a different angle."

Well, he understood that. It was happening to him right now, and no matter how hard he tried to straighten his head out, it remained all mixed up. He shoved himself aside to take care of Marisa. "Don't let this affect your memories," he said quietly. "Maybe all that's happening is that you're realizing you needed some things in your marriage that you didn't get. Probably pretty typical."

"Maybe."

"I mean, I'm no expert. Hell, I'm not even a beginner. I avoided all that. But I do know that John loved you. And I can guess how hard his absences must have been. But that doesn't diminish the love, does it?" He was floundering here and increasingly aware that he was building an internal list of all the things this woman deserved…and that didn't include being abandoned for months at a time or raising a kid without its father. John, he thought, you were one selfish jerk.

So he, too, was seeing things differently. Hitherto he'd thought John extremely lucky to have found a woman like Marisa. Now he was wondering if John had ever considered how much his chosen life had affected his wife.

Why the hell had Julie stirred up this hornet's nest? If he got the chance, he was going to ask her to explain herself.

Because at this point it seemed simply cruel, and Marisa had suffered enough cruelty.

As it turned out, he didn't have to wait long to confront Julie. Marisa fell asleep, and he slipped from her side to let her rest comfortably. He was in the kitchen putting together dinner when he heard a car pull up.

Going to the front, he saw it was Julie. He grabbed his jacket and stepped out into the icy air, watching the woman approach him.

"She's sleeping," he said shortly, without greeting.

Julie studied him from green eyes. "Who made you the castle gatekeeper?"

"Me."

Julie nodded slowly, and he couldn't understand why a smile tugged at the corners of her mouth. "So, you're another Johnny?"

He didn't deny it. Instead, he went on the attack. "Why'd you upset her?"

Julie's face changed, the hinted smile evaporating. "What do you mean?"

"Telling her that John was always leaving her. It upset her. It's making her question everything."

"Ah, hell." Julie looked away, stuffing her hands into the pockets of her coat. "I was afraid of that." Her breath blew clouds on the frigid air. "I was just trying to tell her that she had a right to move on. That she wasn't betraying Johnny in some way if she did. After all, he kept walking out that door. She ought to be able to walk forward, at least." She turned her attention back to Ryker. "She's attracted to you."

He didn't reply.

"Go ahead and be a sphinx. But I have some words for you. Don't you dare hurt her. If you're planning to treat her the way Johnny did, then get the hell out right now. It's not right for her to keep living her life waiting for a man to come home. Not right at all. And love doesn't make it right."

Wow, he thought as he watched her walk back to her car. That woman didn't pull her punches. "Julie?" he called.

She turned with obvious reluctance.

"Thanks for being such a good friend to her."

At that Julie moved toward him. He came down the steps so he didn't tower over her.

"I don't know what's with you," she said. "You were Johnny's friend, so I presume you lead the same kind of life. She loved that man. I don't want to see her in this position again. And now there's a kid to concern me, too. You might be a nice guy, for all I know. Just don't drag her and that kid back into limbo. Don't."

He nodded once. "I read you. And that's not my intention at all."

"Intentions are meaningless. Actions count. She's not one to bark and snarl, but I am."

Again he nodded. "Thing is, she makes her own decisions. What worries me is that you made her hurt."

"Yeah." Julie blew a sigh, a white cloud. "I didn't

mean it that way. I really didn't. I know she's attracted to you. I was kind of trying to give her a blessing, so she wouldn't feel guilty about it. But on the other hand… No more Johnnys."

This time he let her go. She hadn't said one thing he didn't already know. Whatever he did, whatever Marisa chose, he had to ensure he didn't put her back where she'd been.

The question was, could *he* change? Because he definitely didn't want to make Marisa change. Or maybe the better question was simply whether he should just clear out of here after the baby came. She'd have plenty of girlfriends to help her out, women who knew a helluva lot more about babies than he.

As he was combining ingredients for a pot roast, he suddenly froze and wondered why the hell he was even thinking of such things. Soon he'd hit the road again, go back to his life and leave Marisa behind in hers.

Some questions didn't need answers. In fact, they shouldn't even be asked.

Marisa's nap revived her. She awoke to a house full of delicious aromas, then suddenly remembered she had fallen asleep with Ryker holding her. Okay, the guy could be sweet. Even understanding. But he was still a box full of secrets, and really, she'd had enough of that. Julie could say whatever she wanted about a fling being okay, but Marisa wasn't buying it.

She wasn't the "fling" type. Johnny had been her one and only, and with her looming responsibilities to a child, she'd be a fool to change that.

Rising, she freshened up, then headed toward the front of the house to find out what was going on. Ryker was sitting on the couch, reading a book. He looked up and smiled.

"Feeling better?"

"Much. I don't know what got into Julie."

He put the book aside. "I do. She came by while you were sleeping. Apparently, she was trying to tell you to seize the day and then realized later that you might have taken it wrong. She also had a message for me."

Marisa slowly perched on the other end of the couch. "What is she doing messing in my life like this?"

"Being a friend," he said truthfully.

"So, what was her message for you?"

"That I'll be drawn and quartered if I harm a hair on your head."

At first Marisa gasped, then a laugh spilled out of her. The baby stirred, kicking hard. "She'd never have said such a thing."

"Not exactly in those words."

Marisa laid a hand over her stomach, feeling the pokes and prods. Nobody had shared this with her. Nobody. And all of a sudden she had a crying need to share it with someone.

"Come here," she said. "Just scoot closer."

His gaze narrowed a bit, but he did as asked. Then she took his large hand and pressed it to her belly. "Just feel her."

He drew a breath. "Wow," he murmured.

"Wait. Sometimes it feels like she's turning over in there."

He closed his eyes, waiting as she had asked. "Such life," he said quietly. "So much life."

His eyes opened and met hers squarely. She felt electricity zap between them, as if she'd just been connected to a battery. Then every cell in her began to hum with desire. She wanted this man. He might be trouble, but she wanted him, anyway.

Not good, she reminded herself. Ryker would soon leave. He had a job to get back to, a whole life buried in the secrets he and Johnny couldn't share with her. But for now...for now she needed someone to share her joy in this growing baby. Put everything else on the back burner, just savor this moment, a moment she should have been sharing with her husband. Sharing it with his friend at least assuaged some of her need.

"What do I smell cooking?" she asked eventually.

"Pot roast. I hope it's not too salty."

"I'll drink a lot of water."

He removed his hand, then clasped hers. "Marisa? That was special. Thanks for sharing with me."

"Well, I can't share it with Johnny." She meant to say it lightly, but it came out sounding rather different.

Ryker stood up. "I'm not Johnny." He was halfway to the kitchen when he called back, "You want water or something?"

"I'll get it." She sat there feeling almost stunned. The way he had said *I'm not Johnny*. It had sounded angry. Maybe bitter. What the hell was going on now?

She waited a while, trying to compose herself, running her palms over her tummy in a soothing motion that probably did more for her than her baby. Eventually, however, she needed a drink and had to venture into the kitchen, where Ryker seemed to have ensconced himself.

He was seated at the table, staring out the window at the wintry day. Snowflakes had begun to fall, and she wondered vaguely how much accumulation they'd get.

She went to the refrigerator for a glass of orange juice, then paused. "Dinner smells really good," she offered.

"Thanks."

Okay, this wasn't working. "What did Julie say to you exactly?"

"Only the truth," he said grudgingly.

"Which was?"

"That you don't need another Johnny."

Marisa caught her breath and felt her heart slam. "She had no right…"

"She's your friend. She's concerned about you. She has every right."

She pulled out a chair and sat facing him. Standing too long these days made her back ache a bit. "You'd think the back muscles would keep up with the pregnancy," she remarked.

That drew his attention toward her.

"Meaning?"

"Apparently, they don't. I can't stand for long now without my back aching. It's mostly mild, but why flirt with a bigger problem?"

"Oh." He drummed his fingers lightly. "I'm sorry if I upset you more."

"You didn't upset me, you confused me and made me wonder what Julie said to you. I know you're not Johnny."

"I didn't quite mean it that way." But maybe he meant it in the most important ways. "I told you I want you. I know you want me. That's ordinary human interaction. Feeling desire is normal. We all do. What concerns me is… I don't want to do anything that might hurt you. However accidentally. From the way Julie tells it, you're finally emerging from your cocoon. I'd like to help with that, not drive you back into it."

Marisa nodded slowly, running her finger along the side of her orange juice glass, collecting condensation. The ache was returning, and this time it wasn't sexual. She felt as if another loss hovered right around the corner. "Are you telling me you're not trustworthy?"

"Depends," he answered shortly.

"On what?"

"Whether I can provide what's needed." His face darkened, and she thought he looked almost frightening. "Tell me to take a hike and I'll expend my last drop of blood to do it. But this…you… You need things I've never had to provide. Never even *tried* to provide."

"Sheesh, Ryker, what does it matter? You don't know what I need, and I'm not asking you for anything, anyway." Her heart was racing now, feeling something important was going on, but danged if she knew what. This guy had barely entered her life. Whether she wanted him sexually was irrelevant. They didn't exactly have a relationship for him to be worrying about.

"It matters," he said. "Because I'm not going to turn you into a casual conquest. You deserve better. And whether or not you want it from me, I still need to know if I can give it. So forget casual. Forget a fling. It ain't gonna happen. I care too much." He shook his head as if to shake something loose. "I care too much," he repeated quietly. "And that's the hell of it. Never did that before, either."

He stood up. "Another hour or so on the slow cooker. I'm going out."

She looked up at him. "Will you be back?"

"Hell if I know."

Then he was gone, leaving her alone in the silent, empty house, the only trace of him the aromas from the slow cooker. What had just happened?

She pushed her orange juice to one side and put her head down the table. Hot tears burned in her eyes and fell on her hands.

She cared, too. *I'm so sorry, Johnny*, she thought. *I didn't want to betray you.* It hadn't even been a year. Not even a year, and already she was somehow crazily tangled up with another man. And it was crazy. Ryker? Who the hell was Ryker? Would she ever know? Did it matter?

She gave in to the tears, just let herself sob them all out. She'd been safer in her cocoon of grief, but somehow Ryker had yanked her out of it, making life all too close again. No muffling between her and it. She was smack-dab back in all the confusion, pain and upset of being alive.

And this time it wasn't grief.

Chapter Seven

Ryker drove for hours along back country roads, feeling as if a Pandora's box had been opened inside him. All the soul-searching he'd failed to do over the years, all the decisions he'd made or had refused to make, the truncated personality he'd become…they all leaped out and screamed at him like unleashed Furies.

Why the hell had John Hayes asked this of him? More than anyone else on the planet, John had to have been aware of Ryker's lacks. His narrow set of emotions. The secrets that would always stand between him and anyone else.

"What were you thinking, John?" But of course there was no answer. Of all the people John could have asked to check on his wife if anything happened, there were a million better choices than Ryker.

John had chosen to lay this on Ryker, and now that

the baby was imminent, Ryker knew he couldn't leave. Not yet. But that was no excuse for what John had caused here, because John hadn't known about the kid.

Or maybe John had been just that selfish. Maybe he hadn't understood Ryker at all. After all, his friend was the one who'd kept leaving a wife behind time and again to go on dangerous missions until he got himself killed. The guy who wouldn't leave the Rangers until he got himself a dangerous covert job with the CIA.

Ryker could hardly hold himself blameless, though. He hadn't *had* to get John that job. He could have told the guy to go home and settle down. But, maybe just like John, he hadn't given any thought to Marisa. She wasn't *his* wife. What did it matter to him?

Oh, hell, it mattered. It mattered in ways he wasn't used to and didn't know how to handle. Or even sort out.

What did John think Ryker would do? Pull into town, make a little recon, find out if Marisa needed anything, then head out again?

Cussing, Ryker turned into the parking lot of a roadhouse and slammed the car into Park. Maybe that was the Ryker John thought he knew. A man who could come here and leave everything untouched. Leave Marisa in her misery. Barely touch the edges of her consciousness. A gesture, nothing more. A way to speak from beyond the grave and remind this woman he'd loved her.

Well, it hadn't worked that way, had it? What's more, he was beginning to agree with Julie's unspoken assessment of John. Selfish and always walking out the door.

The ugliest thought popped into his head. John had known Ryker wouldn't be able to make it until months after the funeral. Maybe this had been John's way of keeping her grief fresh, of keeping her to himself, because he knew Ryker's rule on women.

Could that man have really been so ugly inside?

It was possible, much as he hated to believe it. But he knew as well how much the kind of life they led could breed ugliness in some. And how possessive some men could be.

He cussed again and switched off the car, heading inside to get a beer. Just one, because he had to get back to that house to look after Marisa. John's other legacy. One that was probably turning out very differently than John had expected.

Ryker tried to shake the thought away. Maybe John had been trying to make a point to Ryker. It was possible. He'd often tried to persuade Ryker that marriage was a good thing.

Ryker was having none of it. And after seeing what it had cost Marisa, he was having even less of it.

He'd have to change himself in ways he could scarcely imagine before he would feel right about sharing his life with a woman.

And that was that.

Ryker was gone so long that Marisa finally helped herself to a small bowl of pot roast, then went into the living room to watch whatever was on TV. She loved to read, but lately reading put her quickly to sleep, and she didn't want to sleep. Not again and not yet.

She found a sitcom rerun and left it on for some background noise. When she glanced out the window, she saw that it was snowing again, a little harder than earlier. She hoped Ryker was safe on the roads.

With her hands resting on her tummy, feeling the

occasional movements of her child, she tried to parse through what had happened that day.

First, Julie had encouraged her to have an affair. Then, she'd apparently come over here to warn Ryker off. Why?

And what had put Ryker in such a turmoil? Why should he be worrying about whether he could provide what she needed? He was just passing through. A friend of Johnny's performing a duty.

That was it, and the sexual attraction that had flared between them didn't change any of that.

Regardless, she got the feeling that something was tearing Ryker apart, and she couldn't imagine what or why. It certainly couldn't be her. He'd been up front with her about his casual approach to women. *Love 'em and leave 'em*, he'd said. Very uncomplicated.

She wondered if she could handle that kind of uncomplicated, or if it would somehow become complicated for her. She had no way to know.

She *did* realize that she was feeling badly for Ryker, though. She sensed that Johnny had somehow put him in an untenable situation. Should she try to get him to talk honestly about it, or was it better just to leave it alone?

But one thing she knew for sure—the clear-eyed, decisive man who had arrived here had vanished. Troubles lurked in his gaze the way they had in hers for so long. Troubles like that didn't go away overnight, as she ought to know.

Emerging from her grief was proving painful in its own way, and she wondered if Ryker was experiencing something like that. He'd been Johnny's friend, after all.

Speculating wasn't at all helpful, though. Not at all. She'd thought Ryker was a man full of secrets, like

Johnny, and he was. But different from Johnny. Johnny
had mostly seemed untroubled. Ryker was striking her
as a man who was being ripped apart from the inside
by something.

At long last she heard him come back.

"I'm in the living room," she called. Lying on the
couch with her feet up. She reached for the remote and
turned off the TV, hoping he'd join her. She was done
with solitude, she realized.

"Hi," he said. "How was dinner?"

"Fabulous. Get yourself some." She turned her head
just a little, catching only a glimpse of him in the doorway.

"I wanted to put your laundry away, but you have to
tell me where."

"Later. It can wait. You folded it so neatly it seems a
shame to disturb it. Eat something."

Five minutes later he returned with his dinner in a
bowl. He took the rocker across from her and started
eating. "You've been okay?"

She snorted. "It may surprise the world, but I've been
breathing successfully on my own for over thirty-two
years."

He flashed a grin at her, then resumed eating. Between mouthfuls, he spoke. "I've been driving around.
Beautiful country here."

"I got a little worried when I saw the snow was growing heavier."

"The roads are getting slick," he agreed. "There is,
however, a roadhouse that I'd advise you to avoid if you
should ever get the urge."

She pushed herself up against the arm of the couch.
"Did something happen?"

"No, I didn't let it happen. I stopped to get a beer, and you could say the atmosphere changed."

She blinked. "But why?"

"Look at me, Marisa. I learned long ago that something about me seems to challenge other men. Not all of them, but some. So I drank half my beer, gave them my best killer look and got the hell out. Some help I'd be to you sitting in a cell for brawling in a bar."

She put her hand to her mouth, afraid she might smile at the silliness. "Really?"

"Really. It happens. I don't know what it is. Anyway, nothing occurred, so it's unimportant."

"Have you ever brawled?"

"Hell, yeah. Sometimes you can't avoid it."

She nodded slowly. "Johnny told me about one or two."

"See? Put a little alcohol in some guys and they suddenly start looking for a place to plant their fists."

"But not you?"

He looked up again. "I told you. I don't have anything to prove."

He resumed eating. She bit her lip, then decided to risk it.

"Why did Johnny ask you to check on me?"

He scraped the last bit from his bowl and set it aside. "I told you I don't know. I've been wondering the same thing. Why?"

"Because you seem so uncomfortable."

"Sometimes I am," he admitted frankly. "I took care of my men, but that's a whole different thing from looking after you. John knew that. He knew I had little to do with women, except casually. Call me stunted. I guess I am. So I don't have a clue."

"But this doesn't seem fair to you."

"Fair?" He arched a brow at her. "Really? You know fair doesn't enter into it."

"But I can tell…something about me is making you uncomfortable."

"Wrong." One single word. A few seconds passed before he elaborated. "You're not causing my problem. You may have made me aware, but you didn't cause this. I'm trying to figure out how to relate to a world I haven't been part of since I was a kid. Change is always uncomfortable, but maybe it's time I made a few. Haven't decided what yet, but there it is. I'm shedding a skin, I guess…growing, I hope. But I'm not sure of much right now."

"You don't need to do this."

His black eyes bored into her. "Actually, I think I do."

His gaze made her heart speed up. Almost as if he reached out physically and touched her, she felt desire begin to drizzle through her entire body, hot and exciting. "Is that what you decided while you were out?" She hoped she didn't sound as breathless as she felt.

"Not exactly. Let's just say I accepted it. Something about walking into that bar. Déjà vu all over again, as they say. I'd been there before, too many times, all over the world. The threat creeping up my neck as eyes fixed on me. My entire body crawling with adrenaline as I waited for it to happen. I'm tired of it."

Well, that was one amazing statement, she thought as she studied him. Tired of it? But it was his life. She'd thought Johnny was making a huge change when he moved out of the army to the State Department, but apparently not. Not considering that he had been killed. Not considering what Ryker had just said. Did the State

Department put people in harm's way as if they were soldiers? Or were there just some jobs... She stopped herself. She'd never know. That had been made abundantly clear to her. Ask as she might, no one would tell her exactly what had happened, what Johnny had been doing. No street mugging, of that she was certain, but what if he'd been doing something decidedly more dangerous? What if all he'd done was find another way to live on the edge he loved?

She sighed, twisted her fingers together and looked at them. Somehow she just had to let go of all that. No amount of knowledge would ease the loss. "What would you do?" she asked suddenly.

"What?" He sounded surprised, as if his mind had moved on.

"If you left your current job?"

"I don't know," he said frankly. "I have a lot of skills that are useless in the civilian world. Well, mostly useless. Occasionally I've toyed with running a survival school or becoming a hunting guide. What I couldn't do is plant myself behind a desk."

In that instant, a light of understanding flared in Marisa's mind. No desk job. State Department? He said he'd run security. Wouldn't that mostly be a desk job? What the hell had Johnny been doing? Because all of a sudden, her imaginings evaporated, and she knew with certainty that Johnny hadn't taken a desk job, either. He hadn't been sitting in some cozy little embassy or consulate somewhere doing routine translations. That wouldn't have suited him at all.

"Ryker? Johnny didn't have a desk job, did he?"

His gaze grew hollow, but he didn't answer.

"What the hell was he doing?"

"I know exactly what they told you. Not one thing more."

"But you know more about the kind of work." Angry now, she struggled to her feet and began pacing. "Everyone's lying to me. Everyone, and that includes Johnny. My God, I can't believe he let me ramble on with all my excited imaginings about the exotic places we could visit with the State Department! He knew I'd never go with him, didn't he? Didn't he, Ryker?" She faced him.

He just shook his head. "I don't know what he thought."

"But you know what he did. And that didn't include bringing a family."

"Actually," he said, rising, "I *don't* know what he was doing. I can't even find out!"

She glared at him, then turned her back on him, accepting that in this, at least, he was telling the truth. "Secrets," she said bitterly. "So many secrets. Did I even know my own husband?"

She felt his hand grip her shoulder gently. She half wanted to shake free and half wanted to turn into his arms.

"You knew the man he was when he was with you," he said quietly. "That's the only part that matters."

"Really? How many lies did he tell me?"

His grip tightened a bit. "I know he loved you. So he never lied to you about that or about your relationship."

"But he never told me anything about what he did, and now I'll never know, and that was such a big part of his life. Now there's you, the same secrets, only you're sweating them. Wanting to change. Johnny never wanted to change."

He turned her then, wrapping his powerful arms

around her, holding her close. Clearly he had no answer for her, but right at that moment she was simply grateful to have someone holding her, because inside she felt herself shattering into a million pieces. Who had she been married to?

His chest rumbled beneath her ear as he spoke. "He was a good man, Marisa. He loved you. A little reckless, maybe, but a good man. I'm sorry I can't tell you any more. I warned you from the beginning, there are operational secrets. Johnny told you that, too. I don't know what Johnny was doing or what his mission was when he died."

But her mind was already straying in a different direction. God, it had been so long since she'd been held like this, comforted like this. Not even knowing that Ryker was just another man full of secrets could change the way he was making her feel: cared for, protected, supported. She'd been alone and lonely for way too long.

She was also pregnant, and before long, leaning into him was making her lower back ache. She didn't want to pull away, but as the ache grew, she knew she had to.

It was almost as if he read her mind. He let go of her, gently eased her back onto the couch, then sat beside her, lifting her legs so his lap cradled them.

"Comfortable?" he asked as she leaned back against the armrest.

"Thanks." It was the best she could manage when she felt as if her insides had been shredded. When Johnny had been in the Rangers, she'd had some idea of what he was doing. He was a soldier, and he went on dangerous missions. When he'd joined the State Department, she'd apparently built castles in the air that had nothing whatsoever to do with reality. Living proof now held her legs in his lap.

With strong hands he began to knead her lower legs through her fleece pants. It felt so good she couldn't have stopped him. Life seemed to be shattering and flying in a million directions, and from what he'd said, he was feeling much the same. What was going on here?

But she was growing awfully tired of unanswered and unanswerable questions.

"I'm sorry I don't have your answers," he said a while later.

"That's not your fault, is it? I'm beginning to really get it."

"In what way?" His hands continued their soothing motions.

"You don't know a whole lot more than I do. Oh, you know what *you* were doing but little else."

He didn't answer immediately, then remarked, "We call it compartmentalizing. Need to know. Each little part is separate from all the other parts."

That was probably the single most revealing thing he'd told her. "So you operate in the dark, too?"

"Much of the time. I know only what I need to."

"Does that seem right to you?"

He turned, his dark eyes catching hers. "It used to."

An interesting choice of phrase. She seized on it, hoping she wouldn't regret pressing him. "And now?"

"Now?" He looked away, still massaging her legs. "I don't know. Maybe there are too many widows like you who don't know the very things they should have a right to know. I couldn't tell you."

"Because you don't know."

"Exactly." His hands paused, then resumed the massage. "It's part of what I've been thinking about, Marisa. I've lived most of my life in the shadows. Do I want to live the rest of it that way? Maybe die in the shadows the way John did? I don't know anymore. And maybe that's why John sent me here."

"What do you mean? You said he loved his work."

"He did. But maybe, like me, he was starting to have second thoughts. I don't know. Maybe he sensed I was having them. Maybe he just wanted me to stop and think about all I was missing. I couldn't read his mind then, and I sure as hell can't read it now. Regardless, he only asked me to check on you if something happened to him. He couldn't have known it would, so all the rest is just speculation and probably had nothing to do with it."

But she sensed a change in him, a slight stiffening. She ran his words back through her mind and then said, her voice taut, her chest so tight she could scarcely force the words out, "He knew."

His head turned sharply. "Knew?"

"Knew he was going to die."

"Marisa..."

"I had a friend in high school. They were on a trip. She told her mother if she didn't go home immediately, she'd never go home again. The next day she drowned." She squeezed her eyes shut. "Sometimes people know," she whispered.

When Ryker didn't argue with her, she opened her eyes again. "You know it, too, don't you? That some people seem to know before..."

"I've seen it," he admitted. "Not often, but I've seen it."

"So when, exactly, did John make you promise to check on me?"

His voice was heavy when he answered. "Right after I got him the job."

Marisa turned her head, looking out the window at the falling snow. The winter night had fully settled in, and the flakes glistened in the light from the street lamp and windows. She felt as if snow was falling inside her, too, frigid and cold. But like the flakes outside, the flakes inside were ephemeral, beautiful at first blush, but doomed to vanish at the first warmth.

She was thawing, she realized. She'd been frozen ever since she'd learned of Johnny's death. Now all her pretty little dreams and thoughts were melting, going the way those snowflakes would go eventually. Fleeting. Impermanent.

Her baby stirred, and she pressed her hands to the mound of her tummy. That was real, but was anything else? Her baby. All she had left of a marriage that had apparently been like a snowfall.

Ryker's hands paused on her legs. "Marisa?"

When she didn't answer, he moved. With astonishing ease, ungainly though she felt right then, he twisted and lifted her until he could settle her sideways on his lap. He wrapped both arms around her and just held her.

"I guess I was the wrong guy to send," he said finally. "Why?"

"Because we're both messed up. I'm no help at all."

She thought about that, about the awakening happening inside her, about the baby that had just decided to become rambunctious, so much so that, without asking, Ryker loosened one of his arms and rested his hand on her belly.

"Hello, Jonni," he murmured.

She looked down at his big hand pressed gently to

her stomach. Life. Maybe most of it was ephemeral but not the little girl growing inside her.

With her head resting on Ryker's shoulder, she thought about the last time she'd seen Johnny. He'd been home for just over two months. When he'd kissed her goodbye and sworn he'd miss her every moment, she hadn't missed the excitement dancing in his gaze. He was glad to be off again. Going on another dangerous adventure. Unaware of the child he was leaving behind.

"Johnny," she said slowly, "never settled down. Never. He never would. If he hadn't died…" Her voice caught, then steadied. "He wouldn't have been home for this," she said. "He wouldn't have. I'd have gone through this entire pregnancy alone. Just the way I have. Until you arrived."

"Marisa…"

"That's why he sent you. At some level he knew he wouldn't be here when I needed him most."

She felt Ryker shake his head, but she knew it in the depths of her being. It was true. The baby was Johnny's legacy, but Ryker was his last gift. She didn't know what to make of that.

"He was doing important work," Ryker offered.

"I'm sure. I never doubted that. But he lived to exist on the edge, Ryker. I knew that, too. What about you? Do you need to be on the edge all the time?"

He blew a long breath. "I think I just told you that's changing."

"Yes, you did. But for how long? How real is it?"

He gently rubbed his hand over her belly. "As real as this child. My gut's saying so."

"And then what?"

"I don't know," he said frankly. "I told you that, too.

I just know I've enjoyed hanging around this town for the last month. I thought I'd be bored, but I haven't been. Nice folks for the most part. I walk down the street without having to be on high alert. People are starting to greet me. I've had some casual conversations where I didn't have to guard every word. It's been like letting go of a suffocating weight."

Her heart hurt as realization sank in. "I feel like I'm waking up from a bad dream that went on forever." Her eyes burned, and she felt one tear roll down her cheek. "I spent most of my marriage missing Johnny. I can't do that again."

"No one's asking you to."

"I know. It's just…I wonder at myself. Why my perspective is changing so much. I thought I'd accepted the way things had to be. Not so much, I guess. I might have lived an illusion for years. But one thing I know for sure now…I loved him. Part of me will always love him, but I cannot do that again. I have a child to think of now, to care for. I need some permanence and stability. Johnny never would have provided that. So it's time to leave all that in the past. Time to look forward and plan. High time."

Ryker lifted his hand and with a finger wiped away the one tear. "Don't give him up, Marisa. He loved you. Keep that part of him."

"I'll never lose that." She closed her eyes, dropped her head and placed her hand over Ryker's. "Nothing can take it away from me. But I'm through railing at the universe and hating life and all the rest of it. Johnny was a bright and beautiful addition to my life. But he wasn't all of it." He hadn't been around enough to be all of it.

She lifted a hand and laid it on Ryker's chest. Through

the flannel of his shirt she could feel heat and hard muscle. Reality.

"No one person," he said slowly, "should be all of someone's life."

"Probably not. I don't mean it as a criticism of Johnny. Like I said, I knew what it would be like. I'm just looking at myself and wondering how much longer I'm going to wallow in missing him. It seems almost like copping out."

"To hell with that," he said sharply. "The man you loved died. Whether he was around much before that hardly matters. This time he's not coming back. A bit weird, don't you think, to dismiss your grief because he wasn't around often? There's a huge difference between temporary and permanent."

And therein resided a huge kernel of truth. Johnny would never come home, and she grieved for that. She grieved because she could no longer look forward to those amazing, bright spots of love that had filled her days when he was here. She had every right to miss him.

But it was dawning on her that she had every right to move on.

Chapter Eight

"It's almost Christmas," Ryker remarked the next morning as they sat over coffee and the eggs he'd made for them.

"So?"

He glanced out the window at falling snow, then at her. "What did you do for Thanksgiving?"

"Stayed home."

He arched a brow. "Really? I'm surprised. All those friends threw you a baby shower."

"And all those friends asked me to join them for Thanksgiving. I said no."

He studied her, drumming his fingers. "How come?"

"Do you really think I wanted to be surrounded by all their families and friends?"

Ryker studied her, beginning to understand something. He wondered if she had any idea how cute she looked with her hair still tousled from bed, wrapped in a pink terry-cloth robe over what appeared to be thermal underwear. Or how bright her almost-lavender eyes looked? Appealing in every way. "Explain," he suggested gently.

"I would have just felt more alone. I can't explain it any better than that."

She sounded a bit querulous now. He felt one corner of his mouth twitch upward. She was definitely shaking free of the paralysis that had been plaguing her when he arrived. Good. Time to tiptoe, though. He was aware that he felt uniquely exposed here, as if his long-protected and buried feelings were now running around out in the world and vulnerable. She was probably feeling the same.

"What did *you* do for Thanksgiving?" she demanded.

"Called my parents. And Maude makes a mean turkey dinner."

"Hah," she said. "Another loner." Then, "Why didn't you go visit your parents?"

"They don't expect me anymore, and…" Did he really want to tell her this? "Frankly, I don't feel comfortable with them. It would have been three or four days of being badgered about the way I live."

Marisa concerned him more. She was truly out of sorts this morning, maybe not surprising, given the thoughts she'd expressed last night, but he had no idea how to soothe her. Damn, he was getting too involved here. Why should he care that she was having a mood? Why should he feel he needed to do something about it? But he did. He just had to feel his way into it. He poured himself another coffee and returned to the table, pondering.

He asked, "Was John home last Christmas?"

"No. He came in February."

"Well, I wasn't home last Christmas either, just like Thanksgiving. In fact, it's been years since I was anywhere near Christmas."

"So?"

He hesitated, then jumped in with both feet. What the hell? He'd been tongue-lashed before. "I want to ask a favor."

She almost scowled at him. "What?"

"Can I get a tree? Some trimmings? Would you mind?"

Some of the irritability vanished from her face. Her mouth opened a bit. "For you, you mean?"

"Yeah. For me." But not just for him. No way. He knew loneliness intimately, and he figured this woman had had her share and then some.

"I have an artificial tree in the attic. Decorations. Help yourself."

"I was thinking of a real tree, unless you object. The scent of pine. God, I love that." He waited. He was proposing to celebrate a holiday in her house, and he'd just dismissed her usual decorations for something entirely different. He knew he needed a change. He wondered if she was ready to really make one.

So much to hang on one Christmas tree, he thought with self-amusement.

"Sure," she said after a minute. "Go ahead."

"Want to tell me where to put it? And better yet, help me pick it out? It's going to be in your house, after all."

Her lips curved, but the smile didn't appear especially amused. "What are you trying to do, Ryker?"

"Change up my life. God knows it needs changing. The last time I decorated a Christmas tree was nearly twenty years ago. In a forward base in the middle of no-where. This scrawny thing we decorated with whatever crap we could find lying around."

She continued to regard him, apparently thinking. Slowly, she relaxed a bit. "Sure," she said finally. "Go ahead. Just don't expect me to get all into it."

"This tree's for me," he reminded her. "If you want your own, I'll get it out of your attic."

That worked. A laugh escaped her, a genuine one. "You are too much," she told him. "One tree is plenty. Yours will be plenty."

And maybe it would help put a different complexion on things for both of them. He'd just have to wait and see.

"Whenever you're ready to bundle up," he said, of-fering a smile. "Dang, I'm getting excited."

"About Christmas?" She laughed again. "Still a kid inside?"

"I think the kid inside me has been locked away for too long."

Her face softened, and she surprised him by reaching across the table for his hand. "Then, let's let the kid out."

She insisted on doing the dishes, so while she cleaned up and dressed to go out, he shoveled the fresh snowfall off her steps and sidewalks. Only a few inches of light and fluffy stuff made it easy. Then he salted every place she might have to walk, brushed off his car and started it to warm it up.

Other people were out shoveling, too, and he liked the way they waved to him, as if he were part of the neigh-borhood now. Friendly folks. He'd been running into that everywhere. Quite a change from his past.

Streets he could walk without feeling exposed. People

with nothing deadly to hide. Something inside him was uncoiling in response, and only as he began to relax into his new environment did he realize how long it had been since he'd simply felt comfortable in any environment.

Yeah, they gave him decompression time after every mission, but looking back now he could easily see that he had never fully decompressed. Too afraid of losing his edge.

Here, somehow, that didn't seem important. He might be making a big mistake, but he didn't care. Life had finally delivered him a small measure of peace, and he made up his mind to enjoy it.

Once he had Marisa safely bundled into his car, he drove them toward a tree lot he'd seen yesterday on the edge of town. Even though Thanksgiving had passed, it had still appeared to have quite a few decent trees in it. A mental checklist began to run of all the other things he'd need to get, from a tree stand to some ornaments. Maybe some lights for outside?

It would depend, he decided, on Marisa's reactions. If she seemed to be enjoying herself, he'd go whole hog on it.

Although it had been plowed, the parking around the tree lot was still covered with snow. No one else was there this morning, except for an older man inside a little hut with a propane space heater. With Marisa's arm firmly tucked in his for support, they began to walk around the narrow paths in the small lot.

"Any particular kind of tree you favor?" he asked her.

"This is your tree."

"I'm kinda out of practice. I'm just asking what you think is pretty."

She glanced at him with a smile. "I like the long-needled ones because they look full. On the other hand, the short-needled ones are sparser-looking but can hold a lot more decorations."

"Some help you are."

She laughed, and he soaked up the sound. "How high are your ceilings?" He figured close to ten feet. It was an older house.

"High enough. The thing is, we can't get a humongous tree unless you want to move furniture onto the front porch."

"Good point. I guess I shouldn't go overboard."

"Just saying." Then she laughed again. She was enjoying this. He could have given himself a pat on the back.

"I never went tree shopping with Johnny."

He almost froze, then caught himself. "Never?" The thought that she'd had to deal with holidays on her own struck him for the first time. Of course she had an artificial tree in the attic. He'd almost have bet that some years she didn't even get it down.

Cripes. They strolled a little farther, then he heard Marisa draw a sharp breath. At once he stopped and turned to her. "You okay?"

"I'm fine." She was staring past him, so he looked and saw the tree that held her attention. In an instant it became The Tree.

"You like that one?"

"I've always loved blue spruce. I've never had one for a Christmas tree."

He studied it. Six feet tall, thick foliage and surprisingly blue compared to the trees around it. "That's wild. I like it."

"Are you sure?"

He'd been sure since he'd seen the sparkle in her eyes.

He didn't care if it was full all the way around, or anything else. If it had bare spots, they had plenty of walls to hide them against. Glancing around, he saw no others of its kind.

"Okay, let's get you back to the car, then I'll help the guy load it up."

She hesitated. "Don't do this for me."

"Did I say I was? I like it, too. It's different."

He was glad she didn't argue. He understood that she wanted to think this was all about him, and to some extent it was. He didn't want to be pushed into a corner where he had to admit he was doing this mostly for her, to break a cycle, because he was nearly certain that would make her uneasy.

But it was time, with the baby's arrival so near, for this woman to find some happiness in life again.

By that evening, Ryker had the tree standing in the corner of the living room and was stringing it with multi-colored lights. Marisa sat with her feet up, watching him and thinking that he finally looked relaxed and content.

If she were to be honest, she was feeling pretty relaxed and content herself. Her baby stirred comfortably in her womb, a Christmas tree was happening right before her eyes, and she spared only a few minutes to think about how she had missed doing this with Johnny. Only once in their marriage had he been home to participate in this. But then she let go of the regret and gave herself over to enjoying Ryker. As he handled the strings of lights, he even taught her a few new cusswords that made her giggle.

"I forgot this was the miserable part," he said at one point. "Sorry."

"No apologies. I'm having too much fun watching."

He pretended to scowl at her as he wound the light strands around the tree. "I hope all the same colors don't wind up in one place."

"You got a problem with blotches?"

"Not unless it means I have to do this all over again."

She laughed again. On one of his trips out for ornaments, he'd brought home dinner again, so she didn't even need to cook. She was beginning to feel like a lady of leisure.

He flashed a smile at her. "You're enjoying watching a tree torture me, huh?"

"Believe it."

On the floor lay boxes of ornaments he'd purchased. She liked their bright colors but was surprised he hadn't purchased any glass ones. Was she thinking of the baby to come? Most were brass or decorated foam, pretty indestructible. Or maybe that was just the way he thought.

"Want some coffee?" she asked.

He left the light strand dangling. "I'll get it. I need a break. I am at war with this tree. You want anything?"

"Milk would be nice. I thought you were going to have fun with this."

"I will, once I get the lights on."

"There's something to be said for fiber-optic trees," she called after him.

"Bah, humbug," he called back, causing her to giggle again.

He was right about the scent of a real tree, though, she thought as she leaned her head back and looked at the corner of her living room where he was installing it. The tree smelled wonderful, carrying her back to happier times, to memories of childhood excitement.

He returned shortly with his coffee and her milk. She held her glass perched on her belly. Like having a handy shelf, she thought wryly. "So," she asked, "did you get excited about Christmas when you were a kid?"

"Believe it." He sat on the edge of the couch, mug in hand, smiling. "There were times I had trouble sleeping, and not only when I was little."

"Me, too," she agreed. "My excitement always started ratcheting with the first snowfall. I could feel magic in the air. I remember when I was fifteen and too excited to sleep, and telling myself that was ridiculous for someone of my age. That was for the little kids. Didn't work."

He chuckled. "I wasn't any better. My sister, however, was a pain. Somehow she slept. Worse, she slept in. I had diabolical ways of waking her up when I got too impatient."

"I had to wait in my bedroom until my folks put on some Christmas music. They always wanted to make coffee before they unleashed me. Mom left a stocking on the door, though."

"You, too? But that stocking didn't tamp my impatience for very long. I used to think there had to be something wrong with my sister. How in the world could she sleep in on Christmas morning? Even when she was young. What five-year-old does that?"

"Your sister?" she suggested.

He laughed. "Apparently so."

She was enjoying seeing this side of him. He looked younger than when he'd arrived, and for the first time, she didn't feel like she was sharing quarters with a cat that was always poised to pounce. Right now he was very comfortable to share space with.

And sexy as hell, she thought with no guilt. As he sat

there in his plain blue flannel shirt and jeans, elbows resting on splayed knees, she felt the sizzle, felt the longing…and he wasn't even doing anything to encourage it. What was it about him? The man in him seemed to call effortlessly to the woman in her.

She remembered the feeling of his arms around her, and admitted that the simple hug had filled an aching hole deep within her. She wanted more hugs, and as she watched him resume hanging the lights, she acknowledged that she wanted a whole lot more than that. She wondered what it would feel like to run her hands over that hard body, to discover his contours. To feel his hands running over her skin, everywhere, touching places that hadn't been touched in so long. She wanted him to fill all her senses until she thought of nothing else.

But as he'd reminded her, they were both sorting things out. Maybe this mood was as ephemeral as everything else. Maybe she didn't deserve stolen moments of happiness, and what if they wrecked her more? Because Ryker would be moving on, back to a dangerous job. The very kind of life she had already lived with Johnny. She didn't think she could do that again.

In fact, she was quite certain. Not with a baby. So, steamy thoughts aside, she needed to avoid anything that could hurt her again. Anything.

When the lights were at last on the Christmas tree, Ryker stood back to eye his handiwork. There were some blotches of color, but not much and not too many. "Okay?" he asked Marisa.

"It's beautiful."

Seeing her smile made it all worthwhile. He would, he realized, do almost anything to keep that smile there.

That expression had been so rare when he had arrived, but now he was glimpsing a new Marisa, one who was no longer totally buried in her grief.

Oh, the grief was still there. He was no fool. She'd spend the rest of her life grieving for John, but the healing hands of time should ease it, lessen it, put it further in the background most of the time. If he could help that along, he would.

"I'm gonna get some more coffee before I start decorating," he said. "Want anything?"

"I need to move around a bit," she said decisively. As she started to wiggle forward, to get her feet properly balanced before she stood, he held out his hands. Without hesitating, she took them, and he tugged her gently up.

"I think I'll keep you," she said lightly. "Getting up is getting harder."

She stood only a few inches from him, and her natural scents filled him. His whole body responded with need. He forced himself to focus on what she'd said. "How come?"

"My balance has changed. It just takes a little more thinking and a little more work now. No biggie."

He looked down into her amazing eyes, saw a smile there. "And how's Jonni doing?"

"She's fine. She's been a little quiet this evening, but still stirring."

"That must be the most amazing experience." Reluctantly, he let go of her hands, reminding himself that there were limits here, wise ones. Limits that protected them both from making a mistake. He didn't want to do anything she would regret, because if he did he'd be living with a pile of regret, too, and he wasn't a man filled with regrets.

He'd made his choices and lived with them. He couldn't see any point in regret because the past couldn't be changed; it could only teach lessons. He had, however, known plenty of people who could devote a whole lot of time to regrets, and he didn't know if Marisa was one of them.

He didn't really know her at all. Nor did she really know him. Worse, his secrets stood between them like an insurmountable barrier. Every time he failed to reveal who John had been working for, he committed another lie by omission. Yeah, he was bound to it, but you couldn't build anything on lies. The whole thing would be rotten, riddled by them. As she walked toward the kitchen, his gaze followed her, and he felt a savage hatred for the secrecy forced on him.

God, he needed to make some changes.

His cell phone rang, surprising him, and he pulled it out. The office, of course. Why the hell were they bothering him?

He grabbed his jacket and called to Marisa. "I'm stepping outside to take this call. Back in a minute."

"Okay," she responded.

Outside, the snow continued to fall. More shoveling in the morning. Making sure no one was within earshot, he answered the call before he even zipped his jacket.

"Tremaine."

It was Bill. He recognized the voice instantly. "You've been rattling some bars, R.T."

"I want to know. And there's a woman who deserves to know."

"Of course she deserves to know. That doesn't change anything. It can't change anything."

"Then at least have someone deliver the letter, let

her know about the star. Someday she might even want to show the star to her child. Is that really too freaking much?"

Bill didn't say anything for a few seconds. "Maybe that's possible. I'll look into it. But stop rattling the cage. Some folks are getting nervous about you."

As if he cared anymore. This had become personal. Maybe that reduced his effectiveness, but to hell with it. The certainty had been growing in him that, given his experience and expertise, he was far more valuable to them than they were to him.

"I'll let you know." Then Bill was gone.

He stuffed his phone into his jeans pocket and stood for a while watching the snow fall. It was beautiful, but tonight it reminded him of frozen tears.

Finally he shook himself, remembering that Marisa was inside, probably wondering what was going on.

He found her in the kitchen, and all the happiness that had been written on her face was gone now. She sat at the table with a glass of cranberry juice and looked hollowly at him. "You have to leave."

It sounded almost like an accusation. "No. Absolutely not. That was just a loose end."

Her hands were wrapped around the glass, her knuckles white. "You don't need to lie to me."

"I'm not lying. I don't have to leave."

"Johnny got calls like that, then he'd be gone."

He blew a loud breath, then said firmly, "I am not John, and I am not lying." Except by all he couldn't say.

Of course he wasn't John. But he was so like John that it made no difference, he supposed. He got his cup of coffee, then sat facing her, tree forgotten. One phone call and her day was destroyed. In that instant he had a clear and ugly picture of what she had endured.

Reaching across the table, he pried her hands from the glass. They were now cold and damp. He swallowed them in his grip, holding on to her. He had a bridge to cross here, and he needed to do it quickly.

"You want the truth?" he asked.

She nodded, her face drooping.

"I've been trying to find out what happened to John."

She caught her breath. "And?"

"And nothing yet. In fact, I got told to let it go. I can't say more than that."

Her expression changed suddenly, her eyes widening a bit, despair replaced by worry. "You're not losing your job over this?"

"No." Flat and firm. "But I guess I made some folks uneasy."

All of a sudden her small hands gripped his back. "Don't do this, Ryker. Don't get yourself in trouble by trying to answer my questions. I'd hate it. I'd hate myself."

"I've pressed it as far as I can," he said honestly. "So don't worry about me. Besides, I think I'm close to shoving this job."

"Really?" Her expression lightened a bit. "But what will you do?"

"If there's one thing I know I can do, it's take care of myself. I'm not worried about it. Now, how about we get back to the tree?"

Marisa helped decorate the tree. Well, the middle section of the tree, she admitted, feeling her mood improve. She couldn't bend over too much, didn't dare squat, and Ryker wouldn't let her reach high for fear she might lose her balance. He was big enough to work over her head, and he clearly had no difficulty squatting.

"This is turning out pretty good," he said halfway through. "Did I buy enough ornaments?"

She eyed the tree and the remaining boxes. "More than enough," she assured him. "If we use them all, we won't be able to see much of the tree."

He laughed. "Can't have that. You like blue spruce."

He was squatting beside her, and as she reached to the side to hang another bauble, she teetered a bit and quickly grabbed his shoulder for balance. Muscle stirred beneath her hand, and heat stirred between her thighs.

"You'd better take a break," he said. "You don't want an early Christmas present."

So she returned to her chair to watch as he finished up. So many bright colors, and the LED lights sparkled everywhere. He'd spared nothing on this project.

But he didn't seem like a man for half measures. Why would she be surprised by that? Johnny hadn't been one, either. The similarity at once disturbed her and comforted her.

If there was one thing she'd learned about men like Johnny and Ryker, it was that they did what they said they'd do, with full commitment. She liked that.

"There," he said finally, stepping back. "What do you think? I don't want to bury it."

She studied it, the smile coming back to her face. "It's beautiful. I love it."

He grinned at her, started to gather up boxes and unused ornaments, then paused. "How about lights outside? Do you want me to do them?"

Amazement filled her, then humor, which unleashed

a laugh. "Are you crazy, Ryker? It's cold out there, and that would be a whole lot of work and expense."

"True," he agreed, settling across from her. "On the other hand, I haven't decorated the outside of a house since I was a kid."

"Oh. I never did…before. I like looking at other people's houses, but I've never done it." He'd missed a lot, she thought, and she didn't want to deprive him of this if he wanted it.

"Well, we don't have to. It crossed my mind."

Why was she raising objections? The Christmas tree delighted her, had brought a breath of fresh air into this house, one she had needed. Because of a Christmas tree, she had enjoyed nearly the entire day. Was that so wrong?

Then she understood something else. "Would you decorate outside because you want it, or because you think I'd want it?"

"Both, actually. I was thinking about how pretty it would be, and how I haven't done it in so long. But it's up to you." He glanced at his watch. "Maude's is still open. Want some hot chocolate? People have been raving about it. Apparently she's spiced it up a bit with cinnamon."

She wondered if he was having trouble holding still. "I'd like that," she said finally.

"I'll be right back, then. In the meantime, you think about outside decorations."

Maybe that call from work had bothered him, she thought as he went out the door. Certainly he hadn't seemed quite as lighthearted since then. But he could just be tired, too. He'd been out in the cold an awful lot today, going for the tree, cutting it before bringing it inside, then running to the store for all those ornaments…

Or maybe she was looking for benign explanations where there were none. She had a habit of doing that.

He said he wasn't in any trouble for trying to find out more about Johnny's death, but he might just have said that so she wouldn't worry. She didn't want him to have problems because of her. But would he admit it if he were?

Probably not. He seemed hell-bent on protecting her. Her friends had been trying to care for her all along, and she'd kept a distance, denying them the right to do something that would probably make them feel good. But then this man Ryker came out of nowhere, and somehow he'd worked his way past her resistance. She seemed more aware of what he might need as Johnny's friend than she had been aware of what *her* friends might need.

Gloom settled over her as she contemplated the selfishness that grief had created in her. She had some serious making up to do.

Ryker returned quickly with the hot chocolate and put a foam cup on the table beside her. "I picked up a couple of crullers, too. Want one?"

"I'd love it." At least he looked as if his troubles had fled while he was out. She leaned her head back, staring at the beautiful tree they'd made together, thinking she needed to apologize seriously to some friends. Maybe have them over for a little Christmas party. Let them know how much she loved them.

"Outside decorations?" he asked as he settled himself with his own cocoa and cruller.

She thought about how it would brighten up the place, how it would welcome her friends if she gave a small party. "If you really want to do it," she said. "And I was thinking about having a small get-together with some friends. I've been pretty much leaving them out in the cold for a long time now. Would you mind?"

"You're asking *me*? Your house, Marisa."

"I'm still asking."

He shook his head a little, then smiled. "Party away. Won't trouble me at all. But let me get the stuff outside up first."

A smile surprised her, tipping up the corners of her mouth. "It would certainly look like an invitation."

One she hadn't issued in forever, it seemed like.

He turned off all the lights except for the tree, and she sat in its magical glow, feeling everything inside her beginning to shift, as if something elemental had changed. Almost without knowing it, she had reached a decision.

At last she rose from the rocker and walked over to him, standing right in front of him. He looked up at her and put aside his own cup.

"Ryker." Her heart beat so fast she wondered if she would collapse.

"Yes?"

"Take me to bed, please."

A hundred emotions seemed to run over the face she had once thought looked like granite. "Are you sure?"

She nodded. She was sure of one thing: she was awakening, and she wanted to complete her awakening wrapped in Ryker's arms.

Chapter Nine

For Ryker, sex had always been easy to come by, easy to enjoy, casual and meaningless. As he rose and took Marisa's hand, he knew this was different. Very different. First there was her pregnancy. Then there was this woman's ability to shake him to his very core. This would be no casual encounter, but rather one that could change everything.

In his life he'd taken a lot of risks, but suddenly none of them seemed as huge as this. Worse, looking into her face he understood to his very core that turning her down would inflict a wound. She had taken a bold step, reaching for life again, but he suspected she didn't feel especially attractive right now, and he hadn't spent any effort on trying to make her understand that she was attractive to him in ways no other woman had been. He'd been avoiding all the build-up to this moment because he didn't want to harm her. With one word, right now when she was so vulnerable, he could have gutted her.

She had taken the decision right out of his hands.

He spoke quietly. "You *did* talk to your doctor?"

She nodded, her gaze hopeful and even a little frightened.

"That must have knocked him sideways under the circumstances."

He was relieved to see a slight smile dance around her mouth. "If it did, he didn't show it."

"Restrictions?"

"I have to lie on my side. Ryker…"

He could see it. She thought he was looking for a way out. That pierced him painfully, and he wasted no more time. For whatever reason, she needed this, and he wanted it. "Well," he said forcing a smile of his own, "there are plenty of ways to give pleasure."

Relief filled him as he saw her relax a bit. One thorny hill surmounted. All of a sudden, though, he became aware of his own inadequacies. He'd never made love to a pregnant woman. He had no idea how this would roll. No mission plan other than giving her a wonderful experience. A daunting task under these conditions. He wondered if he'd be good enough, careful enough, considerate enough…

And all the while he was wondering, he was leading her to her bedroom. The prepared baby crib at the foot of her bed seemed to glow with warning. A dangerous situation.

But it didn't dampen his desire for her. That had been plaguing him, and like a smoldering fire it had refused to go out. Now those embers were glowing, beginning to heat him throughout. He couldn't let them take control.

If ever his self-control had been tested, this would be one of the rare times he wasn't certain he had enough. Inside him flames were leaping. His body was already burgeoning and throbbing. Marisa became the sole focus of his universe.

He left the lamp on because he wanted to see her. He slipped his arms around her as they stood beside her bed, trying to support her back, and leaned in for their first kiss.

To have come to this point without any kisses, without any touches... A dance like this usually had some lead-in time, but not this time. It had arrived with a bang, like a herd of thundering horses. Everything he'd been avoiding, everything that should have preceded these moments, was missing, and he had to make it up to her.

Her mouth tasted sweet, of chocolate and cruller, but her tongue showed no shyness. He felt her hands grip his shoulders as their tongues dueled, as he swept the inside of her mouth and felt a shiver run through her. Her lips clung to his, drinking from him, speaking in a way no words ever could.

He could have lost himself right then and there, but he couldn't forget her precious cargo or her back. He didn't want her to start hurting, to lose these moments with a backache or other discomfort.

Tearing his mouth from hers, he took a half step back to reach for the hem of the shirt she wore. Johnny's shirt, he was sure. For an instant he wondered if he was betraying his friend, then dismissed the notion. Johnny was gone. He and Marisa were here.

No buttons fought him. He pulled the shirt away and filled his gaze with the sight of her full breasts, cased in white cotton, and the smooth bulge of her belly just below them.

Bending, he kissed her belly. "I'll take it easy."

Marisa's hands cradled his head, holding him close as he rested his cheek on her belly. She caressed his hair, making him feel utterly welcome. Still kissing her tummy, he hooked his thumbs in the waistband of her pants and panties and pulled them down.

A gasp escaped her, further enflaming him. God, he wanted this. When he got her pants to her knees, he urged her to sit.

"I want to look at you," he murmured. "But first we have to get rid of some stuff."

A breathless laugh escaped her as she settled on the edge of the bed. Getting rid of her pants and slippers was easy. Then, kneeling in front of her, he pulled her head to his shoulder and reached for the clasp of her bra. As he released it, she drew a sharp breath. "Ryker..."

"I know," he said, as his entire body pulsed. "I know." If she was feeling anything like he was, they were going to light the night with their explosion.

Leaning back, he took her in. Her breasts were full, looking so firm as they readied for the child. Her areolae were slightly brown, unexpected, given her coloring. The secret place between her thighs was partly hidden. He'd never seen a more perfect picture.

Rising, he shed his own clothes quickly. "Condom?" he asked gruffly, wanting to be done with the last necessity.

"Bedside table," she whispered.

He found the drawer and put the box on top of the table, beside the bed. Then he faced the woman he wanted with every cell of his being.

He realized she was sweeping him with a hungry gaze, taking in every detail. She could no longer miss how much he wanted her. But she also had to see the scars, and he hoped they didn't turn her off.

"Ryker," she murmured, "you're beautiful."

"That's my line," he said. "You're the beautiful one. Stand up?"

The moment and passion had gripped her, he realized. She stood boldly, letting him see her delightful curves, unashamed of her swollen belly. That delighted him, but with so much passion hammering him now, he tucked away the memory for later.

He reached out to cup her heavy breasts, feeling how firm they were, brushing his thumbs over her engorged nipples. As he did so, she gasped.

"Hurts?" he asked, concern pushing hunger briefly aside.

"No, oh, no," she said faintly. "Feels too good, so good…"

The image of her seared his mind. He knew he would never forget this moment, this gift. Then she lowered herself to the bed, stretching out, giving him another gift of her complete trust.

Something was being born in him, but he didn't want to think about that now. A beautiful woman was offering herself to him, a priceless offering. It touched him and stoked the blaze inside him, and he knew he would never be the same.

Carefully he stretched out beside her and, propped on one elbow, he began to explore her with his hand, stroking downward over every hill and curve. She responded to each touch as if it was electric. He dropped more kisses on her, sparing not an inch of her. She kept reaching for him, but with the last remnants of reason he remembered he must be careful. Supremely careful.

When at last he put his mouth to her breast and sucked, she arched and groaned and her fingers clawed at him, trying to drag him closer. Hammered by his own need, it was almost impossible for him to resist. Had he ever ached so hard for any woman?

His body wanted to take over, but he couldn't let it. The baby. He kept reminding himself, the last sane thought in a world spinning rapidly out of control. In near desperation, he urged her onto her side so that he lay behind her. His hand made another trip over her, causing her to cry out with pleasure, finding her breasts exquisitely sensitive, so sensitive that she finally clasped her hand to hold it there.

"Never stop," she begged, sounding as desperate as he felt.

But he had other plans in mind. Pulling his hand free, he dragged it lower until at last he found the dewy place between her thighs. He slipped his own leg between hers, separating her, opening her to his touch.

The instant his finger found her sensitive nub of nerves, a deep groan escaped her. She reached back with one hand, seeking to hang on to him while he stroked her repeatedly and listened to her breathing grow more and more ragged. Her nails found his buttocks and dug in, driving him crazy with renewed hunger. He refused to give in. First her. He wanted to bring her to completion before anything else, to show her that he could give her everything while taking little for himself. He needed to give her that.

She rocked gently against his touches, her cries coming more often. He kissed the nape of her neck, savoring each movement she took toward satisfaction. He could feel her electric response inside himself as if they were wired together.

Then, finally, one great spasm took her. A beautiful cry escaped her. Satisfied, he cupped her with his hand, pressing hard, drawing the last drop out for her.

Her ears almost felt as if they rang from the intensity of her orgasm. Ryker had given her a wholly new experience, and as she slowly drifted back to earth, she listened to them both breathe raggedly. Gradually she came back, feeling the cool air of the room on her heated skin, feeling the man behind her keeping her warm with his own body heat. Holding her so gently and intimately. Feeling his erection hard against her bottom.

"Ryker?" she whispered.

"How are you?"

"Wonderful. Fantastic. But what about you?"

"Don't worry about it."

She stirred, grabbing his hand, bringing it to her lips, smelling herself on him. A new arc of desire passed through her. "Please," she murmured. "I want... Fill me. I need it."

For long seconds he didn't reply. Maybe he couldn't figure out how to do this. She didn't really know herself. She just knew that a part of her had been empty for too long, and she needed a man to fill it. This man. Not just anyone, but Ryker. She didn't question the need, she just accepted it.

"Just a sec," he said finally. He pulled away. She heard him open a condom, and her heart began to race again. When he came back, he slipped his leg between hers again and started caressing her from breast to belly. Never in her life had her breasts been so exquisitely sensitive. Something else good to say about pregnancy, she thought distantly as desire began to sizzle through her with renewed power.

"Promise me," he murmured as he kissed her neck and caressed her breasts, "you'll tell me if anything hurts even a tiny bit."

"Promise," she answered with the last bit of air she seemed to be able to find. She was flying again, rising to the heights with this man. His hand found her center and the knot of exquisite nerves. For just an instant his touch almost hurt, but then her body began the inevitable blossoming.

"Ryker?" Impatience began to drive her.

"Shh…" A mere whisper as his fingers lashed her back to the precipice. Then, she felt him enter her, stretching her, filling her, answering a need she had forgotten she had. It felt so good to be filled with him, so good.

Then he drove her crazy by continuing to caress her and move very slowly within her. Gently. He didn't look like a gentle man, but his tenderness with her was amazing.

Little by little he carried her up, refusing to increase his pace, making her want to cry out for more. But he didn't give it to her, drawing the experience out, taking half a lifetime in which she reached new pinnacles of longing and pleasure, until the ache became too much to bear. Then, at last, the explosion rolled over her, leaving her nearly blind with its intensity. Only dimly did she feel him stiffen behind her, followed by the throbbing of his member as he reached his own satisfaction.

Replete, exhausted, she tumbled with him into utter bliss.

* * *

She fell asleep almost instantly. That amused Ryker, but he figured she'd had a long day, and she hadn't taken her usual nap. He reached across the bed, trying not to disturb her, and managed to pull most of the blankets over her to keep her warm.

Then he lay holding her, staring at the wall beyond her bed, dealing with the sense that something inside him had just changed permanently. No other sexual experience had left him feeling that way, except his very first, but Marisa had somehow changed him.

Or maybe the change had been coming on for a while. He'd certainly begun questioning himself in ways he never had before. Deep inside him resided an uncomfortable feeling, the sense that he was unworthy to hold this woman.

She didn't make him feel that way, but the very fact that he was feeling it acted like a warning flag. At some level he was trying to deal with a basic fact: he could go back to his regular life, or he could make a drastic change so he wouldn't feel unworthy of the gift Marisa had just given him.

He needed to be wary of such questions because they could blunt his edge, and all too often his life depended on his edge. So, pretty soon here he was going to have to answer the question: Was he going back or taking a different direction?

His hand rested over her belly, atop the blanket, and he felt the baby stir and kick. Absolutely magical. He spread his hand so he could feel it better and thought about a new little girl coming into this world, all shiny and spotless and eager for life. He'd like to feel even a touch of that eagerness again. He supposed Marisa would, too.

Life left no one shiny and spotless, though. Everyone got dinged and picked up some stains. Life sometimes shoveled manure as if it were a game.

The question was what you did about it. He thought he'd been accomplishing good and important things, that the inevitable stains didn't outweigh the good he'd done. Then he thought about a fatherless child who would soon enter this world and wondered whether any of his past missions could ever outweigh the importance of caring for a child.

Maybe Johnny had missed his boat to redemption.

Ryker sighed quietly and tried to wipe the questions from his head. He had grown increasingly certain that he needed to change something, that he was getting tired of his mission-oriented life, but he had to be careful about what he chose.

His parents kept nagging him to settle down, especially his mother. Sometimes he was quite certain that she believed he was a changeling. They didn't know any more about what he did than Marisa, but they knew it wasn't "normal." His mother's worried gaze popped up in his mind's eye, and he felt her concern for him reach across the miles. He could never answer her questions, nor erase her fears for him, not as long as he kept his job. His missions were important, but maybe he'd failed to consider how they affected others. The way John had apparently never given any real thought to what might become of Marisa.

On the one hand he was making sacrifices for his country. On the other he was stealing something from the people he cared about most. Facing that, he knew the time for change had come. No ifs, ands or buts. The attitude shift in him answered the question.

Now all he had to do was figure it out.

Marisa slept through the entire night. When her eyes popped open and saw the digital clock beside the bed, she started. She was alone in the bed, and now she was embarrassed. What a way to treat Ryker after their incredible lovemaking. Hurrying, she popped out of bed, showered and dressed quickly in one of Johnny's old sweatshirts and a pair of stretchy fleece pants.

She found Ryker in the kitchen enjoying coffee with a stack of toast on the table. He looked at her with a warm smile. "Sleep well?" he asked.

"I can't believe… Ryker, I'm sorry. That was rude."

"Rude?" He shook his head, laughing quietly, and rose to wrap her in his arms. She leaned into him, loving the way it felt to be held by him. Then, gently, he turned her around so that she leaned back into his embrace. One of his hands settled over her swollen belly, the other cupped her breast boldly, causing her to gasp with instant pleasure.

"No apologies," he said, dropping a kiss on her neck. "It was wonderful. You were tired. How are you and how's your little passenger?"

"We're fine. We're better than fine," she admitted, relaxing into him. "It was so beautiful."

"It was," he agreed, his voice nearly a deep purr. "Perfect. But now I need to feed you."

She felt reluctance as he released her and urged her into a chair. As she sat, she realized she didn't want him to let go of her. She wanted him to take her back to bed and bring that miraculous magic to her once more.

Just looking at him made her ache with hunger. She no longer cared why it had happened; it had just happened, and right now it made her feel happy. She was allowed that, right?

He fed her scrambled eggs and toast, along with a cup of coffee and a tall glass of orange juice. He sat across from her with his own coffee, just smiling.

There was a peace to this morning, the kind of peace she hadn't felt in a long time. For once she didn't even remind herself that he'd leave her the way Johnny had so often. This morning none of that mattered.

Her appetite seemed to have reawakened with her, and she ate heartily…at least until shyness began to overtake her. She wasn't usually a shy person, but so much had changed last night. The intimacy they'd shared… All of a sudden, the memory of how she had cut loose, how she had asked Ryker to take her to bed, overwhelmed her. How did they move forward now? She didn't have a thing to say, even though her body was still vibrating at his presence.

"Marisa? Are you regretting last night?"

She glanced up and saw that his face had shadowed, lost some of its relaxation. "No," she said swiftly. "I'm just…it's just…" She bit her lip. "I don't know where we go from here. I just feel…shy, I guess. Unsure. Last night changed things, and I don't know quite what to say or do."

She darted a look at him and was amazed to see him smiling. "Ah," he said as if he understood that garble.

"Ah?"

He tilted his head to one side briefly, a kind of shrug. "I think I get it. Well, this doesn't change anything you don't want it to change. I'm still the same Ryker, except that I happen to be feeling quite special this morning."

"You feel special?" The idea amazed her.

He nodded and leaned forward, reaching for her hand. "You gave me an incredible gift. Why wouldn't I feel special?"

"But…you gave me something special, too."

"I hope so. Just relax and be yourself. I wouldn't change one hair on your head, Marisa Hayes. Not one. You're beautiful, you're generous with yourself, you're a loving person. You deserve every good thing in life. If I gave you one of them, then I'm a very lucky guy."

Wow, that was overwhelming from a man who had often seemed to her to live behind impenetrable walls. Except those walls had been coming down, like with the Christmas tree yesterday. For whatever reason, he was reaching out for something. Maybe not her, but he was reaching, and she suspected he was trying to regain something he'd lost.

She turned her hand over, clasping his in return. "Thank you."

His smile deepened. "Today's a good day for just basking in the glow, don't you think?"

"Carpe diem?" she asked.

He laughed. "I take 'em where I can get 'em."

Which reminded her of when he had said that he *loved 'em and left 'em.* He'd warned her, and she'd reached for him, anyway. But certainly she wasn't naive enough to fall for him. She knew their time together was limited. No, she wasn't foolish enough to do that.

So why not just enjoy the day?

They cuddled on the couch much of the day, taking time to eat, enjoying the tree and desultory conversation that just kind of rambled. It wasn't as if either of them were in a mood to dive into deep emotional waters.

Hardly surprising her, he admitted to having been a bit of a daredevil as a kid and showed her the scars to prove it. Stitches and broken bones had been common for him as a child, and he recounted the time his mother had stood beside him in the emergency room and just burst out with, "Will you, please, just live long enough to grow up?"

"I think I was hard on her," he admitted. "She tried to shrug a lot of it off as natural high jinks, but finally it really started to get to her. I behaved a little better after that."

"Really? I'm supposed to believe that?"

"Well, there were only a few more stitches and no broken bones."

She sighed, feeling his shoulder beneath the back of her head. His arm wrapped around her, beneath her breasts and just over her belly. She spoke. "I think I'm glad I'm having a girl."

"Nothing says a girl can't be a daredevil, too."

She laughed. "I guess not."

"What about you?"

"Nothing like you. I was kind of a geek or a nerd, or whatever it's called these days. Always buried in books. Part of the chess team and debate team. Editor of the school paper. A bookworm, in short."

"You're one helluva pretty bookworm."

"I didn't date," she admitted. "I'm not sure, but I think I scared guys off."

"I can't imagine it."

"Well, I sure didn't appeal to them."

He lifted his hand, cupping her breast. "Say that one more time, I dare you."

"What are you going to do?" she demanded.

"This?" He rubbed his palm back and forth across the peak of her breast. She wasn't wearing a bra, and her nipple hardened instantly. Shivers of longing poured through her. "Ryker…" she gasped.

"Let me tease you. I think we need to be careful." He stopped caressing her and instead gave her a gentle squeeze.

"My doctor said…"

"I'm sure your doctor was right. But I'm not sure he was imagining a marathon. For your sake, I can wait. How about you?"

She sighed, closing her eyes, clamping her thighs together to quiet her hunger. "I suppose you're right."

"Maybe better than finding out someone was totally wrong."

She couldn't deny it.

"Besides, I'm really enjoying this, holding you like this. Sad truth about Ryker Tremaine?"

"Sure."

"I don't do this. Ever. But here I am, and I'm thinking about all I chose to miss until you came along."

Her heart filled with an odd combination of pleasure and pain. Pleased that he was content with holding her like this, sad that he had missed so much. "That was sweet," she said.

"Just the unvarnished truth. Any other time in my life I wouldn't have been here this morning."

She caught her breath. The swelling in her heart no longer contained any pleasure at all. She couldn't tell which of them she hurt more for, him or her. This was ephemeral, she reminded herself. A passing moment he might well forget as soon as he left. Meaningless. It had to be meaningless, because she couldn't return to the life she had lived with Johnny. Not now. Not with a baby.

"Anyway," he said presently, "don't you have a party to plan? We could talk about that. And about whether to do the front of the house and how much decorating we should do."

"You want to go to the store?"

His arm tightened a bit around her midsection. "Not today. I don't want to lose one second with you."

Warmth flooded her, banishing the phantoms of fear that had started to hover nearby again. Take it for what it was. Enjoy the day.

For the first time since the funeral she honestly believed that the future was worth living for. She was alive again, and regardless of what loomed, she didn't want to lose a second with Ryker, either.

Chapter Ten

"Good morning."

She awoke to feel Ryker's breath on her neck, along with a peppering of light kisses. He'd made love to her again during the night, gentle yet explosive love, and she felt cherished to her very soul.

"'Morning," she said sleepily, stirring happily to his touches. She was tangled in the blankets, and when she tried to turn over to face him, he had to help her. He was smiling.

She felt herself smile in response, felt her heart lift. A surprisingly tender man, one she hadn't thought he could be when she first met him. Ryker had exposed a whole side of himself to her that she would have bet he rarely shared.

"How's the passenger?" he asked.

"She's fine." A poke answered her, as if the baby was saying good morning, as well.

"I'm still in awe," he admitted. First he ran his hand over her belly, then swept it down her back, pressing her bottom to bring her closer. "You are irresistible," he murmured before stealing a long, deep kiss.

When she could breathe again, she asked, "Even with bed head?"

"Especially with bed head." He flashed her a grin. "Should I make breakfast?"

"I could do it," she offered.

"I know you could. But I like to feel helpful."

"What do you call last night?"

That drew a belly laugh from him. He stole another quick kiss, then rolled out of bed in all his naked glory. She lay there smiling into her pillow as he took a quick shower, then headed for the kitchen in jeans and a T-shirt.

Her turn now, she supposed, but she hated to leave the bed just yet. She could still feel his warmth, could still detect his scent and the scent of last night's lovemaking.

She closed her eyes and let Johnny's memory surface. She hoped he wouldn't be upset with her but could no longer imagine why he should be. Julie had been right. He'd been the one who kept leaving. And finally he had left for good.

Sighing, she at last pulled herself up and into the shower. Everywhere she rubbed herself with soap and a washcloth, she found herself remembering Ryker's hands on her.

She realized as she toweled off that he had wedged himself into her life, and that when he left, the sorrow was now inevitable. She'd miss him. But she would survive.

For the first time, she appreciated the fact that while

she had withdrawn from life for so long in her grief, she had gotten through the worst of it. She was strong. Selfish in some ways, but strong in the important ways.

Strong enough to be left again. Strong enough to raise her baby. Strong.

She and Ryker were just finishing breakfast when Julie bounced in through the side door. She grinned at both of them, bringing a blast of frigid air in with her before she shoved the door closed.

"My, don't you two look cozy," she remarked cheerfully, shedding her scarf and jacket. "How's it going?"

Then she peered at Marisa and shot a sharp look at Ryker.

"My, my," she said.

Marisa felt her cheeks heat. "Cut it out, Julie."

"Why?" Julie headed for the coffeepot, filled a mug and came to sit with them. "You look more relaxed than I've seen you in forever. Your face doesn't look pinched."

Marisa didn't know how to respond to that. All she knew was that she didn't want to discuss with Julie what had happened. It was private, a secret to keep to herself and savor.

"Vast improvement," Julie went on. "It had better stay that way. So how are you feeling, other than relaxed?"

"I'm fine," Marisa answered promptly. Better than fine, but there was no point saying anything that would only draw out more questions. "I was thinking of having a party for my friends. I've been so withdrawn, and I think I owe you guys all an apology."

Julie became instantly diverted. She waved a hand. "You don't owe any apologies. But a party in your state? What kind of party?"

"Something simple."

Julie flashed another grin. "I could manage it for you."

Marisa shook her head. "If you throw the party, how am I thanking all my friends for sticking with me? No, I'll just do something simple. Coffee and Christmas cookies. I just want to let everyone know I still love them. They must have wondered."

Julie reached for her hand and gave it a quick squeeze. "Everyone understood, hon. And what kind of friends would we be if we didn't stick beside you? It'll do us all some good to see you start taking steps out of hibernation. That's all we need."

She sniffed the air. "Do I smell pine?"

"Ryker put up a Christmas tree."

Julie turned her attention on him. "For real? A real tree?"

He smiled and nodded.

Julie grinned hugely. "Fantastic! The last few years Marisa didn't even bother to put up that fiber-optic tree of hers. As if it was too much trouble when Johnny wouldn't be home. Now, that was sad."

Marisa watched something pass between the two of them. What was it? A warning? An understanding?

"Well, this I've got to see," Julie announced, bouncing up out of her chair and carrying her coffee to the living room.

Marisa looked at Ryker almost apologetically, but he simply smiled and shrugged. Well, if he wasn't disturbed by this intrusion, she certainly wasn't. Julie had a habit of popping in at odd times, and ordinarily Marisa was glad to see her. It was just that this time…this time, what? She wanted to be alone with Ryker? Foolish hope.

They followed Julie into the living room, and Ryker turned on the lights for her.

"Awesome!" was Julie's pronouncement. "And you finally got your blue spruce. I love it!"

"Well," she said, turning to Marisa, "a gang of over-hyper five-year-olds awaits me. Christmas turns them into demons, I swear. I envy their anticipation and excitement, but controlling it is a job for a whole army."

She gave Marisa a hug, set her coffee cup in the sink and vanished through the door.

"Is she always such a whirlwind?" Ryker asked, sounding almost bemused.

"No, but sometimes. I think she's worrying about me."

"She doesn't have anything to worry about," he said with a firmness that surprised her.

Now what the hell did that mean?

But Ryker had returned to sphinx mode and left her wondering.

Three days later, Ryker was out in the cold hanging the lights Marisa had agreed to, along with a wreath for the front door. The day was bitter, and he ducked inside often for a cup of coffee and a few minutes to warm up. Marisa was calling her friends, inviting them over for coffee and cookies. As he watched her chat with them, smiling and looking content, he knew he was in trouble.

He needed to start pulling away. She was showing signs of caring for him, like the way she always had hot coffee ready for him when he came inside. Other little things were mounting up, too.

Nobody had ever cared for him this way, and it worried him. But every time he told himself to start forging some space between them, he discovered something that troubled him even more: he couldn't make himself do it.

As he stood on the ladder outside, receiving occasional help and advice from friendly neighbors, he took a long, hard look at himself. He had a weakness, a serious weakness, for Marisa Hayes, and the self-control that had marked his entire adult life vanished the instant he got close to her.

Weakness of any kind was a dangerous thing, for himself and others. He hadn't missed Julie's significant look of warning the other morning. He was determined to heed it but kept failing. Apparently the only way he could separate himself from this woman was to leave, and he refused to do that until after the baby was safely born.

Only then would he feel he'd kept his promise to John.

But as for paying his penance...hell, this all felt too good to be penance. All of it, from standing at the foot of the ladder and talking to the guy next door, to going inside and seeing Marisa's happy face.

He just hoped she wasn't still worried about betraying John. Too bad she'd probably be the one who felt betrayed after he left. Damn, he should never have given in to her, should never have taken her to bed, even though he'd known how his refusal would wound her.

Talk about a rock and a hard place.

He was standing at the foot of the ladder, the job nearly done, when Ray from next door came over for the second time. "It's nice to see Marisa decorating," he remarked. "Fiona likes it. So, you were Johnny's friend, huh?"

Some friend, thought Ryker. "Yeah."

"Good of you to come see her through this. I wonder

if Johnny would have been here? He almost never was."
Then Ray shook his head. "Not my business, especially
not now. Fiona would kill me for mentioning it."

Fiona would kill him? The thought amused Ryker,
since he had gathered that Marisa thought Fiona was a
huge gossip.

Just then two kids tumbled out of the house next door,
laughing and shrieking. School was out for the day. The
holiday vacation began next week, he gathered.

"My call," said Ray. "Time to take them to the skating rink. See you around."

Ryker watching Ray round up excited children and
pile them into the car. The sight both amused him and
appealed to him. Maybe there were some complications
in being a father, like kids who wanted to play tag when
they needed to be getting into the car.

When the car was gone, Ryker stepped back to survey his handiwork. It looked okay, actually. Spaced well,
nothing hanging loose. Pleased, he took the ladder to the
detached garage, then went in the side door.

When he entered the kitchen, he knew immediately
that something had changed. Shucking his outerwear,
he dumped it over the kitchen chair and went hunting.
He found Marisa standing in the living room, staring
at the tree.

"Marisa?"

She didn't answer immediately. Concerned, he walked
up behind her and put his hands on her shoulders.

"What's wrong?" he asked.

"Phone call," she said in a thick voice.

"What?" An extremely rare sense of panic began to
fill him. "Did something bad happen?"

"I don't know. Maybe. Probably not." She shook herself a little, but he didn't let go of her. "A man from the State Department is coming to see me on Saturday. He has a letter for me."

Ryker felt gut-punched. He'd gotten it for her, but he hadn't expected it. He knew exactly what she was going to receive, and it didn't offer much information that she didn't already have. When it was over…when it was over, she was going to know the extent of his duplicity.

He cleared his throat. "That's the day of your party. Maybe you should postpone it."

"I tried to postpone him, but I couldn't." She turned, facing him. "Is it a letter from Johnny?" she asked, whispering.

"If they had something like that, you'd have gotten it with the rest of his belongings."

"So, this official?" Her eyes seemed to have sunken, and she wrapped her arms around herself. "More information?"

"I doubt there'll be much." Just the most damning information of all…for him.

She placed a hand over her mouth, closing her eyes, swaying a bit until he steadied her. "I guess you rattled those bars pretty good," she said weakly, then pulled away from him and went back to the kitchen.

Standing alone in the living room, he hated himself. She'd wanted to know, he'd believed she deserved to know, but at that point he hadn't considered all the possible ramifications. She was about to be wounded anew, and he might as well pack his bags and head back to the motel. After this she'd never be able to trust him.

But he couldn't leave her alone with this. Time for his atonement. All the lies he lived were about to come back to haunt him. He was going to pay big-time.

But he deserved it. He absolutely deserved it.

When he finally went out to the kitchen again, Marisa was back on the phone, telling all her friends that something had come up and she needed to postpone the party. Promising to reschedule.

But what he heard in her voice was the rending grief he'd heard when he first arrived. The escape from reality was over.

They were both about to revisit hell.

Marisa felt the change in Ryker from the instant she told him about the call. He knew what was coming, but wasn't about to tell her. Damn these men and their secrets.

Anger bubbled quietly in her as she thought about all the years lost to secrets. All the things that she would never know about her husband, about Ryker. And whatever was coming on Saturday, Ryker clearly felt it could be a problem.

She hated secrets, most especially operational secrets. She half expected that what would come on Saturday was another pile of secrets, this time secrets that *she* would have to keep. God, she hated it. She wanted it over. She wanted the life she had just been starting to rebuild.

Now some guy from State was going to come and destroy it all one way or another. Yes, she wanted to know more about what had happened to Johnny, but she'd begun to make peace with never knowing. Now they were going to sweep that away, and she'd have to start all over again.

She'd begged for this, and Ryker had tried to give it

to her, and now she was wishing she hadn't asked and he hadn't tried.

That wasn't fair to him. She knew it. But even as he was keeping his distance, she realized she was doing the same. They went to bed together at night, but no more lovemaking. She accepted him holding her, and yet she couldn't let him any closer than that.

He seemed to feel the same. He didn't even try. She wanted to badger him, hoping for something to prepare her, but she could feel he would offer no answers. None. Maybe he didn't have them. Maybe he was just giving her space because he knew this was going to reawaken her grief.

How could it not?

Saturday dragged toward them on leaden feet. Hours seemed to stretch endlessly. It seemed now that two strangers lived in this house, the way it had been when he'd first arrived. She hated it, but she skirted anything personal as assiduously as he did.

God, she just wished Saturday would get here so she could deal with whatever it was. It might not be half as bad as she imagined, but from the way Ryker was acting, she doubted it. He knew something—damn him. Didn't he at least owe it to her to prepare her?

She'd have felt a whole lot better if he'd acted as if this visit were a meaningless formality. Instead, she couldn't escape the sense that he knew something bad was on the way. Sometimes she could have hated him. He was part of the secrecy that had taken such a toll on her life. She'd accepted that once, but she refused to accept it again.

Truth. God, she needed truth in her life.

Maybe that was what was coming on Saturday. Truth. But even as she quailed and railed internally, she kept remembering making love with that man. That had been honest. Maybe the only truthful thing about him. Little enough.

When Saturday arrived, she pulled on the only maternity dress she had bothered to buy, a simple dark blue with white piping at the neck. For the first time in countless months she used makeup. She didn't know what this guy from State was expecting, but he wasn't going to find a washed-out hag...even if she felt like one.

"I should be here," Ryker said as she emerged from the bedroom. "I can stay out of the way if you want, but in case..."

"In case what? I already got the worst news."

The bite of her own voice shocked her, and she watched Ryker's face shutter. He might have pulled into himself, but she was driving him away.

She drew a long breath, but she wasn't about to apologize. "Keep your secrets," she added bitterly, then marched into the living room and sat waiting.

"I'll get the door," he said, remaining in the foyer.

"Fine."

Why did she feel as if her life was about to end again? She was probably making too much of this, being unfair. But as she sat with her fists clenched, her baby stirring in her belly, she was through with making excuses for herself or anyone else.

The doorbell rang, and she stiffened. She heard Ryker answer it. It even sounded as if they were exchanging credentials.

Moments later a man in a dark suit entered the living room, carrying a slender portfolio. Behind him she could see Ryker hanging his overcoat on the hall tree.

"Mrs. Hayes?"

"Ms."

"I'm sorry. Ms. Hayes, I'm Dan Crandall. May I sit?"

She waved him to the couch. He sat facing her. Ryker remained standing in the doorway.

"First, I need to lay some groundwork. You were married to John Kenneth Hayes?"

"Yes."

Crandall nodded. "All right. I'm going to show you a letter and a couple of photographs. They're classified, so I won't be able to leave them with you. Do you understand?"

"Oh, I understand secrecy," she said, reaching for pleasant and barely succeeding.

Crandall gave a fleeting smile. "I imagine you do. I also have to tell you that you won't be able to discuss this information with anyone. Your child can eventually know, but no one else. This information could endanger the lives of others."

For the first time she understood that there was more involved here than her own loss. She nodded, her mouth turning dry.

"All right." He opened his portfolio and passed her a photograph of a wall with black stars on it. "See the star circled in red? That's your husband's. His name will never appear on it."

She swallowed hard, staring at it.

"In front of the wall in that case you see is a carefully guarded book with all the names of our fallen agents inscribed. The public can't look. The only time families can is during our annual memorial service. Henceforth, you will be invited to attend. It's up to you whether you come or not."

She drew a long breath, nodding as he took the photo back.

"This," he said, handing her another, "is a photo of your husband's inscription in the book. I'm sorry we had to black out the other names, but I'm sure you understand."

She wasn't sure she understood any of this. Stars without names? A book no one could see? But staring down at Johnny's carefully inscribed name, she felt the pain pierce her all over again. At least others would never forget him or forget his sacrifice.

When he took that photo back, he offered her a sheet of paper. As soon as she saw the letterhead, her world turned black.

When she came to, she was lying on her back with a worried Ryker over her.

"Marisa?"

"I'm okay." Although she wasn't sure of that at all. "Help me up."

He did so carefully, and soon had her seated in her rocker again. Crandall still sat on the couch, his previously expressionless face now displaying concern.

"I'm sorry," she said automatically.

"You're not the first person I've seen faint. I'm just glad you didn't fall."

"Lovely job you have."

"You had the harder one," he said frankly. "Do you want to see that letter again?"

She nodded, accepting it. The blue CIA logo adorned the top, beneath it the words "Office of the Director."

Now that the shock had passed, she scanned the words below. Not very different from the first letter she'd received from the State Department. A true hero, died in the line of duty serving his country, a sacrifice that would never be forgotten, deep sympathy for her loss... Meaningless.

She stared at it, the words coming in and out of focus. CIA. That was the shocker. It was also an amazing clarifier. She looked at Ryker. "You, too?"

He hesitated, then finally gave her what she needed. "Yes."

"Why the lies?" she asked.

Crandall answered. "State is a cover story. It protects lives, Ms. Hayes. More than you can imagine. Right now, your husband's associates abroad are at risk. That's why we have to ask you to keep this secret. That's why we don't name the stars and why we keep the book so well guarded. A single identity could cause deadly ripples, costing the lives of men, women and children who knew him."

Again she nodded, barely absorbing this. "I need some water." Ryker hurried out and returned swiftly with a glass. She drank half of it in one draft. "How much can I ask?"

"As much as you want. But I'll tell you right now, I know nothing beyond what I told you." Gently, he reclaimed the letter and slipped it into his portfolio. "I'm sorry it took so long to get this to you, but I was assured there were unfolding events. Again, that's the extent of my knowledge." He gave her a half smile. "For obvious reasons, they keep me in the dark."

Another dead end for her. Truth, at last, but a dead end. Except for one thing: Ryker.

Now she knew who he was and how he had lied to her, too.

Rising, she left the room and headed for bed. She was done.

Secrets, Ryker thought as he watched Crandall drive away, were secrets. Omissions. Things not spoken of. To say he worked for State was an outright lie. His cover was blown, the lie revealed, and he wouldn't blame Marisa if she never spoke another word to him.

She had trusted him in so many ways, inviting him into her house and into her bed. He couldn't imagine she would ever trust him again.

He wanted to blow it off. He was used to the price his life exacted, but this was somehow different. He ached for a woman and a fatherless child, and thought that maybe some prices were too high.

Too late now. He'd mucked this up big-time and couldn't see a way back from it. When she'd asked him if he was CIA, too, he'd seen the betrayal in her gaze. Lies. More lies. A big lie from him.

He had told her he wasn't Johnny, but now she knew he was. A liar. A covert operative who couldn't tell the truth about anything. A man who went into danger without telling those who loved them, who might leave them with nothing but an anonymous star and a condolence letter they couldn't keep.

He suspected that, except for his pushing, Marisa might never have received a letter at all. It had happened before. God, he hated it, and the hate was growing deeper by the day.

He knew he'd accomplished important tasks, knew he had helped his country in countless ways, but he had done so while living uncounted lies. Sometimes he wondered if there was a real Ryker inside, or just some amalgam of all the people he'd pretended to be.

For all he knew, deception had become so deeply ingrained that there was nothing real left of him. Except for his feelings about Marisa and her baby. Each time he touched them, he knew they were real. He couldn't afford them, but they existed. They weren't invented. They weren't a part of a job or a ploy.

And he should have known better than to stay here. Once those feelings had reached past his guard, he should have realized the danger in remaining. Not the danger to himself, though this was going to be painful enough, but the danger to her.

Once again he faced the fact that secrecy was different from a lie. He had lied to her. From the instant he had said he worked with Johnny at State, he had sacrificed everything. She would never forgive him.

Oh, she claimed to understand secrecy, and she probably did, but for a long time she had suspected she'd been told lies about John's death. And she had, although he had no idea what the truth was. He was just certain she'd been given a cover story, like everything else.

Then he'd waltzed in, gained her trust and had been proven a liar. Secrecy was no excuse for what he had done to her.

God, he had to get out of this business. He needed to salvage some honesty and decency before he was nothing but a house of someone else's cards.

Or maybe he was already there, about as real as some

figure in a video game, an avatar that called itself Ryker but didn't even really exist.

Not knowing what else to do, he washed off the chicken they'd thawed that morning and started to cook dinner.

He was sure she was going to throw him out. He could at least leave a decent meal for her behind.

The rest of the day passed slowly. Roasting chicken filled the house with delicious aromas. He found the asparagus he'd bought a few days ago and prepared to cook it. He'd make some rice to go with it. After so many years spent mostly abroad, he favored rice over potatoes now.

Pointless exercise. The entire dinner might sit here and spoil.

But then he heard a sound behind him. He turned and saw Marisa. She'd changed into royal blue fleece pants and a top, her belly stretching the fabric. Her eyes had that sunken look again, with big circles beneath them. She'd washed off all the makeup, and he was glad to see it gone. She needed no enhancements.

When she just stood there staring at him, he finally took the plunge, sure that he was going to be crushed on the rocks below. "I'll leave."

"No." She stepped into the room and sat at the table. "No," she said again. "You stay here. I need someone to yell at."

"Fair enough. Milk or something else?"

"Milk. Thank you." Icy. Removed. That hurt more than an eruption.

He brought her the milk, then sat facing her across

the table. He didn't want to loom over her, seem threatening in the least way. Not even unintentionally.

"How's the baby?" he asked presently.

"Better than her mother."

There was nothing he could say to that.

She sipped some milk, then sat staring at the glass, turning it slowly on the table. "You lied to me when you arrived."

"Yes." His chest tightened as if preparing for the blow of a sledgehammer.

"But you didn't lie to me when I asked you earlier."

Where was this going? He couldn't imagine but knew he was going to find out.

"Why?" she asked.

"Why what?"

"You could have lied to me again. Could have told me you were with the State Department, that you had no idea about Johnny. But you didn't, Ryker. That must have broken some kind of operational secrecy."

It had. Most definitely.

"How many other lies did you tell me?"

"None."

"No," she agreed, staring at him now. "No lies. Just a whole lot of omissions and half-truths. How can I ever believe you again?" Her voice had risen, and now she stood, taking her glass of milk and heading for the living room.

He set up a TV table for her in the living room, then brought her a plate full of food, a napkin and utensils. He retreated to eat by himself, but he was only halfway through the foyer when she called him back.

"Ryker. Eat with me."

Well, that amazed him, considering that he figured just looking at him must make her feel sick. Reluctantly, he set up a table for himself, then sat perched on the goosenecked chair with his own meal.

For long minutes she made no move to eat, then with an almost visible shake, she picked up her fork and knife and sliced into the chicken. Only then did he begin to eat himself.

"So, tell me," she said as she ate.

"If I can."

"What's the real reason you don't visit your family and you haven't married?"

"I think you know," he answered.

She surprised him with a glare. "I want to hear it."

The moment of truth. He put down his knife and fork and wiped his mouth with the napkin before he answered. "The truth?"

"As much as you can tell me," she answered bitterly.

"The truth is that I didn't want to leave someone in your position. Because what I did was dangerous and secret, and I refused to be responsible for leaving someone behind to wonder forever. I don't visit my parents because the whole time I'm there I have to skirt the truth and make excuses about why I'm never home, why I've never married, why I haven't given them grandkids. Because the goddamn lies follow me every waking minute of my life!"

The last came out of him with a vehemence that surprised him. He hated the way Marisa shrank back a little as his voice rose.

"Sorry," he mumbled, stabbing at a piece of chicken so hard the fork hit the plate with a clatter. "I wasn't shouting at you."

"Johnny didn't have those qualms."

"Oh, hell." He'd done it again. Awakened a new pain in her. But when he glanced her way, he didn't see anguish. He saw something else he couldn't identify.

Then she abruptly changed the subject. "So you and Johnny are heroes."

"That's debatable. I guess it depends on what side you're on, which parts of the secrets you know, which parts have been hidden from you. John was doing important work. Never doubt it."

"I don't," she said calmly. "Just as I don't doubt that you've done important things. But what the heck? I'll never know, will I? So I guess you have to be your own judge and jury."

That stung. The chicken became tasteless in his mouth. He continued eating only because he needed to.

"Can you tell me just one thing?"

"Ask and I'll see." Even now, he couldn't tell. Even now. God, it sickened him.

"Did Johnny, do you, believe in what you're doing? Or is it all about the thrills?"

The question could have infuriated him, but he didn't let it. "I believed in what I was doing. So did John. It wasn't just for a thrill. Those kinds of thrills nobody needs. The kind of work John and I did…well, you could say we were in the trenches. Not at the embassy balls."

She gave him a half smile that didn't reach her eyes. "No James Bond."

"Not a chance. Pure grunt work and intelligence gathering for the most part. Some infiltration. And now I'm saying too much."

"I can keep secrets, too." She pushed her plate aside. Part of him was sorry about how little she had eaten, but another part was relieved because now he could stop eating, too. It might have been a good dinner, but he couldn't tell. Everything tasted like sawdust.

Which he supposed was another warning. He'd been in worse situations without feeling like this. Situations where he might die at any moment. Nothing had ever reduced him to this abject level of misery. He'd have cheerfully cut out his own beating heart. He'd spent his entire adult life trying to avoid exactly this, but he'd walked into it, anyway. A woman's pain. Her betrayal. Her child. He disgusted himself.

He cleared away the dishes but returned quickly, a niggling fear working on him. She was too calm. At some point... What did he think she was going to do? Kill herself? Not with that baby inside her. He didn't think he'd misjudged her that much.

But he was still worried.

The phone rang. "Want me to get it?"

She shook her head. "It'll be Julie, and I don't want to face the barrage of questions."

"Then, let me." He could do that much for her at least. Julie was indeed full of questions, apparently worried about Marisa, why he was answering instead of her.

"She's feeling under the weather," he answered. A lie or a half-truth? Damned if he knew anymore. "Can I have her call you back tomorrow?"

When he hung up, he knew Julie wasn't satisfied. She'd probably be here soon. Then what?

He sat again, facing Marisa. "I'll give you odds that Julie will be here in the next half hour to check on you."

"I don't want to see anyone."

"I can understand that, but if you think I'm going to be able to successfully hold her off if she shows up, you've got another think coming. She'll be convinced I've murdered you and have your body half hacked up in the bathtub."

Marisa's eyes widened. Then to his absolute amazement, she started to laugh. She laughed so hard that she bent over a little and held her stomach with both arms.

Hysteria? he wondered. She was making him feel so helpless, more helpless than he'd ever felt in his entire life.

But gradually her laughter trailed away, and she wiped tears from her face. "She would," she said. "That's exactly what Julie would think."

"Then let her come. Sorry, but you're going to have to put up with her."

She eyed him. "Then I guess we need our cover story."

The way she said it, she put him on edge. Now she was going to lie to her friends? No way.

"No," he said. "Tell her the whole ugly story. You got news about Johnny today and found out I'm not the guy you thought I was, and you're keeping me around until you're done yelling at me."

"Really?"

"Really. Truth is always better when possible. Don't start covering for me."

Her face softened for the first time in ages it seemed like. "Ryker? Did you make love to me because I wanted it, or because you wanted it?"

That she would even doubt that made him feel as low as a slug. "Oh, I wanted it," he said firmly. "Believe me. The only thing that held me back for so long was that I didn't want to hurt you. I've hurt you, anyway. Story of my life."

"That's not fair," she said quietly. "You just told me

you did without a full life because you didn't want to hurt anybody. I can't say the same about Johnny. He wanted it all. He took it all." She looked down at her stomach and ran her hand over it. "He did leave me something beautiful, though."

"Yes, he did."

She looked up. "And he sent you."

"Marisa…"

She shook her head. "I'm getting past it, Ryker. Why wouldn't I? I've lived with this secrecy for years, and I understand why you couldn't tell me the truth about who you are. I get it. It was just such a shock. CIA never entered my head, but you know what?"

"What?"

"I understand so much now. I'm glad I do. It all finally makes sense."

He wished he could believe this transformation, but he wasn't sure it would last. Maybe she was in a state of shock?

But she sat rocking gently, smiling faintly, her hands protectively over her belly. If today hadn't been such a ride into hell for her, he could have believed that she'd finally found some peace.

And just as he'd predicted, Julie showed up. She stormed past him and surveyed Marisa. "What happened?" she demanded.

"I learned something today," Marisa answered serenely. "Johnny was a true hero. And so is Ryker."

Julie sat slowly. "Really? What did he do?"

"I can't tell you. But it's true." Then Marisa looked at Ryker and smiled. He felt his heart crack wide open. She was one hell of an amazing woman.

Chapter Eleven

Christmas Eve dawned clear and cold. Ryker had returned to Marisa's bed, although he refrained from making love to her. She was content to be held by him, however.

And finally she answered his question. "I do feel peaceful," she said after breakfast. "It's like...just knowing who Johnny worked for, who you work for...it answered questions for me. I get it now, all the secrecy. I get why he could never tell me anything. I suppose, from what you said, that when he was in the Rangers he worked a lot of missions with you."

"That's right," he agreed as he washed the dishes. "His team did a lot of my insertions and extractions. And you didn't hear that from me."

"I didn't hear anything at all." Standing beside him, she shook her head a little and swallowed her prenatal vitamin. "And now I know why nobody would tell me anything. That makes it easier."

He dried his hands and turned around, leaning back against the counter as he drew her into his embrace. He loved looking at her, loved the way the shadows had withdrawn, leaving her face unclouded. Hard to believe that such a parsimonious bit of information could create such a change.

He felt the baby kick against his abdomen and smiled, lifting a hand to stroke her ash-blond hair back from her face. "You're one beautiful, amazing woman."

"Big as a house, too," she retorted.

"An awfully small house," he answered before dropping a kiss on her lips.

"So," she said, shifting her gaze to his chest and resting her hand on him. "When do you have to leave?"

"I don't. Well, I have to go back and resign, but I can do that anytime."

Her head jerked back, and she gaped at him. "Resign? But you said…"

"If you've been listening, I think I've been emitting rumbles of discontent and a desire to change, sort of like a volcano getting ready to erupt. I've made up my mind. I'm done. Cooked. Finished. I'll find something else to do."

"But what?"

He smiled. "I told you, I can take care of myself. Always have. I'll find something."

Ryker was smiling more since Crandall's visit, as if he'd unloaded a burden. Marisa guessed he had. A huge secret had been shed, and she suspected that it had bothered him from the first moment he saw her.

For her own part, she realized now that she trusted him. All the doubts about Ryker had vanished in a searing instant of honesty. Now she knew who he was. Now she knew who Johnny was. Knowing that, it was easier to accept all the things she couldn't know.

Of course, Johnny hadn't died in a street mugging. Her suspicions and doubts had been justified. She'd never know what had really happened, but somehow it was easier to accept knowing that she'd been given a cover story. In some ways, the idea of a cover story to protect lives was a whole lot easier to deal with than the idea that people were wantonly lying to her in order to cover some misdeed.

Now Ryker had decided to resign. She wondered what that would mean for him, for her. Would he stay here in Conard City? Somehow that didn't seem likely to her. He was a man accustomed to traveling the world, to always being in action. How likely was it that he could be content in this backwater?

So she was going to lose him anyway, which saddened her more than she had anticipated. It almost felt like Johnny all over again, but not quite. When Ryker walked away, he was going to live. There'd be no death in this loss, no finality. Maybe they'd be able to keep in touch.

At least she'd know he was out there somewhere in the world, maybe filling all the gaps in his life. Maybe finding a wife, having those kids his parents wanted. She hoped so for him, because more than once she'd gotten the sense that he felt those gaps acutely. He didn't say much about it, but Ryker didn't say a whole lot.

His actions spoke volumes, however. He took care of her, treating her as if she were precious. So, he was a caring man, a rare find. And some of the edge was gone from him, some of the darkness she'd originally sensed. Ryker was waking to a new world.

Just as she had. And looking down at her belly, she felt that she had yet another awakening ahead of her, a joyous one. She and little Jonni were going to build a new, beautiful life. One without secrets. One lived in the bright light of day.

"I'm going out," Ryker said. "I have to pick up a couple of things. Will you be okay for an hour?"

"We'll be just fine," she assured him. Then she said something she never thought she'd say to him. "Hurry back. I'll miss you."

She half expected his face to darken, to react to the implications in those simple words. A man who was about to leave could hardly be happy to realize a woman wanted him back.

But he astonished her. His own face softened, and he came to drop a kiss on her forehead. "I'll hurry," he said huskily. "Want some milk before I go?"

"Ryker!" He pulled a laugh from her. "I'm pregnant, not sick. If I need something I can get it."

"Just don't let me find you on a step ladder."

"On my honor. I think my nesting phase passed."

"Thank God."

She laughed as she heard the door close behind him. After a few minutes she rose and went into her bedroom to look at the crib. Soon a baby would occupy it, turning everything on end. She could hardly wait. She loved picking up the tiny little clothes her friends had given her, still finding it hard to believe they were big enough to fit a baby. Such little bits of clothing, it just didn't seem possible.

But her back had started to ache again, so she returned to the rocker. It wouldn't be long now, she thought, closing her eyes and savoring both her anticipation and impatience. With each passing day, she wanted this baby more, wanted to hold her in her arms, to see the small face, hear the cries. The waiting was becoming intolerable.

Her thoughts wandered to Johnny, and she felt a twinge of familiar guilt. He hadn't even been gone a year. Shouldn't she still be in the pits of grief? But somehow, despite all, she was emerging.

Surely Johnny wouldn't begrudge her that?

But the guilt remained, stinging. Of course she still missed Johnny. Hated the fact that he was dead. Hated that he wouldn't be here to see his child. Sometimes resentment swelled in her, huge and ugly.

But he'd left her here, and she had to keep going. Originally she had done that only for the sake of their child, but now...now she needed to do it for herself, as well.

But she'd always miss Johnny. Always. With him she had forever lost a piece of her heart. But there were pieces left, she realized. A piece for this baby. Pieces for her friend. Maybe even a piece for Ryker.

The ache in her lower back remained. She rocked a little trying to ease it, then, with a gasp, she realized she was sitting in a puddle of water.

Now. Now? Now.

Half-crazed thoughts raced in her head. She picked up the phone Ryker had left beside her, wondering if she should call for an ambulance.

Then she tapped in Ryker's number.

"Hey, you okay?" he answered.

"I think my water just broke."

* * *

Ryker got stopped by a cop for speeding as he raced back to the house from Freitag's. He didn't even wait for the deputy to reach the side of his car.

"Marisa Hayes," he called. "You know her?"

"Yeah."

"Her water just broke."

In an instant he had a police escort with flashing lights and sirens clearing the rest of his way. "God, I love this town," he muttered, his hands gripping the steering wheel until his knuckles were tight.

They pulled up in front of the house, and the cop came inside with him. They found Marisa in her rocker sitting on a towel.

"Ambulance?" the deputy said, ready to key his radio.

Marisa shook her head. "I called the hospital. A ride will do. Ryker?"

"I'll take you."

"Get more towels or I'll ruin your car."

Like he cared about that. But he didn't want to upset her in the least way, so he grabbed a stack of towels and laid them on the passenger seat. The deputy remained to ensure they got safely to the car.

"Any pains?" Ryker asked as they drove toward the hospital on the edge of town.

"Not yet. Just a flood. Ryker…after you leave me there, call Julie. She'll take care of everything, okay?"

"Sure thing." He wished he could take care of everything, but he wasn't family. They probably wouldn't let him anywhere near.

God, he hated it. He had no rights with this woman or her child, and that ate away inside him along with worry.

"Quit looking like this is the end of the world," she said. "It's a baby. Happens millions of times every day."

"Not to you. Not to me." Something perilously close to panic was riding his shoulder.

She laughed quietly. "I feel good. Dang, I feel good! Finally!"

At the emergency room, they helped her into a wheelchair. She gave him her purse. "In case they need any information. And later, I have a small suitcase packed in the closet."

"I'll bring it."

The last thing he saw was her smile and wave as they swept her away.

He stood there feeling helpless, feeling there ought to be something he could do. Hating that he couldn't.

"Be all right, Marisa," he whispered. Then he pulled out his cell phone and called the whirlwind named Julie.

Julie arrived fifteen minutes later, meeting him outside the ER. She walked up briskly, smiling.

"You look awful," she told Ryker. "Relax."

"I can't," he admitted.

"She'll be fine. I'm her coach, so I'll be with her every minute. You get to join the pacing people in the waiting room. Come on up with me and we'll get the news."

That was better than no news at all.

The maternity nurse met them in the waiting room, smiling as if she had the happiest job in the world. "Just in time," she told Julie. "Her first contractions have just started. They warned you first babies take longer, right?"

Julie nodded. "A few of my friends have been down this road. How long do you think?"

The nurse shrugged. "Everyone's different. It might be as long as twenty-four hours."

Oh, God, Ryker thought. He'd had a lot of time lines in his life, but never had twenty-four hours looked longer.

Julie turned to him. "Get some coffee. Go for a run. It's going to be a long haul."

"Just tell someone to keep me posted."

The nurse regarded him. "Who's he?"

"Family," Julie said, surprising him.

"Well, then, I guess we can let you know. But don't hold your breath. First babies take their time."

Locked out, left in a waiting room with an older couple who seemed to be waiting for the same thing, he decided to take Julie's advice. A long run. Then he'd bring back some decent coffee. Maybe he could even slip one to Julie.

As his feet pounded the pavement and icy air stung his face, he wondered how many changes he could make and how fast. Life was suddenly bearing down on him like a freight train.

He needed to get his head straight fast.

Johnna Jayne Hayes was born at 12:07 a.m. on Christmas day. She arrived with one long, loud wail, and then began looking around with bright eyes as if she were delighted to see the world.

A minute later, wrapped in blankets, Johnna was laid in Marisa's arms. Marisa forgot everything else as she stared into that tiny face, into those incredibly piercing dark eyes. *Oh, Johnny, I wish you could have seen her.*

She held her daughter, weariness washing over her in waves, accompanied by a happiness she had scarcely imagined she would find in this moment.

If she hadn't been so tired, she was sure her heart would have burst with joy.

"We have to take the baby for a little while," the nurse said, reaching for Johnna. "The pediatrician needs to check her out. We'll move you to a recovery room. You need some sleep and then you can see her again."

Marisa yielded her daughter only reluctantly. She understood the reasons, but she didn't want to let go. A crazy fear filled her that something bad would happen while the baby was out of her sight.

But even in her weariness she knew that was just a flash from the past. Johnna would receive excellent care; she knew almost everyone who worked here and trusted them. Julie, who had coached her all the way through, sagged against the bed.

"I need some sleep, hon."

"Go home. You were wonderful."

Julie bent over her and dropped a kiss on her forehead. "You get some sleep, too."

"Ryker?"

"Pacing like a caged lion. You want to see him?"

"Please."

"I'll see what I can do."

The fatigue hit Marisa then, and she barely remembered being trundled down the hall and moved to a new bed. Her baby was here, she thought as sleep claimed her.

The world seemed right again for the first time since she got the news.

She awoke later from the deepest of sleeps with no idea of the time. She turned her head a bit and saw Ryker dozing in a chair beside the bed, his eyes closed, his chin propped in his hand.

He must have heard something, because his eyes popped open. "Welcome back," he said, smiling. "By all accounts, you did very well."

"My baby?"

"They won't tell me a lot except that she's perfectly healthy. Oh, and they're going to move you to a regular room soon, and you can have her in a bassinet beside you until they release you."

Instinctively, she reached out a hand, wincing a little as the IV moved. He caught her fingers gently, still smiling, and leaned in to press a kiss on her lips.

"How are you feeling?" he asked softly as he pulled back.

"Exhausted but so very happy."

"Me, too. They let me see her through the nursery window. She's perfect, Marisa, and she looks a lot like both you and John."

A tired laugh escaped her. "How can anyone tell that this soon?"

"It shows." He winked.

She drank him in, thinking she'd never seen him look more rumpled. He looked like he'd gone through a worse time than she had. Maybe so.

A nurse bustled in, throwing Ryker out for a few minutes. "I need to examine her," she explained.

Afterward, the nurse assured her everything was fine, and she'd be moved to a proper room in the next few minutes.

"And my baby?"

"Right behind you," the nurse promised.

Ryker followed her down the hallway to the regular room and then was evicted once again. "Go home, rest, clean up," the woman said. "Marisa needs her rest. Come back in the morning."

Marisa wanted to protest, but Ryker nodded, promised to return first thing in the morning and departed meekly enough.

Marisa watched him walk away and thought that didn't seem fair at all. Mostly, she already missed him.

In the morning, Marisa chose to sit up in a comfortable chair while she nursed Jonni. She was hungry and eager, and Marisa watched her continuously, hardly removing her eyes from the little girl.

Her friends showed up one after another, oohing and aahing and agreeing that Jonni was one of the most beautiful babies they'd ever seen. Marisa accepted their judgment with delight, even though she knew they'd all said the same things about their friends' babies.

But no Ryker. After the girls left, she sat alone with her baby in her arms and felt oddly bereft. He must have left. Certainly he'd been made to feel like an outsider.

But just as she was about to rise and put her baby in the bassinet again, she heard his voice.

"Good morning."

She looked up and saw him standing there smiling, a bouquet in his hand. He added the flowers to the ones the girls had left, then edged closer. "Can I see her? You're looking great."

"I look like a hag." She lifted one hand to try to comb her hair back.

"No, you look beautiful." He stepped closer, and she pulled the receiving blanket back, revealing a small, sleeping face. "Awesome," he said quietly. "Just awesome."

A nurse bustled in—Mary, a woman she knew. The

former sheriff's daughter. "So this is the guy who's been looking after you? Nice to meet you." They shook hands and exchanged names. Then she reached into the cabinet beside the bed and tossed him a folded blue square. "You need to put a gown on before you hold her. We try to send them home healthy." She grinned at Marisa. "It works."

After she buzzed out, Ryker hesitated. He gazed longingly at the baby, but she could tell he didn't want to overstep. And the truth was, letting anyone else hold the child had been impossible so far. Not even her girlfriends.

But something deep within her shifted. "Put on the gown and sit down, Ryker."

He quickly tugged it on so it covered his front and sat in the other chair. Then Marisa rose and carried Jonni to him. Surprisingly, she didn't have to show him how to hold the infant.

Then she returned to her chair and simply watched as a miracle seemed to happen. Ryker's face changed, softening more than she had ever seen it. It was instant love, and she knew it.

She sighed, closing her eyes, and realized she'd just leaped a hurdle. It was okay. Johnny's baby in Ryker's arms. It was as if a circle had been completed.

"Are you tired?" he asked.

She opened her eyes. "A little. But mostly I'm delirious with joy. Come home with us, Ryker. Will you?"

"I never thought of doing anything else."

Three weeks later, life had settled into a comfortable routine. When Jonni woke for her nighttime feedings, Ryker hopped out of bed and brought her to Marisa. Then he'd sit beside them and watch as she nursed. Afterward, he changed the diapers and walked with the baby on his shoulder, gently burping.

"How did you learn how to do all of this?" she finally asked him.

He smiled over Jonni's downy head. "My sister. I was ten when she was born. I have to admit I resented being pushed to take care of her, but I learned a lot even though I tried to avoid it."

"Are you resenting this?" she asked.

"I'm loving it."

The answer warmed her to her toes. During the days he often went out for a while, always returning with some tidbit of food. He took down the Christmas tree without her help while she sat rocking the baby, then spent a couple of hours outside in the cold taking down the lights. Everything was carefully stowed in her basement.

But as settled as he seemed, she worried this was transitory. A man like him couldn't be content with such a bucolic life, she was sure. Like Johnny, before long he'd be running off on his next adventure, never mind what he'd said about resigning from the agency. She didn't really believe that, although she believed he'd meant it when he said it.

Then late one afternoon, Julie popped over unannounced. "I'm babysitting," she announced. "You two need to get out for a while. Take her to dinner, Ryker."

Ryker smiled. "Sounds good to me. Marisa?"

She still hadn't completely regained her shape, and even with the exercises she performed religiously she wondered if she ever would. But she managed to find a pair of slacks with a stretchy waistband and a sweater that covered her worst sins. She liked the way Ryker's eyes devoured her with approval, but she hated knowing this was only temporary. Soon it would be just her and her daughter, and maybe an occasional Skype from some place far away.

Life could be so unfair in some ways, but even as the feeling dampened her mood, she thought of Jonni. Life could also bring amazing joy.

It would be all right, she promised herself. She had a new life to build with her daughter.

The weather was about to turn bad again, and when they arrived at Maude's the place was only half full, a rarity.

She was ravenous these days, and even though her doctor had warned her to be careful, that, yes, she needed more food but not that much, she ordered a steak sandwich and fries. Ryker did the same.

They talked about Jonni for a little while, but then Ryker shifted the conversation.

"I need to go back to DC," he said.

Marisa's heart plummeted. "I thought you must need to," she answered, although she'd been dreading this moment more than she could say...or dared to say. She had no claim on this man. He had come only because Johnny asked him to, and for no other reason. He had a life elsewhere.

"Only long enough to resign," he said firmly.

"Then what?" she asked. "Did you find something?"

"Actually, yes. That cursed ski resort they keep trying to build?"

"The one in the mountains here?" Her heart began to hammer nervously. He was coming back here?

"They're working on it again. But they've decided

they want to lead backcountry hikes during the summer. I've been hired."

Now her mouth started to grow dry. "Really? Will you be happy with that?"

"What I'll be happy with is being with you on weekends all summer, and then every day in the winter."

She felt her jaw drop a little. "Ryker?"

He looked down at his plate. "You know, there can't be any place less romantic than this. There's a storm brewing outside and a baby and Julie waiting at home. So, please, excuse me if the atmosphere is lacking, but what I'm trying to say is, if you'll have me, I love you and want to marry you."

She couldn't find her voice. Her heart had climbed into her throat, where it nearly suffocated her. She hardly dared believe what she was hearing.

His expression turned rueful. "Guess this doesn't make you happy."

She fought for a breath, knowing it was now or never. This man would vanish as soon as he took her home if she let him believe that.

"No," she burst out.

His face sagged a little. "Sorry if I made you uncomfortable."

"Ryker, no. That's not...not what I meant." She dragged in another lungful of air. "God, I'd been so afraid that you'd leave me. I love you!"

Watching his expression change was one of the most beautiful things she'd ever seen. A smile was born on that harsh face, and every line lifted.

"To hell with it," he said.

The next thing she knew he'd slipped out of the booth

and was kneeling beside her, heedless of gawkers or the sudden complete silence in the diner.

"Marisa Hayes, will you, please, marry me?"

"Yes," she breathed. Then she threw her arms around his neck. "Yes, yes, yes!"

She hardly heard the applause from those around them. She felt nothing except a heart full to bursting with a dream come true. He loved her. He was going to stay.

All she had ever wanted had just swept into her life and carried her away to the joy she had never thought she would feel again.

Thank you, Johnny, she thought. He'd given her a child, and now he'd sent her love. A legacy and a gift.

The tears that rolled down her face now were purely happy, and Ryker's arms around her were a promise for a brighter future.

Epilogue

They were married on Valentine's Day. Julie and her friends had taken over completely, and Marisa, wearing a simple white gown, walked down the aisle in Good Shepherd Church, surrounded by what seemed like half the people in town. Ryker's father escorted her, to stand in for her own long-gone father.

Ryker awaited her along with the pastor. Julie wore a red bridesmaid dress and held a tiny Jonni, who was also swaddled in red. Beside Ryker, Hank stood as grooms-man.

Snow fell outside the tall windows, but it fell gently, purifying the world. Inside, no shadows reached any corner. As Marisa passed the front row, Ryker's mother suddenly stood and leaned over to kiss her cheek.

"Welcome to the family," the woman said warmly.

Marisa smiled at her, her heart so filled with joy she was certain it must encompass the whole world.

I love you, Johnny, she thought. *I will always miss you. Thank you for Ryker.*

She could almost feel him on her other side, as if he too walked her down the aisle. Then she reached Ryker, and every other thought fled as magic touched her once again.

Full circle. Life and love had returned.

* * * * *

Look for the next book in
New York Times *bestselling author Rachel Lee's*
CONARD COUNTY:
THE NEXT GENERATION *series,*
coming in 2017 from Mills & Boon Cherish
Special Edition.

And don't miss out on previous
CONARD COUNTY: THE NEXT GENERATION
books

A COWBOY FOR CHRISTMAS
THE LAWMAN LASSOES A FAMILY
A CONARD COUNTY BABY

MILLS & BOON®

Cherish™

EXPERIENCE THE ULTIMATE RUSH OF FALLING IN LOVE

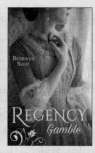

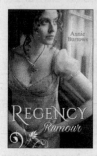
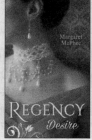

MILLS & BOON®

The Regency Collection – Part 2

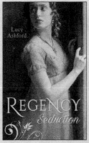

Join the London ton for a Regency
season in part 2 of our collection!

Order yours at **www.millsandboon.co.uk/regency2**